TIPPING

Also by Anna George

What Came Before
The Lone Child

TIPPING

anna george

VIKING
an imprint of
PENGUIN BOOKS

VIKING

UK | USA | Canada | Ireland | Australia
India | New Zealand | South Africa | China

Viking is part of the Penguin Random House group of companies
whose addresses can be found at global.penguinrandomhouse.com

Penguin
Random House
Australia

First published by Viking in 2021

Cover illustrations and design by Louisa Maggio © Penguin Random House Australia Pty Ltd
Typeset in 11.5/16 pt Minion Pro by Midland Typesetters, Australia

Printed and bound in Australia by Griffin Press, part of Ovato, an accredited
ISO AS/NZS 14001 Environmental Management Systems printer

A catalogue record for this
book is available from the
National Library of Australia

ISBN 978 1 76089 778 9

penguin.com.au

For Jason,
Jem and Lachie

1

Liv

Forty-five, married and healthy, Liv Winsome was increasingly dismayed by her lot. Life wasn't as she'd imagined it twenty years, two degrees and three children ago. Only moments earlier, her husband of almost two decades had forgotten her. With a jaunty flick of his wrist, Duncan had clicked his keys at their car behind him. Sitting in the car, finishing a call, Liv had taken a second to understand and try the handle. Then she'd clambered across to the driver's-side window and thumped. She'd called out. This can't be happening, she'd thought, pushing buttons. But it was. Duncan and Jai, one of her fourteen-year-old sons, were dashing towards the office at Carmichael Grammar, without her.

The morning was getting warmer, and the car park full. Sunlight was pouring across the roof of the recently completed Wellbeing Centre. Other families had already arrived, presumably in their full contingent, to watch their beloveds play sport. Their cars, mostly SUVs, the odd sedan or station wagon, looked in reasonable condition. Probably nothing faulty about any of them – no dodgy latches or hidden defects. Newly bought, the Winsomes' car was second-hand but luxe for them. Liv had spent the last few weeks of summer researching, avoiding suspect airbags and dud transmissions. Not one review had mentioned this.

Pressed up against the glass, Liv searched beyond the car park to the school's immaculate sportsgrounds. Though her three sons attended Carmichael, she didn't recognise a single, sweaty child. She tried Duncan's phone. She tried Jai's phone; but, of course, it was still off – and, she remembered, in her handbag. She tried Duncan's again. Often, when she rang, her husband's phone was on silent, or in a distant pocket. She peered into the brightening sky. Usually, she didn't mind Duncan's not answering. But, this morning, it was getting hot.

Children were locked in cars, she thought. Not adults, not *wives*.

Duncan did have form, though. When the twins were babies, she and Dunc had gone on a much-needed short break interstate. Taking pity on them, a close friend had set them up with staff travel. Duncan and Liv were separated in the terminal as they waited on their seat allocations, and she and the twins had boarded the aeroplane without him. Liv was breastfeeding the boys then, and in a nonstop state of exhaustion. With a baby at each breast, she'd sat at the rear of the plane, near the toilets. Liv had fretted when she hadn't seen Duncan board. It was only as the flight attendants performed their final checks that one of them whispered, 'Are you Liv?'

'Yes.' She smiled above the slurping babies.

'Duncan wants you to know he got a seat.'

'Thank you.' Her relief was instant.

'Up the front.'

'Oh.' Liv craned her neck to look far down the aisle.

Polite, with a ready grin, Duncan was the sort of man other men liked, women befriended and old ladies called 'perfect'. Fifty minutes later, when the flight ran out of food, Liv was offered an apple by the apologetic staff. When the plane landed, Liv learnt that Duncan had enjoyed an egg and bacon roll, a blueberry muffin and an orange juice. For the entire flight, Duncan hadn't thought to check on her or swap seats. Or nurse a baby. It was as if he was travelling alone, which, to be fair, he usually did. He'd felt terribly bad afterwards, when he heard about the apple.

A corkscrew of panic twisted in Liv's chest. Though autumn had begun weeks ago, it was expected to reach an unseasonably warm thirty-two degrees today. When they'd left home, it'd been twenty-six. For their short, tense trip, Duncan had set the air conditioning on high, but the air in the car was no longer cool. Liv clambered back into the passenger's seat for a better view of the oval. Two sets of boys in footy jerseys were deep in a game. Liv thought she recognised one of the pink-cheeked midfielders – someone's giraffe-like big brother. She waved. But no one was giving her, or the car park, any thought. She reassessed the multi-level buildings, the curving driveway. Past the ovals, the buildings appeared to be empty. Between the buildings was a glimpse of the bay. Usually the water calmed her. Simply looking at a poster of the sea made her feel better. But looking at the water this morning was not helping.

Duncan had only been out of sight for a minute or two, but it seemed like twenty. Already, the car was getting stuffy.

Liv elbowed the horn.

Twelve hours earlier, the Winsome family's current woes had begun with a phone call. It was 10.40 pm on a Friday, and Liv was driving home from Oscar's disappointing representative basketball game in Bendigo. The standard of these games could be quite high, as each club chose their best players for the teams. But tonight's game was a shambles. After giving Oscar a light roasting, Duncan had fallen asleep. Oscar had sung himself to sleep as well by the time the phone rang. Liv assumed it would be Jai, the team's star point guard, home sick with a sore throat. But the number was unfamiliar. She'd pressed the button on the steering wheel and a woman's voice had burst into the dark cabin.

'Is this Jai Winsome's mother?'

'Yes.' The silence gaped like a ravine. 'Is he okay?'

Liv eyed Oscar snoring, open mouthed, in the back seat.

'That's a matter of opinion.' The woman's tone, while nasty, didn't suggest tragedy.

'Who is this?'

'Jilly Saffin, Bella's mother.'

Liv tried to recall either the woman or the girl. Had Bella started in the twins' year at Carmichael in Year Three, five years ago? The Jilly that Liv could remember was fine-boned, with ironed, yellow hair.

'What's this about?' Liv turned down the volume.

'Tonight, Jai and that Blake Havelock . . . posted . . . the things they've written . . .' The woman's voice was breaking up but Liv caught her drift. 'Bella . . . and Jai's girlfriend, Grace . . . humiliated . . . and some girls are only twelve!'

'Jilly, Jai won't have done any of that,' said Liv. 'He's sick.'

The younger of her twin sons, her secret favourite, was also a decent, sensitive child, who didn't have a girlfriend.

'Blake told his mother. They did it together, all right. I just got off the phone with her.'

Liv pictured her son's best friend: narrow, stooped and wan. Oh, Blake. A complicated kid, he wouldn't have been her choice for the job. Liv first met Blake Havelock when he was seven years old, and even then he was trying. It was day one of Year Two and, slyly, he'd been kicking balls over fences and up-ending rubbish bins. His chatty mother, Stella, had quaffed coffee while laughing wildly at Liv's jokes. Hard not to like, despite her crafty son, who, unfortunately, Jai had loved on sight: 'Mum, he's so fun!'

Liv could remember the Saffins better, then. Jilly Saffin was a fragile woman with a retired, compliant husband and an odd set of children: Bella (frumpy, kind, reserved), aged fourteen, and a son (sporty, social, popular), aged sixteen, who'd been sent to the Australian Institute of Sport in Canberra.

She tried to follow the threads of the conversation. 'But Stella's in the Northern Territory.'

'That was her excuse. What's yours?'

Liv swallowed. Was it for her to have an excuse, or simply for her son? And what of her napping husband? 'Jilly, I'll look into it.'

She'd ended the call and planted her foot. 'Duncan?' she whispered. 'Wake up. Where's your phone?'

Not one person was responding to the horn.

Liv watched two boys running for a loose ball, from opposite directions, and she winced. Nearer the car, on the driveway, three girls in

Carmichael sports uniforms sashayed past. Four boys propped on a fence took their eyes off the game to yell and gesture at them. The boys were from the opposing school: some inner-city Grammar. One girl tugged at the hem of her netball skirt. The others grew pinker with each step. Laughing, the boys shoved each other until the smallest of them fell.

Like a demented child, Liv continued tooting.

Last night, as paddocks dashed by, it'd seemed to Liv she was constantly rushing. Constantly time-poor. Constantly exhausted. That morning, she'd risen at six to ready the boys for school and herself for work. At eight, once the boys had left, she'd driven across town to interview the former workmates of an injured truck mechanic. Around two, hot and hungry, she'd interviewed their defensive motor-head boss. By six, she was rushing home again to pick up Cody from Harry's house and make veggie burgers.

She looked to Duncan, who was hunched over his phone.

'This Grace girl . . .' he said. 'Crikey. She really fourteen?'

In the rear-view mirror, she glimpsed Oscar, still asleep. You could just make out his wispy moustache.

'Put it away,' she whispered.

She rushed, she supposed, to fit everything in and keep everyone happy. As if her husband's and children's happiness were her KPIs. Of course, Duncan's happiness was ultimately his responsibility, but Liv did what she could, and much of the boys' happiness fell to her. And her boys were happy – or so she'd thought. Their happiness was measured in activities and grades and goals, friends and haircuts and shoes. Each day, she attended to their breakfasts and school lunches, their clean washing and stainless steel water bottles, their home-baked after-school snacks and healthy, colourful dinners. Each week, she scheduled the boys' basketball training (for two teams, their local, domestic team and repre-sentative team) and their football games, clarinet/trumpet practice and maths tutor, swimming lessons and play dates (for nine-year-old Cody). Until recently, she'd patched their six knees, cut their thirty toenails and sponged their countless stains. She still chased a filthy Cody around the backyard with a hose. Listened to his eternal, illogical stories. Stemmed his bloody noses. She washed the boys' bed linen, admittedly not often enough, and hung their towels. Nightly, she scrolled through the twins' messages and monitored their screen time. (She'd never seen anything alarming. Not like this.) To preserve her sanity, and her marriage, she organised annual holidays, dinners with friends and date nights. Twenty-five years ago, she was a high-achieving student, and today she was a high-achieving mother (and wife). A super-doer. Or so she'd thought.

She'd been living, she realised, as if one day someone was going to grade her efforts, and that A-plus would make everything worthwhile.

Arriving home around 11.30 pm, Liv had been relieved to see the house lit up and Jai sprawled on the couch. He was watching the Milwaukee Bucks play the Toronto Raptors, with one hand on his phone, the other in Duncan's chocolate stash. Stirred by the ceiling fan, shreds of silver foil danced about the orange carpet. The carpet, like the flat-roofed house, was only a few years older than she was. Built in the early 1970s, their house was large and airy and in need of updating. And she loved it. Its unpretentiousness. Its liveability.

She surveyed the rest of her tired home as if on the lookout for a sniper. You can do this, she told herself.

'Hi Mum, did we win?'

Jai was smiling his usual smile, which involved most of his face. His large white teeth were chocolatey. He seemed better. She shook her head.

'Did Oscar score?'

'Nope.'

She studied him for signs of knowing. His eyes, like hers, were over-sized, dappled hazel and rarely deceitful. He swept his hair across his forehead. She took in the sprinkling of freckles across his nose. His throat, where his glands were down. Yes, he looked better. He also looked like the sort of boy she would've fancied at high school, and therefore avoided. Fortunately, he and Oscar seemed unaware of their looks.

Duncan entered then, carrying Oscar's basketball backpack. Confusion was scrawled on his face, and something else – horror, or awe? Oscar's expression, too, was complicated.

'Why's everyone looking at me funny?'

Liv abandoned the horn for her phone once more. Dialling, she reminded herself that this school was run by professionals who fell over themselves to help. The teachers at Carmichael, though not perfect, were the best money could buy, which meant *highly engaged* and *terribly responsive*. If you emailed them at 7.39 pm on a Sunday with a homework or excursion query, you'd have a response by 7.43 pm. The office staff were similarly efficient.

Twenty seconds later, her call rang out.

No doubt the office was having an especially busy Saturday.

Liv remembered then a study, done in the 1960s, after a woman was murdered outside her apartment in New York City. Thirty-odd people in the surrounding apartments had heard her screams, but no one came to help, apparently. Why? It turned out, because everyone assumed someone else would . . . if it was necessary. The study found that if you wanted to be helped or rescued, it was optimal for fewer than four people to be nearby. One was best.

On and around the ovals, Liv could see more than sixty people. She was stuffed.

She pressed the horn again, long, insistent bleats. Perspiration dotted her cheeks. Eventually, a lonely winger turned in the direction of the car. A breeze lifted his fringe from his eyes. When she tooted again, he took a step towards the car park and she beamed; but then, in the midfield, a boot connected with the ball, sending it high and his way. And he was off.

The TV was black and Jai was perched on the couch when Liv said, 'You wrote that Grace Charters *loves cock*.'

'I did?'

Jai took Duncan's telephone and flicked through the images. He looked, at most, puzzled. His gaze lingered on the one of Grace, his apparent girlfriend. Then he flipped through the others, while Liv talked. As he listened, his eyes flared, but not with major distress or mortification. Watching over Jai's shoulder, Oscar's eyes were wide, yet wounded. This girlfriend caper seemed new to him too.

'What do you have to say?'

Duncan shot Liv a *go easy* look as he switched off lights and the fan. For ten whole seconds, they sat in vacuum-sealed silence as Jai seemed to process the night's developments. Then he returned the phone.

'They're not the best of Bella,' he said softly.

Liv frowned at the photographs of girls in various modes of dress, ranging from school uniforms to barely there bikinis; thankfully, none was topless or explicit. But, beneath each image, foul comments vied for attention, like scrawls on a toilet door. Girls were given ratings of 3 out of 10, called 'skanky ho's' and 'ugly bitches' . . . Liv recognised many of the kids' handles: these were boys from school. Her sons' friends and acquaintances; the children of friends and acquaintances.

Liv's stomach roiled.

Jai drew his heavy eyelids down. Sometimes, Liv thought her handsome sons resembled thoughtful lizards. But, tonight, this son's silence was baffling her. She'd been chatting with her boys for years about *respect* and *equity*, since the twins were eleven and Cody was six (and not meant to be listening). She'd been determined to create young men who owned their emotions *and* articulated them. Men who had friendships with men and women. Men who didn't touch anyone else's body parts without clear permission. Long before #MeToo, Liv and the twins had talked about sex and consent, condoms and pregnancy, nudes and dick pics. Often reluctantly and squirming . . . but she'd done it. Liv had talked with the twins and Cody about the number of female characters in the board games they'd played and movies they watched. They'd talked about how the women in music videos wore far less than the men – who were often noticeably plain-looking, pudgy and covered up. Liv was trying to make her sons critical thinkers. Responsible humans. But, somehow, had her son become *that* boy? Jai, one of their reliable, sensible twins, who'd been nothing but compliant his entire life.

Jai returned to his phone.

'Jai!'

'Bedtime,' Duncan said, flicking off the final light switch.

Wisely, Oscar made for the shower. When Jai looked up, Liv was disconcerted by the intensity of his gaze. It wasn't malicious or angry. But it was unfamiliar. Like looking through a hole in the wall and finding an eye staring back at you.

'Chill, Mum,' he said. 'It's not a big deal.'

Liv rested her forehead against the car's warm window.

After a few seconds, her obstetrician popped into her head. Almost fifteen years ago, at the thirty-six week mark, he'd said, 'Are you ready for your life to be changed forever?' He'd been trying to be cheery, she supposed, to normalise the impending birth of her first and second children. But he'd been an obtuse fellow, referring to himself in the third person. 'Elliot wants you to lie back and relax . . .' This said while holding an instrument as long as his forearm. To his question, she'd smiled politely, thinking he was overstating matters. Back then, she and Duncan were both third-year solicitors, working in neighbouring top-tier firms. They were paid similarly, had similar ambitions for partnership. But Elliot had been right. Since the birth of the twins, *her* life had changed completely. Had Duncan's? Well, yes, but not in the same way.

And had she been ready? Looking back, she'd have to say, Fat chance, Elliot.

Another, more recent doctor appeared in her head. Liv wondered what her subconscious was trying to tell her. Only yesterday, Dr Helen, her GP, had asked, 'You still tired?'

Ha! Eight uninterrupted hours of sleep was a thing of the past for virtually everyone Liv knew. But Liv's problems, it turned out, were greater than lack of sleep. Dr Helen had the results of Liv's recent blood tests. Cholesterol, iron, vitamin D, thyroid thingies, menopausal whatsits; you name it, it was out of whack. This was one of the few tests in Liv's life she had failed spectacularly.

'Your hair still falling out?'

Liv had run her fingers through her hair, producing rusty strands of evidence.

'Liv, you need to slow down,' said Dr Helen, more kindly. 'Look after yourself . . . rest.'

'Are you serious? I work four days a week, I've got three school-age children and a husband.' Liv had laughed.

But Dr Helen hadn't seen the funny side. 'You are at risk of burning out. Focus on what is important and forget everything else.'

Soon, Liv supposed, she'd have to smash a window.

She was considering what in the car she could use when an elderly man in a sunhat came through a side gate. He was tottering, with a forward lean, across the car park. Liv bashed on the window and honked the horn until he registered her. He studied her as if she were a mystifying exhibit in a glass cage. Breathless, she yelled through the window, 'My husband's in reception, about to meet the principal, with our son, Jai. My husband has loads of springy hair on top and long teeth . . .' She pointed at her own teeth for emphasis. The old man seemed suitably alarmed and set off, unsteadily, at speed. Liv could have cried.

Within seconds of the man doddering inside, Duncan reappeared at a run, his curls bouncing, his arm outstretched towards the car.

And then she was out. Wiping perspiration. Gulping air.

'Are you okay?' said Duncan. 'Liv? What happened?'

She was having trouble looking at him.

'I thought you were still on the phone.'

She inhaled deeply. He glanced at the boys playing football.

'Mr Crisp is waiting – but are you okay? Why didn't it open?' He examined the car's door as if to spot the problem.

Liv breathed slowly until her eyes focused. The world beyond the car looked new, more distinct. The birdsong sounded louder, the sun brighter. Even her husband, looking worriedly from the car to her, seemed made new. Duncan's best feature was his loose curls the colour of chocolate mud cake, worn long on top but short on the sides. His eyes, a lighter tan, were small and deep-set yet warm. His teeth were on the long side, but his smile was quick. At university, in the Law faculty, they'd found each other and stayed put, figuring they'd done as well as they ever might. They were nineteen.

'Liv, say something. I'm sorry about the car.'

He scowled at the Audi as if it had betrayed him.

She inhaled. 'That must never, ever, happen again.'

'Yes. Got it.' He smiled. It was hard to dislike Duncan, unless you were irked by amiable neutrality. Her husband had been invited to more twenty-firsts and weddings, thirtieths and fortieths than anyone she knew. A pleasant, human stocking filler.

'Are you okay?' He leant towards her.

'No.' Liv made herself smile. 'But I will be.'

Jai appeared on the grass. Her beautiful, oblivious boy waved. The twins had thick blond hair on their long limbs but nutmeg-coloured hair on their heads. A tall boy, Jai looked as if he'd grown taller since they'd arrived. She wiped her eyes.

'The keys . . .' she said. 'Please give me the keys.'

Duncan passed them and Liv clasped them tight. As she set off, she wobbled, and Duncan took her arm. His grip was strong and his step steady. Mustering some dignity, Liv entered the chilly administration building and smiled at the receptionist.

'I'm terribly sorry for the delay,' she said.

2

Duncan

Unannounced, Tony Crisp burst into the office and extended his hand to Duncan. A small man, white haired, with boyish, plump cheeks, Crisp was stylish in a black suit and blue silk tie. Duncan rose, a split second late, to grasp the principal's soft palm. 'A pleasure.'

He'd always wanted to meet Crisp, one on one, though not under these circumstances. He was still struggling with the car fiasco, too. Later, at home, he'd have to re-enact it to believe it.

'Good morning,' said Crisp, with a nod to Liv and Jai.

Duncan eyed a nearby grandfather clock. Technically, it was now afternoon. The principal sat and read a sticky note on his desk. Though he'd not met Crisp before, Duncan had heard him speak. A passable orator, the principal tended to bang on about his dream of making Carmichael Grammar 'the best school in the world'. Admirable, thought Duncan, if over the top.

He wondered how long this would take. Liv had googled how other schools in Melbourne had dealt with these dime-a-dozen Gen-Z scandals. Expulsion seemed most likely, accompanied by counselling and a burst of pastoral care for the students who remained. Effectively, the naughty children were shuffled out of one school and into another. The parents' embarrassment faded. The End.

Sayonara, Blake.

•

Duncan crossed his legs. Crisp's cool office felt familiar, like that of a senior partner in a top-tier firm, which made sense. The Winsomes could buy a stately house in the country for what they were paying to send their sons to Carmichael. They'd certainly be more liquid without the school fees. He wondered if the principal knew they couldn't make the regular term-by-term payments, that they were on a payment plan. He hoped not. But it was worth it; he'd never heard another parent say it wasn't. The school had an exceptional reputation and achieved phenomenal results, far better than when he and his brother had attended. Carmichael turned out all sorts these days, too: actors and astrophysicists as well as footballers. Plus, it was co-ed now, relatively close to home, and the uniforms suited his boys: light blue, silver and grey.

Since the twins had started high school, the years were flying by. Duncan felt as if this year had just begun, but already it was Term Two.

Prior to Carmichael, the twins had spent two mind-numbing years at the local primary school, where they'd dozed through the alphabet. Duncan had been shocked by the patchy teaching and low expectations; the early switch to Carmichael had been his idea. They'd originally planned to wait until high school, but Duncan didn't want to risk it. He wasn't making a call on the entire public school system. He wasn't like Liv, who'd cross-referenced studies, and casually interviewed everyone. Her education and their socio-economic status were more predictive of the boys' educational outcomes, apparently; but for him, it was Carmichael Grammar or else. The stand-off had been one of the few hairy moments in their marriage. Liv had briefly flirted with the idea of homeschooling the boys through the primary years. But, luckily, they'd all liked Carmichael when he'd dragged them here for a tour. Best of all, both the twins and Cody had stepped up since the family had been paying exorbitant fees. Over the years, the boys had gone from goofing off, not caring less, to buckling down – even Cody, a bit, at nine. Were the two related? Who could tell? But whatever had happened, it was working, and Duncan didn't want it ruined by an idiot and his Insta account.

•

Duncan could hear Liv deep-breathing. She hadn't recovered from the car thing either, he supposed, and he couldn't blame her. That car shouldn't have any glitches. It could've taken a nasty turn out there, in the heat. Liv's ability to talk was legendary – on and off the phone. He'd been prepared to give her another five minutes. He'd been on the phone himself when he'd locked the car.

When Crisp looked up, Duncan was taken aback by the man's green eyes. While one of those eyes was on Jai, the other was quite possibly on him. Duncan tried to listen as the principal began. But his mind quickly wandered. It'd been a hectic week. Fortunately, Liv was an excellent listener. Within seconds, he was checking out the photographs on Crisp's desk. A large black-and-white print showed male students circa 1960. Bright, white faces.

'There it is: a sorry tale,' said Crisp, a few minutes later. 'What do you have to say, Jai?'

Jai blinked.

'Just tell Mr Crisp what you told us,' Liv said, gently.

Duncan stirred. Liv still looked rather damp.

'Okay. Um, my side's kind of . . . I, um, was home sick, and, like, Blake came over.' After a bumpy start, Jai recounted what he'd eventually told them. 'I was watching the Toronto Raptors. Winning by a stack. Blake was on his phone.'

Duncan eyed a smaller black-and-white picture: muddy boys in rugby uniforms. Duncan had loved getting muddy.

'Doing what, on his phone?'

'I don't know. Being all gloomy about Bella. Looking at pictures of her, I guess. Then he wanted to go on the PlayStation and I didn't. So, yeah, he left.'

'You didn't create the Instagram account together before he left?' said Crisp.

'Nope,' he said, sheepishly.

Liv nodded and Crisp leant forward. 'How did Blake get that picture of your girlfriend, Jai?'

'He must've got it off my phone. Sent it to his.'

'I see.'

'Yeah.' Jai looked suitably crestfallen. Betrayed by his best friend.

Liv gave Jai a quick, reassuring pat on the back.

'Nope? Yeah?'

Jai blinked until his brain kickstarted. 'I mean, *yes*, Mr Crisp.'

Duncan smothered a yawn. He'd hoped that his sons would've met the principal at some stage before this and impressed him with their brains, their coordination, their easy charm – especially Jai. Jai's jump shot was a thing of beauty. Today, though, he simply hoped his son seemed credible.

'*Top Ten Sluts by the Sea* . . . are these, or any other words on this account, your words?'

Crisp was impressively direct. Jai glanced at Liv. She flashed a high-beam stare.

'Yes. I mean, no. But I did say Bella was a top slut. I was trying to make him feel better. A slut isn't necessarily a bad thing,' said Jai. 'It can be, you know, jokey. You can call your friends sluts.'

Duncan's turn to wince, as he studied the ceiling. Jai's obliviousness was excruciating.

'You call your friends *sluts*?'

Duncan jerked at the principal's tone and Crisp's gaze strayed to him. He gave a weak smile.

'Yeah. I mean, yes, sir. Everyone does. Sometimes.'

Crisp's stare returned to Duncan's dopey son, while Liv clenched her mouth.

'This is not a debate in which I intend to participate. Language of this ilk is unacceptable at Carmichael Grammar.'

Liv's high-beams flashed again at Jai.

'If I am to understand you correctly, Jai, you are saying Blake was looking at pictures at your house, because he was *gloomy*? But he didn't create an Instagram account there, with you?'

'Yes.'

Duncan nodded. This was an open-and-shut case. He swivelled his eyes to wake them up.

'I'm afraid none of that correlates with what Blake Havelock is saying,' said Crisp. 'He said you did it together, at your house.'

'Yes, but we didn't.' Jai's voice cracked with emotion. 'I didn't.'

Liv prodded Duncan with a sharp look. But what was there to say? He didn't understand why Blake said and did what he did. Neither did Jai, and they were meant to be best friends. Duncan focused on the other frames on the desk. As the images became coloured, more recent, girls appeared.

Liv cleared her throat. 'Blake's . . . got a good heart, but—'

'Why would he take your girlfriend's picture?' said Crisp.

Jai shrugged.

Crisp put a hand over his weak eye. 'Unfortunately we have your word against Blake's.' He removed his hand and his eye roved. 'But just as troubling, I have to say, are these girls, posing and whatnot. It's a big problem.'

This last was to Duncan.

'I couldn't agree more.' Duncan whistled. 'Glad we don't have daughters.'

Liv scowled. 'Actually, Mr Crisp—'

'From Blake Havelock – well, we all know about Mr Havelock.' Crisp pouted. 'But from you, Jai? You're quite a smart boy, quite pleasant and, from what I hear, quite handy with a basketball . . .'

Liv's frown deepened. She wouldn't be liking those 'quites'.

'Jai's a kind and moral boy,' she said. Then she glared at Duncan. What was he meant to say?

'Yeah, he is,' said Duncan. 'He's a good, *honest* kid.'

'Yes, so I've heard.' Crisp shot a quick smile to Duncan. 'But why would Blake bring you into this?'

Jai shrugged again. Duncan had asked himself the same thing. Presumably, Liv would get to the bottom of gloomy Blake and his motives. But she was sitting back, as if she'd given up. For the life of him, he didn't know why.

Crisp turned both eyes to Duncan.

'Oh. I, ah . . . I don't see how this affects the school,' he said. 'It happened on a Friday night, at a private house.'

'It is *fundamentally* about the school,' said Crisp. 'Unfortunately.'

Liv's stare swung between Duncan and Crisp as the principal went on about the school's uniform being visible in some photos; about how each of the girls was a Carmichael student, whose *reputation* was at stake; about the many Carmichael students who posted those obscene comments or voted, especially on the more ill-judged of the photographs; about the school's expectation that its students conduct themselves appropriately *at all times*. And, finally, about the blurred line between private and public personas these days. How these young people had crossed that line.

Crisp, thought Duncan, seemed pained by that last fact. He didn't envy the man's job: corralling twits into adulthood.

'I do hear what Jai is saying,' continued Crisp. '*But*, if the matter proves to be as Blake has attested, then, as I am sure you are aware, Duncan, this behaviour puts Jai's presence at Carmichael Grammar in jeopardy. Expelling a student is not something we do lightly.'

Liv folded her arms. Duncan waited for her to say something. But she turned to look through the window. Wrong-footed, Duncan sat up straighter.

'Ah . . . to be fair,' he said, clearing his throat, 'the account was up for, what, five hours? Even if Jai was involved, it was a brief lapse of judgement on the boys' part.'

While Crisp nodded, Duncan felt Liv's glare, though it made no sense. He was doing his best here. This was more fraught than he'd expected.

Crisp rose and stepped to a sideboard, where he straightened a coloured picture of a group of boys, and a smattering of girls.

'For the time being, the boys are suspended,' he said. 'We will be in touch on Friday. In the meantime, please do not engage with the media.' He smiled at the three of them.

'You can count on us,' said Duncan, though Friday seemed a long way away.

Duncan stood. He thought of the post someone had sent to Liv on Bayside Rocks, a public neighbourhood Facebook page. Grace's mother, Jess Charters, had vented there: something about the girls having been disrespected, the boys needing to pay a price, and so on. Overnight, the post had exploded, mostly with support. How big would that fury be by Friday?

Liv was back to looking through the window.

'The sooner this blows over,' said Duncan, 'the better.'

'Your father has a good head on his shoulders,' said Crisp to Jai.

Duncan beamed as he shook the man's warm hand again. 'Thank you, and we are sorry.'

'Indeed.'

Liv stood, with her arms still folded. Jai shook Crisp's hand too. 'Yes, I'm sorry too, sir. Very.'

Duncan didn't really know what Jai was apologising for – taking up the man's time or being friends with wayward Blake. But, for a second, he was proud of Jai, of the boy's eye contact and firm grip. His son was growing up.

3

Liv

Stepping into the foyer, Liv felt deeply dissatisfied. Just as her sons had never been in trouble at school before, neither had she. Perhaps that was it. Her school had been small, the buildings unobtrusive and the oval pockmarked; it'd been surrounded by inexpensive real estate, including a train line and a piggery. By the end of her first term there, she no longer noticed the trains rattling the pencils in their jars and she couldn't smell the pig shit. She had always remembered that: how easily you could become desensitised, to the point that something that shook your entire body or made you gag could, over time, be forgotten or disregarded. But today, something . . . stank. And not just that Instagram account.

Hesitating, she surveyed the reception area and the clean windows facing the ovals. Last week she'd investigated the bullying of a graduate teacher at a country primary school by a parent, and she'd read research around the current challenges in education: the escalation in parental expectations and bad behaviour, the rise of the toxic parent, et cetera. She didn't want to be that parent. She'd learnt a lot about the pressures on new teachers and experienced principals alike. She'd learnt, too, how pivotal the role of principal was in setting the tone for the entire school.

Liv rubbed her cool arms and studied Tony Crisp again. Something about the small man rankled.

The school was forever corresponding with parents and asking for feedback, particularly from newcomer families with 'fresh eyes'. Liv's family wasn't new but, this morning, she'd managed to get her hands on a pair of *fresh eyes*. She felt as if she were a character in a movie who'd had a blow to the head and was transformed.

'Goodbye.' Tony Crisp smiled at her, paused in the no-man's-land between the front desk and exterior door.

Liv looked from him to the walls of paintings. There was something seriously amiss here, she decided, whether Blake was lying or not. Being in that meeting had reminded her of being a junior solicitor. An oversized white man in a black robe loomed at her from the wall, and she frowned. His scalp was shiny, with streaks of white, and his eyes were dabs of indigo blue. His expression was sombre, appraising. The plaque read *Edward Fenton, Principal, 1939–1947*. Alongside Ed were two other stern figures. Liv looked along the hall – more portraits, large and framed. Principals. Assistant principals. Chairmen. Every face was white and bore the same toothless half-smile of the self-satisfied. Every body wore a suit: grey, brown, black. Each painting contained bookshelves, ornate wooden chairs or grandfather clocks. None of these former principals had a personality, as far as she could see. And not one a . . . uterus. Of course, the school was old, she told herself. Decades of principals and assistant principals had ruled and retired. Died. These walls were not representative of today, or even of the twenty-first century. Liv searched for a portrait of the current principal and could not find one. She turned to face the full-bodied man himself and cleared her throat.

'Mr Crisp,' she said. 'How many assistant principals do you have?'

'We only need the one.' He gave his most charming smile.

Liv's boys spoke of Mr Palmer, renowned for his ukulele playing and football coaching. 'Yes. And how many of your heads of year levels are men?'

The principal's eyes aligned as he considered her. 'Men? Why, seven, I believe.'

'And that's out of?'

She saw Duncan frown.

Tony Crisp looked at her as if she was fraying at her edges. 'Nine.'

Yes, she was onto something. Duncan opened the exterior door. 'Liv?' he said.

'Nine.' Liv tried to swallow the gristly lump of a word. 'And who are the two women?'

Jai began grinding his jaw, a long-forgotten habit.

'Mrs Wattletree, Head of Junior School, and Miss Patterson, Head of Early Learning.' Tony Crisp nodded, like an adult placating a child who'd dropped her ice cream and wanted another. He motioned towards her husband at the exit.

'Of course.' Liv gathered herself. 'And the ratio on the board?'

'Why, two of nine again.' Tony Crisp smiled as if he'd conjured a bunny from a hat. 'The board is a significant, voluntary contribution to our community.'

Liv planted her feet. A neat coincidence? She was pretty sure thirty per cent was the magic ratio needed to avoid tokenism. A few of her friends' husbands were on the board. She'd never considered how they came to be there. But what of the leading teachers? How had she not noticed this before? After all those parent–teacher interviews and whole-school assemblies, sports carnivals and performance nights. She'd never bothered to count teachers' heads, or their other bits. She looked beyond this cool island of administration on its manicured lawn. Outside, hot children were still being entertained by balls.

Tony Crisp retreated, to stand framed by the doorway to his office. He raised his hand in farewell.

'Liv?' Duncan tipped his head to the world outside as warm air seeped in.

'Mr Crisp?' she said, her voice sharp and rising.

Duncan's eyes snapped towards her and he shut the door. He seemed to have recognised her tone: not her bedroom voice, but a voice usually reserved for home. Jai was grinding pre-emptively. She'd never done anything like this before; but today, for imprecise reasons, she couldn't *not*. She could see the entire interconnected reality of what Blake had done. It seemed she was the only one who could.

'You have a woman problem. Or, rather, a too-many-men-at-the-top problem.'

'A wo— Oh, no.' Tony Crisp's smile tightened, and the word *handler* sprang into her mind. 'Rest assured, Olivia, we do our best, but the talent pool is remarkably small at the top end of the profession,' he said. 'We do have Mrs MacBeth, of course. While not in a leadership role as such, Mary is one of our most beloved and talented senior teachers.'

Liv crossed her arms. The warm and highly capable Mrs MacBeth had taught the twins Year Five English. Liv may have assumed Mrs MacBeth was a head teacher. The pause grew like a warm puddle. Duncan and Jai were locked in a shocked silence.

Tony Crisp opened his mouth but a slight delay ensued. Liv hoped he wasn't going to use the m-word.

'We are absolutely about *merit* here at Carmichael,' he said, benignly.

Liv exhaled deeply. She tried to give the man the benefit of the doubt. Old-fashioned soul that he was. Tony Crisp's gaze strayed to the receptionist, a grey-haired woman around Liv's age, who was busily trying not to listen.

'Olivia, our school is renowned for its teaching and rigorous programs. We expect a great deal from our staff. Naturally, we demand over and above from our leaders, to which I'm sure you and your sons can attest.'

Liv's eyes narrowed. Tony Crisp was choosing his words as she'd observed many an interviewee do, when navigating her questions.

'I understand your concern,' he went on. 'But around twenty-five per cent of all workers in this country are women who work full time, and women sit in around thirty per cent of leadership roles. Our numbers reflect that general trend.'

Liv's fresh eyes began to smart.

'We are committed to making the leadership team "representative" in the long term, I assure you.'

Tony Crisp turned to Duncan as if he might find an ally. But Duncan's mouth was a small, empty cave.

Liv wondered what to say, how far to go. She wasn't by nature disagreeable, but how well had being agreeable served her? Today, her husband had locked her in their car; a dozen families watching one-sided football had ignored her; her son, guilty or not of this Instagram debacle, was a fledgling Neanderthal. In recent weeks, she'd begun to go bald. She didn't want to have an outright argument with the principal or, god forbid, *rock the boat* at her boys' fancy-pants school – especially not in these circumstances – but, then again, the present circumstances stank like a teenager's week-old socks. And this – this was important.

The matronly receptionist slipped away. Perhaps to call security.

When Liv began, her voice was shaking. 'Women make up around seventy per cent of the full-time *teaching* workforce in this country.' Her voice rose. 'Teaching is one of the industries where women predominate! I would bet the numbers here reflect a significant majority of women in the teaching staff, full-time and otherwise.' She paused, tried to calm herself but couldn't. 'Mr Crisp, it's inexplicable for the school to be unable to attract and *hire* women in positions of leadership. It's inexcusable, particularly in a co-ed school. What sort of message are you sending to the girls and boys at Carmichael? Do you not see a link between the way some of your male students are viewing girls and the culture of this school?'

She let the question dangle like a sledgehammer on a rope. Tony Crisp's mouth slipped open unbecomingly.

'What you said before was spot on. This issue with the Instagram account is *fundamentally* about the school. It's not about one or two *ignorant* boys or *foolish* girls. It's about a culture. A culture that lives and breathes here. Whether Blake created it alone or with Jai, that Instagram account was liked by ninety kids, most of whom go to this school. Kids who wrote disgusting, sexual things. Jai and Oscar and Blake have been at this school since they were seven. They are now fourteen. While we will take responsibility for our part in what Jai may have done, we expect you and the school to do the same.'

The man closed his mouth. Stared. Blinked. As if he'd been doused with icy water.

'What have you been teaching these kids these past seven years, about boys and girls, men and women? How is it they can think there's nothing wrong with calling girls *sluts*, making sexualised slurs about them and publicly rating their looks? How did that happen?'

She was breathless and her voice was well and truly high-pitched. Duncan was bug-eyed and pale. Jai was grinding hard. But there was no stopping now.

'I would hardly call these students well-rounded and right-thinking human beings. We aren't paying obscene fees for this school to turn our three sons into misogynists. Whatever you decide to do about Blake and Jai, this school has a problem and you need to fix it!'

4

Liv

The afternoon sun was putting a sheen on the bay as they drove in silence. Liv's gaze skimmed across their suburb. A 'lifestyle suburb' in one of the most liveable cities in the world, and in the heart of Bayside, Hampton was flanked by the water and neighbouring golf courses, and, mostly, it was as clean and well-tended as a putting green. Today it was busy with walkers and runners and late-season beach goers. Locals called the whole area 'the Bayside bubble', as if those within were safe and protected. Liv loved the place – less for its occasional mansion and tennis court, more for its natural beauty and jaw-dropping sunsets. But, today, everything about it felt . . . compromised. The bubble, Liv feared, had popped.

The silence in the car was profound by the time Liv pulled in. She'd lost it at her sons' principal. Rendered him mute. Her embarrassment flowered on her cheeks as she stared at her property – nay, her mid-life – as if seeing it for the first time. An unmown lawn, cascading junk mail and a protruding fence paling greeted them. The vessel carrying the Winsome family had been slowly running aground, she realised, despite her super-doing.

Their chocolate labradoodle, Pickle, bounded to the car and barked at them. Liv and Duncan didn't move. Their other boys had been dropped home by kind parents. Visible through their home's front windows, still in his footy jersey, Oscar was on his phone, while Cody was watching TV, as the overhead fan whirred. The engine was still running as Jai shot out of the car. 'They'll expel me for sure now,' he muttered. 'I can't believe you did that.' He bolted inside, leaving the front door open.

'On the whole, that went well.' Duncan gave a half-hearted smile as he reached for the door. 'Crisp seemed reasonable enough. This'll blow over.'

'Reasonable?' Liv's eyes filled. 'Blow over? Oh my god.'

Worry streaked across Duncan's face. 'What's the matter now?'

Cody marched onto the porch and yelled, 'Mum, I'm hungry!' then dove back to the couch.

Idly, Liv wondered whether Harry's mum had fed Cody morning tea after collecting him from golf. Then she looked at her children. Cody seated again – on someone's phone – the twins in headsets now with their noses presumably to the PlayStation. They resembled, from this distance, underage and uncooperative call-centre staff.

'The man ignored me,' she said. 'And you didn't even notice.'

'What are you talking about?'

She took a breath from the deep sea of her gut. 'Duncan, things need to *change*. Not only at school.'

'Liv, you're . . .' Duncan shrugged. 'I don't know. Stressed or anxious or something.'

Liv sighed again. Her inner world was like Tasmania: a place she'd always wanted to explore but had never found the time. But what she felt wasn't anxiety. She was pretty sure.

As the engine purred and air-conditioning blew, Liv didn't move. Instead, she tried to describe to Duncan how she was feeling. How her malaise had crystallised in the car. How Dr Helen was right. She needed to do less. To focus on what was important – like their sons, and their friendships and education. How, today, she could see the link between her overwhelmed life and the school's culture, and what Blake had done and Jai didn't understand. She explained how the problem was structural. How she and Duncan were like job-sharing shift workers, who'd misplaced not only their sex life but their values.

By the time she'd finished, Liv understood herself a little better.

But Duncan said, 'Huh?' And then, 'Come on, things aren't that bad.'

She and Duncan had been married, mostly happily, for eighteen years, and had known each other for twenty-six. They'd spent a significant part of their lives together, even if they now spent a significant chunk of their weeks apart. They'd met at law school when Liv, a starry-eyed second year, had shown first-year Duncan around the campus. Duncan had climbed into Law through a window in the Arts faculty, and was awed by anyone who'd walked in the front door. Anyone who scored more than a Pass average impressed him beyond words too. And Liv had impressed him. She'd blitzed her degree, finishing with first class honours, while Duncan had meandered through his as he played open-mic nights and jotted dreamy lyrics. Liv, partial to musicians, had happily traipsed along. His muse. Once, Liv and Duncan had been a couple who did everything together.

'Twenty years ago, we were on the same page, you and I. These days, I have to explain everything to you, including our sons.'

Duncan's face was a blank Scrabble tile. It was the face of a weary man who'd lost the thread of the conversation. The face of a man who'd spent most of the week at his desk. But it wasn't the face of doubt, or nastiness, or – that death knell of a marriage – contempt. Importantly, he did not roll his eyes.

'It's been a tough twelve hours. Come on. Turn off the car, let's have lunch.' He peeked at his phone.

'Mum!' screamed a twin. 'Cody's hungry. We are too.'

Liv shook her head. Inside, Cody was now jumping on the coffee table.

The problem wasn't her children, she told herself. Despite recent events, the twins were 'good kids', much like Duncan was a 'good bloke'. Everyone said so, and Liv believed them. Jai and Oscar had had few friend-ship dramas – until now. They lived in each other's pockets but managed to get along, despite Jai outshining Oscar in most sports. They still shared a bunk-bed and walked together to and from the school bus. They were identical but Liv could tell them apart. Duncan could too, after a few seconds, particularly if a ball was involved. Not so much their teachers, nor sometimes their friends, who didn't overlap. It was the voice – their voice.

If one of them was in the shower and sang out, kudos to you if you could tell who it was.

And Cody was a nice enough kid, for a talkative, hyperactive nine year old whose favourite word was still 'NO'. The only time Cody stopped bouncing was when he was deliriously tired, and then he'd sleep anywhere – under the table at a restaurant, on the dog. Alas, he talked even during his sleep. When Cody came along, the finely poised balance in the Winsome family collapsed and Liv became a super-duper-doer.

'We want a toastie!' yelled, quite possibly, the other twin.

Late bloomers, the twins hadn't disappeared into teenage-hood yet, but they were on the brink. They'd both recently sprouted a few spots, a couple of hairs, and had begun to stink. Proud of himself, Jai had said, 'Gross, we smell like Dad.' Oscar had marked the occasion with a primal roar: 'We need more deodorant! One that smells!' Liv didn't want her boys to disappear into grunts and acne, moustaches and wet dreams. She enjoyed their conversations and their hugs and their softness. She could still get away with the odd tickle. But, while she didn't want them growing up too soon, the twins (and even Cody) were able bodied and highly coordinated: capable of moving from one room to another and opening the fridge, buttering bread, even cutting cheese. Liv knew this, but hadn't implemented this knowledge for . . . well, forever. Why? Because she'd wanted to care for them, to make their lives easy? Possibly. If she was more honest, though, it was probably because it was quicker and tidier if she did it.

Liv yelled across Duncan, from the car. 'Make it yourself!'

'What?!' A three-child yell.

'*Make it yourself!*' She sounded angrier than she thought she felt.

From the passenger seat, Duncan was regarding her as if she'd told the boys to take the Audi for a spin.

'Mum!' screamed Cody.

'You want me to go?'

In spite of his offer, Duncan wasn't moving. Her husband, her children's father, had offered to get up, like a visitor who was displaying good manners but had no intention of doing so. Liv felt an internal lightning strike.

'Liv, what's going on?'

Liv remembered then what a psychologist friend had told her once: marriages change shape over time. The psychologist had said every couple of years she badly wanted to get a divorce, and this was normal. The psychologist told Liv that she and her husband grew on their own trajectories, and sometimes their growth lines took them far apart, but in time the lines would come together again. They would then track in parallel for a while before growing apart once more. She said their lines formed the shape of a plump Greek vase. The psychologist said she and her husband had made three vases so far, and she expected them do that forever – with at least one, if not both of them, seriously considering divorce every few years. Liv had been shocked and relieved when she'd learnt that. She'd been married about four years then. The twins were in kindergarten, she was pregnant with Cody and she'd tried and failed to return to work part-time as a solicitor. The vase she and Duncan had been creating was a lot like a platter.

Detached from their screens, the boys appeared in the foyer. They'd moved off the couch as one.

'Why are you still in the car?' yelled Cody.

'What's wrong with Mum?' said Jai.

'Yeah,' said Oscar, 'why do we have to do *everything*?'

If Liv wasn't feeling so angry, she would have laughed. Cody looked from his brothers to his parents. The look of puzzlement on the three boys' faces was a magnified version of their father's. The few remaining clouds in Liv's mind cleared. The events of the past twenty-four hours had been calamitous, yet constructive. Suddenly, she had a new super power. Women's vision.

'There's nothing wrong with Mum.' Duncan bent forward to examine her. 'Right, Liv? Are you . . . do you know where we are?'

'That's it,' she said. It was time to focus on what was important. Slow down. 'Boys, we've lost our way.' She smiled. 'But, starting now, we're realigning.'

Worry and indignation streaked from face to face.

'No, Mum!' Cody shrieked.

Oscar said, 'What does that even mean?'

Jai shrugged. The boys stepped closer, craned their necks to look into the car. Liv was tempted to lecture. She wanted to squish about in her sons' brains, like a vigneron in grapes, before their grey matter was permanently gender-coded. She wanted Jai to understand the context of Blake's Instagram account, and what respect looked like. She wanted to undo what that school and the world at large and, maybe, ahem . . . they had done. And she wanted to do it now, before another year got away from them. Oscar glanced at Duncan, who wiggled his caterpillar eyebrows.

Where to start? Something tangible was needed. Doable . . . and small. Something the boys would understand. Something that would *stick* in a real and meaningful way. Otherwise, what was the alternative? More of the same? She'd be bald by Christmas.

She turned off the car.

'Gentlemen,' she said, 'after you've made lunch, we're each going to write a list.'

5

Liv

Yes, Liv's first major act of change was a call for the making of lists. They would each make a list of everything they did around the house. This wasn't radical but it was a start. For the first time in twenty-four hours, she felt mildly optimistic.

After eating her too-cheesy toasties, made mind-numbingly slowly by the boys, Liv sat on the toilet and devised her list. Beyond the bathroom, her sons screamed. 'Mum, where have you hidden the Milo?' and 'Mum, have you seen my orange hoodie?' and 'Mum, Cody's punching me again!' followed by screams – from Cody.

Liv answered their questions through the closed door: 'In the Tupperware cupboard, go easy on it!' and 'In the laundry on the clothes horse,' and 'Stop punching, all of you!' Years ago, when this first started happening, she'd wondered why they didn't call for Duncan. Why they hunted her down to the smallest room in the house. Was it, perchance, because she couldn't escape? Over time, she'd become used to it.

She had to admit, Duncan had become extraordinarily good at stepping into his Tardis-like home office and disappearing.

'Mum?' Someone grumbled through the door. 'I need my phone.'

'Jai, can you give me five bloody minutes!' she yelled, yanking toilet paper.

To her surprise, Jai scurried.

Win number one.

An hour later, Liv sat, showered and refreshed and nursing her own phone. On its screen was a photograph of Stella Havelock in a wig and gown. Liv took in her friend's high forehead, oversized red glasses and thick marbled-grey hair. Liv was missing the sound of Stella's horsy guffaw. The two of them and their children had spent hundreds of meals together, especially in the early days. Stella was there when Cody was inconsolable the day he'd decided he must be adopted because he didn't look like his identical brothers. Stella was there when Duncan said, one time too many, 'Why are you cutting it like that?' (This said every time Liv took to an orange, a tomato or an apple.) Liv was there to witness Lindsay's refusal to be driven by his wife, anywhere, anytime. Odd, as when Liv and Stella had holidayed together with the kids, when the men were working, Stella had driven often without a bingle. Yes, Liv and Stella were as good as married but better. They were like sisters, but better. They were also the odd couple of parenting styles, but it worked.

Liv's finger hovered over the green call symbol.

Liv knew her friend thought her over-protective. Stella used to let it slip, sometimes, when she didn't get what she wanted – like Liv's sons' presence at an 'inappropriate' movie (MA+) or a birthday party at a fast food joint (KFC). Or, more recently, when Liv quoted parenting books at Stella – like *Smart Phones, Smart Kids* – or the latest research on Instagram fuelling anxiety, or the perils of online gaming, or the distorting influence of porn on boys today. And Liv was forever running around after her children. The term 'concierge parent' had been coined to describe a parent poised to meet their children's every need, and Liv was guilty as charged. The old Liv. Today, her concierge uniform was at the drycleaner's and she didn't intend to pick it up.

But Stella was the opposite of a helicopter–lawn-mower–concierge parent. She wasn't a permissive parent, either, as that implied a philosophy. Stella was a passive parent. She'd told Liv recently that neither she nor Lindsay could be bothered with the kids. 'Why should I do anything if he won't?' she'd said, and Liv had laughed. As if Stella was counterintuitively striking a feminist mothering position: equal rights to do nothing. Which

Stella *was* entitled to do, as was Lindsay, of course. Liv had thought Stella's crack funny, without completely believing it.

In the Outback, Stella and Lindsay were childless, and it was cocktail hour. But Liv desperately wanted to hear Blake's side of this and try to understand it. Their friendship worked, however, Liv realised, because most of the time she held her tongue.

Liv pushed the little green button.

That night, Duncan prepared a Greek lamb dinner (win number two). At the table, as he served up the dry, stringy meat, each member of the family produced a list. Liv expected hers to be longer than the boys' and Duncan's, though Duncan did do some housework – and more than he used to. The boys did chores too; they emptied the dishwasher, picked up Pickle's poop and threw clean washing at beds. What Liv hadn't expected was for her list to be nine pages long and contain three hundred and twenty-two items, while Duncan's was a page and a half, and the boys' half a page each, in a very large font (Cody's was enormous). Duncan, too, was caught unaware.

'What have you put in there?' He eyed her list as if she'd laced it with adjectives.

More to the point, what did *he* do around the house? Well, according to his puny list: the bins and the lawns and all things dog, along with occasional grocery shopping and the eviction of spiders. Jobs his dad would have done, and quite possibly his grandfather. About both the nature and number of these jobs, Liv was astounded. Duncan too.

Going through the pages, Duncan shook his head. 'You've included everything from checking their breathing each night to running spreadsheets on co-curricular activities, and Christmas presents?'

Liv passed the yoghurt to Cody. 'Uh-huh. I've put headings: daily, weekly, monthly, yearly.'

'Come on – *yearly*?' He put the mega-list aside.

'Buying the gifts and decorations, setting up the tree, preparing Christmas lunch, shopping and cooking . . . there's a lot in it. If you did any of it, you'd know.'

'But . . .' said Duncan, dealing pita wraps around the table, 'other people's presents and Christmas pudding?'

'Yeah, Mum, we don't care about that stuff.' Oscar was on his feet and lunging for the tomatoes.

'Oscar, sit down. If I didn't do it, you wouldn't like it. It's the same for birthdays. When was the last time any of you bought a gift?'

Duncan frowned as Liv passed Oscar the tomatoes, the lettuce and the yoghurt. She'd always prided herself on buying thoughtful gifts – things the kids wanted rather than something they needed, like a desk lamp or dental plate. If it was left to Duncan, the kids would receive a pair of socks apiece.

'Mum's right,' said Jai, chewing with his mouth open. 'We wouldn't.'

Liv pointed to Jai's mouth, which was spinning lamb and tomato like a front-loader washing machine.

Oscar said, 'Try us.'

'No, Mum!' Cody yelped. 'I like Christmas!'

'Cody, stop yelling,' Duncan said.

'What do you make of this?' she said to her sons. 'Half a page?'

'Told you, you mollycoddle them.' Duncan gave a half-smile, which Liv shot down.

'We were being concise,' said Oscar. 'What's the point, again?'

'Your mum's had a bad day.'

Liv wondered whether to deliver her lecture now. To link domestic duties and sexism and slut-rating Instagram accounts. She wondered if Jai and Oscar would see it.

'It's called a reckoning,' she said.

Oscar chewed noisily, nonplussed, while Jai flipped through her nine pages for a second time. He seemed softer today. Swinging on his chair, Cody watched his older brothers. Liv watched Jai. What sort of empathy muscle was he developing? He was her more sensitive child, the one who had come out second by a margin of eleven minutes. Today, hopefully, in the midst of a moment of growth.

'Sucks to be you, Mum,' he said.

Liv snorted her white wine. 'Thanks.'

Duncan laughed.

'But not for much longer,' she said, recovering with a cough. 'From now on, you lot are doing more and I'm doing less.'

Duncan's laughter dried up, as Liv beamed. The twins ate, with their mouths open, as was their untrainable habit; and Cody, now on his feet, jiggled around the table as if his motor was running too fast. Which it was. She waited, hoping for more insight. Gratitude? Compassion? If only she knew the origins of the division of labour in the home. On this stuff, she and Duncan and her boys needed to be educated. But Oscar pushed his plate aside and said, sheepishly, 'Wanna shoot around, Jai?'

'Yep.'

Jai kissed her on the ear before bouncing into the twilight. She sighed as Duncan tucked into his lamb and Cody ricocheted outside. The link between Blake's captions, those girls' sexy selfies and her lists was far from plain to her boys. Just as frustrating, no one seemed that perturbed or particularly interested. Jai didn't even seem overly concerned about his fate, or that his best friend had wronged him. Once he'd explained to them what Blake must've done, Jai had seemed to return to himself. Now the only clue to her son's possibly altered mental state was his unfinished souvlaki – which, she supposed, was a relief. It could have been much worse.

After dinner, Liv cut her list into four and a half pieces. She'd take them at their word. It was only March, but for Christmas, she'd give one gift each. Duncan was clearing up when she passed him his extra list. He looked at it, lost. 'I can't do all this. Why don't we get a cleaner?'

'Okay, moneybags. How about a gardener too?' said Liv. 'And a driver? A concubine?'

Duncan tugged his ear.

Sometimes Liv wondered if she shouldn't have given up the law for good when Cody was born. But the investigating gig worked well enough, despite the lower pay grade. The hours were flexible, she was paid by the file and her income helped feed that school-fee beast.

'You'll manage. It's not that bad, is it?' She arched an eyebrow.

Duncan poured himself a strong lime cordial. He did work hard for them. But so did she. This was for her peace of mind. Otherwise . . . Weren't women the backbone of the family? The Winsomes couldn't afford to have hers broken. She stuck the boys' new lists on the fridge, with extra duties for Jai, the Suspended. Then, though the dishes were mountainous and Cody was booting a soccer ball into the garage roller door, she steeled herself and went for a walk, alone, which she didn't particularly enjoy. But Stella wasn't around, and she had to get out.

Later that evening, while brushing her teeth, Liv searched her book-shelves until she found a book she'd bought three years ago and not read: *A Dummy's Guide to Changing the World.*

She climbed into bed, as Duncan wandered in. 'You've given me pick-up from footy training on Mondays and pick-up from basketball on Wednesdays.'

'Yep.'

Between community sports times two, school sport on Saturdays and footy on Sundays, the twins were rather busy. Thank god the school carted the twins around on Saturdays.

Liv flipped the book open. 'I'll do the rest of the twins' trainings and take Cody to swimming Tuesdays and golf Saturdays. We can take turns to watch the twins' basketball games on Friday and Saturday nights.'

Duncan's lips parted but no words came.

'Unless you want to take Cody?'

'Ah, no,' said Duncan.

It was an open secret that Cody's high energy was an acquired taste. After nine years, Duncan could take small sips.

'But footy *and* basketball . . . Every week? What if I'm in the middle of something?' He proffered the List as if she might read it, correct it.

'Duncan, work around it. You're a boss.'

Duncan huffed as he climbed into bed. 'It's not that easy, and you know it.'

Liv narrowed her eyes.

'Tell Michael your sons need you.'

'Sure, that'll do it.' Duncan tugged his forelock.

Liv picked up another book from her bedside table – *How to Say No and Mean It*. 'When you get stuck, you can text the other parents,' she said, 'set up a ride share. It's not difficult.'

Duncan looked at her, disoriented.

'I don't remember having a conversation about this. Ever,' she said. 'And I'm calling time out.'

She lay the book down, and made the referee's T-shaped gesture with her hands.

'This's about more than you feeling overwhelmed. Or . . . iron deficient,' said Duncan.

He frowned at the book draped across her chest.

'Duncan, look around you. Sexism is everywhere! Its groping tentacles need to be prised off one by one before they bring us down.'

Duncan stared. He could be quite slow sometimes. She wondered if it was a tactic. She could feel a rash prickling beneath her nightie.

'You picking up the kids from basketball is a tentacle of—'

She cut him off. 'Yes!' Cutting people off was one of her known vices, but she couldn't wait for his predictable words. 'Research has shown that crime against women is more common in countries where women lack power.' (If you don't count Iceland – or was it Denmark?)

'What's that got to do with us?'

'Here's the thing: your work pretends it's more family friendly these days. But you still work all the time!'

'No, I don't.' Duncan took off his glasses. 'I'm here much more than I used to be.'

'Yes – working!' Liv's voice was rising again.

'I get we're not . . . Norway? But, we're doing okay!'

Liv felt hot, perhaps with a hot flush. She let the heat peak. 'Are we?'

Duncan flinched, as if she'd poked him in the ribs. He leapt out of bed.

He looked almost as rattled as the day she told him they were having twins. But Liv's thoughts were leaping from her compromised career and their unbalanced home life to Duncan and his partners' workaholism, enabled by stay-at-home wives or part-timers. She didn't know why she hadn't raised this before.

She tried to deepen her tone, to make it more persuasive. 'How many female partners do you have again?'

'That's not my fault.'

Of the eight, none was a woman. In her mind's eye, Liv saw these eight white, clean-shaven faces as if for the first time. How had that happened without anyone seeing the problem?

'Your work needs to genuinely step out of the dark ages,' she said, her pitch getting away from her. 'Call your partners on it, especially now you have a vacancy.'

Duncan's group recently being raided by another firm had come as a shock – to them both. He'd lost a partner, a rainmaker, unfortunately, and two talented female senior associates. But it did present an opportunity.

'Yeah, right.' His tone wasn't exactly kind. 'Like you did, with Crisp?'

'Duncan, your work and our home life are not sustainable.'

'Been sustainable for fifteen years; it—'

'No, that's not true.' She'd survived, thanks to her super-doing and close friends. She gave a final poke. 'Duncan, even when you're in the house, you leave virtually everything up to me. Your "work" is like a get out of jail free card.'

Duncan sat, concussed, on the end of the bed. She was more serious than he'd grasped. She was more serious than she'd grasped. This was bigger than pick-ups, grocery shopping and Pickle's poop. Despite Jai's predicament, Liv felt slightly better. Less . . . squashed.

She'd read once, in a book called *Should You Leave*, that people unhappy with their lives tended to blame their spouses and leave their marriages, when in fact they would do well to change their lives first – by changing themselves. If the marriage was alive, it would change, too. Easier said than done. But Liv was up for the challenge. Over the past fifteen years, she'd lost something fundamental; today, she had an inkling of what it was.

6

Monday

Jess

Jess's top three fears:
1. Grace is abducted;
2. Grace is addicted to: drugs, alcohol, dangerous activities/men;
3. A catastrophe strikes: terrorism/natural disaster
(less relevant in Bayside?).

At 10 am on Monday morning, in a small room in Middle Brighton, Jess Charters adjusted the large microphone before her and licked her lips. This would be her first ever radio interview, and she'd forgotten to bring water. She glanced at her two hosts, who were chatting as they set up. It was too late to ask, she supposed.

'Here we go,' said Kristy Thompson. 'Thirty seconds . . .'

Morrie's second cousin, Kristy, was a colourful, big-earring person; but Jess and Kristy didn't see each other often, not even at Christmas. Jess had introduced people to Kristy over the years: friends from choir, friends from Save the Bay and Neighbourhood Watch, and they'd been on her show. This morning, Kristy's energy seemed to fill the cramped studio. Far more people listened to community radio than you'd expect, Jess reminded herself. More than twenty thousand listeners in Bayside; she'd read that on their website. By starting small, Jess hoped to get her eye in, and go bigger if she had to.

As the intro music played, Mark said to Kristy, 'You lead. It's your baby.' Around Jess's age, forty-five, Mark was wearing a tan leather jacket and a big, smarmy grin.

Jess reminded herself to smile when she spoke.

'Welcome back to Bayside FM,' said Kristy. 'You're listening to *Fresh and Local* with Mark and Kristy. Today we have a special guest, an aggrieved mum who we'll call Ruby.'

Kristy smiled encouragingly at her. 'Ruby' had been Jess's idea. People could be very nasty in Bayside, she'd realised. The things they'd written on Facebook, over the weekend! The grown-ups were almost as bad as those boys. She wondered who of her friends, acquaintances and co-workers were listening to the show. She'd told that many people about it.

'Ruby's here to discuss her daughter's treatment by local boys on the internet this past weekend. Hello, Ruby.'

The more Kristy said that name, the stupider it sounded.

Jess made herself smile. 'Hello everyone.'

'How's your daughter coping, Ruby?' asked Kristy. 'It must've been very upsetting for her, seeing that picture made public.'

'Oh, that picture . . .'

Jess swallowed. Her mouth didn't seem to be working, as she saw Grace again in her mind's eye. Grace standing, side-on, hand on her hip, her lovely, mahogany hair free. Her eyes wide and playful, her tongue curled. The girl in that picture was nothing like the girl who slept in the single bed upstairs at home. That girl wore dotty pyjamas, messy top-knot buns and see-through braces. Not cut-away bikini bottoms and teeny-weeny tops. The girl in the picture was sassy and bold, knowing and cheeky. Like a girl in a music video – though not as slim, and with sticking out ears. On Friday night, upon seeing the picture, Jess had made the strangest noises. But it wasn't until she'd read the caption – *Loves cock* – that the angry genie she'd had corked within for over thirty years woke up.

'Ruby?'

'Yeth, it wath.' Jess's mouth felt full of glue.

Jess tried to swallow again. Couldn't. She opened her mouth but didn't dare speak. *Save me, Kristy*, said her big, dry eyes.

'We'll be right back after this break.'

Music played as someone rushed in with a glass of water.

Mortified, Jess drank.

A minute or so later, Kristy said, 'Are you okay? Good to go?'

Jess nodded. When the music faded, she sat close to the microphone again.

'Tell us, what would you like to happen now?' said Mark.

Jess prayed for her words to be clear. Silently, Kristy was moving her lips, like she was praying too.

'I'd be happy to, Mark . . .' Her mouth felt better; she smiled. 'We feel, for starters, these boys need to be named and shamed.'

Kristy gave her a big thumbs up.

'That sounds . . . vengeful,' Mark said. 'Naming these young boys could have very serious consequences for them.'

Jess sucked in a lungful of air. Boys. *Carmichael* boys. They were like regular boys but worse. Normal boys were, at best, puppies, or at worst, mongrels. That sounded bad but it was true. They needed to be run, fed and kept on a short lead. They were uncomplicated, especially compared to girls. How many times had she heard boys' mums say this? But Carmichael boys were different again. They were purebreds. Their lives were gold-plated and fast-tracked. Long before Grace had started at the school, Jess had noticed those boys out and about in their uniforms, especially the older, handsome boys. They jostled, taking up the footpath. They had it good: very good.

On the school tour, she'd read the names on the plaques and trophies around the school and realised some names echoed through the generations. After Grace had been offered the scholarship, Jess noticed the fathers and grandfathers on the television, in the newspaper. Sometimes for winning a big case, or being made leader of the opposition. Sometimes for tax evasion or insider trading, or not paying their staff. Some people thought they could get away with anything. So, yes, name and shame these boys. Bring them down a rung. At the end of the day, they'd be fine. Somewhere else.

'Ruby?' said Mark, with his car salesman's smile.

Jess took a quick sip of water. 'On Friday night, these boys exposed our girls to the entire world and called them . . . *sluts*. Not only to the people of Hampton or Middle Brighton. But before the *entire world* of *seven-point-eight billion people*. Do you know how unsafe it is out there? On any given day, how many predators are on the internet, Mark? No? Me neither. But it's *millions*.' Her heart sprang into a gallop. Kristy donned that worried smile again. 'Why should these boys be protected?'

'Your daughter's picture,' said Mark. 'I'd call it a very saucy selfie.'

'Oh, goodness, Mark. I'm disappointed by that picture. I am. But I wouldn't call it that.' She heard her nervous laugh. 'It wasn't indecent or anything. Not like the disgusting captions and comments . . .'

In a clear voice, Jess explained how this Instagram account was one of her worst nightmares. How she'd spent years making sure everyone, from the school to her friends, didn't photograph her daughter and upload the images. How you could never be too careful.

'We've been very lucky,' she said. 'She's very sensible. Isn't fussed by social media. Or boys.'

'How do you explain that pic?' said Mark. 'She did take it, didn't she?'

Jess stretched her neck until it cracked. The picture had been taken in Grace's bedroom, one-handed. Jess recognised the honeycomb doona cover, the running trophies, and Grace's self-portrait that Jess still didn't get. But this Jai Winsome must've forced Grace. This *boyfriend* must've badgered her. Jess's Grace, normal Grace, was too busy studying, fretting if she received less than 90 per cent on an assessment, or outside, practising her free throws, to take pictures of herself. A sweet child, Grace mustn't have been able to say no. Obviously they needed to talk about that. Later.

Jess could feel her legs jumping. Giving Mark's question the silent treatment probably wasn't ideal for radio.

'While we won't name the boys today,' Kristy said, quickly, 'we can name the school. How is Carmichael Grammar dealing with this?'

Jess looked at the posters of dirty-haired, scowling musicians on the wall. On Saturday morning, the school had heard her out, she supposed. It had programs around social media use and respectful relationships. It had a huge wellbeing department set up for mindfulness and yoga and counsellors, and lots of lovely teachers. Mr Crisp had been quite under-standing and had offered Grace 'support'. The school was doing its best. The real problem was the parents. Those oblivious mums at pick-up time in their pretentious cars. Double parked. Letting their boys run free.

'Ruby?'

Mark and Kristy were both holding their breath.

'No, the principal has been very good,' she said, slowly. 'The school is considering its options. It is. But I'm sorry. The boys behind that Insta-gram account need to go.'

'Carmichael Grammar is a powerful school,' said Mark. 'They look after their own, you know.'

'Mark, my daughter is one of their own.'

Mark laughed. 'Time for a tune. Here's Simon and Garfunkel's "Mrs Robinson".'

Jess had heard 'Mrs Robinson', though she'd never seen the movie and didn't really get it. She'd never listened to *Fresh and Local* before either, or Bayside Radio for that matter. Not even when her friends were on.

Mark said to Kristy, 'You lead in with the community's response to her post.'

Something about that sentence put Jess on edge. When the song finished, Jess waited for Kristy's lips to move.

'We're here with Jess Charters, a local mother who's upset,' said Mark.

Wrong-footed, Jess switched to look at Mark.

'A racy photograph of her teenage daughter, along with those of other local schoolgirls, has been posted on an Instagram account called "Top Ten Sluts by the Sea". Before you go looking for it, the site's down now.' Mark chuckled. 'But it was created by two boys who go to the same school as the girls, apparently, and it invited people to rate the girls' looks . . . But, hey.' Mark made a hangdog face. 'I don't know about you; but, for me, despite a few off-colour comments, this isn't a big deal. Everyone's okay, aren't they?'

Jess's brain was in logjam. He'd used her real name, and called her *upset*.

'I . . . um, Mark. This is a very big deal. If . . . If . . . If a man flashes at a woman on the beach, is everyone *okay*?'

Morrie's second cousin was scrambling through her notes.

'I'm not following,' said Mark.

'What I mean is . . . a person doesn't need to be *hurt* hurt. The man on the beach is breaching common decency, isn't he? Making it unsafe. Like these boys. I mean, they're the same, aren't they? Like flashers.'

Kristy flinched. Jess felt her body heating. This wasn't coming out right. An image of a dick pic popped into her head, though she'd never seen a dick pic. And didn't want to.

'What I mean is,' she said, 'they've breached that same code.'

'What code?'

'Yes, sorry, whose code?'

'It's all of our code, isn't it? It's . . . the law. What the boys have done is illegal; I'm fairly sure. People can go to jail.'

'Fourteen-year-old boys?' said Mark. 'You wouldn't send them to jail? Have them expelled *and* jailed?'

'Why not?' Jess's voice was loud. 'We need to protect our daughters from boys like this! They're little—'

'I think we'll leave it there. Thanks . . . for coming in, Ruby,' Kristy cut in.

Mark grinned at Kristy, who responded with an eye-roll. Jess probably should've had more Christmases with Kristy over the years.

'Thank you for having me on.'

Jess sat back, wondering what had just happened. She gulped the rest of the water.

None of this was going how it was meant to – not her Facebook post, not this interview. Not even Grace's reaction. First thing Saturday morning, when Morrie explained what had happened, Grace's face, though perfectly still, had become pinker. In Grace's bedroom, as Morrie spoke, Jess could feel Grace's energy getting bigger. Here it comes, Jess had thought, passing the tissues, as Grace's tears welled.

She'd whimpered, 'Do you know who did it?'

'We think it was two boys from school,' said Morrie. 'Blake Havelock and Jai Winsome.'

But then Grace had frowned, dabbed an eye. Sniffed.

'Sorry, what photo was it?' Grace said, sitting up.

'Here,' said Morrie. 'The account was taken down pretty fast. But your mum took a few screenshots.'

Jess held her breath as Grace took the phone and flicked. This is it, she thought, as Grace's gaze lingered on the image of herself. But then Grace flipped through the photos of the other girls, of Bella – more selfies, some with actual clothes. When Grace examined the photographs a second time, read the comments and ratings closely (some were complimentary, mainly beneath her picture: *This really u? Your smokin!*), Jess frowned.

When she'd finished, Grace had stared dreamily into space. Her lips curved and her tears dried up. She returned the phone. 'Bella won't be happy.'

Grace slid out of bed and stretched.

Where'd the tears gone? Where were the sobs?

Bewildered, Jess could see the effort on Morrie's face too. While they both wanted to know about this Winsome boy and this picture, neither of them wanted to push their luck. Grace's meltdowns could go on and on, and were terribly distressing. On the other hand, Jess at least wanted to see Grace upset! For a second time in twenty-four hours, Jess hadn't recognised her daughter. Her beautiful, long-legged daughter. As she sprang towards the wardrobe, Grace had been wearing pyjamas covered in tiny red hearts, the ones Jess had given her for her last birthday. The pyjamas stopped, Jess had realised, ten centimetres above her ankle.

Jess paced outside the single-fronted building that housed Bayside FM. She was due around the corner in fifteen minutes. If only she had more time, she'd go home for a jog on the treadmill. Instead, she looked down the narrow street. What had her mum said? 'Be the woman you want your daughter to be.' But how did that sit with 'Keep yourself nice' and 'Words spoken in anger rarely win arguments'? Especially when the enemy was hiding behind modern technology, or a microphone. Jess retraced her steps. On the one hand, Bella's mum wanted the embarrassing business over. Jilly was, like Morrie, relieved the account was down and hadn't been up long; though of course those pictures were out there now. Grace hadn't mentioned it again. Jess hadn't discussed her Facebook post with

Grace, and she sure wouldn't be discussing this radio interview. The sooner Grace's life went back to normal, the better. But another of Jess's guiding principles was 'Do the right thing'. They'd taught Grace justice was important. Consequences too.

Jess closed her eyes and tried to listen to her heart.

When Jess had taken the screenshots, Grace's photograph had forty-two comments and an average rating of eight out of ten, while Bella's had eighty-five nasty comments and mostly zeros. Poor thing. Bella's photograph had been as upsetting as Grace's, but in a different way. Her daughter's best friend had been dressed in a lacy black singlet top and denim shorts that were so short they were virtually legless. She was wearing high-heeled silver sandals, and each toenail was a different shade of blue. Her face, painted from brow to chin, looked shimmery and somehow plastic. If Jess didn't know better, she would've thought Bella had had a boob job. But Bella was thirteen, and the boobs were real. It was the look in Bella's eye, though, that'd made Jess most uncomfortable. Though Jess wouldn't admit it to Jilly (or Grace), she could guess why this photograph scored less than Grace's. Bella's wasn't playful and sassy like Grace's. Bella's stare was uncertain as she thrust herself at the lens. Touch me, she seemed to be begging. Touch me.

Jess shivered.

She imagined taking a picture of herself, right now. What would people see? A woman, five-foot-five and fifty kilograms, whose rich red-brown hair was silver at its part. A fit woman in a black-and-white mini-dress and high-heeled red sandals. What she looked the most today, Jess supposed, was tired. She stretched her arms, cracked her neck. She still had an opportunity here though, didn't she, to make this dangerous world safer? For all girls' sake. She might not be good at it, but she wasn't done yet. Those boys had chosen to humiliate the wrong girl. The wrong mother.

7

Jess

Forty minutes later, Jess rushed into the cafe. She'd taken longer than she'd intended; the young constable had been a fumbler, and at one point she'd almost leant over and typed the thing herself. But it was done and, finally, she was among friends. At The Provedore, two seats were left at the long table. As Jess approached, the ten or so women fell quiet then burst into applause. Everyone was smiling. Taking a seat, Jess looked to Charvi, who raised a finger to the air. 'Jilly texted me. We asked them to put it on. You could have heard a pin drop.' After a moment, the applause stopped and Jess heard it: the radio. If only radio had died back in the 1980s when everyone said it would.

'Morning, ladies.'

'Hi, Ruby,' said a smiling chorus.

Jess made herself smile in return as she looked at the other faces around her: Hannah's mum, Penny; Coco's mum, Alison; Meili's mum, Zhu; and Camille's mum, Christina. The table was stacked with the mums of girls. Carmichael (and basketball) mums. Half of them had last been together on Friday night, watching the girls lose, again. Jess's telephone beeped. Five times. Her smile dipped.

'Are you okay?' asked Penny. 'That man was a tool.' Penny was a sharp-featured woman with icy blue eyes and a wardrobe of sportswear. Penny's daughter Hannah was one of Grace's friends.

'I'm perfect, thanks. Shouldn't have let him get to me.'

'No, you were amazing,' said Charvi.

'*Amazing*' echoed around the table.

The more they said it, the less Jess believed it. When the pretty waitress appeared, Jess was grateful for a break from their attention. The women ordered, quickly.

'Are you going to the police?' said Zhu.

'Not going, gone.'

'What do you mean?' asked Penny, with a thin-lipped smile.

'On my way here.'

A collective intake of breath. A few women looked aghast. Mostly the faces were assessing, before smiles were reapplied.

'Good for you,' said Christina. 'Taking a stand.'

'That's not like you,' said Penny.

Jess frowned. She didn't know what to say to that.

'You're very brave,' said Alison. 'Doing it for our daughters.'

'Hear, hear,' chimed in another voice.

Heat blasted Jess's cheeks. She was doing what had to be done. Nothing brave about it.

'Calling them "ho's" and "sluts"!' said another mum. 'Those boys should be shot, along with the parents.'

'Here's hoping they're expelled,' said Penny, raising her water glass.

Jess heard the support and saw the smiles but didn't, on a deep level, believe them. Did these women know the boys' mums? Was that it? Some of these women had boys in other year levels, though none of her close friends did. Mums of boys and mums of girls didn't tend to mix. She tried to remember Blake's mother, and Jai's, but failed. She shuddered, sweeping thoughts of the boys away.

'Andrew's furious,' Christina whispered to Alison.

'Nimish too,' said Charvi, leaning across the table. 'Bags not telling Bettina Low . . .'

The women smothered giggles.

Jess focused on her coffee. Husbands. Old boys. The rumour mill. She didn't have time for it. This was the most exposed she'd felt in her life. She tipped sugar into her cup while the women nearby nudged each other.

She needed to give the next coffee morning a miss, she thought. This was maybe her thirtieth time attending. She needed to mix with people beyond the Carmichael/Bayside bubble. She was wondering how to get better at public speaking (maybe Toastmasters?) when a latecomer arrived: a bony woman, soft around the middle. The woman's auburn hair was damp and her eyes blotchy. You could see oblong goggle marks around her eyes and practically smell the chlorine. But, despite a touch of weariness, this face was attractive, in a freckly and milk-fed kind of way. Jess narrowed her eyes; she was always leery of grown women who didn't wear make-up.

8

Liv

Liv's ponytail dripped as she faced the dozen chatting and laughing women. It'd been months since she'd exercised vigorously, and the effort had brought on asthma she didn't know she had. But, in the pool, her agitation had dispersed. She'd become conscious again that she had a body. Limbs. Breasts. Skin. In the noisy cafe, she murmured 'Hello' to no one in particular. She hadn't made it to one of these get-togethers last term, but the Carmichael mums were generally pleasant, switched-on women. Though their conversation usually didn't stray far beyond chitchat, today she intended to raise the subject of those sucking tentacles of sexism in their lives. She was interested to hear their thoughts. To have a laugh and a gripe about the boys' stupidity too. She was toying with the idea of starting an action group: Mums for Equality. She couldn't be the only one who had twenty-twenty vision, and she needed all the help she could get. And, she hoped, Carly, one of her inner circle, might drop by after tennis.

As Liv settled, the group's chemistry shifted. Conversation spluttered. Liv's skin rose into goosebumps as she picked up a menu. This morning had been organised weeks ago. There was usually no need to RSVP. There'd been a spare chair. But the women on either side of her were reading their menus as if they'd never been to The Provedore, even though The Provedore was the school mums' local haunt. Half the mums practically showered here.

Liv had never been comfortable with acquaintances – people you encountered in life but didn't properly befriend. Friends of friends, ex-work colleagues, even work colleagues themselves (and, for that matter, ex-friends). Over the years, the more you saw these people, the more uncomfortable you felt. If you'd liked them more or they'd liked you more, you would've become (or stayed) friends. Usually, Liv didn't bring this angst to the school mums.

But, ever since the Night of the Pics, Liv had been an astronaut bobbing about in space, connected to her old, safe self by a long, thin tube. She could see her home base, the mothership, the Good Ship Winsome, but she was far away from it now. She wasn't keen to go back, but being adrift in space was pretty spooky too. Which was why, on an impulse, she'd taken the day off work, although she wasn't paid for sick days, and she'd disconnected from the world – no radio, no newspapers, no online snooping. She'd intended to unwind and treat herself, and perhaps find some comrades.

She re-read the menu.

Earlier that morning, Liv had watched the Lists at work. One of the jobs she'd shed was the making of school lunches. The boys probably should've been making their lunches from the moment they could hold a butter knife. But Liv had kept doing it for three reasons: first, she liked to be helpful, and the kids didn't want to make them; second, she preferred to be in charge of what her children ate (and her tidy kitchen); and, third, she'd wanted to maximise their sleep, as they caught an early bus. They got so tired! There was good evidence that teenagers needed around nine hours sleep, especially between 11 pm and 8 am. That was impossible for her boys, given they headed to the bus at 7.25 am. So, each morning, she'd hopped out of bed and prepared their lunches. But this thinking was old hat. Gone!

Liv glimpsed a passing plate of scones and her mouth watered. Everyone was still actively pretending she didn't exist.

Her thoughts returned to her morning. She was also no longer waking her sons. The three of them could set their alarms and take ownership of their routines. No more rushing the twins from their phones to the shower, from phones to breakfast, from phones to the bus . . . No more breakfasts of eggs fried, scrambled or poached to order. No. If the boys were going to miss valuable sleep because the bus left at 7.27 am, that wasn't her problem. The school day could start later to meet the sleep needs of hundreds of thousands of teenagers. There was, truly, a truckload of research on this issue. But changes to the school day at Carmichael Grammar? No. So they might as well lump it. Besides, it wasn't as if her children had appreciated her daily efforts.

As the waitress approached, Liv decided she needed scones, with jam and cream, urgently. Once she'd ordered, she leant to one side. 'How have you been, Coco?' Coco didn't respond, and instead began whispering to the person on her right. Liv tried the woman on her left: a sharp, tall woman in a tracksuit. Hannah? But the waitress intervened. Once the girl had gone, the woman began a conversation about nearby vacant land with the pair of women across the table. As the seconds mounted, Liv tried to identify a friendly face. These were women she'd seen over the years, in the playground at pick-up time, and smiled at, or waved to, or stood along-side. People whose children had been in class with the twins but with whom friendship hadn't bloomed. At the other end of the table, a woman sat back to reveal, at the table's head, Jess Charters.

A rogue drip of water trickled down Liv's spine.

Liv hadn't seen Jess Charters in four years, though she'd stalked her online on the weekend. Jess had one child and worked part-time as a book-keeper in a fellow school mum's spice business. Liv and Jess had met when Jai and Oscar were in Year Five. Liv didn't think Grace and the twins had been in the same class since. Jess's one public photo on Facebook had been a flattering and rather old headshot. Jess didn't look like Grace, though Liv could see a family resemblance in Jess's slender neck and startling blue eyes. But where Grace was tall and curvy, Jess was smaller and trim. Jess had the look of a seasoned runner: wiry and tightly coiled, as if she'd be twitching without her daily ten-kilometre fix. With arms as angular as diamonds, she looked impressively fit. Yes, Jess Charters wore her fitness like a badge. It read high-functioning, and, on the flip side, obsessive.

But today Jess Charters looked like someone who had recently given birth – depleted, dirty haired, and dark ringed about the eyes. And the women around her seemed tentative and deferential, as if the labour hadn't gone well.

Sitting up, Liv tried to catch Jess's eye. But Jess was stirring her coffee with seemingly insoluble sugar. Liv considered Coco again.

'Excuse me, Coco?' said Liv.

Liv was about to try a third time when it dawned on her. Coco was the name of the woman's *daughter*. Mortified, Liv studied the ring of faces again, but few of the mothers' names came to her. And of the students' names she could recall, there was not one boy's . . . She really needed to make more of an effort with these people.

Liv smiled at the faces that were studiously looking elsewhere, and understood. But, girls' mums or not, these women weren't the enemy. As the silence around her persisted, Liv considered eating toast at home. By the next coffee morning, this would've passed. And hopefully Jai would be reinstated at the school. She was snaking her hand towards her handbag when huge scones arrived. The cream was pearly and thick; the jam glistened with raspberries. Her mouth watered again. She picked up her knife. Surely what happened between the kids was the kids' business?

The conversation around the table fell to its knees and face-planted. Everyone was looking at their rings or coffee cups or phones.

Liv put down her knife and leant forward. 'Jess, hello? I'm Liv, Jai Winsome's mum. We met years ago.'

The air at the table contracted, as if they were in a soundproof booth. Jess gave a pained smile. 'Hello.'

'I just want to say how sorry I am. About this business with the kids.'

Jess was sitting up straight, as if on high alert.

'We're hoping it's resolved quickly.' Liv smiled. 'And the kids can put it behind them. We are very, very sorry. Jai will be writing Grace a letter.'

Jess was smiling rigidly. Liv looked to the other women but, apparently, she'd become a blinding sun.

'We feel . . .' Liv wasn't sure whether to continue. 'Jai needs to apologise personally for—'

Jess grimaced. 'I don't . . .' She shook her head. 'This isn't the time or place.'

A murmur of agreement skimmed around the circle.

'Yeah, you're probably right. Sorry.'

Liv felt a tug of regret that she'd begun this exchange. But she also felt a tug of regret she was letting it go. Shouldn't they discuss this complex situation like grown-ups? Weren't their children being taught to talk and listen respectfully? Weren't they sitting in beanbags once a week in that Wellbeing Centre to discuss their feelings, their issues and wellness?

'But, hey, we're here now,' Liv said, looking around the table of women. 'We might as well get everything out in the open.'

'What your son has done is disgusting!' said someone, possibly called Alison.

'Thinking with his dick!'

Liv couldn't identify this voice over the sound of titters. A louder, more disapproving murmur ran around the table and stopped at Liv's plate.

'Well, yes and no.'

'*No*?' said Coco's mum. 'In what way?'

'I've got to go,' said, maybe, Meili's mum, and Camille's mum followed. They rose so quickly a chair crashed to the floor.

The cafe fell silent.

'But you don't know the full story,' Liv said, too loudly, as someone picked up the chair.

Jess reached for her handbag. 'Thank you, but I don't need to know any more.'

'Wait, please. Jilly Saffin had it wrong on Friday night,' Liv said, and immediately regretted it. Jilly Saffin wasn't at the table. Jilly was a frail, unwell woman. Quite possibly, Jilly was in bed. 'She only had one version . . .'

Liv hesitated.

What did these women need to know? Liv looked around the table again. Didn't other parents know Blake? Yes, he could be disrespectful and hard work, but deep inside, he was a quirky, funny kid. Which didn't excuse his recent spectacularly poor form. Liv wasn't about to defend him, but she wasn't about to crucify him either.

'You need to know that Jai's part in this wasn't large. He showed Blake a picture of Grace. That was it. He did it without thinking, when he received it. He was so surprised. He knows he shouldn't have. But he didn't *send* it to Blake. And, well, I'm sorry to say, Blake nicked it.'

Jess Charters was standing. 'I don't understand. Are you putting this back onto Grace?' She was doing a bizarre smile–grimace.

'Ah, no.'

'Jilly said Blake and Jai did everything. Together,' said Hannah's mum (Penny?), with an arm around Jess now. 'That's what Blake told her.'

'I know. And I can't explain that.'

Slumped into her tracksuited friend, Jess Charters looked like she had been struck on the head.

'What has Grace said?' asked Liv. 'Hasn't Jai explained?'

Another mum scrunched her mouth into a knot. Eyes turned to Jess. She seemed to have lost the power of speech.

'Are you saying Jai didn't make that account?' said a woman beside Jess.

The remaining women rose. A couple extracted themselves to settle their bills.

'Yep, exactly,' said Liv. 'Jai was at home, on his own.'

The women tossed about disbelieving looks. Someone muttered '*Top Sluts . . .*'

'Look, the whole thing's awful, but . . . on that word . . .' said Liv. 'You know they all use it, don't you? Your girls probably do. I mean we did, didn't we?'

Someone gasped. More of the mothers scurried from their coffee cups. Even the waitstaff were keeping away. Liv had assumed the boys and their parents would be seen as separate entities, with their own agency, their own distinct culpability; but obviously she'd been naive. Her body tensed, as though she could feel all five foot ten of Jai sitting on her shoulders. The relaxation she'd brought with her from the pool was gone. These women were so quick to condemn. None of the young people caught up in this situation were old enough to fully understand what they were doing or saying. Or what was done. Not their daughters, not her son. Not Blake Havelock.

'Where's your compassion?' Liv said. 'These are children.'

Jess's head was shaking, her mouth flapping.

Liv knew, with certainty, she ought to stop. Leave. But she really didn't want to. It was like having another scone when you knew you shouldn't. But you loved scones! Besides, she'd known some of these women as acquaintances for years. From a distance, they'd all been so pleasant: making chitchat about real estate and each other and their brilliant children.

'We need to look at the bigger picture.' Her voice grew louder.

'We've seen enough pictures, don't you think?' said a voice from behind her.

'Ha . . . but there are degrees of culpability here, there always are. The school has a big role to be play in this, don't you see?' Liv appealed to two women by the counter, who pretended she was inaudible. 'That's what I wanted to talk about, this morning. This isn't only about one or two boys! It's all of our children, living in our skewed culture. They're using a language they don't even understand. They don't know its etymology. They've inherited it without critically examining it. This is an opportunity to teach all of them. Boys *and* girls. We need to talk about sexualised selfies as well, while at the same time taking away the link between shame and sexuality for g—'

'I don't have time for this shit,' said one mum, tapping her phone.

Liv might as well have been reciting a piece of tax legislation. She returned to look at where Jess had been standing, but the table was abandoned, with cups half full and cake barely eaten. Liv reached for her wallet as the cream in her stomach curdled. At the counter, defeated, she paid for her scones and three unclaimed coffees.

9

Duncan

Duncan was putting in a six-minute appearance. Around him, a dozen people were eating Black Forest cake. One of his juniors, Julia Hogg, had just turned twenty-four and loved cherries, apparently. They hadn't had one of these mini-celebrations for a while. Once, Duncan had eaten a lot of cake. Most partners at W&U tended to work through these events, but Duncan couldn't do it. He distributed a plate or two then stopped to chat with Maia, his assistant. He looked at the female legal staff in the firm – solid solicitors, every one. Contrary to Liv's grievances, the world had come a long way. Fifty years ago, a firm like this would've looked completely vanilla, he told himself, especially the legal team. These days, the lower ranks of solicitors at Winsome & Ueland were sixty per cent female (and diverse, to boot). Everyone started on the same salary and was given the same opportunities. Everyone could work flexibly if they wanted to. Though only a minority opted to be mostly at home – mums with school-age kids. Mums with preschoolers, surprisingly, wanted to come in. Yes, all in all, today had to be the best time in history to be a woman, thought Duncan. True, the firm could do with more female senior associates, and a female partner or two, but it wasn't his fault a senior associate was on maternity leave. Or that those other two had jumped ship. But a female partner would happen one day soon. He watched two of the younger solicitors from Michael's team pass around the cake: clever girls, both of them, with bright futures. If they stuck around.

But, at home, he'd toe the line, he supposed, for a week or two. Though things were picking up, he wasn't flat-chat this week. His workload was unpredictable, but hopefully he could juggle it. In a month, this agenda of Liv's would be gone. Crisp would have forgotten her spray. Stress did strange things to people. He had a mouthful of cake. Made a mental note to get the car checked. A piece of fruit squished between his teeth. He considered his plate: purple layers overflowing with cream and dusted with chocolate. He surrendered it to a passing admin girl.

'Thank you.' He made sure to look her in the eye, and smile.

He had four minutes left. Maia was telling a story: something about her toddler, who was a bolter, and a creek. Duncan's mind wandered. Today, none of his partners was here eating cake. He glimpsed his brother, Michael, bailing up Xavier Yuen, one of the senior associates, in his office. Xavier was taking it on the chin. This firm was a boutique version of the upper-mid-tier firm where Duncan had first made partner, after years of sweat and grind. Somehow, when they set up W&U, the hyper-competitive, 'high performance' culture had come with them. His partners prided themselves on that, and on the complex, more interesting work that came with it. Which did attract a certain kind of person. Michael was W&U's managing partner.

Duncan checked the time and began his retreat, waving, giving the Black Forest a thumbs up.

By the water cooler, he congratulated the birthday girl again. A slight person, with curled shoulders, Julia had a button of cream on her nose. He smiled, tapping his own nose, and she blushed. He could remember being twenty-four, university finally over, moving out of home. His first suit. Nothing but world-building ahead of him: marriage, family, partnership. So much to look forward to. He wanted to say something useful to Julia. Something like take your time, savour your youth. But it'd probably sound trite. Besides, she seemed a little scared of him.

Second serves of cake were going out and no one looked miserable. If only Liv could see them, he thought, as he snuck away.

10

Liv

Liv spent the early afternoon prowling around the house. 'Last time you were like this, you'd given up sugar,' said Jai. 'We were ten, remember?' And she did. Since the clash at the cafe, Liv had half-made her bed, left washing in the machine, and boiled the kettle every quarter hour. Every time she paused, mid-activity, she'd check her phone, call Stella, or Blake, the Parent-less. She even called Chandler, Blake's manny-nanny. No one answered. She caught herself staring at Jai as he caught up on homework. *Are you telling us the truth? Am I getting this wrong?*

At one stage, Jai confronted her by the fridge. Pointing a carrot at her heart, he said, 'What's up with you?'

She was inclined to ask him the same question. Instead, she quizzed him on whether he'd heard from Blake. Nope – nothing on text, Insta, Snapchat.

'Have you actually called him?' she said.

Jai shrugged.

'Or even messaged?'

Jai couldn't meet her eye. Liv couldn't blame him, really. 'How are you feeling about all this?'

'I dunno.'

She sighed. 'Try again.'

He gave a half-smile. 'Like, confused. Disappointed.'

Liv nodded as Jai's phone beeped; they both fell silent as he checked it. His expression – bashful, guilty, chuffed – told her who it was. Without responding, he put the phone in his pocket. Of Grace, Liv didn't have a firm opinion yet. She was confident Grace and Jai had been texting over the weekend. Those messages would be worth a read. But unfortunately, if wisely, Jai had changed his passcode.

'Ah, Jai-Jai, about Grace . . .'

As succinctly as possible, she confessed to her run-in with Grace's mum.

'Are you trying to ruin my life?'

'I'm trying to make it better!'

'You're joking, right?'

'The best person to make it better is you,' she said, dodging that debate. 'Have you actually apologised to Grace?'

Jai shrugged.

'I want you to write a letter to her, now. On paper. With a pen. And another one to Bella. You explain your side of the story properly, tell them how you feel. Apologise to Grace for showing Blake her photo, and ask if there's anything you can do—'

'No way, Mum.'

'And then I want you to write to Blake.' She pointed at him. 'Tell him how you feel too; ask him why he did it. While you're at it, ask him how he is. Ask him to write you back.'

'Not a chance.'

Half an hour later, Jai sat down to write, on paper, with a red pen. After four false starts, his single-page letters were beautifully heartfelt, tinged with regret and penned with care. He read his final versions to her before tossing them into the bin. She made him do them again. The briefer, sixth drafts were no less heartfelt. He delivered them incognito while on a jog.

No letter to Blake, though.

Meanwhile, determined to stick to her List, Liv gave herself permission to set up on the couch and binge on other people's lives and imaginings. She stumbled across a Nordic detective series, set in a charcoal grey and constantly rainy Sweden and Denmark. Through the drizzle, Liv tried to identify the region's superior attitude to women. The show's main character was a sallow female detective who didn't move her face or speak a lot, or say please or thank you. Liv studied her closely. The woman was whip-smart but impassive, mildly drone-like, but very effective. Authoritative. Leaning heavily on subtext seemed to work for her. The more Liv watched, the more she liked the woman's no-nonsense, take-no-prisoners style.

Two episodes later, Liv felt better as she and Jai headed off to school, though Oscar had texted – *bus sucked this morning.*

With radio-pop blaring, Liv pulled up outside Carmichael Grammar and tried to spot the moving target that was Cody, the human pogo stick, and Oscar, the meandering softie. Without Jai, Oscar could be lost, and unsupervised, Cody could be anywhere. Seeing the flow of students, Jai stopped singing and hunched to focus on his phone. Soon, Liv supposed, someone would recognise their car. Shoes and cars were things kids noticed. Had been since primary school.

Some distance ahead, a skinny boy in new Nikes and torn jeans was striding along the footpath. The shoes looked like the latest design, probably self-styled. Otherwise, his outfit was like something Jai would have worn: vaguely retro, second-hand, sourced at op-shops. The boy was waving his arms about as if he was rapping. There were probably AirPods under that hood. Though Liv didn't recognise the shoes, there was something familiar about the faded, rose-pink hoodie.

That afternoon, a bite in the air was heralding the proper onset of autumn. Little kids in too-big uniforms tumbled out of a nearby gate and surrendered their bags to waiting parents. The children looked like freshly hatched chickens. It was hard to believe Liv's sons had once been that cute. A long time and a lot of money ago. Before iPads and smartphones, Instagram and memes.

Bigger kids began to appear on the footpath. Dozens of students walked with their necks bent and their eyes on their phones, like poorly designed robots. One of the school captains was rolling his double bass behind him. Apparently Dylan Low was good at everything, from footy to debating, which parents and teachers loved, but his younger brother, Taj, not so much. Being in Year Eight, Liv's boys didn't know the older kids unless they did something notable like lead the school, conduct the choir, or run amok on an overseas trip.

The boy in the pink hoodie had reached the main gate and was looking in.

Groups of kids were passing their car now. Still no Oscar or Cody. Oscar, the most conflict-avoidant of her children, was probably keeping a low profile somewhere. A few metres away, one kid glimpsed the Winsomes' car, then Jai, and nudged his mate. The mate turned and flicked the finger. Jai's gaze was still on his phone, but Liv bristled. Usually no one bothered the twins and they bothered no one. Jai and Oscar weren't cool and they weren't nerds. They were young for their year level, but good enough at sport (even Oscar, just). They were handsome but not preening. They were smart enough. Occasionally one of them was amusing.

Dylan Low was observing the boy in the hoodie. On the older boy's plain, spotty face, Liv read concern. Her phone rang as the hooded boy began to pace. Something about the intensity of his movement was off. He lunged at kids who were walking by, and a few started to cry. One of the mothers snapped at him but her words had no effect. Liv answered her phone as Dylan Low left his double bass unattended to shepherd smaller children past. Up close, Liv saw the nose he was renowned for: long and pointy, like a wedge of brie. Cruel.

Jai looked up then, and started.

In her ear, her boss was describing an urgent new file. One of those off-the-books jobs Ryan did for friends, usually involving a delicate HR matter with a senior bully or a disgruntled ex-lover. Ryan called these his 'Mr Fix-it files'. He did some himself, but these days gave most to Liv: Ms Fix-it.

The skinny kid was spinning, drawing closer to the car. To her dismay, Liv recognised then the milky forehead and what her boys called his 'butt chin'. Her stomach clenched. The anger she'd been feeling changed hue.

'What's Blake doing?' she mouthed.

Jai gave an exaggerated shrug. Then Blake began to yell. Dylan Low ran, double bass in tow, back into the school.

Ten metres away, Blake was trying to pick up a rubbish bin. He started kicking it, but it was bolted to the ground. Most students and parents gave him a wide berth, but some lingered as if he were zany street performer.

'Mum . . .' Jai was peeling himself from his seat.

'Yes, tomorrow,' said Liv, into her phone. 'But, Ryan, I really need to go.'

Liv searched for Chandler, Blake's uni-student manny. Chandler was always late, or on his phone. Today, he had definitely gone AWOL. And Stella and Lindsay were still interstate. Liv braced herself as kids stopped to laugh.

Then Jai sprang out.

Yes, Blake had been a turd over the weekend (Jai's word). But Blake had been Jai's best friend since day one of Year Three. Blake always shared his endless cash and sugary stashes. Yes, Blake could be disrespectful and ignore rules; but, to Jai, he was loyal and fun. In that regard, the events of this past weekend were an aberration. Jai liked to think the best of people, and was a good influence on Blake. He calmed the boy and coaxed him off screens. But Blake was still karate-kicking nothing much, which explained Jai's slow-motion, tiptoeing jog.

By the time Jai reached the bin, students had their phones out. Jai stalled.

Mid-kick, Blake noticed Jai. His leg dropped. 'Jai-Jai . . .' Blake lifted his hood, hunched his shoulders.

Alongside Jai, Liv moved quietly, as if Blake were a spooked brumby. Abruptly, Blake said something to Jai that Liv couldn't hear, then in a swoop whipped off his hoodie to stand, pointing at his creamy skin. His nipples were like two tiny press-studs. Blake's eyes were blazing, red-rimmed marbles. Suddenly, he pulled down his trousers.

'Whoa there, buddy!' said Jai.

Blake staggered about, bare chested and with his trousers down. More kids congregated and laughed. Blake wasn't wearing any boxers or under-pants. At the best of times, Liv didn't really understand Blake but today he seemed seriously screwy. True, he was known for pulling down his pants when excited, but it had never happened at school.

Liv felt for him, then, in his unloved nakedness.

'Mum, do something!'

Liv cast about for backup, as Jai managed to tie his own hoodie around Blake's waist, to cover the front of his friend's body. On the other side of the school fence, Dylan Low was on the phone, looking towards the admin building. Carly's son, Rowan, Oscar's plodding, bucktoothed pal, was joining the ring of spectators. Unusually, Liv hadn't seen him all weekend. She caught his eye. She needed to keep her cool, not panic or rant. She thought of the Nordic noir detective. How she got things done.

'Rowan,' Liv said, deadpan. 'Get a teacher.'

'Wait, what?' Rowan's overbite was truly astounding, in his mouth of metal.

'Rowan. A teacher. Now.'

Rowan blinked like a startled nocturnal creature, then ran. Which was rather extraordinary, for Rowan. Heartened, Liv took a deep breath as more kids appeared, and with them, more overpriced phones.

'Put that away.'

Mildly shocked, some students put their phones away, but they were quickly replaced by others. The kids were like zombies pointing weapons. Liv left Jai and Blake to address a boy around eleven years old, whose phone was newer than hers.

'Give me that.'

The kid's eyes bulged and he slunk off. As Liv bent to accost another smaller child, she noticed a teacher approaching at a run. She could see the suited legs through the trees of students. Thank god. The small ring parted to admit him. He wouldn't have been her first choice of backup. But Tony Crisp wasn't wearing his elegant jacket; his shirt was rumpled, its sleeves pushed up. He looked concerned, like a regular man caught on the hop, or a country vet facing a difficult delivery.

'Olivia.' He gave a small nod.

In Nordic mode, Liv acknowledged him with a lift of her chin.

Seeing the principal, the students pocketed their phones and receded into the crowd like the innocent bystanders that they weren't. Some ran. Those photos and videos could be uploaded within minutes. (How robust were the school's social media policies?) More kids arrived to fill the holes left by those who had scarpered. Liv began to shoo onlookers away as Tony Crisp stepped forward.

'Hello, Blake. You seem to have a lot to say today. How about we go someplace quiet and have a chat?'

As if considering the idea, Blake looked from Tony Crisp to the pale and sombre Jai.

'Blake?' Mr Crisp gestured towards the gate. 'This way.'

Blake sighed grandly, as if preparing to make an announcement. Tony Crisp observed the boys. The shuffling ring of students quieted.

'Jai-Jai – sorry, man, for taking that pic of Grace and making shit up . . .'

Jai's face broke into a smile. 'That's okay, buddy.'

Tony Crisp was staring at Blake, as if lip-reading, but no more words came. Whispers animated the watchers as Jai patted Blake's arm. Liv exhaled audibly. Tony Crisp glanced at her, his gaze soft. Then he said, 'Very well, Blake, let's walk this way.'

Tony Crisp led the shuffling Blake into the school. The boy's trousers remained at half-mast while silently Jai walked behind him, like a human shield. Amid her dismay – and relief – Liv felt a pang of pride.

11

Jess

Jess paced the fence line near Carmichael Grammar's side entrance, as students poured from the Middle School building. Since lunchtime, she'd been on the phone. Liv Winsome seemed to know the details of Friday night better than she did. And Liv had sons! Everyone knew adolescent boys didn't speak, and mums and daughters were meant to be close. As if that wasn't embarrassing enough, Jess wasn't any nearer to an answer. It seemed the only people who really knew what had happened were Blake Havelock and maybe Jai Winsome. But today, hopefully, Grace would know more and would spill the beans. Grace and Bella walked home together each day, but this afternoon Jess couldn't wait for the pair of them to stroll in.

Scanning the sea of teenagers, Jess recognised girls from basketball and the big band, as well as the odd boy. Off to one side, she spotted someone who had to be a Winsome twin. He looked just like his mum, though with a longer face: freckles, big teeth and bigger eyes. The Winsome twins were identical, but this would be Oscar. Jess felt a fresh pinch of doubt, watching him lug his bag and instrument case. His narrow shoulders were slumped, his head bowed. He didn't look like a jock or a smart-arse. After a moment, Oscar was joined by Rowan Whittaker-Smith, puffing and pointing towards the main road. Rowan had woolly hair and no chin to speak of. Behind them, watching, was Taj Low, an athletic man-child. Those two boys she knew; everyone did. They couldn't be more different. Their dads were old boys, and probably their grandads too.

James Whittaker-Smith was the Chairman of this and his wife, Carly, was President of that. Though only about forty, James had thick silver hair and, like his tennis-mad wife, was often tanned. James and Carly were an attractive pair; their son, not so much. Taj's dad, Owen Low, was on TV sometimes – she couldn't remember why. Near Oscar and Rowan, a group of mums waved to Jess and, vaguely recognising them, she waved back. A second later, Oscar and Rowan darted past her.

Jess checked her phone again: nothing.

Groups of teenagers stood laughing near the front gate. Parents were speaking behind cupped hands. Grace's favourite teacher, Mrs MacBeth, called these gangs the Carpark Yakuza. Jess turned away, hoping they weren't talking about Grace, or her. Over the weekend, she'd been waiting for the humiliation to hit Grace. She'd been gearing up for tears and regret. But Grace seemed to be coping, which was as confusing as it was worrying. Maybe now, after a day at school, the upset would come.

From a distance, the students were hard to tell apart. Jess stepped onto the path that snaked around the grounds. Hunting for Grace's long ponytail, she walked among children from the Junior School as they greeted their mothers (and fathers, and grannies and au pairs). A mother squealed, swirling her daughter in a hug. The child's face crumpled in pleasure and Jess swallowed a hiccup of emotion. Grace was too big for those hugs, not that Jess had ever given them. Too public, too showy. In the Prep area, Assistant Principal Palmer was farewelling four mums in gym gear and big sunglasses. He towered over the laughing women as he held open the gate. The AP was what you'd call a man's man, thought Jess, though women liked him too. It was the muscles, Jess figured, and the big grin, the deep voice. He wasn't her type. Two suited men – teachers, wearing lanyards to identify them – passed by.

'One of the perks of being a lead teacher,' said one to the other. 'Prep-mum gate-duty.'

The men laughed. With a tut-tut under her breath, Jess headed away from the Junior School towards the basketball courts. Most men were simply overgrown boys, she thought.

•

By the edge of the basketball court, Jess spied a familiar, curvy brunette. She was about to call out when Bella snapped, 'Are you coming?'

Jess stopped. Bella was looking down at a girl tying her laces, a basketball by her side.

'Grace?' said Bella.

Jess looked again. Grace must've redone her hair. The simple ponytail she'd been wearing this morning was gone, replaced by two low, coiled braids.

'I think I'm going to stay and shoot a round,' said Grace to her laces. 'You want to join?'

Nearby, boys were playing three-on-three, among them Taj Low, who had an impressive jump.

'Since when do I play basketball?' said Bella.

'Since now, maybe?' Grace said.

Jess could hear the smile in her daughter's voice. She frowned. Since when did Grace walk home alone? Children moved around the pair like traffic manoeuvring around roadkill, but Grace didn't seem to notice them – or her, a handful of metres away.

'What's with you playing basketball with the boys?'

'It's nothing,' said Grace. 'They asked me, and it'll make me better.'

Irritated, Bella tucked a finger into her skirt's waistband and tugged, as if her skirt had shrunk. Jess ducked behind two students as they walked around the girls. Jess was torn between taking Grace home and letting this scenario play out.

On the ground, Grace's phone vibrated, and she read the screen. Tapped. A tiny spear of rejection passed through Jess.

Another ripple of laughter came from the Prep area and a man's voice boomed. Lloyd Palmer was on the move, waving his large hand. Jess's radio interview echoed in her head. She hoped he hadn't heard about it. Her face was warm as she stepped towards Grace, and Bella stomped off.

'Bye then,' said Grace, springing up.

Jess watched Grace jog away, around big and little children. Grace seemed oblivious to the pointed stares of the older students. From the group of basketball-playing boys, Taj bounced his ball to Grace and she dribbled and laid it up, with a left-hand finger-roll. The boys whistled.

Jess wanted to call out, 'Hello? Over here!' She wanted to take Grace by the hand and tug her away as if she were four. Then Taj grinned. A startlingly handsome boy. A tier-one boy, according to Grace, Jess remembered; while Bella was most definitely a tier-three girl, as Grace was. Or had been. Grace's smile transformed her face.

For the second time that day, words dried up in Jess's mouth.

12

Jess

Stuck in after-school traffic, Jess was officially more worried than confused. As the cars rolled forward, she prayed Grace would make it home. Young girls alone, day or night, was never a good idea. Jess turned in her seat to search the footpath in case Grace had changed her mind; but no. After a moment, she glimpsed Bella shuffling along. She could ask Bella to go back and get Grace, she supposed. To plead. Walking head down and phone in hand, Bella looked like every other teenager: vulnerable to poles and holes. Abruptly, Bella stopped and Jess tried to read her face. What was she seeing on that little screen? Four young Carmichael boys on bikes were racing along the footpath.

'Get out of the way!' yelled the leader.

'Yeah, fatty!' said a second boy.

Bella leapt onto the nature strip as the boys zipped by. They looked around eleven years old, scrawny and in training to be trouble. Further down, at a bus stop, they skidded to a halt. Walking again, Bella looked from her phone to the boys' bikes strewn across the path. Jess inched closer in the traffic, as a bigger, meaty boy, tossed a lolly wrapper at Bella.

Bella flinched and Jess sat up, lowering her window. In kindergarten, the children had been taught to say, 'Stop, I don't like it' and 'Hands to yourself'. But that was ten years ago. Back in kindergarten, Grace had had a lot of spunk. Bella probably had too.

The boy tossed a lolly at Bella and it pinged off her leg. The group sniggered. Jess wondered where to park, if she had to. The chunky boy had something sticky in his mouth. Jess could see him munching as he eyed Bella. If Jess didn't know better, she'd have thought he was leering. He could've been someone's little brother, she supposed, with access to things he shouldn't have. Then Jess thought back to primary school, when her breasts were first spotted by boys: she'd been eleven, wearing a sports shirt, just like Bella's. In a split second, she'd felt stripped.

'Nice titties,' said the boy.

Jess snapped on her indicator.

Bella looked from her phone to the boy to the image on the bus-stop shelter. A reclining blonde woman was half-naked, impossibly stunning and slim as a pencil. Suddenly, Bella ran at the boy and pushed him over. The boy's limbs flailed as he landed, with an almighty crunch, on his bike. The other boys were silent at first, then laughed, then jeered, while he tried to get up. Though he seemed unhurt, the boy was tangled in spokes and pedals and handlebars.

Stunned, Jess looked around. In her rear-view mirror, an older man driver was arguing with a child, while other drivers were staring ahead, oblivious to the drama at the bus stop. On the grass, the boys had formed a circle and were taunting Bella. One boy helped the fallen child, who, on his feet now, dirty and grazed, limped to join the others. Uh-oh. Jess put on the parking brake and hazard lights. She checked her mirrors again, then climbed across the passenger seat and out of the car.

The grandpa tooted as she dashed onto the nature strip.

'Leave her alone! Be quiet!' she yelled, waving her arms. 'Go away. Yes you. Get! Before I call your mums!'

The boys flew onto their bikes and pedalled away. The limper glowered as he picked up his. Despite his size, he did look young.

'You too.' She sweetened her voice. 'Have a salt bath, hon, you'll be fine.'

Jess smiled as she and Bella watched him pedal gingerly away.

'Little shit,' said Bella.

'Are you okay?'

Bella nodded as more cars tooted behind Jess's unmoving vehicle.

Jess sighed. 'Can I give you a lift?'

'I'm good, thanks.' Bella eyed her phone.

'Bella, hon, please? Are you sure? It's no trouble.'

The grandpa and a dad in a sports car were tooting out of time now. Jess ducked her head. 'Oh, shut up, you jerks.' She muttered to her feet.

Shock and delight wiped the tears from Bella's eyes.

13

Jess

The traffic was clearing as Jess buckled in. She hoped no one she knew
had seen any of that – yelling at other people's children could get you in
trouble. Beside her, Bella looked tired and slightly different to when Jess
had last seen her. Her features were still mid-change – some too big, some
still small. But today Bella had puffy eyes and a large, blind pimple on her
nose. Jess could remember those pimples. How they pulsed beneath the
surface. How badly you wanted them to pop. But fiddling only made them
worse.

She patted Bella's knee.

'I shouldn't have pushed him over.'

'No.'

'It felt good though.' Bella gave a weak smile.

'I bet.' Jess beamed.

Bella's smile grew and their silence warmed. When they passed older
Carmichael students in footy uniforms, Bella eyed her phone.

'I'm sorry about the weekend.'

'Yeah.' Bella rolled a shoulder as if flicking off a hand.

Jess wondered if Bella bore her any hard feelings. If her post had made
it worse. But Bella was watching something on the screen. A wriggly ring
of children.

'How's your mum?'

Bella gasped. 'Huh?'

'Your mum, hon, how's she coping?

Bella paused the footage on what looked like a bare bottom. 'Um. Yeah. Not great.' Bella flipped her phone over. 'First thing Saturday, we had to go meet Mr Crisp.'

'We did too.'

Bella looked at her.

'Awkward, wasn't it?' said Jess. In Mr Crisp's office, the silences had been careful. Jess hadn't said much. Mr Crisp had prattled on, mainly about risky behaviour and bad eggs.

'How was it?'

Bella twisted to face her. 'You mean once Jilly stopped saying how devastated she was? And what bad timing it was, with her stupid clothes shop shutting down.'

Jess tore her focus from the road. Bella was nothing like her fragile but elegant mother. The word 'indulged' came to mind, when Jess thought of Jilly. Though that wasn't very nice. While their daughters became besties, Jess and Jilly hadn't progressed from small talk and waves at pick-ups and drop-offs. Fortunately, Bella tended to come to their place. Jess had always felt bad for Bella, who was the opposite of indulged.

'Once Jilly shut up, Mr Crisp said he was sorry, blah blah, then he gave me a lecture. Told me not to send photos of myself, wearing, you know, not much.' Bella touched the pimple. 'It's not like I was naked! But he said, "If you don't want boys to see you in this fashion, don't give them photos." He was sort of nice about it but it was embarrassing. He said, "You need to rethink how you're choosing to dress."'

Bella had Mr Crisp's posh voice down pat.

'Oh, Bella.'

Jess had wondered about Mr Crisp's manner with Grace, who'd blushed, deeply, under his wonky gaze. The most ashamed Jess had seen her.

'Mr Crisp loves a speech. I wonder if he memorises them. Says them in the morning, to the mirror. In his jocks.'

Jess smiled. 'You do know, hon, it's not your fault, what those boys did?'

'Yeah.' Bella wriggled on the leather seat. 'You know what else he said? "Adolescence is terribly confusing, and heartbreak, the loss of a first love, is a very trying time for any young man."'

'No!'

'Kept banging on about testosterone, too. Ego. But it's not even like that! Blake's a sad dude but inside he's gentle. You'd never call him mean. What he wrote, it doesn't make sense. Not that anyone asked me.'

Bella sank into the passenger seat, hot and spent.

'I'm really sorry to hear that, Bella.'

With a shrug, Bella turned her phone back over, frowned at it. They were outside Bella's home: a two-storey townhouse with a modest, parched garden and empty driveway.

'What have you got there?' Jess gestured to the phone.

'Oh, nothing.' But Bella's glance to her was complicated – accusing? Guilty? Sad.

With a melodramatic sigh, Bella opened the car door. She had a lot, too much, on her small plate.

'Bella, how are you now?'

Bella's eyes fired, like hot coals. 'To be honest? Over it.'

Bella's snark was refreshing. 'I can understand that.'

'Think I'm going to disconnect for bit.' Bella tossed her phone into her bag.

'Fair enough,' Jess said. 'But, well, what do *you* think the school should do about Blake and Jai?'

'I don't care about the sluts thing. Or that the pics were public. But the captions, and everyone voting – that was shit.' Bella pulled at her waistband. 'I don't get why Blake would do it, and Jai definitely wouldn't . . . I don't know. To be honest, those two aren't the problem.'

Jess bit her lip. 'What is, then?'

Bella picked up her phone and looked at it again. 'School's like *Lord of the Flies*, most of the time.' Bella frowned across to Jess, then her face closed. 'You get used to it. Thanks for the lift.'

Bella climbed out. *Lord of the Flies*? Was that a movie?

'Bella? You get used to what?'

Bella shook her head.

'What about Grace, how's she . . . you know, coping?'

Inwardly, Jess cringed. But it wasn't her fault Bella was easier to talk to. 'Dunno. Good, I guess.'

Bella looked across the top of the car, and Jess couldn't see her face. 'It was better when we were invisible. Now Taj Low's poked his nose in and . . .' Bella bent into the car. 'And Grace's all . . .' Bella pouted and flicked her hair. 'I guess she got what she wanted.' Bella winced. 'Sorry. That was harsh.'

'Oh, no, hon, it's okay.' Confused, Jess gave a small smile. 'But I mean, what's she doing? Taj Low?'

Bella pulled a face. Jess pictured Taj bouncing the basketball to Grace. The boy's pretty smile had matched Grace's. Tier ones. She wondered what tier Jai Winsome had been. What he was now . . . Which one was worse?

'Is that why you girls take those pictures?'

'Uh, duh . . .'

Jess felt very old again. Fishing for praise she understood, but wanting to be an amateur bikini model? To be popular? Hadn't the school talked to the girls about this?

Bella ducked back into the cabin. 'Sorry, no offence, but everyone does it. Why am I the skanky one?'

Bella's huge brown eyes were wet again and Jess wanted to soothe the girl. But she didn't want to lie. Or say it was because Grace was prettier or slimmer or had better hair. Or because Grace's picture had conveyed sass, not need. Because she wasn't sure that was it. What would she know?

That pimple seemed to be getting bigger.

And that's when it hit Jess. The world wasn't fair. Jess hadn't realised the great depth of the unfairness and the ocean of lies filling it until now. She restarted her car.

'Bella, I don't know about skanky. But, hon, you dress how you like.'

14

Liv

Liv drove home as if she was following a hearse. No singing. No music. Beside her, Jai sat, unspeaking, as did Oscar and even Cody in the back seat, as if under a dark spell. She'd been hoping, in terms of the boys' daily school life, that Friday night and its aftermath would blow over quickly. But the Havelock family was in cyclonic and uncharted waters. Blake's distress had been terrible to witness. With his chalky legs, and trousers around his ankles, Blake had looked at once like a very old man and a very young child. And Jai . . . Both boys had looked so vulnerable, but in completely different ways. Blake was always so guarded by his precise, ill-fitting clothes, his subtle stoop and his indifference. Seeing him half-naked and flailing had been a revelation. Like seeing the insides of an intricate yet large machine and finding them soft and made of gel. Liv had been reluctant to leave Blake on his own at the school, but she'd had two other sons to find and a car in the two-minute pick-up zone. Tony Crisp had insisted he'd stay with Blake until someone came – probably Stella's mum. Conflicted, Liv had relented. Returning with Jai to the street, Liv spied one said missing son crouched in a bus stop, the other jumping from a tree.

'But I don't get it. Where's his mum?' Jai whispered. 'Where the fuck is she?'

'Hey, I get you're feeling anxious but cool it. And I don't know where Stella is. I can't find her.' She looked into the sky. She'd been trying to reach

Stella and Duncan, all day. Her husband in particular had mastered the art of being unreachable. 'But his Gran'll be here soon.'

Blake's Gran was almost as passive and uninterested as her daughter. At least she lived nearby. Tears filmed Jai's eyes. Sensitive children didn't miss much.

'Look what you've done,' Oscar had snapped at her. 'You and Grace's mum.'

Silence was the best response to that. (You had to pick your battles.) In the hush, Liv felt herself drifting away from her sons. Far, far from the mothership.

Jai stared ahead, grinding his jaw. She hoped if she let him be, he'd return to himself as he had over the weekend. His brothers seemed to be adopting the same strategy. She was, yet again, making this up as she went along. As her children had become older, their problems had changed. The mild relief she'd experienced in that sweet spot when the twins were ten – when the worst of it was grazed shins and nose-picking – was gone. For a few years, she had her children worked out. Then puberty struck. And mental frailties. And perimenopause.

As they approached home, another car pulled up. Cody screamed, which was nothing new, except this time, his scream was, 'Mum! Watch out!'

Liv swung into the driveway as two police officers – a man and a woman – hopped out of their car. The police looked little more than a year older than the twins and as though they were wearing dress-ups. Not so long ago, Liv had been younger than a large chunk of society, and that was normal and appropriate; but then a point came when she was on the other side of the age mountain. Hers was one of the older faces. Shop assistants and waiters called her 'Madam'. This came as an unfortunate surprise. Somehow she'd slipped up and over by mistake. Though she looked in the mirror many times a day, she was still unprepared for it. As she switched off the car, Liv was having these thoughts, along with a bunch of others like, What sort of trouble were these boys in? What was wrong with Blake? Did Tony Crisp definitely believe Jai's story now? And why was this mess hers to deal with, on her own? Liv could think about a number of things at the same time – something Duncan found peculiar, the one time he thought about it.

'Mum?' Jai's hazel pupils were like two new planets in a white sky.

'It's okay. Deep breaths. Just tell them what happened.'

Jai nodded, but blotches of red were appearing on each cheek. Possibly hives.

'Take three.' Liv breathed in and out and Jai copied her. 'Let's go.'

She unlocked his door.

'Is Jai going to jail?' Cody whispered.

'That's what Blake said,' Jai whispered, getting redder.

'He did?' said Liv.

'Is Blake going to jail?'

'Nope.'

Liv smiled bravely and climbed out of the car. Whatever law Blake may or may not have broken was, hopefully, a sensible one. Created by politicians on a rare good and wise day. Unfortunately, social media post-dated her law degree by decades.

'Mrs Winsome?' said the young woman.

'Yes, *Ms* Winsome.'

The officers introduced themselves and greeted the boys, and Liv invited them into the house. She was hoping at least part of the front room was tidy. It wasn't. Liv grabbed armloads of washing and threw them onto her bed. Cody's turn to do the washing, she thought. Then she dragged the dog's bed and the dog out of the room, and closed the door.

Everyone sat on the edge of their seat, even Cody, as the lounge suite was overly low, an op-shop surprise. (Last year, Pickle had vomited on their better settee, which'd been banished to the boy-cave garage.) Liv sighed. Like most people's, their good room was rarely used. In their next house, there wouldn't be a good room.

'We'd like to talk about Friday night,' said the fresh-faced woman, who may have introduced herself as a senior constable. 'About what you got up to with Blake Havelock.'

Liv looked at Jai, who was nodding but blotchy. 'Jai?'

'Yep, yep,' he said.

Liv shot him a steadying look.

'I mean, yes, that's okay. Yes, sir.'

Jai flinched, realising his error, then took a deep breath and answered the questions, as he had with Tony Crisp. The woman asked the questions. The earnest young man jotted notes as Jai spoke. Watching, Cody hadn't been so focused or stationary in years – his jitters shocked out of him, perhaps. Oscar was ghostly, like a hologram of Jai. No one mentioned jail. Listening to Jai, Liv tried her hardest not to answer for him. A few times she was mouthing the words as Jai spoke them, but Oscar waved at her and she made herself stop. Once the questions were exhausted, Liv asked her own.

'Could you tell us, please, what law Jai may have broken, if any?'

If only Duncan had specialised in something useful, rather than mergers and acquisitions. If only he was home today to shoulder this.

'If Jai's involvement is limited to him showing Blake that one photo, it changes things. But, if not . . . well, we need to see. There could be a few possibilities, from child pornography and sexting offences to cyber-bullying.'

As Liv listened, words like *intimate* and *distribute*, *nasty* and *embarrass* washed over her. She didn't dare look at Jai until some moments later, when the young policeman chimed in with the words '*age-based exceptions*'.

'How old are you, Jai?' he asked.

'Fourteen.'

'Same as Grace Charters?'

'Yes.'

He jotted in his notepad, as if that detail made a difference.

Jai was blinking hard and Liv could see his mind whirring. He did not, she felt reasonably confident, have any idea of these offences. Or relevant exceptions.

'The picture of Grace wasn't particularly intimate or . . . or indecent,' said Liv, 'and Jai didn't share it or distribute it.' Though he did *show* it to Blake. What did these words mean exactly in this context? Liv's legal brain was very rusty. 'And Jai definitely didn't write any of those things.'

Jai shook his head adamantly.

'Worst-case scenario, what's the punishment for . . .?'

'Yeah, it can be serious.'

As the woman continued, Liv's mind jammed. She thought she caught the words 'youth detention'. 'Criminal record'. But also 'formal caution'. Oscar began to cry. Cody put his puny arm around Oscar.

'We need to get the message out,' the man was saying. 'The malicious use of intimate images or nasty comments online to embarrass or belittle a person is not on.'

These words went straight in. Jai stopped moving.

'Do you understand, Jai?' said the woman.

'Yes, ma'am. But I promise I only showed Blake my phone, like once. I had nothing to do with that Insta account. I swear.'

The police officers exchanged a glance, as Liv put her arm around him.

'Can we have a look at your phone please, Jai?' asked the woman. 'And any other devices where you store photos?'

Jai yanked his telephone from his pocket and his iPad from his school bag as if they were contaminated. The police spent some time flicking through pictures: boys playing footy, boys playing basketball. The boys' bedroom ceiling, window sill, doorknob. For the life of her, Liv couldn't fathom the point of those.

Oscar was now sobbing. Cody was patting Oscar's back. Any second, Jai would be crying too.

'The photo of Grace is not here.'

Jai shook his head. 'I deleted it.'

Liv exhaled quietly. Thank god. The police officer's nod at Liv was an encouraging full stop.

'Cody, can you take Oscar and Jai into the kitchen.' Words she'd never thought she'd utter.

'Are you okay, Oscar?' Cody whispered. 'Want an apple?'

Snotty and distressed, Oscar sprang up like a well-trained monkey to follow his sombre little brother. Glum, Jai traipsed behind them.

'Is that the end of it?'

'Not quite.'

Liv pictured Blake back at the school gates. His pale butt. 'About Blake Havelock. Outside school today, he was . . . behaving strangely . . . acting out, I guess, for attention or help. He seemed . . . fragile.'

The pair exchanged another coded glance. Liv waited for more. For clarity. For permission for her life – her family's life – to return to normal. Or at least the shape it was in four days ago.

'Thanks,' said the man, straightening his uniform. 'Bye-bye.'

Liv watched the youngsters leave.

15

Duncan

Duncan hurried in before Liv could call him again. He took one look at her and his three sons in various modes of oddness: one spotty, one dripping and one inanimate. No one was dressed for the footy training for which he'd dashed out of the office. Outside it was daylight – glorious, midweek daylight! In here, though, the air seemed to have been sucked out through a giant straw. 'Has someone died?'

'No. But the police have just left,' said Liv.

'That why the car doors are open?' He frowned, confused. 'You locked in again?'

'No, no.'

'Oh, good-o.'

Patting the dog, Duncan gave his customary half-smile. Once, apparently, Liv had found that smile bewitching. His boys eyed him coolly, as if he'd turned up too late. Or uninvited.

'Where have you been?' Liv said.

'Where do you think? In traffic.' He helped himself to a glass of pineapple juice. 'It's beautiful out there, though. What's up? Aren't you boys going to footy?'

'They're investigating Blake's Instagram account.'

'Right.' Duncan shrugged. But, in that solemn kitchen, the new Liv seemed to want more from him. 'You don't need to worry. Jai's done nothing wrong. We know that.' He downed the juice.

'Hopefully Blake sticks with the truth,' said Liv. 'Otherwise, if they don't believe Jai, he could go to jail. For cyberbullying, I think.'

Cody seemed to turn whiter.

'Jail?' Duncan ran his tongue across his furry teeth. 'Jail, for fourteen-year-olds?' A cloud crossed his heart. Was it possible?

'You know, juvie or similar. I'm simply telling you what the police told us.'

'Right.' Had the police really said that? Or was Liv over-worrying again? He looked to Jai. 'What do you think?'

'I'm hoping it's like school. They tell you off, give you a scare, then forget about it.'

'You feel sufficiently scared?' said Duncan.

'Yes, sir.' Jai stuffed his trembling hands in his armpits. 'I'm never leaving my phone alone again.'

'There you go. Good boy.'

Hearing his tone, Duncan cringed inwardly. Sometimes Liv accused him of speaking to the boys the same way he spoke to Pickle. He didn't mean to and didn't know why he did. It wasn't as if he couldn't tell them apart. The dog was much easier to be around.

He smiled at their sad faces. His family, he decided, needed him to hold it together. 'Anyone hungry?'

Liv crossed her arms. 'Jai, I don't care that "send pics" is now a normal part of teenage relationships, *don't get any more*. And, for god's sake, don't send any!'

'I won't. And I haven't. I promise.'

'Thank you.'

Duncan tickled Pickle's belly as Liv stepped in front of their sons. 'Everyone, listen up. Let me tell you again. You need to *think* before you act – in real life and online. What you do has *consequences*. Look at Blake!'

'What about Blake?' Duncan looked up. Had they expelled him, already?

But Liv wasn't finished. Often, he felt like this: a step or two behind the action in his own family. A downside of being engrossed in making a living most of the week, he supposed. He'd exit as one drama was unfolding and return to a totally new one. Emotional jetlag, Liv used to call it.

(In between he'd have his own dramas, at work; though no one cared about them.)

'Promise me you will *think*,' said Liv. 'I know parts of your brain aren't fully grown yet but for god's sake! You know how people learn to paint with their toes when they lose their hands? That's what you've got to do! If your frontal lobe's useless, use another bit!'

Duncan had no idea about his boys' brains: what worked, what didn't, when the right bits would kick in. He hoped it was by the end of the week. 'Good,' he said again. 'Right-o, I'm starving . . .'

He considered the kitchen. Bereft of action, there were no pots on the stove, no vegetables partially chopped, only one lonely onion. Quite possibly, he'd forgotten a task again.

'Oscar, it's Monday,' he said. 'What's for dinner?'

Oscar moved half of his puffy face. Liv was hunting through her pockets. Jai was making that noise with his teeth again. And Cody looked . . . well, lobotomised. A small mercy.

It looked like Dad was cook.

'Check the board,' said Liv. 'I'm going for a walk. It's been a crappy day.'

'Stella back?'

'Nope.' Liv held his eye as if to say, *You don't know the half of it. And you will.*

Duncan washed his hands. 'Let's see . . .' He consulted the whiteboard on the wall. 'That'd make it Mexican?'

Mexican Monday. They hadn't wiped that whiteboard in weeks. They also hadn't had Mexican in weeks. As far as he knew. He wasn't always around at dinnertime. Jai and Oscar managed half a smile between them.

'You can do the guacamole,' said Liv to Cody. Normally, that would've seemed ambitious, or malicious. But tonight . . . it didn't rouse the boy.

Liv squeezed Cody's narrow shoulders. 'Toodles.'

Whistling for Pickle, Liv stuffed plastic bags in her pocket. Duncan took a second to congratulate himself for defusing the tension, and for taking on the cooking again. He tried to sustain his enthusiasm for dinner, but it wasn't easy. He'd had tacos for lunch, and, well . . . *The Shawshank Redemption* was one of his favourite flicks.

'Take your time, sweetheart,' he sang out, too late.

16

Jess

Climbing the bleachers, Jess Charters watched the point guard in Grace's team dribble up the sideline. Training was due to finish, but the 1's were playing the 2's in a practice match. The smallest girl in Grace's rep team (the 1's), Hannah Appleby, was taking high, sweeping bounces as she half-ran in a generally goal-ward direction. The other four players, including Grace, were positioned around the key. Pass it, hon, Jess thought. Pass the ball. Sitting to watch, Jess crossed her legs. Within seconds, her right foot began to swing. Grace darted about, signalling, silently, for a pass. Grace wasn't the tallest but she was a strong, fast and selfless player. When she was in the play. Jess wasn't a basketballer (too small) and neither was Morrie (big, but unco), but they'd heard the other coaches say that passing the ball down the court was quicker than running it. Hannah's hogging had been going on week after week for more than forty weeks. Half the parents couldn't bear to come to games anymore. Everyone had worked it out, apart from the coach. Who was, incidentally, Penny Appleby.

Jess thought of the roast chicken she'd thrown together for dinner, along with raspberry crumble. How she'd salvaged her afternoon by turning off her phone and listening to last year's Eurovision winner as she peeled and chopped. How she planned to sit Grace down for a chat, after dessert.

Down below, Taj Low swaggered in, glanced at Hannah's over-dribbling and kept moving. The Applebys and Lows had known each other since

Penny and Bettina met in mothers' group with their eldest sons. The allegiances between families in Bayside took you by surprise, sometimes. Especially the random links like mothers' groups or these out-of-school sports teams. The children in the area played in many teams: domestic basketball and representative, school basketball and football, local football, soccer and netball. Almost everyone active knew each other somehow, eventually. Penny and Bettina were different but similar, too. Passionate about their children. If you were unkind, you might say one-eyed. Briefly, when Hannah and Taj dated last year, it'd seemed incestuous. Somehow it'd ended without the mums' friendship busting up.

Taj Low looked to the bleachers and saw Jess sitting alone. You wouldn't call the look on his face friendly. Feeling assessed – by a fourteen year old – Jess sat up. She didn't like Taj Low, she decided; his long-limbed grace and blond good looks irked her. He had it too easy, already. He was in the 1's too, of course. The boys trained on court one when the girls finished. But the boys' 1's had the whole court. Didn't have to share, like the girls. Jess frowned: that hadn't occurred to her before.

Back on court, the ball was behind Hannah's back. Between her legs. Then Hannah's counterpart got a hand to the ball and ran. A fast break. A lay-up. Drat. Jess's foot continued to swing. 'No one's saying anything because there's no point,' Morrie had said when she'd last grumbled. 'Wait for next season.' But this *was* next season. The good news, Jess supposed, was these days Morrie didn't have to carry Grace into the stadium. Back in Year Five, when Grace had first made it into the representative team, on game nights, she'd been too terrified to get out of the car.

Four minutes to go. More boys were arriving. Jess couldn't see the Winsomes. Maybe they weren't in the 1's. She made herself look at the adults. Waved across to the few parents coming in, and mostly they waved back. She tried to watch the end of the girls' game without blowing a gasket. Grace would've seen Jess arrive, she decided. Grace would've seen Taj, too. Grace was doing a great job of not looking at anyone. Perhaps Grace had seen her at school. They hadn't discussed that, when Grace had wandered in half an hour late. Jess had been ready to send off a search party. They hadn't discussed that, either. Jess had been too relieved, and Grace too perky. Below, in the stadium, a man who had just arrived looked up at her sitting alone. He was tall, in a cap and tracksuit.

The whistle blew. The 2's won by six.

Silently, they left. Ignoring Taj's stare, Grace darted past her teammates and other waiting boys. Hopping into the car, Jess rehearsed her opening line: 'Hon, we've had a few days to think . . .' But she was too irritated by watching Hannah. The car growled to life as Grace tapped her phone. That tall man appeared in the car park. Walking alone, speaking into his phone. He was wearing sunglasses, though it was dusk. Jess had a feeling that he was looking at her. At them.

He walked slowly, onto the road behind the parked cars. Jess waited for him to move. Her frustrations were smashing into each other like cars on a freeway. Basketball was on top.

Grace was messaging, with that new, small smile. Her face was scarcely hot or damp. What a waste of time. Jess was desperate to snipe about Hannah Appleby. To tell Grace, you are so much better! Call for the ball! But . . . Grace was a sensitive and modest child. Jess didn't want Grace to feel bad about herself or her friend; friends were hugely important at age fourteen. What's more, Jess didn't want to sound like one of those nasty, competitive parents. No one had been taken hostage, she told herself. No one was hurt. Basketball wasn't important. Even Under-16s basketball at the club representative level wasn't important. Good health was. Kindness was. Keeping safe.

Hurry up, she thought. She had her foot on the accelerator, and the man had almost moved on when a chatting Penny and Hannah came out of the stadium. Penny called to the man and he waved, stopped. In that moment, Jess wanted to smash Penny Appleby in the face.

Instead, she slammed her idling car into park again and it hopped.

With a scowl, Grace looked up from her phone. 'What the hell, Mum?'

17

Tuesday

Liv

Some days in Liv's life as a mother felt never-ending; some weeks – filled with illness, injuries and other mortal wounds – felt like years. Other days, uneventful, healthy and happy days, vanished in a blur of same-same weeks. This day was in the first camp. Waiting on news of a son's potential expulsion or incarceration did tend to make the seconds drag. Liv spent most of the day writing up her interview from that morning, with a remorseful bully (or a very good actress), compiling her report and keeping an eye on Jai, who'd abandoned his iPad and deleted various apps from his phone. Outside, at the basketball hoop, he seemed to be managing, though there was a new intensity to his repetitive shooting. Labelling her report's attachments, Liv wondered what the school and police were doing, and how she could possibly change the world. She also needed to wash the bed linen.

Changing the world took time, she'd realised. Most women Liv knew didn't have a lot of that to spare once they'd earned some cash and kept their household afloat. It was hard enough to see your friends, do a plank and avoid losing your hair. Liv wondered how she could fit it in, even after her redistribution of the Lists. It was easy to get overwhelmed again thinking of the scale of the work required. The sheer energy. How did women do it over a hundred years ago, to get the vote? Back then, they didn't have washing machines and refrigerators or the pill. They had to contend with hordes of children, untreatable infections, and lifelong marriage.

At least back then, she supposed, women weren't juggling part-time or full-time work and work-obsessed husbands, multiple high-needs children and sky-high mortgages. No one knew about anxiety disorders or peanut allergies or screen addiction in those days. Women weren't trying to be A-plus mothers and ageless lovers. Today's woman had that many jobs, it wasn't funny. Yes, they were doing it all, and they could; of course they could. But it wasn't fun. Why would you want to?

Men sure didn't. At least not the ones she knew.

At her desk, at 3.45 pm, Liv was ploughing through chapter 4 of *How to Change the World* when she heard Jai answer the front door. Fleetingly, she thought it might be Blake. Time then perhaps for afternoon tea and a frank chat. But no. Heading downstairs, Liv saw Jai and a girl gliding through the house. Liv hadn't met a girl through her boys before. In her school uniform, the girl was as tall as Jai, and natural looking – no fussy hair or preciousness. She had thick eyebrows, as Jai and Oscar did, large teeth and a mocha-hued, long, fine ponytail. Liv couldn't detect any artificial fingernails or laborious make-up. However, the girl's eyes, the colour of denim, fairly exploded from her face.

In the kitchen, subtly appraising the girl, Liv thought she did look vaguely familiar.

From the fridge, Jai tossed an apple and, one-handed, the girl caught it.

'Mum, this is Grace.' Jai looked at Liv intensely: *Don't mess this up, Mum.*

Grace? This girl had sticking-out ears and little exposed skin. Liv headed for the kettle. Jai had mentioned that Grace had been grateful for his letter. Perhaps it was what had inspired this impromptu visit. Liv tried to be as cool as she was able, which was not terribly.

'Hi, Grace, how was your day?'

After ten years of asking this daily you'd think she'd have learnt. But perhaps Grace's mum coaxed out more from Grace than the mind-numbing *fines* Liv got from Oscar and Jai.

'We had a Health session.'

'Okay, good to know.'

Liv fought the urge to yank the girl onto a seat and snuggle up close. It wasn't that Liv didn't get *any* information from her sons; she did, but usually much later when she was kissing them goodnight and wanting desperately to be alone. But then, like cats sensing her disinterest, the boys were similarly desperate, or at least inclined, to tell her about basketball or their latest scabby wound; occasionally about forgotten homework.

'What's a Health session, exactly?' said Liv.

'It's new, but we do a term on respectful relationships, sex ed. Stuff like that.'

Liv nodded energetically. 'And who teaches Health?'

Behind Grace, Jai was running a finger across his throat.

Grace chewed her apple, with her mouth closed, much to Liv's delight. The girl swallowed. 'Miss Lee, the new PE teacher. You can tell she hates it.'

'You can?' said Liv. 'That's a shame. What did you learn today?'

'Mum, Grace can't stay long. She's got band practice.' Grace's school bag lay alongside a sports bag and two instrument cases.

Liv wondered if Grace's mum knew where she was.

'Mostly stuff we already know.' Grace glanced to Jai. 'But it goes from bully-busting and safe sex to trans people.'

Munching, Grace sidled towards Jai. She waved her apple at Liv, a fruity farewell.

Liv considered the Lists on the fridge; and thought of that fleshy pic. 'Do you learn about men and women, and, you know, the roles they get cast in?'

'I, um – not sure.'

Grace looked to Jai for support, the way married people did when bailed up by a third person, who might be a touch odd.

'Grace, come on, I'll show—' Jai attempted.

But Liv had a whiff of something meaty and wasn't letting go without a wrestle.

'What about the gender pay gap, and gender bias?'

Grace frowned, prettily. 'I don't know. I don't think so. Not yet, anyway.'

'Mum, if she's late for band she has to sing a song in front of everyone.'

Liv considered Grace's array of bags. 'What instruments do you play?'

'The piano, saxophone and guitar.'

'Aha.'

'Grace is in three bands.' Jai gave Grace a look that said, *come on, quick.*

'Is she.'

'She's the busiest person I know,' said Jai. 'And the smartest.'

Grace bowed her head with appropriate oh-shucks modesty, the authenticity of which Liv couldn't decide.

'Well done you, Grace,' said Liv, sincerely.

Liv benched her tea. Here in her kitchen was, she suspected, one of the super-girls she'd read about lately. The type of girl who intuited the secret to her future success was to be extraordinary at virtually everything. The sort of girl who, yes, played multiple instruments and several sports, and debated for her school; while also reading poetry to old people and racing off letters for PEN International. The sort of girl who scored ninety-plus per cent in every subject. These girls had somehow imbibed the message that they had to outperform the boys to earn their place in the world. But, equally, such a girl was probably torn between popularity and outright brilliance – because completely outshining the boys was a problem (one to which Liv could attest, though Jai seemed to be coping, as his dad had). This young girl was also probably stressed by her jam-packed life, but hadn't yet understood that about herself or didn't admit it to anyone, except perhaps her mother. These super-girls tended to live in a post-feminist bubble, oblivious to the unequal realities awaiting them beyond school. The type of girl Liv had been reading about was aged fifteen and a half. Grace had the jump on that prototype by about a year. Grace was the type of girl Liv would've been, if she'd been born this millennium. Liv couldn't let her slip away.

Liv also had one additional question: what'd prompted Grace, plainly a super-girl, to take and send a pouty picture of herself in a mini-bikini?

'Grace, we need to go. It's four o'clock already.'

'Wait a tick . . .'

Jai scowled at her. But, having little exposure to real teenage girls, Liv was desperate to sit Grace down, peel off the top of her skull and squish around in her brain.

And Grace wasn't moving. 'What's the gender pay gap?'

Liv pulled out a chair.

'Mum, you made her fucking cry! Like, a *lot*!'

'Yes, Jai-Jai, and I'm very sorry.'

How was she to know how badly Grace would react to the roughly fifteen per cent pay gap? Not to mention the miserable ratio of women to men on company boards and in federal parliaments. Or the reality that leaders in Western democracies tended to come from just six per cent of the population: white and male, married and university educated.

'She'll never come here again. Ever!'

'I'm sorry, darling-heart, what more can I say?'

'She's the most determined person I know. And you just knocked her out with your stupid statistics.'

Liv doodled in her book. Being direct and disagreeable was definitely an art. Should she have led the girl to the facts sideways? Let her glimpse them out of the corner of her eye, rather than banging them over her earnest, overloaded head?

'You've wrecked it!' Jai's rant escalated to the wild flapping of arms.

He was rather fragile at the moment, too. And he was right, she supposed. But it wasn't Liv's fault the world awaiting Grace Charters wasn't as the girl had blithely assumed: with male and female school captains in equal numbers. Liv was only trying to equip Grace with knowledge of what lay ahead. Of the mountain that she, Grace, along with Liv and everyone else who was *switched on*, needed to move. It wasn't Liv's fault the girl hadn't already been disillusioned by someone else. She hadn't expected Grace to flush deeply and liquefy copiously. She hadn't expected the noise that Grace had made, like a stepped-on mouse, which put an end to their exchange. But she was proud of her son. He'd scooped Grace up in his hands and plonked her on the couch. Eventually, he'd managed to get a sentence out of her: 'I want to go home.'

Liv had driven her home in silence. Jai had walked Grace to her door and then bolted back to the car.

'I'm sorry,' Liv said, a sixth time.

Jai's stare dug a ditch in her conscience. Had she been heavy handed in order to get back at Jess Charters? She didn't think so. What else could she say? Other people's frailties were so difficult to predict and understand. In the books she'd read, when the psychologists explained the gendered world we lived in to the super-girls, the gender pay gap in particular had made the super-girls *angry*. Anger, she would have been prepared for. But not disintegration. Or discombobulation.

'Why'd you tell her she'd end up working for someone like Rowan Whittaker-Smith?' Jai was close to yelling.

With a sigh, Liv pictured Oscar's pal, bucktoothed, flat-footed Rowan. Heard his catchcry: 'Wait, what?'

'Because he's a plodder: an average, well-connected white boy, a C-minus.'

'But she didn't need to know that! She could learn it later. In ten years' time, at work! You've ruined her life! And mine!'

Liv was growing weary of her placating role. 'For goodness sake. Take a breath!'

But Jai was having none of it. For a boy who struggled to find his voice socially he could be very communicative at home. He stomped his way from the kitchen to his bedroom. His anxiety was taxing at the best of times, and these weren't them. What was she thinking? She needed to be more careful. More sensitive. Her heart began to pound a Morse code message: it said, *Nice one, Olivia; nice one, Olivia.* She always called herself Olivia when she screwed up. It gave her a sliver of ironic distance.

18

Duncan

It was around 8 pm when Duncan glided through the intersection of South and Beach roads. The drive from his office to his driveway was sometimes the best part of his week. Some people were glad to see the demise of their commute. Not him. Day or night, he loved that ribbon of road curling by the bay. He'd note the mood of the water, and the sky, and he'd drift away. That evening, if you asked him how many times he'd stopped at the traffic lights, or what was the make of the car ahead of his, he couldn't have told you. His mind was perfectly . . . blank. Once, Liv had said he was paid to think and if he wasn't being paid, he didn't. A little unfair. But he smiled; he'd trained himself to decompress. Besides, Liv thought enough for both of them. Five minutes later, he swung into the driveway. Too quickly, sometimes, he was home.

He found his family in the kitchen, bickering. It was Jai's night to cook but for some reason he'd boycotted the List business. The thing was about to collapse and result in a walkout – possibly to the nearest pizza joint – which would've been fine by Duncan. But Liv was taking the blow-up to heart. His wife was having a notably bad week. Much like his day. A client had called to say their deal had gone to a third party. They'd been a stalking horse, which basically meant used. Lots of brain-power, lots of billable hours, for nothing. Those fees were going to sting. Duncan shrugged off his jacket.

On the upside, it didn't look as though the police had returned.

In the kitchen, Duncan juggled lemons to lighten the mood while Liv brokered a new deal. Jai would trade the meal-making to a hangry Oscar in exchange for the car-washing, which Jai would on-trade to Duncan in exchange for the vacuuming. And twenty minutes later, after Duncan had showered and spent some time lolling about with Pickle, Oscar was finishing the most exquisite-smelling spaghetti dish which he'd drummed up from the dregs in their kitchen. The things he'd found! Sardines and broccoli, pine nuts and withered sultanas . . .

Incredibly, Cody had watched the whole thing from a stool. 'What's that?' Cody whispered, pointing, when dinner was almost ready. Cody's hair was still damp, Duncan guessed, from swimming. Liv had been busy.

'What?' Duncan followed Cody's finger to Oscar's face, where an eye was puffy.

Oscar shrugged.

'Oscar?' said Duncan.

Draining the pasta, Oscar was giving himself an impromptu steam mask.

'Oscar?' Often Liv came in like the second strings behind him. As if his parenting needed bolstering. Or undermining.

'Not much.'

Everyone examined Oscar. A pocket of puffiness underscored Oscar's right eye. A small red tick emanated from its corner. If Duncan didn't know better, he would've thought Oscar had been punched. But Oscar had never been punched – as far as he knew.

'Taj Low punched me.'

Jai winced, flicked his hair.

'Taj Low?' Duncan tossed three lemons, kept them airborne. 'Bettina and Owen's son?'

'Are you all right?' said Liv.

Oscar nodded.

'Why'd he punch you?' said Duncan.

Oscar shook the pasta. 'I guess he had his reasons.'

'Did you do anything to make Taj punch you?' cut in Liv.

This was always Liv's first line of response to a brother-inflicted injury. She'd dig out the provocation rather than fly off the handle, up front, at the aggressor. Hear both sides, et cetera. In her defence, often one of them had said or done something to provoke the attack. But Duncan didn't have the time for a full-blown investigation. His response was mostly 'Go to your room', or the confiscation of technology, or a toothy growl. Sometimes it was more hardline.

But violence at Carmichael? Duncan hoped Oscar hadn't punched, kicked or 'accidentally' kneed Taj Low. The last thing he wanted was another chat with Tony. Or the attention of Owen Low, the pompous overlord. Duncan had gone to school with Owen's younger brother, Scott, who'd been a little sadist.

'Nope.' Oscar ladled pasta into bowls with a shifty zeal.

'Glad to hear it,' said Liv, rubbing Oscar's back. 'Where'd it happen? On the bus? At the bus stop?'

'In Home Ec.'

'But why?' said Jai.

'You're doing Home Ec.?' Duncan tossed a lemon at Jai.

Jai snatched the lemon as Oscar eyed Liv through the steam. 'In front of everyone, Taj said that I was a girl for getting into cooking.'

Liv gasped. 'Who's your teacher in that class?'

'Mr Waring – head of Year Nine. He's the Pom with the beard.'

Jai flashed a look at Liv, while, on his stool, Cody was still paused.

'And what did this hairy Pom say?' said Liv.

'He said young men today would have babies, too, if we let them; and everyone laughed.'

'Oh Osc, how did that make you—'

'So I poured my pancake batter down Taj's back.'

Cody blinked rapidly, while Oscar shrugged. Like Jai, Oscar wasn't much of a liar. Unless Duncan was mistaken, Liv looked practically gleeful. 'Then what happened?' she said.

'Taj punched me. And we both got detention. Had to write an essay on what it means today to "man up".'

Duncan tossed lemons, one by one, into their bowl.

'Are you serious?' said Liv. 'This Neanderthal is your Home Ec. teacher?'

Jai was grinding his teeth. Oscar scowled at him. 'No,' said Oscar. 'He was filling in.'

'There you go. A relief teacher,' said Duncan. Though how that made it better, he wasn't sure.

'Is Oscar going to jail too?' whispered Cody.

Duncan rolled his eyes. That was too dopey to answer.

'No. I've got him for English, remember?' said Jai. 'He told us the other day to make the openings of our essays like a skirt: not too long, 'cos that's boring, and not too short, 'cos that's sketchy . . . but short enough to be interesting.'

Duncan laughed. But Liv didn't seem to appreciate the joke. She was searching Oscar's face, while reaching for her phone, as if Crisp's number was now in her contacts. 'What's this man's name again?'

'No, Mum,' said the twins in unison.

'Put down your phone!' said Jai.

The intensity of the boys' anger was another surprise, but Duncan was with them. This was a hiccup, and conflict clearly wasn't a Winsome strength. Alongside him, Cody was completely unmoving, as if his motor had been flicked off. Permanently. He wondered what Liv was doing about that.

Liv lifted the phone to her ear and Oscar's face reddened.

'Liv, please . . .' Duncan shook his head as if she'd raised a vase and was about to smash it. 'Don't.'

Liv surrendered and instead gave Oscar a hug. Relieved, Duncan tossed his final lemon at Cody. Still nothing.

19

Liv

After dinner, the twins were at their desks, Cody was in bed, and Liv was doing the dishes. In no fair and equitable kitchen did the chef also do the dishes. Unfortunately, though, Oscar had scattered dirty pots and pans high and low. When Liv cooked, she diced and scrubbed, fried and rinsed all at once, like a human Thermomix.

'Tell me,' said Liv, peeling spaghetti from the base of a pot, 'do you think you're available to our boys' emotional needs?'

Duncan was committed to drying the new garlic press. 'They don't seem to have any.'

'Ha-ha.'

Liv tugged off her rubber gloves. Waited for a proper answer. Huffed.

'Obviously Jai's anxiety is spiking,' she said, 'while Oscar's acting up, and Cody's shut down.'

Duncan held the garlic gizmo in pieces in his fingers. 'Give them a few days.'

Liv slapped the gloves onto the sink.

In the past, when Cody and then Jai's behaviour first tipped from normal-difficult into indecipherable, Liv had read the books, met the psychologists, walked beside her sons. Ostensibly because she and Duncan had agreed, without discussion, that he didn't have the time and wouldn't know how, anyway. (Outside of work, he hadn't consulted a book that wasn't a biography of a musician in decades.) When the boys' behaviour first flared, Duncan had diagnosed Jai's anxiety as old-fashioned attention-seeking and Cody's hyperactivity as straight-up naughtiness. What they both needed was to be ignored; and, if that didn't work, yelled at and possibly chased with, say, a wooden spoon. A stunned Liv hadn't seen that coming. She'd since realised that Duncan's emotional literacy was what you might call low. (Which possibly also explained his song-writing chops.) Otherwise, of course, he was a lovely fellow.

Duncan was eyeing the garlic gizmo as if it were an IQ test.

Liv's hair was stuck to her brow and she shoved it out of the way. 'I'm doing all the heavy lifting here.'

Duncan gave up on the press. 'Because you're a natural at it.'

'What you mean is it's easier for me to do it.'

Duncan's phone rang but, pragmatically, he ignored it.

Liv rearranged the drying rack. Easy wasn't a word she commonly used when discussing her children. Dealing with the boys' mental health issues had actually been harrowing. Bewildering. Devastating. It occurred to Liv then, the Lists had missed a fundamental item. This was different to booking their dental appointments or buying their friends gift cards. This was attending to their hurts, joys and frailties. Being attuned to your children's emotional needs and mental health wasn't a chore, but it was taxing. And fundamental.

'They need more of you,' she said. 'They're not little anymore but they still need a proper, hands-on dad.'

Duncan's phone fell silent as he busied himself drying a sieve.

'You need to think and behave like a parent.'

He put the sieve in front of his face. 'You know, Darth Vader was a parent.'

'You need to *parent*. Verb. I'm not joking.' Verbs were much more important than nouns: Love. Respect. Parent.

Liv stared through the mesh. Why didn't he care their parenting was so extraordinarily lopsided?

Suddenly Duncan was searching for the pots and pans cupboard, as if he'd mislaid it.

'I mean, do you even know your sons?'

Bent at the knee, he stilled.

'*Tune in*, Duncan. You need to do more than throw a lemon at them. You need to teach them how to back themselves. Stand up for themselves, without pancake batter. How to open up, too. Be vulnerable. Be brave. And ignore the other crap, told by the likes of their numb-knuckle peers and that Pom, Waring.'

He straightened. 'Right. Yeah. Thanks for the tip.'

Liv put her gloves back on. 'You take Cody and Oscar,' she said. 'I'll take Jai.'

'What?' He blustered. 'Are we horse-traders now?'

She glared. 'I'm not doing three on my own anymore.'

'Right.' He flipped the sieve back into the water. 'You missed a spot.'

20

Jess

Jess was packing the dishwasher when her phone rang again. It'd been ringing more often than usual since Saturday morning, but this evening it hadn't stopped. It was her op-ed, she supposed; the one she'd dashed off overnight, which had been published online two hours ago. She didn't know what had come over her. But friends, acquaintances, relatives, everyone had an opinion on teenagers today. And she'd wanted to add to hers – namely, that this wasn't about one or two bad eggs but groups of indulged, feral boys. She'd sent the article to the journalists who'd been calling. One group got in touch. Her article was entitled 'Lord of the Flies' (which she'd googled), and she'd sent a link to Bella. She wondered who was ringing now. It felt like the only people she hadn't heard from were Jilly, who'd disappeared, and Grace.

Oh, Grace. An hour ago, Grace had come home from band practice early, red-eyed and clutching her tummy, and gone straight to her bedroom. Ordinarily, Jess would've thought Grace had a nasty period. Or a test coming. But maybe, finally, that humiliation had hit. Whatever it was, tonight, Jess planned to smoke the girl out with chocolate caramel slice and. Have. The. Talk.

Last night, Jess had tiptoed into Grace's room when Grace was asleep and gone through her phone. Grace was more involved in social media than Jess had realised. After wading through homework confusion, photos of cats and dogs, and too many girls in bikinis, Jess could see the benefit of sneaking. On each platform, it was mostly the same boring conversations between the same children, with two exceptions. The first was Jai's, *Wtf, what's this?!* And Grace's, *What? Don't you like?* This happened last Friday, which added up, though Jess couldn't see the picture. The second concerned Taj Low. He'd sent his first ever message to Grace after school yesterday, via Instagram. Something Jess couldn't open. Something Grace hadn't answered. Then he'd sent, *Your turn.*

After her snooping, Jess had gone for a long, long jog on her treadmill.

The phone continued to bleat. It could be Morrie, she supposed, on his way home. Whenever he rang, around this time, she answered, thinking, Sweetie, what couldn't wait another half an hour? This evening, as always, she was midway through her peak hour. Potato and leek soup was simmering; the washing machine was spinning; and she needed to sweep the floor. Still in her work clothes, Jess hadn't managed to escape the kitchen, let alone the telephone.

The call rang out, but, after a moment, started again. Jess bent, bowl in hand, over the dishwasher. Out of nowhere, she thought of the Bayside Rocks again, and how on Sunday night trolls, those mean, soulless people, had crawled out and onto the Facebook page.

'You want me to answer, Mum?'

Jess jumped as Grace watched her. Her clear, peachy skin was pink, as if she'd had a shower.

'It's okay, poppet.' Jess lunged at her phone. 'Hello?' Best case scenario, it was a friend.

'Jess Charters?' This voice was muffled, as if the words were being spoken through a blanket.

'Yes, how can I help?'

'You need to leave our boys alone!'

'Who is this?' Her voice squeaked.

'Call me an old Grammarian.' The line crackled on the final word.

'Sorry?'

'An old *Grammarian*.' The voice reminded her of a grumpy, posh politician.

'Who is it, Mum?'

Jess turned her back to Grace. 'How did you get my number?'

The man's laugh was scoffing. Was he one of the awful boys' fathers? Or grandfathers? Beneath the laughter, she could hear heavy breathing. The caller must have been walking, asthmatic or dying. She tried to gather her words. Use some of the anger she felt, without being mean or offensive.

'Please do not ca—'

'How dare you turn our fine school into a media circus!' he said. 'It was a lark! A fucking lark! You humourless bitch!'

Tears blurred Jess's eyes; the few words she'd assembled shattered like glass.

'You need to shut your mouth.' The man ended the call.

Grace tugged at her. Grace, her fragile and confused goodie-goodie. '*Who* was that?'

Grace's wet eyes were wide. Jess could hear her fear. And a hint of accusation. 'No one, hon.'

Jess gave a discreet sniff. Grace seemed to be waiting. But for what? The truth was, that man could've been any of a hundred men Jess knew.

Later, once Grace was in bed, Jess scrubbed the spa bath. German death metal blared in her headphones. What had she started? When Morrie appeared, she banged her shoulder into a tap.

'Is she okay?' Jess asked.

A nod. 'How much longer are you going to be?'

Jess pushed off her headphones and considered the gleaming room. 'Another half an hour.'

Morrie shut the toilet's lid and sat on it. 'Did you speak with her?'

Jess shook her head.

'You can't keep putting it off.'

'Tonight wasn't—'

'She told me about the phone call.'

Jess returned to the plug hole, and the unintelligible screaming in her ears. Her fear and embarrassment were almost gone.

'After what happened on the Bayside Rocks, why'd you go off and write that?'

Jess squeezed clean suds from the sponge. Ran the water and watched the suds swirl away.

'I guess I had more to say.'

Morrie's bushy eyebrows met.

'You think I should let those meanies shut me up?'

'I think you have to be sensible.'

Morrie's idea of sensible was head down, work hard, hope for the best. Hers had been the same, until recently.

'You're telling me to pull my head in too.'

Morrie stroked an eyebrow. The one with the extra-long grey hairs.

'I forgot to tell you.' She smiled at herself in the tap. 'I went to the police yesterday about those boys.'

'What? Why would you do that?' Morrie was grimacing.

'I was cross.' She attacked the shining soap holder.

Morrie knelt beside her and took the sponge from her hand. 'Jess, please. Stop. You're a wonderful mum. Patient and selfless and kind. But you're not yourself. Your thinking's muddled. You're scaring Grace. Those boys'll be terrified. Jilly will be mortified. The school's going to be mad as hell. Have you forgotten Grace's scholarship?'

He was looking at her with more intensity than he had in years.

She wiped her forehead with the back of a gloved hand. She was feeling bad; she hadn't anticipated this pushback. But what did Morrie expect? She didn't have the hang of anger.

'I hope, for our sake, the police let this go,' he said.

With a pointed stare, he returned the sponge. Then he washed his hands and put on his moisturiser. The wimp.

21

Duncan

Liv could be quite critical and was getting worse with age. Duncan wished he'd known that twenty-odd years ago, but faults are camouflaged when you're young. He was still smarting as he jotted onto a pad and his mind whirred. He was a better father than his dad had been: he watched the boys' sports, made them laugh, fried up their Sunday breakfasts. Sometimes, when he worked from home, he opened the door to them coming in from school. Plus, he praised them – how many 'good boys' had he said already this year? A hundred? Two? And they were good boys. Even Cody, especially in his current go-slow mode. Tonight, he'd gone down like a dream.

Ignoring the letter of advice open on his screen, Duncan re-read his notes. Beneath two columns, he'd written whatever he could think of. He'd been at it for around twenty minutes. Under the heading 'Oscar' he'd written: pigeon-toed; slow to shoot; fouls easily; a follower; pacifist; sleepy. Lazy. He crossed that out and wrote: lacks initiative. Gentle; could be fitter; daydreamer; easy; smart enough; loved those novels about the kid lawyer; a sweet tooth. Introvert . . . like me? He re-read those last two words a few times.

He could hear Liv, singing out, 'Bed in five, guys!'

He supposed he should help, *again*. But how hard was it? Cody was already asleep and the twins were fourteen! As far as he knew, the only real job left was prising Oscar's technology off him and locking it up overnight. Though Liv would do her nightly watch later. He wondered if Liv didn't make her workload bigger – by doing too much, thinking too much, expecting too much. No wonder she was worn out and easily disappointed.

He spun the pencil on his thumb.

Underneath 'Cody' he had written: loud; boisterous (normally); exhausting (constantly); stubborn; explosive; kind to animals and littler kids; likes fish and chips and pepperoni pizza with pineapple. Fidget ball/octopus. Annoying . . . He crossed that out. Wrote: loves funny/over-the-top characters/novels. Something about red food dye. Silly, floppy/shaved soccer player hairdo. A weak swimmer. Michael Phelps a hero. Allergic to rye grass? Not a lot of friends.

When he was finished, one column was longer than the other. But one child had been alive longer than the other. Getting up, he was tempted to show Liv. See? Though, he hadn't written a single emotion. His children had them. Everyone did. What else was there to know?

He should get back to work, he supposed. Tighten up that letter. He could hear running water. A late shower. He vaguely wondered who was in it, yawned. Then he tapped his phone; saw a notification for Word Scramble. One game ought to do it. Then back to work.

22

Wednesday

Liv

The Winsome family's new and improved routine held, more or less, until Day Four. On Days Two and Three, Cody had sorted and delivered the washing, give or take a bra. A glum Jai had vacuumed around the furniture and a solemn Oscar overfed the dog. But Liv wasn't complaining. Her house was clean-ish, and her sons were becoming her personal Oompa Loompas. What's more, on Day Three, after her pep talk, Duncan had seen Cody into the shower and put him to bed. He'd even read him a story – a short one. Then he'd chatted with Oscar about the Lakers before retreating to 'do some work'. Liv had been impressed, although afterwards Dunc seemed to want a Nobel Prize. She suspected he was putting in a big effort before pulling the pin. That talk had definitely left him wounded.

Last night, Liv had coaxed a sentence out of Cody: Miss Laghari plays with Harry's hair. On that, Liv had nothing. She was similarly silenced by Oscar's new, centre-parted hairdo. And, somehow, having a smidge more time, Liv had taken on extra files: a degloved scalp from a roof fall, and an electrocution; soon she'd be hard at it, interviewing hostile and mostly amnesic people. Even so, things were, she told herself, on the up.

On Day Four, Liv left early for the office while the boys slept. Once her school-going sons roused, they burnt their raisin toast, spilt their mango smoothies and forgot their honey sandwiches, apparently. They also missed the bus and resorted to walking to school – which was unheard of. As a consequence, a very late Oscar missed a Humanities test. This was, it turned out, a Big Problem. Particularly as Oscar explained to Mr Humphries: 'We're not used to getting ourselves up or to school. It's not my fault I missed the test. It's *Mum's*.'

Upon receiving the teacher's email, Liv agreed to dart between interviews to the school for 'a quick chat'. A slight overreaction, perhaps. But while there, she could possibly eyeball the Neanderthal Waring and hopefully get the inside word on Jai's future. Outside Carmichael, Liv hesitated. This afternoon, she needed to be taken seriously. She thought again of her effective, Nordic detective. What was her name again? The only Nordic name Liv knew was Gunhild.

At 2 pm, Liv strode into the Middle School building. When Liv was a teenager, her mum (and dad) spoke with her teachers, yearly, at parent-teacher interviews, if they remembered. In Year Nine, a teacher had called her 'capricious' on a report card; and they'd had to look it up. But that was as far as it went. Her parents didn't have a clue what she was being taught. No one talked about 'pastoral care'. Thirty years ago, school and home were far apart. Today, Liv felt like a stakeholder. Her sons' education and her parenting were interlinked. Until recently, she'd dropped forgotten lunches, sports shoes and instruments at school. She'd clarified homework tasks via email. She'd swotted up on her boys' assignments; she'd learnt minute details about the levels of government, the lymphatic system, how to keep plants alive. Today, parents and children and their schools seemed far more entwined thanks to the performance and speech nights, the coffee mornings and working bees, the dinners and cocktail parties, and fetes and fundraisers. The fees. School loomed large in their life. Well, this school had, in hers.

Which made it all the more extraordinary that she hadn't paid close attention to who was running it.

Fifteen seconds after her arrival, Mr Humphries appeared, bowing before holding open the door. 'Please come in.' His voice was deep, with a touch of vampire.

'Thank you.' She winced, remembering Gunhild.

Ethan Humphries was both a Humanities teacher extraordinaire and head of Year Eight. A pale thirty-year-old with small hands and sculpted facial hair – goatee, sideburns, eyebrows – he directed her to take a seat at a round table. The room was wallpapered with books. Liv wondered if Mr Humphries remembered her name. At times, to certain staff members, she'd been MUM. As in, MUM has a question about the camp's safety assessments; or MUM mentioned a bump on the head; or MUM's here to collect the boys due to the storm. Somewhere at the school, at least one man had referred to her thus. She couldn't recall his name. Let's call him TEACHER or COACH. In the past, this shorthand hadn't bothered her; people were, like her, busy.

'Very good,' said Mr Humphries, apropos of nothing. 'How is every-thing?'

'Everything is fine.' If you didn't count the son, suspended at home. Liv tamped down a smile.

Not smiling was a gamble. You were meant to build rapport in meetings, then impress people with your brain. You were meant to be likeable, much like characters in fiction and women generally. Liv thought of her Nordic heroine. Her smiles weren't cheap. People worked hard for them. Why? Maybe because people didn't respect freebies.

'But busy, busy, eh?' Mr Humphries leant forward.

A pilot light of wariness flickered on inside her. She decided not to respond. This was more difficult than you'd think. But subtext was import-ant too, she realised; in this way, words were like smiles. People probably didn't respect gushers either.

'Let's get down to brass tacks, shall we?' Mr Humphries shuffled his notes. 'Oscar can sit the test at lunchtime tomorrow. But this leeway won't be allowed a second time. In future, he must be punctual. Make his bus.'

'I agree.'

Mr Humphries' nod was a businesslike jerk. This was to be a quickie, particularly if she played it Nordic. But then he lowered his voice. 'Oscar has been scavenging for money at lunchtimes. Young Cody, too, I have been led to believe.' His too-pink lips turned downwards, like a sad child's.

She took a moment to process this information.

'They don't need to do that,' she said. 'They have lunch.'

'Of sorts, as I understand it.'

Was that a sneer?

Mr Humphries explained that Oscar and Cody's pocket money had been rorted during days one to four. They were in debt to the more malleable staff and their remaining friends. What with the punch and detention, Oscar was having a less than optimal week. Perhaps, the man mused, Oscar was playing up in support somehow of Jai?

'I . . . doubt that.'

His look to Liv became pitying. She opened her mouth again to explain. Apologise.

'The boys are in transition,' she said, 'from being mollycoddled to being independent.' She made herself speak slowly. 'We are sharing the load at home. Equally. A few glitches are to be expected.'

Mr Humphries curled a shapely eyebrow. 'Glitches?'

Liv decided not to elaborate. Difficult, but she managed it. Besides, mistakes were a part of life; she would get used to them. But this development was a concern. She steeled herself. 'I will speak to the boys. People must not give them money.'

To her ears, she was sounding Nordic. She quite liked it.

'Oscar tells me he's been swamped with jobs—'

'I would not call it swamped.' It was getting easier to not smile.

'He seems worried . . .' He stroked his goatee. 'He seems to think you're having some sort of . . .'

His focus seemed to shift to her patchy scalp. Liv rose, willing away a blush. Since when did Oscar open up, and to teachers?

'We see it more that you'd think. Mums not . . . Do reach out if we can help.'

Mr Humphries was on his feet. He squeezed her hand, as if she were a teabag.

'I must say, you're very lucky – you have quite a husband, to be taking on new jobs too.' Mr Humphries face was a pantomime of jollity.

Liv told herself he was a young man and didn't know any better. Her heart did a nervous tap dance. But her feet refused to move. If her boys weren't so happy at this damn school, she'd pull them out tomorrow. If you didn't have to give a term's notice. Times three.

With her feet planted hip-width apart, she put her hands on her hips. She'd read once certain poses made you feel more powerful. She waited a few seconds, until she was truly channelling Gunhild.

Mr Humphries was still smiling vigorously.

'First, luck has nothing to do with it. Second, Danish men do more housework than any other country's men. You Australian men need to catch up.'

Mr Humphries's face dropped, as if she'd tugged a cord affixed to his chin. 'I'm very sorry, I didn't mean to . . . I'm sorry. Here, allow me.' Eyeing her warily, he held the door open. 'I'll let everyone know not to give the boys money. Or lunch. Thank you again for coming in.'

'Bah.'

Liv strode out. Her exit, though perhaps more French than Nordic, felt fabulous.

23

Duncan

Duncan winced as the voice on the phone grew louder. He moved one earpiece and stuck a finger in the tight, fleshy cave. Deep within was a new itch he couldn't reach. He turned down the volume and put two dots next to his notes. It'd been a long day in a long week; and it was only Wednesday. He'd like to work from home tomorrow, and take Liv's car to the mechanic's himself, but he had to go to Sydney. Through a glass door, he could see two young people. He gave them a signal to indicate he'd be one minute. Sometimes he waved them in when he was finishing a call so they weren't waiting outside like room service with fresh towels.

On his desk, his mobile phone was vibrating.

He stared up at the bush-scene painting on his office wall. Liv wanted more of him too, but not much was left. Often, while he was on the phone, he would walk into that camp site, sit by the fire and imagine the birdsong. If he concentrated, he could smell the smoke. He tried now but couldn't. Ted was nearly done. The deal that had finally been struck yesterday was in danger of unravelling. It needed restitching. Tonight. Yes, he'd do it himself. He waited. Looked at his computer screen: 5.15 pm. When did that happen? 'Yes,' Duncan said. 'Yes.' A word he said a lot. 'First thing.'

Liv did have a point – he did work a lot, his working hours (like everyone else's) bled across the entire week.

Another minute later, Ted hung up. Henry Ueland, one of the founding partners of W&U, had gone to school with Ted, at Carmichael, and the

CEO was one of Duncan's most difficult clients, which was saying something. Phone calls from Ted alternated between the standard complaints: Took too long! Cost too much! And the flip-side demand, that Duncan do the work himself, immediately, all night if necessary. When Duncan's time was the most expensive in the mergers and acquisition group. Duncan removed his headset as if it were a heavy crown. A second later, the door opened, and his mobile phone began vibrating again.

He suspected he was due somewhere.

'Howdy, Dunc,' said Red Jackson, elbowing ahead of the queue.

Red shoved a joint venture agreement under Duncan's nose. Duncan tried to concentrate despite Red's idle chatter. But the page in front of him contained exactly two typos, a formatting glitch and some seriously sloppy thinking. Duncan considered the moustachioed sapling. A third-year solicitor, eager, overconfident and slightly lazy, Red probably wasn't really W&U material. But Red was fun; played footy at the Christmas party with uncoordinated zeal.

Duncan placed a red dot above each typo; circled the wonky indentations; and put a line beside the dodgy clauses.

'Have another think.' Duncan gave a weary smile. Of course, Red wanted him to do the thinking.

Duncan tugged his ear. Red had been eavesdropping for more than ten minutes with that paperwork. One day he ought to give it to the boy. Michael wouldn't stand for this. Red didn't move to take the document. With a sigh, Duncan scribbled in the margin. 'Here, something like this . . .'

The next person in line was Julia Hogg, lover of cherries. Duncan read her freshly drafted clauses a second time. 'Very good!' he said, 'Send it out.' Julia beamed, flushed and scurried. They'd had roughly ten conversations in her twelve months at Winsome & Ueland – mostly about his kids and her competitive fencing. People tended to devalue the quiet ones, but she was a gun; unlike Red, who was forever chasing Duncan to chat about his career or the orientation of his office. If only Duncan could mix Red and Julia together.

Duncan rose to stretch his legs.

His office faced the car park too, a fact that Red had evidently not considered. Outside, it looked warm. Out there, people were playing tennis, running their dogs, canoodling. Twenty years ago, on a day like this, Duncan would've corralled his mates into an evening staggering around the city. Tonight, he was on the hook for dinner again. Mates were thin on the ground. And he'd be working late.

He checked the time. This week, he'd managed to leave early for footy training; he'd bought green groceries and cleaned the car; but he'd totally forgotten rep basketball this afternoon. That explained his phone's demented buzzing. Swearing softly, he read: *Where are u? Walking. Train. Bus. Forget it.*

Duncan rubbed his face. His first major stuff-up. He hoped Oscar and Jai hadn't waited long. But what more could a man do? He turned off his phone. This List business was another screw on the rack of his already screwy life. It had been unsustainable, even before Liv had bundled two sons onto his responsibilities too. But he'd give it one more week – until Jai was reinstalled at school. Then the whole thing could go away. Liv was forever decluttering or rearranging the furniture. Last summer, he came home to find their newish couch on the nature strip. He and the boys had carried it back in when Liv was at work. This current burst of redesigning was on a grander scale. Maybe a change or two would last; the boys could do more around the house. Though he'd never understood the source of Liv's restlessness, it had kept them attaining new goals, he supposed. She'd been the one agitating to have children, to move back to Bayside, to set up Winsome & Ueland.

Duncan wilted as another person appeared at his door. He needed to go, but instead he moved to the window. Often, he glimpsed his staff coming and going down below. He knew who drove what and when they needed an upgrade. Michael drove a Jag. Henry drove a low-slung Lexus coupé. Julia had a tragic Honda Civic. A SUV was reversing awkwardly into its spot: George Lambe, perhaps returning from a client meeting. A senior associate, who'd been working in the UK, George had started two months ago and was another one in litigation, who reported to Michael. He was a wiry, sunny man, who ate delicious-smelling lunches brought from home. In tracksuit pants and a T-shirt, George strolled across the bitumen. He'd been at the gym. Good thing Michael's office faced the park. Duncan had heard Michael earlier – 'Anyone seen George? Bastard's not answering his phone!'

Michael liked his staff within arm's reach, where he could see them in a heartbeat. Duncan's view was that their people were adults and free to decide where to be. However, wherever they were, he supposed, people needed to be accessible.

A knock.

'Come in,' said Duncan, over his shoulder. But the person was already in.

The Winsome brothers were two of the three founding partners at Winsome & Ueland. Henry Ueland was an old friend of Duncan's father. By rights, when they were setting up, it should've been Winsome, Winsome & Ueland; or Winsome, Ueland & Winsome; or Ueland, Winsome, Winsome; but it'd seemed both pedantic and like a stutter. Though Michael had more clout, Duncan liked to think it was his last name on the letterhead with Henry's. After all, the firm was Liv's idea. Michael's inclusion, on the other hand, had been Henry's suggestion. One Duncan hadn't loved but didn't resist. Back then, Liv was pregnant with the twins, and they'd tossed around making her partner too, but neither he nor Liv could see how it'd work. Michael was older than Duncan by just under two years. Michael passed by Duncan's open door, his sky-blue eyes flickering in. These eyes were pinched together and small, like Duncan's brown eyes, but Michael didn't have Duncan's untameable hair. Michael's was a silver, monk-like ring.

The person at the door was Henry, a fit sixty-two-year-old with a fine, grey buzz cut.

'What can I do for you, Henry?'

Henry raised his finger as shouting erupted across the hall. Duncan recognised the voice, tone and scale. His heart rate spiked. George was a new dad; his baby girl was six weeks old but had been born prematurely, and he'd taken a fortnight of paternal leave as soon as he started. Only yesterday he'd been spotted dozing at his desk. Not a good look, but who could blame him? His life had been completely upended. Duncan could remember those early months, with the babies staring wide-eyed at the downlights at 2 am. But Michael, himself a father of three, had selective amnesia. And two ex-wives.

Henry paused, as if waiting for a train to pass. Usually, Michael's PA, Trish, closed his door. Michael could work for hours, undisturbed, in the office – despite the number of people he supervised. When the yelling eased, Henry waved a piece of paper at Duncan. Meanwhile, at the door, another person appeared. Duncan wouldn't be alone again until he was in the car. Red wasn't the only one guilty of following him into the Men's. He wouldn't get to his own work again here today, either. Michael's roars were sentences beginning with 'You . . .'. Soon a door would slam and it'd be over. Duncan told himself Michael's bark was worse than his bite. But someone should have warned George.

Henry closed the door. 'Sally-Anne's resigned.'

Duncan tugged his hair. Sally-Anne was another senior associate in Michael's litigation group. Talented. She'd lasted two years.

Seemingly rattled, Henry shook his head. 'Wasn't she at the wellbeing talk the other day?'

Duncan shrugged, and Henry went on. Everyone knew the life of a senior associate was brutal, if you wanted to make partner. Duncan's partners didn't call it 'sweating the assets' for nothing. Sally-Anne was going in-house. Another one. Oh dear. Duncan's mind was wandering to the evening's redrafting when he saw George recrossing the car park. Their newest senior associate was carrying his suit and briefcase. Duncan was shocked George wasn't at his desk, if also slightly impressed by the guy's tenacity. But then George lurched, as if on a boat, clasped his left shoulder and sank.

24

Liv

Nursing a prosecco and deep in the school's website, Liv was ruminating on her meeting with Ethan Humphries when a dishevelled Jai arrived. Jai, her darling, sensitive son. He would never suggest she was having a breakdown. He was also an excellent source of information. Surely Humphries and Waring couldn't be typical of his teachers? In primary school, the boys' teachers had been excellent, a few duds aside, and female. Waring, Liv suspected, was a hangover from Carmichael's all boys' days.

'Hello, Jai-boy, how was basketball?' She sat higher on the kitchen stool.

He gave her snarky stare. 'It's seven-fifty.'

'Is it?' She squinted at the screen in front of her. 'Where have you been?'

Her youngest son had been quiet a long time! This particular silence struck her as too deep. Either Cody had found last year's Halloween loot or he was on the roof. Which meant he was better but . . . not ideal. She rose.

'On the bus and then the train.' Jai was trying not to look at her. The way he did when she tried to go back to work, part-time, the first time, when he was one.

She hesitated. 'You mean public transport?'

'Dad forgot to pick me up.'

'Oh.' Where *was* Duncan? 'Did you call him?'

'He never answers his phone.'

'Very true. Where's Oscar?'

'He skipped training and went to Taj's. He texted you.'

'Taj Low's?' She eyed her phone on the kitchen bench. 'But don't the 1's train with the 2's?'

Jai shook his head.

'Why didn't you text me to come and get you?'

Jai scowled at the Lists on the fridge. And Liv loved him for it. Her semi-compliant son.

'Well, you're here now.' She was at risk of sinking into an abyss of guilt that was opening in the floor. Then she remembered Oscar's reasoning: Mum's fault we slept in, missed the bus.

She hopped up and flung open the laundry door. No Cody.

Jai dropped his sports bag as he walked, as if it was a deer he'd hunted, and it'd been a tough and bloody battle. He poured himself a glass of vegetable juice.

'Are you okay?'

Jai gulped juice. She watched his Adam's apple working. 'People are still saying I did that stupid Insta account with Blake. I don't get why Mr Crisp hasn't called.'

She'd wondered the same thing. 'He will.'

Jai set the glass down.

'You been in touch with Blake?'

'I've tried. I have. But he's not answering, like, anywhere.' He shook his head, dumbfounded.

'So strange . . .' Liv finished his glass of juice.

'Mum, Oscar texted me that Mr Humphries was talking to Mr Crisp about you.'

'About me? Are you sure?'

Jai did the not-looking thing again. Was this the time to broach Oscar's contention that she was cracking up? And how to do that with someone who'd cracked up a little himself, once?

'What do you think of Mr Humphries?'

'Not much. He's creepy. Why?'

Liv avoided his eye. On her screen was Carmichael's fifteen-page anti-bullying policy. She'd read a few anti-bullying policies for work – as usual, the section on bullying from teachers seemed to be missing.

'Mum, Oscar's super-pissed. Mr Crisp wants the dirt on us. Wants to know our friends, activities, grades. They're going to kick us both out, you watch.' His anxiety seemed to be kicking in. He also had a thin orange juice moustache, which was distracting. 'What'd you say to him?'

'Nothing.'

'He wanted to know what country you're from!'

'What?' Liv cringed, on the inside.

'I know that face,' he said. 'You did say something! And now Mr Crisp's setting his spies on us!' Jai flapped his arms. She needed to talk him down. Soothe him.

Gunhild had other ideas. 'Don't be ridiculous.'

Jai began to circle. 'I'll do my stupid list. I'll do the vacuuming, clean the toilets, but keep away from school! It's not perfect, but we like it! I want to go back!'

Liv wobbled her head noncommittally. She didn't like to lie to her children. But, that evening, she intended to watch her show again. Once she'd found Cody.

'Have a shower, Jai,' she said. 'And chill out.'

Inwardly, she winced, but she couldn't be all things to all people. Not anymore.

25

Duncan

Around 10 pm, closing his eyes, Duncan tried to hear the bubbles popping. The bath was the one place he could flop, alone. He'd shed his shirt and tie on the landing and run for it, like a child for the sea. After his soak, he'd get back to work. But for now, on the underside of his eyelids, he could still see George, the colour of smoke and distressed. He saw the ambulance and its silent siren. Thank god the heart attack had been mild: there'd been no need for heroics, no CPR or devastating news to pass on. Duncan could have wept, there in the car park. Not that it was over. The doctors were running tests and monitoring. George's future as a road-racing cyclist was looking iffy. Matters at W&U were becoming more complex by the minute.

Duncan was waiting for the bubbles' soothing spell when Liv appeared. They'd spent the minutes he'd been home apart; he'd glimpsed Oscar's Maths and kissed Cody in bed. Cody had taken himself to bed, apparently, hours ago: another anomaly. But at least the evening had been uneventful. A moment ago, Liv had put on the television to watch some foreign show. It'd looked dour and soggy, and he couldn't have concentrated on the sub-titles, even if he'd wanted to. This bath needed to be a quick one, but here she was in an oversized towel. As far as he could recall, they hadn't had a bath together since Cody was born. His eyes slid shut. A more optimistic man might've watched his wife de-robe. A more lively man might've said something tender. But, after the day he'd had, he couldn't raise an eyebrow.

As Liv slid beneath the water, she gave an exasperated groan, and he recognised the opening refrain of another difficult conversation. They didn't have many, but the one they had was repeating on him. With trepidation, he waited for her to begin; though, tonight, in the waiting room, he'd worked something out. Surrounded by incomplete and upset families, he'd realised he hadn't had the stomach for his boys, especially when they were younger: grotty and messy, loud and unruly. Then, as they'd grown and their behaviour had become stranger, he may have, well, avoided them. Incredibly, it was easier, much easier, to work.

He opened one eye. He hoped she would be able to read his day in it.

'The boys are asleep.' She gave a faint smile. This was one of her favourite times: everyone was safe, undemanding and meeting expectations.

Duncan dropped his eyelid. He'd tell her about his day in a tick. He heard the skid and scud of her flesh on the porcelain. Felt the water recede then rise in a one-off wave.

'I met with an Ethan Humphries today,' she said. 'About Oscar missing the bus. And a test.'

'Who?'

'Humanities teacher, head of Year Eight.'

'Ah.'

'We had a little argument.'

He moaned, despite himself.

Liv sat up, clasping her bubbly knees. 'Duncan! He implied it was *my fault* Oscar missed the test. He said the boys have been scavenging for lunch, because I'm not doing my job.'

'He said that – out loud?'

Duncan doubted this, but what was the point of arguing? People got upset. Said things they regretted. People got more upset.

'He implied I was having a breakdown.'

'Implied, how?'

Why was he having this conversation? George was in hospital! His wife was probably still crying. George was probably still crying.

'He was rude,' Liv was saying. 'And I'm not putting up with rude men anymore.'

'Mm.'

He opened his eyes. Saw his beautiful, animated wife. His family needed more of each other, he'd realised. Not time wasted on unwinnable and unnecessary battles. But, lathering herself, Liv was getting quite worked up.

Duncan let his head sink back, leaving only his face above water. He exhaled through his nose. While he could respect Liv's newfound passion, he didn't have much to add. He wanted a more balanced world too! Who didn't? But *their* world was in reasonable shape. Many people had it much, much worse. Besides, people were rude. And then they died! Boom. Death needed to be front of mind. It didn't give notice. Boom.

He wondered what time he'd get to bed tonight – one? If he didn't start soon, it'd be three.

Long ago, he'd worked out (or maybe Liv did) that he was home, awake and not working, with the boys for, at most, fifteen hours a week, less if you included time when the children were playing sport or at friends'. These days, he worked, on average, sixty hours a week plus. Fewer than he once did. But, daily, he contended with bigger issues than swimming lessons and missed buses and rude teachers; issues like customising hundred-page agreements, keeping demigod CEOs and their subordinates happy, and meeting sky-high targets. Liv didn't sign off her emails as Liv Winsome, Director of Home Affairs for nothing. That was her job. Well, along with investigating, since a few years ago: when Cody started at Carmichael.

Liv was still speaking and lathering. He let an ear poke out of the water. Heard the odd word: 'respect'; 'discuss'; 'policies'. He closed his eyes; the words broke up in the water.

Bottom line was, he felt snookered. Their firm was still fairly old school: ran on billable hours, astronomical targets. The person who charged the most won – and lost. That person, of course, was Michael. By a long shot. Duncan thought of his other workaholic partners. He wasn't really friends with any of them. That left the senior associates, solicitors, PAs. George. He quite liked George. But, no, not much point discussing this with George, right now. He thought of talking to Liv. Could she help? A gap existed now between his concerns and hers. A big gap. No one else came to mind. Softly, he blew bubbles.

As Liv spoke, she was repositioning herself, without touching him. Sometimes, he felt as though he was communicating with his wife through trifle. That he stopped listening did embarrass him. It wasn't who he thought he was. When they'd met, married, it wasn't. But Liv did tend to sweat the small stuff these days. As of today he'd only sweat the big. He thought of his own somewhat detached dad, living it up, now with a touch of dementia, on the Gold Coast. When his dad started again with a remodelled, younger wife, he'd been a better father to batch number two. But Duncan didn't want another batch. He blew his last bubble. He was ready to tell Liv about George, the look in the man's almond-shaped eyes.

'It's not going to be easy from the outside. Not like Winsome & Ueland.'

Duncan stirred. 'What was that?'

'That's your business, our business. You have a real voice. You could make it work better, for us.'

She'd become fabulously soapy. But expressionless.

'Sorry, say that last piece again?'

Liv climbed out of the bath; suds clung to her and the water level dropped. Around him, the water was unpleasantly tepid and the bubbles almost gone.

'You're always at your desk, on the phone, in the office. Wherever.' She nodded once. 'It doesn't have to be like this.'

She was speaking in a bizarre, deadpan fashion; a bit like a Russian spy in a Bond movie.

'How do you mean?'

'Find a new female partner. Then, take a sabbatical. Be home for a few months and do nothing. Just focus on us. And the boys. And yourself. Then think about how to go back, in a genuinely balanced way.'

He felt a tingle as she rewrapped herself. She seemed to expect him to speak. But, gobsmacked, he had nothing.

'Good talk.' She marched out.

Duncan stared at her footprints. Then he lay back, pale and grey, an old man in his liquid coffin. How long was he going to feel this way? How long was she going to be like that? After a while, a word formed above him like a magical ladder: sabbatical.

26

Duncan

When he came out of the ensuite, Liv was now reading *The Way We're Working Isn't Working*. Could a person read too many books? Could it be like eating too many apples? Forty in one hit could kill you. Duncan remembered learning that at school: an English sailor arrived in China, ate forty apples and died. He wasn't sure if Liv's latest crop of books was agreeing with her. These all-knowing books certainly weren't agreeing with them as a family. But reading was one of Liv's happy things to do. She could lie on a concrete slab in a car park and be happy, if she was reading. She could be content in a queue at the dentist, if she was reading. It was a gift. As he dressed, he tried to identify his happy place. By the time he was in his track suit, he'd come up with: poky, dark rooms, behind a mic, with his guitar; and mountain lakes, clear skies, bike riding. As a kid, he'd loved his guitar, his bike and his dog, in no particular order. He'd liked his parents, not so much his brother. But he'd loved his bike. And his guitar. As an adult, he loved his children. His wife. Pickle.

As Liv turned another page, he put these ingredients together; gradually, they blended into an idea. A stupendous idea.

He needed to get to work, but instead he watched her read until she acknowledged him. It took two more pages. The end of the chapter helped.

'What would you like to say?' she said.

'I think you're right.'

She smiled, as he knew she would. Rightness was her weakness.

'We do need a break. I'm thinking a road trip, for a month or even two. The five of us. We could hire a Winnebago. Imagine it – every day together! We could take bikes. Camp. Play music. Dance!'

She was staring as if he'd broken into pidgin English. 'What are you on about?'

'A sabbatical! That's the best idea you've had in—'

'Duncan, you have taken the wrong end of—' She sounded weird again.

He raised his palm. 'This afternoon, at work, George Lambe had a heart attack. Well, in the car park.'

He sat on the bed and raised his chin towards the ceiling, as if he was about to spill. He'd travelled from sad to excited to sad again at the speed of light.

Liv put down her book. 'Oh, Duncan, is he okay?'

'He's doing as well as could be. Should be out of hospital tomorrow.'

'Why didn't you tell me earlier? Are you okay?'

Duncan's top lip quivered. 'I don't know.'

Liv wrapped her arms around him. 'That must've been very shitty.'

'Very,' he said into her hair. 'Henry and I were the first ones there.'

So often they passed each other like housemates; this simple hug moved him. She understood. They were in this together. As he elaborated, he enjoyed the warmth moving between them. She listened, chipping in soft murmurs. He felt himself equalise. He told her about George's cold sweat, and Michael's bloodletting.

'That man,' said Liv. 'One day someone'll sue you guys because of him.'

They lay in silence. Liv didn't return to her book.

A few minutes later, Duncan felt his shock melting into something usable. He would seize the momentum that'd been created by all this upheaval.

'I do want to be there for you, you and the boys. I'll make it happen.'

Her smile was sparkly. 'Thank you.'

He stood up. 'I'd better make a start,' he said. 'But what do you think: South Australia or East Coast?'

As she said, 'Who's George again?'

27

Thursday

Liv

Thank god it was finally Thursday: Liv had friends again. She was greeted at Stella's door with a glass of bubbles. Straight off the plane, Stella was her usual fashionable self, her taste for couture seemingly unaffected by her son's spectacular brain snap and potential expulsion. Today, she was wearing a many-ruffled tent-dress and bare feet. Her Outback tan was virulent. Liv was pleased, if surprised, to see her friend so rested, as she shepherded Cody in. The nine-year-old was dwarfed by the fourteen-foot ceilings and the doors designed for giants.

'Be gone, little person,' said Stella, passing Cody a can of ginger beer.

'Hello, you.' Liv enveloped Stella in an awkward hug.

Liv gave Cody a shove and he limped towards the 'media' room, where little kids could be heard cushion-fighting. The twins were at home. In her text, Stella hadn't mentioned Blake. Releasing her, Stella didn't ask after the older boys or comment on spaced-out Cody. Instead, with a swagger, Stella led Liv in.

'The girls are in the kitchen.'

Liv hesitated. 'Stella?'

Stella turned.

What Liv had wanted was a chat, alone, to tease out what had happened – with the police and at school. And to lighten the mood with her story of being locked in her apparently glitch-free car. But Stella had been impossible to catch. This was their friendship's most dramatic moment. Together, they'd survived food fights and tantrums and bloody gashes – but always with their big boys on the same side.

Warily, Liv lifted an eyebrow.

'Can't keep the girls waiting.' Stella strode off.

Liv followed Stella through her grand house. Girls. Boys. Sometimes it was confusing. When they were seventy, would these women still be 'the girls'? Their husbands, 'the boys'? And their middle-aged sons 'the little boys'? This evening, a grown-up conversation was needed. Liv hoped she could swing it.

Dirty windows flanked the northern side of Stella's house. Beyond the leaf-strewn tennis-cum-basketball court, the covered pool and the forgotten trampoline, Liv could see the bay. Today, its waves looked concreted.

Liv greeted Carly Whittaker-Smith and Bettina Low with a kiss. A proper, lips to skin kiss. Where had these two been? Fleetingly, Liv teared up, until Taj Low sloped into the kitchen.

Strictly speaking, Taj wasn't Blake's friend; and Liv's boys hadn't had much to do with Taj either – not counting Oscar's recent punch and inexplicable home visit. Jai and Blake's group was more a duo, and Oscar mainly had bucky old Rowan, Carly's son. Though Rowan had been lying low lately, Liv realised, which was as curious as seeing Taj. Bettina never brought Taj with her to these gatherings. But here he was, helping himself to the fridge and a blue sports drink. His fair hair was centre-parted, straight and almost at his collar. Liv recognised the 'do.

Slipping onto a stool, Liv hid her reaction by unlocking her phone. No news. Then she asked the question that'd been nipping at her conscience. 'How's Blake?'

'See for yourself.'

Stella gestured to the adjoining lounge room. Alongside a huge couch, Blake was sprawled on the shag-pile. He was eating corn chips and salsa as he read a book and listened to music. His headphones were huge. But most extraordinary was the ostensible reading material: Cyrano de Bergerac, no less! Usually Blake was lost to a screen – whether it was his iPhone or iPad, the PlayStation or the TV. The only sign of tribulation was the shade of him. His milky colour had leaked out, and his new colour hadn't been poured in. Otherwise, he seemed the same: skinny, with ill-fitting clothes and a butt chin.

'Hi, Blake. How are you?'

Liv waved but Blake didn't look up. Taj flopped onto the couch near Blake and picked up an iPad.

'Hi, Taj.' Taj looked at her blankly. 'I'm Liv, Oscar and Jai's mum.'

Taj returned to the images on his screen. Liv glanced at Bettina – on her phone – then smiled at Carly, who smiled back. Thank you, Carly, she thought. A kind woman, Carly had become a friend when dippy Rowan became Oscar's best friend. Rowan, the C-minus. Grace's future boss.

'What did the doctors say?' said Liv.

Stella was studying an iridescent sunset on her phone. 'Hey?'

'About Blake?'

'Oh, he's fine.' Stella whispered, badly. 'He was fucking stoned. I found his cookies.'

'Oh, no,' said Liv. 'Where was Chandler?'

Chandler had never struck Liv as the best manny. Whenever Liv saw him, he was usually watching NBA highlights on his phone.

'Gone to Columbia Uni. We had a fill-in. Blake had never – you know – before.' Stella filled the silence by pouring another round. 'Weed made me feel like total shite too,' she said. 'But Lindsay loves the cookies.'

Stella had told her once that, in his heyday, Lindsay had been quite the party animal, dropping his pants and dancing bare-bottomed on bar-tops. Liv glanced to Blake again, with renewed dismay. What else had the poor kid inherited?

'What do you think the school's going to do?' she said. 'And the police?' It seemed she was becoming abysmal at small talk.

Stella fixed her gaze on Bettina. 'Have you been to Central Australia? I forget.'

'No.' Carly gave a polite smile.

'Not forever,' said Bettina.

Liv studied her friend's stack of Steelo hair as Stella shared her phone. Liv was interested. Of course. But she could hear holiday tales later.

She was worried about Blake. Something was strange, here. For days, Liv had been mulling over his lies. And why he'd come clean and then gone to ground again. It made no sense. And why hadn't Stella (or Blake) called her back? In their one Melbourne-to-Uluru conversation, Stella had claimed she needed to speak with Blake face to face before she could shed any light. That call had been brief.

Stella didn't look particularly concerned about her son . . . or remorseful for his actions.

Liv tried to listen as Stella summarised the pros and cons of glamping, but failed. Liv's drink grew warmer. An inquisitive Bettina and subdued Carly finished their drinks. Bettina seemed especially interested in the spectacular rock and swanky tents.

Liv checked her phone again as Stella proffered French cheese.

'It sounds beautiful, but this is killing me,' said Liv. 'What's happening at school? Have you heard anything?'

Stella chewed slowly. Carly began picking at her lip.

'We're pulling Blake out. Decided this morning.'

Liv gasped, and Taj Low suppressed a smirk.

'Wait, you're what?' said Carly, sounding awfully like her son.

'We've had enough of Tony Crisp's vendettas. We're meeting the principal of Bayside Sec next Friday.'

'They get all the cheeky ones,' said Bettina.

The Havelocks were giving up on Carmichael! Liv's thoughts split into two strands. First, no more Blake. That could be a good thing, a wonderful thing – for Jai. Sorry, Blake. But Jai might make a more sensible, less problematic, new friend. Liv felt a pop of hope. Second, though, she'd been hopeful Blake's emergency might lead to changes in the Havelock household. More attention to Blake's needs and behaviour. A reorientation in the family dynamics. Even a boundary or two. The hope she felt for Jai was burst by the disappointment she felt for Blake.

'But what's going on with Blake?' Liv whispered. 'How is he really? Why did he do it – and make stuff up – then change his story?'

'Don't ask me. He's being a nightmare. Won't talk about it.' Stella's smile was quick, before she looked away.

Over the years, Liv and Duncan had had many conversations about the parenting of Blake. At times, Liv had tried discreetly to mother him; and sometimes, he'd let her draw him out and listened. They had connected every so often, over the weirdness of humans. He seemed to like that she was an investigator, too. Said she asked good questions. But, Liv realised now, Stella hadn't exactly encouraged that connection.

Liv felt a pang of nostalgia. Disorientation. Panic. For everyone.

There was a conversation here, one she and Stella should have had years ago. When high school began. When Blake's oppositional behaviour escalated. His language, his disrespect for property and rules. His late, late hours on multiple screens (detected by Liv when she read his messages to Jai) and his diet of Nutella-and-sprinkles sandwiches – eaten at 1 am, 4 am. You were morally bound to prepare your own kids to be decent citizens. Did you have responsibility for your friend's kids, too? Did you owe it to your friend? Or the kid? Or everyone else? Even if the friend wouldn't like it?

Liv tried to focus. Did other people think like this?

'. . . cheeky git,' said Stella. 'I don't know what got into him . . .' She gave a strangled laugh. When none of the other women responded, Stella added, 'Fucking Tony Crisp. What an overreaction. We can't let Blake stay there another minute while that man's in charge.'

Carly averted her eyes from Stella's. Both Carly's husband, James, and Bettina's husband, Owen, were old boys and on Carmichael's board. Liv vaguely recalled the charming James, a financier, was its chair. The Whittaker-Smiths loved Tony Crisp, for his ambition as much as his rousing speeches. Liv also recalled James and Owen often clashed.

'It's a toughie,' said Bettina.

'I feel for Blake, I do,' said Carly. 'One mistake.'

'Hmm,' said Liv.

For years, Carmichael Grammar had seemed eager to move Blake on. Only last term, he'd sworn at Lloyd Palmer. Called him 'an evil fucker'. Which Stella had laughed off. She half-fancied the man, called him 'The Rock of Carmichael'. Shortly thereafter, Blake had 'accidentally' set the Home Ec. kitchen on fire. But expelling the boy – or sending him away – wasn't the answer. Blake could be reformed. God forbid the school attempt to reach out to him, educate him.

'Has anyone else tried to get through to him?' Liv said. 'A counsellor or someone?'

Liv wondered whether to volunteer herself. Blake hadn't answered her calls, true, but he might talk to her. Alone. The silence became elastic, thin and stringy.

'Nah. No point. He won't go.'

Liv opened her mouth but paused. Stella was actively avoiding her eyes. She needed to mind her own business, she supposed. But where did that leave them? An apology here to Jai (or Liv) wouldn't hurt; or at least an acknowledgement of wrongdoing. Liv didn't want a speech. One word would do.

So much for Jai and Blake, *best friends forever*. Jai's fate alone at Carmichael Grammar was hanging by a shoelace now. But what of the police? Please let Blake have come clean with them.

'That do-gooder Jess Charters just had to make a big hoo-ha,' said Stella. 'None of this would've happened if she hadn't let her skanky daughter pose in her undies.'

Carly and Bettina laughed, while from the couch, Taj smiled. Once, Liv might've laughed too, uncomfortably, telling herself Stella liked to be provocative but had a good heart. This evening, though, Liv's fresh eyes were working overtime.

'Ah, Stella—'

'Girls these days are outrageous,' Bettina said. 'Taj's phone rings hot. I don't know how he keeps up.' Somehow she managed to sound both proud and disapproving.

Taj angled his iPad out of his mother's line of sight. Only Liv seemed to notice. On the coffee table, Blake's phone beeped. A second later, Blake glared at Taj, hopped up and left the room.

'What do they expect, taking pics like that?' Stella pulled a pouty, sucked-lemon face. From her phone, a tiny version of herself in a green bikini grinned.

'The girls are the predatory ones,' said Bettina. 'Aren't we lucky we have boys? So much easier!' Carly and Bettina murmured agreement. Somehow these women were lost to their own sex. They'd crossed the floor.

Upon Blake's return, Taj threw the lid of his bottle at him. Blake didn't react.

'I wouldn't say that,' said Liv. 'Girls—'

But Bettina cut in, regaling them on the plight of men and boys. How tough they had it: how confused and pressured their lives were, thanks to women's oversized expectations, high-level needs and bewildering behaviour. How, recently, everything had gone too far – against men. Usually, Liv didn't take Bettina's raving personally. Tonight, however, Liv realised she felt capable of a pinch or a quick shin-kick.

Stella cleared her throat, and Liv stirred; she didn't need to hear Stella's views on men, again, too. As a family law barrister, Stella saw how men avoided child support, 'upgraded' wives and didn't look back. Her take was that women, armed with this knowledge, must not see husbands as 'meal tickets'. They absolutely shouldn't stay out of the workforce for fifteen years, because then they were screwed. Fifteen years was, effectively, how long Liv had been out of the law. She'd tried to go back a few times but it hadn't worked. As an investigator, she was three years old.

Every few months, Bettina and Stella liked to bang their drums at each other.

Liv watched Carly avoid meeting her eye. She wanted to leave this hand-crafted kitchen. To see her beautiful boys and feed them. But faith in friendship kept Liv glued to her stool. If she couldn't be honest with her friends, what hope did she have? She also wanted Stella and Bettina to know the truth – about these girls and their own sons. Liv had a flash of deja vu – seeing herself at The Provedore lecturing an empty table.

'I've met Grace Charters,' she cut in. 'And she's far from skanky – whatever that means. She's very impressive. Bright. And you know Bella.'

Stella's face lengthened, looked distinctly horse-like.

Taj's eyes flickered from the women to Blake, who was concentrating hard on that book.

'You can't blame the girls for their photos being uploaded. Or their mums. The photos weren't even nudies. Does that make a difference? I don't know. But some of these girls were standing at the bus stop!' Liv laughed, incredulous. 'The point is, what Blake did was wrong. And then he lied. You need to do something about it.'

Bettina shot a look to the lounging boys. Carly drained another glass. Taj was openly smirking now. Only Blake, wearing his earphones, was oblivious. The silence became like a vice.

Liv squirmed. For years she'd endured Jai's whine: 'But Blake's allowed to do it!' Her parenting had been dragged down by Stella's, the lowest common denominator. Not anymore.

'Stella?' She collected her bag. 'I need to go. Walk me out?'

Stella twirled her flute, but otherwise didn't move.

Liv felt a gob of emotion in her throat. 'Cody? We're going!' Liv stepped towards the hall, but Cody didn't appear (which wasn't a surprise).

Liv weighed up her options. She looked to Blake, who was, she realised, reading his book upside down. His head bobbed to his music.

She returned to stand at the island bench.

'Blake's got a good heart,' she said. 'But, well, he's disrespectful. Without boundaries . . . he gets away with murder. He has for years, let's face it.'

This time, Carly and Bettina pretended she was invisible. On occasion, over the years, the three of them might have discussed Blake. Once or twice.

'That's not his fault. But it hasn't made him *happy*. This account and his lies are a cry for help, Stella. It's giving you a chance to turn things round.'

Liv skidded to a stop with a smile. She'd taken a big social risk. And, probably, her technique needed work. But she hoped Stella would hear her: she cared. Stella lifted her chin, then pivoted her gaze from Liv to Bettina. Seconds passed. Tears welled in Liv's eyes.

How did that Nordic policewoman manage? Did she have friends? Liv hadn't watched enough of the show to know. Though nothing in the kitchen moved, Liv could feel the temperature become Arctic.

Stella cleared her throat. 'Lindsay's furious. He was furious with Blake, but mostly he's furious with everyone else, from Tony Crisp to Jess Charters and her pissant husband . . .'

Stella was staring into Bettina.

'Oh, one hundred per cent! That woman should never have aired the school's dirty laundry,' said Bettina, attacking the cheese and crackers. 'The boys have been devastated by the things people are saying, especially Dylan. He puts his heart and soul into that school.'

Liv caught Taj in an eye-roll.

'Did you see the mud-slinging piece in yesterday's paper?' Bettina was saying. 'Jess Charters is running with the *class warfare* angle now. Calling our boys "elite little savages". This is getting personal. I don't like it.'

Liv made for the sink. Ran the water, emptied her glass. Her social experiment had bombed somewhat. Being authentic didn't seem to win you friends. Was it better to be inauthentic and in company, or principled and alone?

'Stella . . .' Liv tried for a neutral tone. 'Listen, hopefully, Blake gets a caution and—'

'That woman should have kept her mouth shut,' said Bettina.

'Loyalty is a precious thing,' said Stella.

A moment later, the huge door swung shut behind Liv, like an enormous page in the book of her life.

28

Jess

You always had to be alert to threats, and Jess was more alert than ever. As the train thundered through Balaclava, she glanced at the other passengers: businesspeople and schoolchildren, university students and daytrippers. She didn't recognise anyone, thank goodness. And nearly everyone was minding their own business, looking content and well-kept, even now, at the shaggy end of the day.

Jess shut her eyes. Pictured the mums and dads lining up to debate her in the street or school grounds. As of yesterday she'd decided, when she wasn't at work, she'd stay home and offline, ignore the TV and radio requests. Stop answering the phone. Her friends had thinned out anyway. If she hadn't had an appointment for a filling today, she wouldn't have left Bayside. Sitting in the dentist's chair, refusing the anaesthetic, it'd hit her: Morrie was right. Letting the genie out of the bottle had been a mistake. The more anger you released, the more you received. And if there was one thing she hated, she realised, it was being hated.

She stirred. So far this evening no one was giving her a second look. Apart from maybe the stylish man seated opposite her. He was tall and dressed in a silver suit, with a fashionable haircut, short but long on top. He would've been around her age, or a few years younger – say, 40. The scent of his cologne was strong. Too strong. He was handsome, but in a spoilt way. She wondered where he'd gone to school. Not a question she often considered of adults. But Carmichael Grammar students and old boys seemed to be everywhere this week. And he did seem familiar. Maybe a basketball dad.

The man's gaze flicked back to her. Was he checking her out? It wasn't impossible, she supposed. She forgot sometimes that, at forty-five, she was still a sexual being. Occasionally, she was reminded by a stare or smile, a double-take. Sometimes, when a halfway appealing man smiled at her, she enjoyed the attention. But mostly she didn't. The man opposite held her eye and it was as if a screen between them dropped; she felt unnaturally seen. She turned away. The energy he was emitting wasn't pleasant. The word 'vainglorious' sprang to her mind. Which was funny, because she wasn't sure what it meant.

Her stop was still three stations away. She lowered her eyes but could still feel his gaze. The faint pressure of his right calf. She could have been imagining it; she moved her leg, adjusted her skirt. One of the downsides of public transport – the odd leer or grope. She thought of Bella and of Grace. How she worried for them. She opened her eyes to the backyards skipping by. Now and then she glimpsed a woman standing by a clothesline.

As the train rolled into Middle Brighton, Jess hopped up. On the platform, she wove through the crowd, eager to be home. She joined the queue at The Provedore buying last-minute 'home-made' dinners. She kept her eyes on her phone. Then, pumpkin quiche in hand, she set off on the long walk home. Within a few steps, she was again rehearsing her chat with Grace in her head. She'd crossed two blocks and was beginning to relax when she heard a noise across the road. Glancing over her shoulder, she saw a man walking two houses behind her. She looked again. *Him.* She picked up her pace and her new shoes began to pinch. But, within minutes, the distance between them was the same, although he was very tall, with a long stride, and she was small, with a fitted-skirt-clipped stride.

At some point, she realised, other pedestrians had forked off.

She looked back to see Mr Vainglorious taking off his jacket, as he walked. Her street was coming up on the right, but, hesitating, she slowed. When she looked back, he was looking at her and slowing too.

Maybe even smiling. Her house was only four from the corner. Grace was home on her own.

At the last minute, Jess took the street on her left. She pulled up her skirt and trotted. Another glance confirmed he'd taken the left too. He might live on this street, she told herself. Brighton was a large suburb of inter-connected people. You're imagining this, she told herself, trotting faster. The sun dipped behind the houses but the street lights didn't blink on. Jess had spent a good deal of her life worrying about this very moment. Trying to avoid it. Was it really happening now? In the middle of Brighton?

She took another left, so she was basically going in a circle. A few moments later, he appeared behind her again. Either he had a shocking sense of direction or . . . She considered the homes around her. Their lights were off, their driveways empty.

With her shoes in her hand, Jess headed towards another T-inter-section. She could use her phone, she supposed. And call who, Morrie? He'd say she was being paranoid, or tell her to call the police. But she hadn't told Morrie that, when she'd complained about the nasty, upsetting comments online, the dorky policeman had said, 'Too easy. Don't read them.'

The street lights blinked on as she ran.

Across the road, Mr Vainglorious was about fifteen metres behind and jogging slowly. What did he want? At the corner, Jess eyed the nearby houses. Picket fences and pretty facades. A house three up from the corner had a lower slatted fence, waist high, with a shrub the width of the garden. A gate on the far side. She made for it before he reached the corner. At the fence, she yanked her skirt high before climbing over; scratched and puffing, she sank beneath the shrubs.

Her quiche copped a battering. Her stockings were shredded and her feet hurt. From the dirt, she could hear the man's footsteps at the corner. She heard him swear. Through the slats, she saw Mr Vainglorious step onto the road, look one way then the other. He stepped in the direction of her hiding spot. Stopped. Then crossed to the other side and searched behind a wheelie bin.

Jess's fear was eclipsed by a fresh blast of anger. She thought of Bella, pushing that boy. Hop up, she told herself, rage at him. How dare you!

Leave me alone! How satisfying that would be, if he did. But what if he didn't? He was big and she was small. She squatted, holding her breath. For five minutes, she watched him through a gap. He crossed the road again then crouched, presumably to better see down the footpath. Then he crossed to her side, did the same thing. On the other side of the fence, he was close. She could smell his foul cologne. See his polished black shoes. Hear him muttering. She could've been mistaken, but it sounded like, 'Jess, Jess, Jess . . .'

Pressed into the dirt, she made herself tiny.

29

Jess

Hyper-alert now, Jess jogged on the road, beneath the streetlights. She ignored the passing cars, which were giving her a wide berth. In her hand, her shoes were banging against her thigh, while her feet were screaming. Her phone was flat. It'd taken Mr Vainglorious forever to go away. It must've been almost eight now. Grace would be worried. Morrie might be too. But her worry had gone. Jess didn't notice the slowing car until it was beside her. Through the open window, she saw a woman. Familiar, but not a friend. She stopped, breathless, though not from the run. The car moved ahead then stopped. She walked the few metres to it, adjusted her skirt.

'Jess? Are you okay?'

She didn't know who was friend and who was foe anymore. Liv Winsome had a little boy in the back, asleep in his school uniform. The Audi's indicator flashed. They had the same car, except theirs was silver, not white, and older. Jess put a hand to her hair and found a leaf. Liv Winsome's face spoke of real concern. Jess thought of a pharmacist she'd seen years ago: when she'd told him of the large ulcer under her tongue, he'd said, 'That must be very painful.' His had been the kindest face she'd seen in weeks. Jess swallowed a shot of tears. Where were her friends: Charvi and Alison, even Penny Appleby? Since Monday, Jess had been thinking about Liv Winsome. Whose side was Liv on?

Jess gave a watery smile, and the central locking clicked.

•

Liv Winsome drove straight to her house, without directions, which was funny. Behind a neat garden, their miner's cottage looked small but immaculate. When they'd bought it, it'd been a dump. An expensive dump. Tonight it looked sad, somehow. Inside, Grace would be worried, but their car was in the driveway. Lights were on. Dinner would be sorted. She could bin the busted quiche. A tear landed on her forearm.

Liv left the engine running as Jess climbed out. She hadn't explained her jog in work clothes. Liv hadn't been particularly warm, but she hadn't been rude either. On the footpath, Jess hesitated. The woman deserved something for her kindness. Jess dug deep.

'I saw Jai's letter to Grace. I didn't know about Grace sending the picture without Jai asking.'

'Yeah, I gathered.' Liv tapped the steering wheel. Her stare was open and direct.

'I'm sorry. I should've heard Jai's side.'

'Yep. Especially before you went to the police. I've never seen my boys so scared.'

Liv's stare sharpened. Jess gulped another tear and apologised again. You certainly knew where you stood with this person. The child in the back seat murmured in his sleep.

'I guess you heard about Blake's meltdown?'

'His what?' Jess dropped a shoe. 'Is he okay?'

'He'll live.' Liv tapped the steering wheel again. 'He was acting out, at the school gate . . . struggling with everything, I guess. But, yeah, he's okay-ish.'

Liv turned off the car, and Jess felt grateful again. She didn't move but she didn't know what to say. She hadn't meant to upset so many people. She had no idea the boys would take it so hard. In her defence, she was one of three girls. Her sisters' children were girls. Morrie was an only child.

She could feel more tears forming. She bent to pick up her shoe. While out of sight, she wiped her face.

'I read your piece in the paper. It was . . . gutsy.'

'Thanks. But I wish I hadn't done it,' said Jess, straightening. 'Any of it.'

'Hey, don't say that.'

Jess gulped. She was in danger of blubbering. 'Liv, would you like to come in?'

On the back patio, Jess and Liv drank black tea and nibbled cranberry nougat. In the intervening half-hour, Liv had dropped Cody home and checked in with her older boys. Meanwhile, Jess had cuddled Morrie and reassured Grace, then showered and eaten leftover shepherd's pie. They didn't need to know what'd happened, so she didn't tell them. (She'd binned her shredded stockings with the quiche, and fibbed that she'd ducked back into work.) Grace was playing her sax in her room now; and Jess had Grace's screens. Morrie was on his computer. The situation had gone back to normal – apart from Liv's presence and an unpleasant smell in the kitchen.

Taking a sip of tea, Liv said, 'You should read V. N. Kovach's *Bringing Up Gen Z*. It'll help get the conversation started.'

'Thanks.' Jess smiled politely.

'Excellent on gender, social media, emotional literacy . . . the whole shebang. Everyone at Carmichael should read it.'

'First thing in the morning, I'll call the police and Tony Crisp.' Jess's smile became rueful. 'If he takes my call.'

'Thanks, it can't hurt.'

When Liv smiled back, Jess felt genuinely forgiven. She'd never had such a direct and honest, if difficult, conversation.

Then Liv took a deep breath. 'I, ah . . . upset Grace the other day. I'm so sorry. I told her about the gender pay gap and workplace bias. How companies in Australia are more likely to be led by a man named Andrew than by a woman.'

'Oh, goodness . . . I mean, no, that's okay. What happened?'

'She kind of . . . melted.'

Jess laughed. 'You mean, went very red, sobbed a lot then shut down?'

'Yep. Didn't make it to band practice.'

That explained Grace's closed door on Tuesday. But Jess didn't understand: who was Andrew? Besides, Grace wanted to be an orthopaedic surgeon.

'Thanks, I guess,' said Jess.

'Forewarned is forearmed,' said Liv, chewing her nougat. 'How was she after? When she got home?'

'Honestly, hon,' said Jess, 'I don't know. She hid. And then . . .'

Over their second cup of tea, Jess opened up about everything, from Grace's behaviour and that phone call, to Mr Vainglorious. As she spoke, she could feel that genie within stirring again. Listening, Liv Winsome demonstrated another extraordinary trait: as well as being a very direct communicator, in twenty minutes, Liv totally listened and didn't speak once.

'I ended up hiding in shrubs,' said Jess.

'Hence the leafy hair.' Liv's eyes were gentle. 'You need to tell the police.'

Jess glanced at her guest, but she seemed sincere. 'He was walking home. That's what he'd say. Besides, he looks like half the men around here. He's probably a Carmichael dad, or from basketball.'

'True.'

'What do you think he wanted?'

'I'm guessing to give you a scare.'

Jess nodded, then sat forward, half-whispered. 'You want to know something? I'm not an angry person, but, on the inside . . . this thing is making me madder and madder.'

'Ha! You're allowed to be angry. My god. You should own it!'

'You think?' Jess looked over her shoulder to her quiet house.

'You bet.'

Jess leant further forward. 'You mean like, "Hello, I'm Jess Charters and I'm angry"?' She laughed.

'Yep, except don't laugh. "Hello, I'm Liv Winsome and I'm over-whelmed. I mean, I was. Now nothing fazes me. I am Gunhild, a driven, Nordic female detective who knows how to say *No* and doesn't need to be liked to get results."'

'*Gunhild*?' Jess's laugh was genuine this time. Liv Winsome was seri-ously strange! 'Nice to meet you, *Gunhild*.'

'You too,' said Liv, completely deadpan.

They laughed.

Taking more nougat, Jess was feeling better.

'We have to keep pushing,' said Liv. 'You're good at this. Getting a profile. I'm wandering around upsetting people but not making any headway.'

'Is being abused, threatened and followed making headway?'

'That's the very definition of it, today, for a woman.'

Jess put her face in her hands. 'That's the opposite of what I wanted.'

'You've been gunning for the wrong people,' said Liv. 'This isn't about teenage boys . . . and their useless parents . . .' Liv smiled. 'Sure, it is a bit. Obviously, Blake's stuffed up and needs to be dealt with and, you know, *helped*. Unpleasant kids and clueless parents do exist . . . But ultimately a lot of this can be traced back to the school.'

'Sorry, hon. I'm not following.'

'Carmichael's an extraordinary place,' said Liv, 'with many excellent teachers, but it needs to be dragged into the twenty-first century.'

It was Liv's turn to open up about the past week. Liv described two moronic teachers, and the out-of-touch Tony Crisp; she talked about Blake's mum and Taj's parents. Listening, Jess had to close her mouth to not interrupt. Listening, she still felt mad and a little guilty.

'The school can do a lot of harm, but it can do a lot of good too,' said Liv. 'I'm thinking of writing a charter on equality. Putting it to the board.'

'Goodness, that won't make you popular.'

'If being popular means living with the status quo,' said Liv, 'I'd rather not be.'

They both smiled again as Liv took the last piece of nougat. Being popular wasn't just a teenage concern, was it?

'You're sure it's the school?' As Jess said this, something niggled: male laughter.

'The school *and* the parents.' Liv chewed. 'But we can get to the parents through their kids.' She grinned. 'You said it before, about Crisp. He's progressive in some ways but woefully backwards in others; those attitudes flow down.'

Jess could see the gleam in Liv's eyes. Any day now, Liv was going to seriously ruffle feathers. She was already arguing with teachers and Mr Crisp. Soon, Liv would be fighting with more mums (and dads) across Bayside.

'I need courageous people like you to join me.'

Jess spluttered. Not long ago she was hiding in a bush.

'If you keep Grace at Carmichael, she has, what, close to five years left? You don't want her putting up with the likes of Humphries and Waring, do you? She's a second-class citizen there.'

'But Grace's on a partial scholarship. If we leave, we have to pay it back.'

'All the more reason to make Carmichael the best it can be. '

Wiping her hands, Jess eyed her silent house again.

'Around seven hundred girls go to that school. And nine hundred boys. These people are tomorrow's leaders.'

Jess was pretty sure Liv was quoting Mr Crisp.

'Jess, please. I can't do it on my own.'

Jess tallied. Helping others was one of her callings. Holding those boys to account hadn't only been for Grace and Bella. But she'd made a hash of it. The light went out in Morrie's office. Morrie wouldn't like it if she were to make trouble. Then again, Morrie didn't know what it was like to be followed or trolled. Grace wouldn't like it, either, though thanks to Liv she may understand it better. The genie within flexed. Jess thought of those phone calls, those random debates on the footpath and Mr Vainglorious.

'One condition. I don't want to be the face of this, anymore.'

'Deal.' Liv flashed another grin. 'We can give the media a rest. Go more grassroots.'

'What do you want me to do?'

Liv slugged her cold tea then wiped her mouth on her wrist. 'Go back to your friends, to Jilly Saffin. Tell them the full story and join the dots for them.'

'Oh, no. Do I have to?'

'Have a go. Clearly I'm lousy at it.'

Jess scrunched her nose. 'Sorry, hon . . . I'm not sure I'm joining the dots, myself.'

'Read *Bringing Up Gen Z*. Kovach puts it beautifully.'

With a grimace, Jess typed the title into her phone. She hadn't read a book since high school.

'I'll put together the paperwork. But we need someone on the inside, too. Someone passionate and persuasive. Do you know any of the teachers?'

Jess raised her eyes to the night sky. 'Heavens, I know loads. Mary MacBeth is a possibility; she's clever and lovely. And Mrs Copeland and Miss Anthony. Wait a tick – Mr Crisp said they're getting in a cyber-safety consultant. Do we know who?'

'It'd need to be someone extraordinary.'

'It would.' Jess raised her eyebrows. 'Like . . .' Jess pointed at her phone.

30

Duncan

In the airport lounge, Duncan watched the crisscrossing planes landing in the drizzle. He hadn't travelled in a while and hadn't missed it. By his reckoning, if his plane took off on time and stayed airborne, he'd be home in three hours. But his family would be asleep; and he had to be off again in the morning before they woke up. Unsustainable – yep, that was the word du jour. That and its antidote: sabbatical. When he closed his eyes, he pictured pedalling himself through South Australia's Barossa region. He couldn't remember the last time he'd been on a bike. Years ago, they'd tried a family ride. The details escaped him, but Cody had been small. Someone had thrown in the towel halfway up a titchy mountain. It could've been Liv. He'd had to ride down to get the car. That'd been the best part. He smiled as he tapped 'women's bikes' into his phone, and up popped Vintage Ladies' Classics. His stomach rumbled. Somehow he'd gone from a too-long meeting to drinks without eating, again. He flicked images, as the weather closed in.

Road bikes or mountain bikes? he wondered. Heading for a seat, he hoped someone would stir when he arrived home. He longed for a chat about his plans. Pickle would do, if she had to. She'd wag in the right places, lick his fingers. He hadn't felt this excited in decades. He hadn't had a holiday longer than a fortnight since he'd been at uni.

Two months should do it, he thought. They'd know each other fairly well by then.

By the bar, a woman was receiving an iced coffee, or maybe it was a cocktail. He'd seen her somewhere, not so long ago. Did she work in the law? There was something about her. She wore a softly draping pale-pink blouse beneath a navy suit. When she passed, he remembered: last year's Mergers and Acquisitions Symposium, here in Sydney. She'd given a talk; some demerger case study. They'd chatted after. He could remember a few of the guys trying it on with her at the hotel lounge. She'd fended them off, from what he could recall. He'd been doubly impressed by her poise. Was she married? He couldn't remember. Not that it was relevant. He looked at her again: elegant and black-haired, sitting now in a quiet corner. Who did she work for again? She was probably a decade younger than he was. He wondered if she was a partner somewhere already, or still slogging. He sucked a mint. Wondered whether to introduce himself. Whether she'd remember. Or he'd come across as creepy.

31

Liv

That night, as her boys mumbled and farted in their sleep, Liv scoured her bookcases. These were her real friends, her like-minded companions. She scanned, high and low, until she found the four she wanted. She'd read them each, several times: *Bringing Up Gen Z*; *Smart Phones, Smart Kids*; *Why Popular is Not the Answer*; and *Power to the Small Change*. Opening their pages now felt like dipping into pools of wisdom. Yes. This was *the* person. She considered the email address Jess had found. It'd taken Jess roughly an hour. Her neighbour's work colleague was friends with V. N. Kovach's assistant! The author and psychologist was originally from New York but had married an Australian academic and was now living in Bayside. What were the chances?

Liv wondered where Duncan was. It was almost eleven.

Then she wrote:

Att: Roxy, a message for V. N. Kovach

Dear V. N.,

I've read almost all of your books, and I love the way your brain works! I can't wait for the next one. Bringing Up Gen Z *changed my parenting forever. (Sorry for the fangirl rave!) My children go to one of the local independent schools in Bayside. You might have heard about this school recently – Carmichael Grammar? It's embroiled in a fairly standard* twenty-first century scandal. The usual moron boys and oblivious misogyny. Two Year Eight boys, to be exact, who've been suspended, and one is not returning. The other one, I must confess, is my son. Though Jai's not a moron. Long story. We learn of his fate tomorrow.

My question for you is: would you be interested in running a series of lessons at the school, in a similar vein to your work in Smart Phones, Smart Kids *and* Bringing Up Gen Z? I could pass your details onto the principal, Tony Crisp, if you were keen. Your fees won't be a problem – this is one cashed-up school. If they have reached out already, do ignore this! Otherwise, please shoot any questions my way. Thank you for your time.

Very kindest regards,
Liv

32

Duncan

By the time Duncan arrived home, it was after midnight. His flight had been circling Melbourne due to the weather, and not even Pickle stirred when he came in. Overtired, and naked, he poked about in the fridge. Somewhere near the Victorian border, he'd sobered. How had he lived like this for years? Skating across the surface of his family's life. He opened a low-fat yoghurt. He wondered about George. Was he home safely, and sleeping as his wife tended to their baby?

He envied George. He had an excuse to stay home. And a baby.

In the air, Duncan had been thinking. The closest he'd felt to his children was in the minutes after they were born. The twins had been skinny and dark, like him, though the dark hair had gone in a flash. Nursing his sons, he'd felt their perfection in parts of his heart he didn't know existed. And, crucially, in that moment, he and Liv had known their sons equally. She couldn't pull rank. This equal status had lasted about as long as the babies' dark hair. After mere weeks of feeding and bathing, dressing and settling, he'd discovered his fingers were too big, his hunches wrong. Like the time, in desperation, he'd put the twins to sleep on their bellies, because he slept on his belly. And it'd worked! But he was taken off settling duties after that – for nearly killing them. Dressing was the next to go, after the babies' lips turned a shade of blue at a work picnic. 'Same as for us, but one layer *more*,' Liv had hissed when she'd arrived with the hamper. He'd thought she'd said one layer less.

Then there was the time he dropped Cody on his head. Bloody baby massage oil.

He shut the fridge, his nether regions cold. In the laundry, he donned a clean T-shirt and boxers.

He'd been trying to remember the last time they'd done something fun together, voluntarily, as a family. Cycling would be good for them, he told himself. Physical, outdoors, in nature. Cycling across wine country would have to be better again. The boys didn't know a soul interstate. Or a wi-fi code.

At the sink, he swallowed spoonfuls of yoghurt. Liv's critical words of Tuesday night still smarted. He tiptoed to the twins' bedroom. Bent over each boy. They were on their bellies, mouth-breathing and alive. Duncan smiled. See?

He crept towards Cody's smaller room. Saw the empty bed. He looked about and found the boy on the floor, wedged between the bed and the wall. With only a pillow, he looked uncomfortable, felt cool, but was oblivious. Leaving Cody where he was, Duncan pulled the doona over him as the boy rolled over. He held his breath but Cody didn't wake. Beneath the pillow, Duncan realised, was a photograph – of the five of them. The same one was on Liv's phone. It had been taken years ago, up far north, at dinner, suntans and smiles and silly sunglasses.

Duncan shook his head. This child was a puzzle he had not tried to solve. But maybe it wasn't impossible. He propped the photograph on the side table.

In the distance, a car hooned, its throaty engine a shock in the Bayside quiet. Duncan hesitated. He wasn't the only one who loved that curling beach road. He smiled. He loved his family as they were, loved this peace, but . . . He tried to imagine what that would feel like: to put your foot down, in the wee hours, come what may.

33

Friday

Liv

At 9 am, Liv checked her email for word from the school or V. N.: nothing. She watched Jai weed the garden with disconcerting gusto. Jai's nerves and her own were rising in tandem. Four times, he'd come in and asked, 'You sure they won't expel me?' The first three times, she'd answered patiently and sent him out again. After the last, she'd locked the back door and hidden in the bathroom. She'd felt awful but, as expected, it'd worked. He'd tried once more then hadn't returned.

She checked her phone, and put on the kettle. Wondered if Duncan was thinking about them; if he'd remembered the school's imminent decision. Going to bed last night, she hadn't left him a note. Once, she would have: *Missed you, sleep well.* Or *I owe you one foot massage.* Waking this morning, she hadn't found any word from him, either, apart from an empty yoghurt tub and some junk mail. Ah, marriage.

At 10.30 am, a proper, personalised piece of communication landed in her inbox. It read:

Hi Liv,

Thank you for your interest in my work. I'm pleased to hear from you! I am currently writing and won't be taking new appointments until the end of the year. Do see my website for updates. In the meantime, you can contact my agent or assistant on the details below. Have a fantastic day!

V. N. Kovach.

Liv whimpered. She felt as if she'd been knocked back for a date. Her natural instinct was to hide in a wardrobe, and beat herself up. Which she did, for around thirty minutes. Then she stirred for a curative cup of tea.

The thing was, she thought, sipping, she'd had a good feeling about that author. A sixth sense. Nursing her mug, Liv read the email again. Noticed, at its foot, beneath the assistant's signature: a mobile number.

She typed out another message, this time on text: *Please, please help . . .*

Yes, she was begging.

At 11.15 am, a message arrived from an unfamiliar number: *Hello! Know of school. Brilliant idea! Liaise with Roxy. Meet Monday morning? Introduce me to the old fogeys. Vic*

Giddy, Liv felt as if she'd received a text message from God. She walked circuits of her garden until she found Jai unearthing carrots in the veggie garden. She high-fived her son, then left a message for Duncan. She thought of Stella but telephoned Jess. Jess's phone was engaged so, by the tomatoes, Liv hugged herself tight.

Liv was still buzzing when, at 11.45 am, her phone rang.

'Yes, hello?'

She straightened her nightie, which was covered in colourful lollipops: a ridiculous gift from the boys, although it had come from a women's nightwear store. Breathless, she listened to Tony Crisp's preamble. Eventually, his point came: Jai was welcome back, effective immediately; and Blake was gone.

'Thank you!' she said. 'Thank you!'

She wanted to kiss someone. Whizzing back outside, she found Jai and hugged him by the overflowing green waste bin. 'We're very, very grateful,' she half-yelled. 'This won't happen again. Jai's learnt his lesson.'

She and Jai stared at each other meaningfully.

'I am pleased to hear that,' said Tony Crisp. 'We do not believe in second chances.'

'No, no. No need for second chances.'

Jai shook his head, mirroring her. Though Liv was feeling guilty now about Blake, as well as worried, she decided not to focus on that. She shooed her happily dancing boy into the house. He'd be late, but she'd be delighted to drive him.

'I've been advised that the police don't intend to lay charges against either of the boys,' Tony Crisp was saying. 'This matter is closed.'

'Oh, that's wonderful news! Thank you for telling us!'

Liv was running on the spot in her ugg boots. A celebration was in order. And perhaps a thank you to Jess Charters. Her cool Nordic detective lay dying on the lawn. Then, remembering, Liv returned inside. Saw, on the bench, those well-thumbed books. She was about to lead in when the principal said, 'Olivia, in light of recent developments, we have done some soul-searching.'

By recent developments did he mean Blake's Instagram account, her fresh-eyed feedback, or Jess Charters' campaign?

'While the school overall is in excellent shape, we could perhaps go further in our teachings around gender and so on.'

Liv beamed. 'Well, yes . . .'

'To that end, we are setting up a working party, to be led by an external specialist. He will roll out a pilot program to the Year Eights, and perhaps beyond. We do want to finesse what we're doing. We feel it's time.'

Oh my god, yes, it's time!

'Would you like to be involved?'

Liv was close to swooning. 'Yes, absolutely. Thank you.' The man was jumping in her estimation with every syllable. 'I've been writing a charter on equality, actually, for the school. I can—'

'Very good. I have spoken with Jess Charters, who I would also like to contribute. Is some sort of mediation required?'

Liv smiled. 'No.' She crossed her fingers and her toes before asking, 'Who do you have in mind to lead the program?'

'A renowned cyber-safety chap—'

'If it's not too late, may I make one more suggestion?'

She tapped one ugg-booted foot on the other. Thought she heard a sigh. 'As you wish.'

Liv steadied herself with a hand to the books. She sensed a big sell now would prove fatal.

'An acquaintance of mine does this very thing.' She cleared her throat, expelling the white lie. 'She's renowned for it.'

Another pause. 'Very well, send her details to my assistant, Jean Anderson. But this is very pressing. We need to get going ASAP, and the chap we've reached out to is the best, world-class.'

'Yes, got it. Thank you.'

Carmichael was in for a pleasant surprise. You wouldn't find better than V. N. Kovach! When the call ended, Liv kicked off her ugg boots and ran outside again. She felt aerated, kilograms lighter. In her daft nightie, she jumped on the trampoline until her bouncing boobs hurt.

34

Duncan

Mid-morning, Duncan had Maia look her up: his symposium speaker with a taste for flavoured milk. They'd had a quick and pleasant chat at Sydney Airport; she'd remembered him too, and commented on his suit, which was flattering. Her name was Maggie Koh. He'd forgotten she was based in Perth – not ideal – but a senior associate, which was helpful. Timing was everything in matters like this. Timing and luck. It was like dating, he supposed. You could find the right one, the perfect fit, early; and you were sorted. Or you could find yourself alone and searching, for months, maybe years. He and Liv had been lucky. Winsome & Ueland, not that much. While Maia snooped, Duncan tiptoed to his door and locked it. He spent twenty minutes figuring out how he'd get the bikes home. It took Maia about the same time to seek out Maggie Koh and find the paper she'd delivered. Ten minutes later, he was pulling down the shade on his glass door, something he seldom did, and reading about her. Liked what he saw. He told himself not to get his hopes up. Maggie was in a well-regarded Perth firm, though not a national, which could prove handy – probably no non-compete. But, still, he'd have to entice her across the country. He wondered what would do it. What her happy place was.

He left a message on her phone. Then he rolled his chair to the window. Thought of the five of them barrelling down an open highway in their motorhome. Pickle included. A minute later, someone knocked on his shuttered door. Duncan covered his face and felt like a child about to be sprung. When the person gave up, Duncan beamed.

He sprang from his chair to stand at the window and contemplate the sky. Its clouds were variously corrugated, fluffy, streaky. He could see a cloud the shape of a Roman nose, and another looked like a great big wheel, spokes and all.

After a minute, his phone beeped; he saw he'd missed two voicemail messages from Liv. He listened to them both, uninterrupted. The first one didn't make much sense – something about reinforcements for Carmichael. But the second was good news. Old Crisp was a sensible man, after all.

That evening, though the Winsomes were off the hook – no patchy basketball in the boondocks for them – Duncan left work early. Pulling in, he found Liv's car was gone. After helping himself to nuts and wine, he wandered through his home. The kitchen was tidy. The laundry baskets empty. He eyed the Lists on the fridge: no need to fold sheets or dust trophies tonight. In the lounge room, he paused. Someone was bouncing a basketball next door. He almost missed the sound of Cody tossing his fidget spinner at the ceiling. His home office called to him, but he ignored it. He opened the back door for Pickle, who bounded in. Flipped through a monster pile of junk mail.

After half an hour, he ran a bath. Waiting for it to fill, he texted each of his family members. Only Liv answered. *You feeling sick?*

Nup, all good.

Turned out Jai was with Grace at the movies, Oscar, at a loose end and in a huff, had gone window-shoe-shopping, while Liv was dropping Cody at Harry's for a sleepover (and having a glass of wine). Most of which was unprecedented, as far as he knew.

Waiting for someone to come home, he tugged his forelock, sipped wine. The emptiness around him was swallowing him up. The house was far too big for one person. Too dark. He switched on a lamp before folding onto the couch. Patting Pickle, he felt like a teenager as well, post-exams, unsure what to do with himself. He checked his phone again. No messages from his boys.

He was starting to feel lonelier as a dad than he had felt, ever.

The bath was on the verge of overflowing when he remembered it. For an hour, he lay, alternately running hot water onto his toes and pulling the plug. He considered getting out, watching a movie; but life needed fewer decisions, not more. Around eight-fifteen, he called it a night. To catch up on some Zs. Besides, he wanted to be at the shops early – avoid any queues. Hopping into bed, he tried to picture his sons' faces in the morning. It'd be like Christmas, he told himself, but better.

The next day, when he got up, Liv was already in the shower. The twins were still asleep. Only one child rose at 6 am these days, and he wasn't home. One of parenting's unexpected bonuses was that teenagers slept in; though, he remembered, the twins had to be up soon for school footy. (Another bonus, of course, was Carmichael's compulsory Saturday sport.) In his boxers, Duncan sat on the edge of the bath.

'Cody's better, hey?'

Liv was shampooing her hair. 'The minute I told him Jai wasn't going to jail. It was like a shot of adrenaline to his heart! He raced outside and kicked the soccer ball over the fence.'

'Look out.' Duncan smiled, making a note to remember his children's *feelings*. Somehow, he did need to factor them in. 'I thought you didn't like sleepovers?'

Earlier that year, Liv had decided sleepovers weren't worth the trouble. Unless you'd signed up the parents to your code of ethics. Otherwise, after the fact, you were left with shattered kids and stories of sneaking out, drinking out of shoes, big brothers' porn. Sleepovers did not become their children, and someone like Cody needed them least of all.

'I still don't.' She cocked an eyebrow; he might've impressed her. 'But he deserved a break. I wanted to give them all a treat after the week we've had.'

'Fair enough. I'm getting something for the boys this morning, too.'

'You are? That's good. Might cheer Oscar up.' She became a statue of suds. 'What?'

'Wait and see.'

She hammed a grimace. Liv was not one for surprises or uncertainty. Or maybe it was his track record on gifts.

'Something for you, too.'

'Oh, no.' She grinned. 'Can't wait.'

35

Monday

Liv

On Monday morning, Tony Crisp and assistant principal Lloyd Palmer beckoned Vic Cato (nee Kovach) and Liv into a small boardroom at the rear of the administration building. This meeting had been set up at an extraordinary speed. It was amazing what could be done in a crisis. Who knew Tony Crisp could be so nimble? The group was deep inside the Victorian part of the building, which had been restored in recent years; it featured enormous, stained-glass windows populated by sombre scholars. Mr Crisp ('Call me Tony'), Lloyd Palmer and Vic chatted about the weather as they took their seats. Through a bay window they could see the Wellbeing Centre, mown ovals and brimming flowerbeds.

'Your school is spectacular.' Vic's smile was wide.

'Thank you, Vic, it is,' said Lloyd, with a click of his pen.

Everyone was on a first-name basis and actively smiling.

Liv had been at the school for meetings three times in the past two weeks, though not in this inner sanctum. She was becoming a many-hatted woman: contrite parent, disgruntled parent and now parent advocate. Today was her favourite. The mood seemed bright, despite the context. She beamed at no one in particular. Lloyd was a handsome, bald man with smooth, unlined skin and biceps that stretched his suit-sleeves. Liv tried not to look at him; handsome men made her nervous. Vic was similarly handsome, which'd been a surprise. The doctor of psychology was flame-haired and fiftyish, with a strong jaw. She was also very tall – say, six-two – and had large, full breasts, not that this ought to be relevant.

'Thank you for coming in at such short notice, Vic,' said Tony. 'And thank you, Olivia, for introducing us.'

'No problem, Tony.'

Smiling stupidly, Liv made herself stop; reinstate Gunhild. No one seemed to notice.

'I'm thrilled to be here,' said Vic, in her charming New York accent.

Tony smiled again.

'As you're aware, we have had a very poor few days. What began with an ill-judged teenage decision has escalated. We need to restore harmony and faith at the Grammar. And . . .'—he glanced to Lloyd—'we'd like to finesse what we're doing here. One never stops improving.'

'It's fantastic you see it that way.' Another smile. Vic's head was nodding; Tony's head began to nod too. Liv had never seen the man so friendly.

'What we are after,' he was saying, 'is a review of our teaching around gender. Are we doing enough? I'm confident we are, but one must always ask. We also want a program for the Year Eights and potentially others specifically speaking to the regrettable behaviours we have seen recently.'

Tony Crisp glanced at Liv. She was stumped and delighted by his turn-around. He gave her a small smile.

'Yes, brilliant,' said Vic. 'A whole-school approach is the best way to go. Teachers need to be brought on board. The leadership team. Parents too, of course.'

Vic was nodding again, and Tony. Even Lloyd started nodding. Vic seemed to emit a contagious, upbeat energy. Liv tried to keep her head still, but couldn't.

'This material needs to be embedded, not only in our teaching and the curriculum but in our practices and the environment too!' said Vic.

'Indeed,' said Tony, with a fleeting frown.

Liv wondered why she'd never seen a picture of the author. The world was biased towards good-looking people. Perhaps, in Vic's line of work – as a serious *thinker* – you could be too good-looking? Watching Lloyd taking in Vic, Liv could see downsides.

Vic grinned again. 'Have you surveyed the staff or students in any of this space lately?'

'Ah, not that I can recall,' said Tony, deferring to Lloyd, who shook his head.

'Okay, not a problem. We could do that. It'd be fantastic to get a reading, take the pulse.'

'Our boys and girls do get along very well,' said Tony. 'We don't have any major issues in that regard, generally; and I don't expect we will again now the bad egg's gone.'

'Yes, Tony, excellent.' Vic gestured to the window. 'I can't wait to get a sense of the physical context of the school; the buildings, décor, images—'

'I see. And why would that be?'

Vic frowned, for the first time. 'Because our environment, and changes to it, can affect our behaviour. Have you heard of behavioural design?'

Liv sat up.

'Ah, no, I'm not following . . .' Tony seemed to remember himself. 'But before you go on, as Lloyd would have explained on the phone—'

'I didn't have the pleasure of speaking with Lloyd.' Vic smiled again. 'I spoke with the very capable Jean Anderson.'

Tony frowned at her résumé, darting one eye to Lloyd, who nodded. 'Ah, given how terribly important this work is, we are looking for someone special. Someone with a profile in this area. Who can give us at least this term, intensively.'

Liv didn't understand the man's point.

Vic's smile took in the photos of suited men, boys in sportswear, and paintings of pelicans. 'I love the pelicans.' She gave a charming, tinkly laugh. 'I understand the scale of it. But, as I'm sure you're aware, great advancements can be brought about by *small* changes. Sometimes surprisingly quickly.'

It was Tony's turn to seem lost. But Liv vaguely recalled this material now, from one of Vic's books.

'I'd love to help. There's so much we can do!' Words gushed out of Vic, spiced with smiles and nods. 'I can't wait to get started.'

Listening, the men smiled back at her. 'Yes, that's tremendous.' Despite themselves, they were being swept up.

'But . . .' said Lloyd.

'Oh, yes, but – as I mentioned to Olivia here,' said Tony, 'we have already reached out to a chap.'

Tony raised his palms. Liv was heating up, perhaps with a hot flush. There was a disjunction here she didn't understand.

'Oh, you have?' said Vic. 'I would love to be involved.'

Tony and Lloyd stared at Vic. Liv could see their brains whirring.

Liv leant forward. Kept her face still. '*Dr* Cato has an excellent handle on the influences on young people today.' Her voice droned. 'Particularly on what boys and girls need—'

'Yes, nice,' said Lloyd.

Tony eyed Lloyd, who was noting the time on the grandfather clock as he clicked his pen.

Dumbstruck, Liv sat back. It'd been going so well, but it'd only been fifteen minutes! When the two men pushed their seats out, and thanked her again for this introduction, Liv understood. They'd agreed to this meeting to humour her, a MUM. A noisy and increasingly difficult MUM.

'But *Dr* Cato—' she said.

As he rose, Tony seemed to hear her: surprise dashed across his face. 'I wonder if you could work with—'

'Why, it's possible. Who do you have in mind?'

Liv willed the men to sit down.

'It turns out we have a *world-renowned* authority in our midst,' said Tony, almost apologetically. 'You may have heard of him.'

Tony turned to the books behind him. Liv felt as if the room was slowly revolving.

'People were discussing his work at a principals' conference recently. Some years ago, he wrote a tremendously useful book on resilience, and another on authenticity – or was it assertiveness?' Tony was saying. 'We have it somewhere.'

Tony frowned up at the shelves until Lloyd pointed. Climbing a ladder, Tony plucked a book.

'Here's one: *The True You*.' Tony was speaking slowly, as if Liv and Vic might have trouble committing the three words to memory.

When Tony offered his find to Vic, she laughed.

'A *New York Times* bestseller, I believe,' he added, puzzled.

Lloyd grinned as if he too saw the joke. Liv looked from Vic's face to her résumé.

Tony's arm holding the book wilted. 'Do you know him? He's quite renowned: V. N. Kovach?'

Vic nodded, wiping her eyes. 'A tall person with red hair, Manuka-honey coloured eyes?' she said, with a glance to the reflection in the window. 'Early forties.'

The latter, Liv suspected, was a fib. Tony crinkled his nose at her unlikely description. Turned the book over. 'I don't believe so. I read about his work again only this year in *The Journal*. Remarkable fellow. A Rhodes scholar.'

'I read that article.' Lloyd nodded at Vic. 'He's unrivalled in his field. We can't wait to meet him.'

'It's *her*,' said Vic.

A frown sprang to the principal's brow. 'Oh, no, I don't think so.'

Tony shook his head, as if bothered by a fly. Not finding a photograph on the book, he appraised Vic, then Liv, then Lloyd. He wore his assurance like a cape. His smile changed its tenor. The room had stopped spinning.

'V for Victoria,' said Vic. 'Kovach is my maiden name.'

'*Your* maiden name?' said Tony.

Vic pointed to her résumé – which bore both names. 'I took my husband's name. I like Cato better than Kovach.' Her grin was at its zenith now.

'You?' The assistant principal fumbled for the résumé.

Tony's mouth fell open and his face coloured; he looked remarkably like a letterbox.

'I write under Kovach.'

'We . . .' Tony cleared his throat. 'We . . . we were aware . . .' His look to Lloyd was of unmasked horror.

At the door, executive assistant Jean Anderson lingered with a tea tray.

'Not now,' Lloyd snapped.

Jean retreated as Lloyd turned to face Vic and purred, 'We've been trying to get in touch with you. Your agent?'

'My agent's a very busy woman.'

Tony slumped into his chair. 'Why the initials?' Though his tone was soft, it was also slightly defensive, as if Vic had sprung a trap – by getting married, changing her name, assuming they'd read her résumé.

'Reflect back on our conversation, gentlemen,' Vic said warmly. 'Somewhere there you'll find your answer.'

36

Liv

An hour later, Vic and Liv were concluding their tour. A most deferential Lloyd Palmer had shown them the marbled science laboratories; the two libraries, dotted with students; the many-levelled Middle and Senior schools, replete with theatrettes and forecourts; the food tech labs (akin to the science labs, except decorated with images of TV chefs rather than scientists) and even the girls' and boys' toilets – at Vic's suggestion. 'You can tell a lot about a school by its toilets,' Vic had informed Liv. And you could: to Liv's surprise, the girls' bathrooms at Carmichael had pink-and-silver-detailed wallpaper and enormous mirrors. The scent of rose was in the air, thanks to a wall-mounted gizmo. The boys' toilets, by contrast, were plain, beige and mirrorless. Happily, they didn't particularly smell. The front of house and back-end of the school were stamped with the same five-star ambience, but something felt off. Unlike when Liv had originally toured the school, years ago, today it was occupied. Then, hand-picked, highly animated mini-adult students had lead the tours. But this morning Carmichael was populated by glum, mildly hostile clones who chortled occasionally. Liv, Vic and Lloyd were largely invisible.

As tour guide, Lloyd was chatty and knowledgeable, a walking, talking school brochure. Following his broad back, Liv was careful not to touch him. Lloyd's attention was primarily on Vic, who was sucking the marrow out of the man, bone by bone. Gulping down the school in one rare, bloody serve.

Afterwards, in a sudden silence, Vic and Liv exited the school's grounds and strode along the street. It wasn't until they were by Vic's Jeep that they stopped and collapsed into laughter. Liv had counted four apologies from Tony Crisp. He'd called the misunderstanding 'an oversight, due to stress'. He'd unearthed another two of V. N. Kovach's books from the shelves. Once, someone at Carmichael had been very familiar with V. N.'s work.

'Imagine not reading the thing!' Vic said.

Liv was still struggling with that herself. Talk about hubris! What would Vic have done if Tony hadn't blundered across the truth?

'I have to confess,' said Vic, sobering. 'Jean Anderson and I go way back.'

'Okay.' Liv smiled. 'I don't get it.'

'We had a hunch they wouldn't read *Victoria Cato*'s résumé. It was a sneaky little test.'

'Oh.' Worry skipped through Liv's thoughts. 'Will Jean be in trouble?'

'It's not her job to read the CVs.'

It turned out Jean had babysat Vic's children when Jean started working at Carmichael around nine years ago – incidentally, a few years before Lloyd Palmer. Jean, like Liv, was a passionate reader, and, with her corkscrew grey hair and thick ankles, was often only noticed when she was absent. As in, 'Where's Jean? I need a coffee.' Or 'Where's Jean, my screen has frozen.' This stood Jean in good stead to know the inner workings of Carmichael Grammar. The things she heard, the things she saw, the things she could do. As it turned out, Jean and Liv had both contacted Vic over the weekend.

'Makes sense, now.' Liv glanced to her own car. 'Thanks again for letting me sit in.'

'You're very welcome. We have a lot of work to do.' Vic Cato stretched her back. 'There's plenty wrong with that school.'

'There is? I mean, yes, there is. But how could you tell?'

'Some of it's blindingly obvious,' said Vic. 'But I'll know more once I get the data. One thing I can tell you now, someone needs to look at how they hire people.'

Vic and Liv laughed again. At that moment, a cherubic sixty-year-old exited the school at speed.

'That's Mary MacBeth, we need her,' said Liv. 'She's lovely and wise. She's taught my boys.'

'Mary? Yes, Jean mentioned her. A crucial recruit.'

Vic Cato clasped Liv's hand and, then and there, Liv decided to adopt the psychologist as her new best friend. She did have a vacancy.

'We're going to need a small army on this. You do have the time?'

Liv wondered how she would fit an intensive nine-week program at Carmichael into her home life, work life, married life. She was only just beginning to feel less overwhelmed, and she hadn't found hair on her pillow in two days. Maybe she could drop more duties, amend the Lists? Perhaps she could hire a housekeeper. Ha.

'I'm paid by the file. I could say no to a few.'

Not that she ever did. Her boss relied on her. She'd have to do her best Gunhild with Ryan. Added to which, their house was old but their mortgage was enormous. (Duncan had been determined to live in Bayside . . .) And they were overcommitted all over the place. Could the Winsome family afford it? Probably best if she didn't tell Duncan.

'I'm happy to do my bit,' she said. 'Community service and all that. Carmichael is big on having us mums involved, fundraising or making jam.'

'Okay?' With a quizzical expression, Vic studied Liv. 'Good for you. I'll draw up our plan of attack. I'll share with you and Jess Charters first. Then I'll sell it to Tony and Lloyd.'

Liv marvelled again that she was about to work with *the* V. N. Kovach. 'But aren't *you* extraordinarily busy?'

'Yes and no. But this is what I love – using insights about human behaviour to create real change, improve lives. For years, Jean's been telling me about this school; I've been itching to get in.' Vic beamed as she revealed this. 'One day, I'll set up my own school, like Oprah. But for now, I can't imagine a better place to be. Because, boy-o, does Carmichael Grammar need me!'

Vic gave a final chortle, then embraced Liv on the pavement like a fairy godmother. Liv wasn't a hugger, generally speaking; but, briefly, the two women stood, happily interlocked.

37

Dear Parents,

You may be aware of a recent incident involving several of our students. We have investigated this matter and are providing support as needed to the students affected. Naturally, we have taken disciplinary action against the boy involved, who is no longer a student of the Grammar.

Moving forward, we are delighted to announce that Carmichael Grammar will be providing a nine-week program run by the esteemed psychologist and author Dr Vic Cato (who publishes as V. N. Kovach). Commencing immediately, Dr Cato's program will run as a part of our Health and Physical Education offering throughout Term Two. It will include specifics on how to treat one's peers respectfully, how to express oneself appropriately and how to obtain insight into one's own behaviour. Dr Cato's work will examine the school, our teaching and our students' interpersonal dynamics through the lens of gender. We envision Dr Cato's program will be rolled out across the school in the coming terms. Dr Cato will also take a critical eye to the Carmichael way, to ensure we continue to provide the best possible learning environment for all our students and maintain our position as a world-leading school.

Dr Cato has our full support in providing this invaluable and timely program, which we are confident will restore harmony and respectful relationships at the Grammar. Her time with us promises to be like her books: creative, colourful and compelling. We are extremely fortunate to retain her expertise.

While we have been deeply disappointed by recent events, we remain optimistic that as a result of this process our students will be ever more mindful of the importance of appropriate social media use and the need for mutual respect between the sexes.

If you have any queries in relation to Dr Cato's program or any other matters raised in this letter, please do not hesitate to contact me directly on the number below.

Yours sincerely,
Antony Crisp BA (Hons) MEd (Intl)
Principal
Carmichael Grammar

38

Duncan

In the twilight, Duncan found Liv typing merrily at their outside table. Beside her was a half-empty jug of water, a glass and a notepad of red scrawls. 'Hello, husband.'

'New file?'

'Ah, no. Writing a charter for Carmichael.' She typed as she read her handwritten notes. 'I called you. The school's retained Vic Cato to bring it into the twenty-first century. I'm part of a working group to support her.'

'Geez, that's great . . .' He frowned. Was he meant to know this Vic Cato? 'They really want to look at themselves?'

'Uh-huh.' She grinned. 'Can you believe it?'

He shook his head, couldn't really. But change was in the air, every-where, these days, he supposed. 'Do you have time for that?'

'Think I'll manage.'

'What a turnaround.' For her. For the school. 'I'm happy for you.'

He was, though he didn't feel it. What he felt was the chambers of his heart closing. He'd spent the weekend waiting for his family to be home together. But on Saturday afternoon, straight after sport, Jai had gone to Grace's and hadn't returned. A solo Oscar had plugged into his head-phones and rapped badly as he made banana bread. Meanwhile, Cody had been transported from Harry's to golf by Liv, who didn't come back. More errands, apparently. Hours later, Cody had returned, rings around his eyes, yelling and slamming things. Liv said something about 'bloody sleepovers, never again'. She'd clean forgotten his surprise. Duncan had given Jai's disused iPad to Cody to watch a movie, and it'd seemed to calm him. On Saturday night, once Cody had collapsed, Liv had fallen asleep during the opening credits of a movie. On Sunday, only he and Oscar had been home. This was new. They'd played one-on-one basketball until Oscar said, 'You're too easy, Dad, it's boring.' Shortly after that, Oscar was sucked into the internet's black hole.

No one noticed he wasn't in his home office. Nor that, on Saturday afternoon, he'd snuck into the garage for hours. Hunted for ages for the right wrench, then struggled to get the wheels to turn without rubbing. For a simple job, it took a long time, times five. But, by sundown, he'd managed it. And still no one had noticed. In the garage, the bikes remained, undiscovered, like stray nuggets of gold, rolling about, between their second fridge and spare couch.

Rousing himself, Duncan thrust a bunch of lilies at Liv. The large white heads were already open, lascivious and pungent. He had an announcement to make. But a flicker of negativity soured her face. She stopped typing.

'Thanks.'

Duncan felt six years old, gifting his mum a wonky mug made in art class. Something *had* pricked his conscience at the florist. He settled into a deckchair. It was another stunning autumn evening – mild and clear and full of promise. He was determined not to let it turn, as the weekend had.

Liv rested the flowers on the table and sneezed.

'You close to finishing?'

'Nope. It keeps growing.'

He could see she was busting to resume. He wondered how long she'd been out here. The lights weren't on inside. They sat in silence. The flowers' scent was intense. But she wasn't springing up to put them in water or prepare their chicken stir-fry. It was her turn tonight, but the kitchen was bare. He wondered where their sons were. Then remembered: footy training. Oops. Luckily, tonight, he'd be able to pick them up.

With a quick smile, Liv resumed typing. He was pleased her Lists had worked; she seemed lighter and – more balanced? Calmer? He wouldn't put money on it. She still walked fast, talked fast, thought fast. Much like Jai. You learnt a lot about yourself – and/or your wife – by having your children diagnosed.

'Liv?'

Her eyes were on the screen as her fingers danced.

If he told her tonight, and linked a prospective female partner to a road trip, he'd probably ruin her mood. The last time he'd kept a secret from her, besides the bikes, was twenty years ago. He'd made a decision then, too, over a period of weeks. One afternoon, he'd planned to share it. In his rental in Elwood, they'd been in bed: her reading, him strumming. He'd had one eye on rental ads in the paper when he'd turned to her and she'd said, 'Yes! Yes! Let's do it!' Once he was an open book to Liv; but, lately, she'd become a lapsed reader. Of him at least.

When Liv sneezed again, he looked to the beached flowers. Took in his garden of low-allergenic plants. Oops.

'Where's Cody?'

'Yikes. The bath.' Liv leapt up.

He thought he'd heard running water. 'I'll go.'

Liv's mouth fell open and his spirits lifted again.

Heading inside, he reminded himself that his life, their life, was about to cleave open, spill with possibilities. Henry had been amenable to the female partner idea. 'I don't buy the diversity-leads-to-greater-profitabil-ity bulldust,' he'd said. 'But we need someone, and it looks bad that we don't have a woman. Not good for recruitment or the staff, either. Try to find one.' Duncan had been surprised at Henry's acquiescence but agreed with his point. He recalled a recent meeting when he and two of his partners had turned up, like the Three Musketeers; the client's female general counsel had quickly become stroppy. Yep, a woman would be good, all round. While he hadn't mentioned the sabbatical to Henry, it was one step closer. He'd already had a chat with a headhunter, and left another message for Maggie Koh. After, he'd felt something shift. Backup was coming. Now, walking down the hall, he felt as if he was flying, high above their house. He was looking down at their huge eucalypts and their double-storey home's flat roof. He was seeing the bay and the heads and the ocean, far, far away. He was taking a satellite view of his life. For two whole months, they could go anywhere. Do anything. Despite the likelihood of some hiccups, Duncan felt electrified again. He wondered how long it would take Liv to notice. Not so long ago, his boys had called something extraordinary 'lit'. Well, tonight, he felt *lit*.

Water spilling across the floorboards greeted him as he turned towards the bathroom. Water, on its way to the twins' bedroom.

'Cody!' he yelled. 'Turn off the taps!'

He flung open the bathroom door, hard, harder than he meant to. Wearing AirPods and half-asleep, Cody lay in the cascading bath. The floor was a pool, centimetres deep. Jai's iPad was propped on a cabinet.

'Cody!' Duncan yelled again, turning the taps. 'Look what you've done! You little twit!'

Startled, Cody sprang up. 'I didn't know! I didn't know!'

'Why didn't you open your eyes!' Duncan bellowed. 'Look at the floor!'

Duncan tossed towels onto the tiles.

'Get out of here! You've lost your technology! For a month!'

'*NOOOOO!*'

Cody ran, howling, his little bottom wobbling.

Duncan swore under his breath.

This life! Was it this much of a roller-coaster for everyone? Or only him?

Returning outside, Duncan found Cody wrapped in Liv, and a towel. Tears were still pinging off Cody's cheeks. The front of Duncan's shirt was soaked; already, he'd deposited eight sopping towels in the laundry. Liv's laptop was shut. He and Liv considered each other. They hadn't had one of these stand-offs in a while. Twenty-six years of intimacy glimmered between them.

'Want to order takeaway? Indian?' he said.

'Sure.'

Now he had her full attention. But he'd lost his enthusiasm for his announcement, as well as his frustration. He needed to get a mop. He turned.

'Why'd you yell like that?'

'Wait till you see the bathroom. The little—'

'Duncan, he's nine years old.'

'Yes, he is.'

Spent, Duncan shook his head. Why did Cody behave like such a . . . a . . . *child*, sometimes? Why couldn't he be more . . . *mature*? It'd make parenting him a whole lot easier.

Duncan remembered then another reason why he'd stepped away from this hands-on parenting gig. Let's just say, in the good old days of his childhood, you didn't flood a bathroom twice. And ADHD? That was definitely not a thing.

Two minutes later, Duncan returned with the mop as, bleary-eyed, Oscar emerged in the kitchen. Where had he been? Judging by the stupefied look of him, online.

'What happened to footy?' said Duncan. 'It's Monday.'

'Shitty shit shit,' said Liv.

'Who's in charge here?' he snapped.

Liv's head jerked.

He'd never known her to forget the kids before. She hadn't noticed his hour-old haircut either, or that he was late. How long had she – they – been like this? Did it predate the Lists? This dawning irked and shamed him, almost as much as his outburst with Cody. Liv also hadn't noticed that in bed he'd started reading one of her books: *Should You Leave*.

'Isn't it your night?' she said. Then sneezed again.

Last night, a page of that book had floored him. Long pencil marks ran by the text – presumably Liv's. The page told the story of a man turning forty. A man who'd been feeling distinctly out of touch with himself, his values and beliefs. A man who decided to take a broom to his life, and actively and consciously sweep away the deadwood. He discarded several child-hood friends. He distanced himself from his mother. He changed his job. He took a long, deep look at his wife. Duncan had found the tale disturb-ing yet fascinating. He'd been particularly intrigued by how the man had appraised his wife. He'd decided to keep her. But, as the man insisted to his therapist, the author, it could've gone either way.

In bed, the word Duncan was left with was 'brave'.

Oscar, Liv and Cody were still looking at him. Not one expression was clear-cut. Each had shades of anger. Or was it disappointment? Fear? His bedraggled youngest was whimpering. He moved to ruffle Cody's wet hair, but the boy pulled back. Tight-lipped, Liv observed the exchange. Oscar folded his arms.

'Don't go, Mummy.' Cody shivered.

She held a finger to her lip, pausing a sneeze. 'What time is it?'

'It's not too late.' Duncan rested the mop against the wall, carefully. 'I'll take the twins.' He turned to the hallway. 'Jai? Footy! We're leaving. Now!'

39

Jess

Jess's new top three fears:
1. Grace stops being excellent at school;
2. Grace is picked on at school;
3. Grace rejects her family and becomes a rebel.

Jess carried clean washing into Grace's room as Grace lay texting. So much for Grace doing her science prac. On Sunday, when Jess had asked after it, Grace had said, 'What's the point?' and sulked away. Today, Grace had been given a B-minus for a Maths quiz, her lowest mark ever. That was something else they needed to talk about. Jess watched Grace's fingers moving. It seemed Grace's phone had become both her second brain and an extension of her hand; it also seemed to have gobbled up her personality.

Watching as she folded laundry, Jess wondered if she ought to keep 'telling her story', as Liv put it, or focus on dragging Grace back from the depths of that iPhone. If Grace didn't watch out, she'd become permanently average. Her friendship with Bella seemed to have hit a snag, too; Bella hadn't been around for a smoothie in days. Hannah Appleby was also missing in action. Grace and Hannah hadn't socialised since the Instagram mess. These were all things they needed to discuss, Jess supposed. She'd made it through one chapter of V. N. Kovach's book, and it said to make an appointment for difficult conversations with your teenager, but that seemed way too formal. Now probably wasn't the time, being Grace's bedtime and a school night, but Morrie was jamming at his mate's place, and Jess had heard from almost everyone in Bayside about Carmichael Grammar and its issues, except Grace.

Jess took in the running trophies on Grace's shelves: 100 metre sprint, 200 metres, 4 x 100 metres relay. She thought of Grace's results last year: a sweep of As and A-pluses. Grace's dreams of studying orthopaedics weren't beyond her, were they? Not if she went back to her old ways and applied herself. If she stayed at Carmichael. How many Andrews were orthopaedic surgeons? There couldn't be that many.

Jess tapped Grace's leg, but Grace did not look up.

Jess folded the final T-shirt and sat down. She'd had a topsy-turvy week, too. She'd gone from being excited about the expert-author-person's appointment to worried, almost overnight. She didn't want to be followed again. Or scared. Also, she liked the school as it was, and so did Grace. She'd spent the afternoon debating whether to call Mr Crisp. Ring and pull out; or bluff and brave it? On the one hand, the working group didn't need her. She wasn't across the statistics and politics, like Liv. She wasn't an expert, like V. N. Kovach. She hadn't even gone to uni. What could she add? Even when she was at school she hadn't read the books; she'd skimmed. The only thing she could remember was that *To Kill a Mockingbird* had something to do with shoes. She wasn't that interested in other people's ideas, or stories. She just wanted to protect her daughter. Keep her safe. At a good school. That was it. She wasn't really angry, like Liv. Liv had mistaken Jess's tiger-mother inner rage for something else. She'd needed to get out how she felt. Nothing more. She'd thought it over and she wasn't that gutsy.

Mr Crisp only wanted her involved to keep her quiet.

On the other hand, she liked Liv. She could do with more fun and clever and refreshingly weird friends. And she did want to do something. She didn't want the bad guys to win, whoever they were. But she'd prefer to fight back *later*. Couldn't someone else do it for now?

Further up the bed, Grace was leaning with her legs crossed and her phone to her nose. From her position, Jess couldn't see Grace's face, only the blank rectangle. Jess sniffed again. What was that smell? Yesterday, she'd cleaned the fridge. But it was back.

In that moment, Jess made a decision. After her chat with Grace, she'd ring Liv. Resign from whatever she'd signed up for. She'd like to help but she had too much to do. It'd been a harrowing week, but it was over now. And the world was . . . *good enough*, as Morrie would say. It was. The school was, too. It could have been worse – heaps worse. Grace was lucky to be there.

Steeling herself, Jess tapped Grace's knee again. 'Grace, hon, please, can you look at me?'

'Mm.' Grace stopped typing on her phone but otherwise didn't move.

'With your eyes.'

'In two minutes.' Grace resumed sending her thumb-tapped code.

'Sweetie?'

Grace lifted her gaze then let it fall back.

'Okay, pass it, please,' said Jess.

Jess extended her hand and counted aloud. Made it to one hundred and twenty-seven before Grace slapped the phone down.

'What do you want?'

The expression on her daughter's face was that obnoxious, Jess could've laughed. Or yelled. In the past week, Grace had been ruder than Jess had been in a lifetime. It was very disappointing. But, of course, Jess would never yell in response. They slipped into silence, as Jess tried to get a run up to this conversation.

'Can you smell anything?' A false start.

'Huh?'

'Can you smell anything?'

'I dunno.'

'Oh, not to worry.' Third time lucky: 'Grace, honey . . . I'd like you to tell me about that photograph.'

She'd done it! But Grace was staring at her kneecaps. Jess tapped Grace's leg again. Grace managed to maintain eye contact by twirling strands of ponytail. What had V. N. Kovach's book said about this type of talk? Something about not making it personal. Avoiding being 'judgey'.

'What about it?'

'Why did you do it, hon, out of the blue like that?'

Grace leapt up and began tidying her room. A radical avoidance strategy.

'Were you trying to, I don't know, fit in . . . or be "cool"?'

'I don't know what that means – "cool".' Grace scowled at her. Jess felt another ping of irritation.

Jess realised then why she'd been avoiding this conversation. This was a teenage experience she knew nothing about. Why, given the risks, would anyone do it?

'Grace, you know what I mean. Popular.'

'What does it matter? It's not as if I'm going to do it again, am I?'

'I don't know, hon. Are you?'

Grace glared as if she'd asked the most ridiculous question in the universe.

'You don't seem very remorseful.'

Grace tossed her clothes into drawers. Watching her, Jess realised, Grace had been both perkier and more upset since that Instagram account. What had the book called it? More *labile*?

'Were you experimenting, is that it?'

Grace groaned. 'You have no idea,' she said. 'None.'

This stung far more than it should have. 'Why don't you fill me in, then?' said Jess, trying and failing to keep her voice calm.

Grace was stuffing clothes into her dirty washing sack, many of which didn't look particularly dirty.

'Did someone talk you into it? Was it Bella?' This idea hadn't occurred to Jess before, but it wasn't impossible. Maybe that's why Jilly and Bella had vanished.

Grace shook her head then sat on the bed with a bounce.

'Was it another boy? Taj?'

'No.' Grace sighed, dramatically. 'It wasn't Taj.' She pulled a sour face.

'If it wasn't Bella, or Taj . . . or Jai . . . or . . . Blake?'

Grace shook her head.

'Well, who was it?'

Grace rolled her eyes.

'People don't do things completely out of character for no reason.' Jess's voice was becoming squeaky. 'Something was going on. Grace, you have to tell me!'

Sounding desperate probably wasn't in the book.

'Why? So you can post about it on Facebook,' Grace spat the word. 'Or write another stupid article?'

Jess sat back as if Grace had given her a shove. Now they were getting somewhere, unearthing truths between teenagers and mums as old as time. Yet it still hurt. When you were the embarrassing mum.

When Grace bowed her head, Jess thought *Oh, no.* Grace began to cry loudly and turn red. Next the sobs would start, and Jess would fly into hugs-and-tissues mode, their conversation over. But Jess remembered what she was supposed to be doing: tuning in to her daughter's emotions.

'Grace . . . Wait up . . .'

Grace wailed and, when she saw no response from her mother, grew louder, screwing up her face. Jess didn't react, though, on the inside, her genie was in a flap.

'Grace, you seem very . . .' Goodness, thought Jess, what the heck was a feeling word? She took a deep breath. Cracked her neck. 'Sad and . . . and frustrated and, well, embarrassed and . . . angry?'

Jess winced as Grace's head snapped up.

'Is that it, hon? Are you angry because of me?'

Grace's wails faded. Jess waited. After a moment, Grace looked at Jess squarely through wet eyelashes. 'Why couldn't you be quiet, like everyone else?'

Jess moved up the bed to sit beside Grace. It was a good question.

'I didn't like seeing you . . . exposed, I suppose . . . and judged,' Jess said. 'I had to do something.' Grace sniffed, and Jess realised something she should've seen earlier. 'I didn't like being judged, either.'

When Grace sighed, the emotion fell from her face. 'To be honest, I didn't understand why you had to go post about it. I thought you were just being overprotective, as per usual . . .'

Jess opened her mouth.

'But . . . I kind of do, now.'

'Oh, good.' Jess smiled.

'Though you stuffed up a bit. Going off what Jilly said Blake said, blaming Jai and bringing in the police. That was over the top.'

'Yes.'

Jess sighed; she still felt sorry for Jai, and even for Blake, though she didn't understand him, what he'd done or how he'd seemed to have gotten away with it – though, she could guess. On the upside, this tuning-in was going quite well. She stood up. It was getting late; she had calls to make.

'But Mum, why didn't *you* tell me what *you* were doing?' Grace said. 'And why didn't you tell me about, I don't know . . . how the developed world is run by middle-aged white guys who employ people who look like them? I thought the biggest problems facing my generation were climate change and global health. And racism and terrorism. And . . . not getting kidnapped.'

'Oh, well . . . um.' More good questions. 'Would it've made a difference, hon?'

'Maybe.' Grace shrugged. 'It helps to know what you're up against. Especially when it's all connected.'

Jess was still struggling to see the connections, herself. Grace's gaze returned to the phone in Jess's hand. They'd come a long way without answering the question. Suddenly, Jess felt struck by a moment of genius.

'What were you feeling when you took that photo?'

'What do you mean, *feeling*?'

'You know, hon: happy, sad or scared? Use a feeling word.' Jess doubted the book called them 'feeling words'.

'I don't know.' But Grace seemed to concentrate. 'Excited . . . and angry . . . and brave . . . powerful. Free.'

Jess tried on each of these for a split second. A few of them didn't fit. 'Why angry?'

Grace appeared to adjust some scales in her mind. 'You sure you want to know?'

'Yes.' Jess smiled, though her shoulders tensed.

'Okay.' Grace gave her a hard stare. 'That day, in Science—'

Jess frowned. Science?

'The boys were joking around, as per usual, and I had my hand up. I, like, waited forever, and then finally he pointed at me and said, "Look at her. Isn't she *boring*! All work and no play keeps the boys away, Grace." He said it that meanly, Mum; everyone went super quiet.'

A sudden shower sprinkled Grace's cheeks.

Jess felt the stuffing tugged out of her. 'Sorry, who was this?'

Grace shook her head as she dripped, turned pink.

'It's okay. Grace, it's okay. Hon, what did you do?'

'Ran to the bathroom.' Grace took a deep breath, and wiped each eye with a finger.

Jess tried for a smile. They were both holding it together remarkably well. 'I thought you loved Science.'

'Not this year.'

Jess exhaled slowly. 'What happened after you ran out?'

'Bella came after me, and later Jai came with my lunch.'

'Lunch?'

Grace nodded her bowed head. The pieces of her daughter's life began to fit together.

'There are better ways to prove you're not boring, hon.'

'That's what Jai said.' Grace smiled through her tears. 'I am kind of popular now, though . . . which means some people love me and some people hate me.'

Grace's face crumpled again. She wrapped her arms around Jess. Touched, Jess didn't move, but inside her genie was stomping. Gently, Jess broke the hug. 'Grace hon, who was it?'

Grace shook her head, sat back.

'Was it Mr Humphries or Mr Waring?'

With a frown, Grace shook her head again. Jess hadn't yet had any parent–teacher interviews this year, and she couldn't picture faces. But, next term, she'd definitely get her money's worth out of those seven minutes! In the meantime, she'd need to speak to someone about this, she supposed. Drat it.

'Was it your regular Science teacher?'

Jess stroked Grace's phone. The school's portal was only two clicks away. But Grace's face was in her hands.

'Hon, I'll tell Liv, she'll take it to the school. I won't make a fuss.' Liv could bring it to the working group too.

'No, Mum.'

Jess frowned, detecting a new tone in Grace's voice. 'There's a consultant coming to work with the Year Eights,' said Jess. 'She'll know what to do.'

'No.' Grace sat upright, wiped her face. Jess could feel Grace's anger making her warm and keeping her heart pumping. 'You do it.'

'But you just said—'

'He said it to *me*. You're my mum. You should do it. Just don't go on and on, and don't post about it . . .'

Jess gulped. 'Honey, I've retired from public life.'

'I know what I said before but, to be honest, I think it's kind of good for you.' Grace gave a weak smile. 'Just, I don't know, Mum. He can't go around talking like that to people or . . . or ignoring them. But be careful.'

Jess swallowed, overcome by her daughter's flattery. It seemed Grace didn't miss much, even when avoiding her. 'All right. But, hon, you have to tell me who it was.'

Like a small child, Grace cupped her hand and brought it to Jess's ear, whispering a name. Then she pulled back to see Jess's reaction. Jess just managed to swallow that mouthful of vinegar and keep her face in check.

'Okay, hon, I'm on it.'

But the relevant feeling word, Jess realised, wasn't only anger. The other one was fear.

40

Liv

Duncan returned from dropping the twins at footy training with yet more groceries. His new motto seemed to be, 'When in doubt, shop'. The house had never been so stocked, nor with such an eclectic range. Liv opened an Aldi bag. Since the Lists, Duncan had developed an intense love affair with the German retailer. He was stripping Aldi's shelves of sweets, chocolate and cookies. Obviously, he hadn't noticed her healthy food choices these past fifteen years. He'd also snapped up a three-person tent. She'd decided not to bite.

Entering the house, he'd seemed pleased that she'd set the table, poured water glasses and mopped the wet floors. Bathroom debacle notwithstanding, she was having too good a day to niggle at Duncan for losing his cool. After mopping, she'd managed to speed-make Cody a toastie.

'Forgot to ask, has Jai gone okay back at school?' The snark had left his voice.

'Absolutely.'

'Good-o.'

From the bag, she pulled out a five litre tub of butterscotch and honeycomb ice cream. She willed herself not to read its label. Sugar was one thing; those artificial flavours, colours and preservatives were another – especially for finely-tuned Cody.

'Sorry about before. I'm a bit rusty.'

'Yup.' Liv dug a hole in their freezer and stuffed in the tub. Transitions were rarely smooth, she supposed. Parenting still tripped her up, daily, and she was the full-timer.

'But, guess what?' His grin revealed every long tooth.

'Okay then,' She made herself mentally move on. 'What?'

'The guys have agreed to open the doors.'

'To what?'

'A female partner – what else, silly? I'll flip her a few clients, too, so I can . . . scale back, and help you more here.'

Her smile faltered. 'Everyone's on board? Even Henry?'

'Yep, Henry.' Duncan smiled across a half-emptied bag. 'And Michael. Obviously we need someone.'

'That's great, Dunc.' Liv became aware of her less than authentic smile. As much as she wanted Duncan around more, she preferred her parenting style to his. Calm trumped grumpy, any day.

Liv grabbed a slab of extra-dark chocolate and a carton of ginger cookies. Good thing Cody was in bed and couldn't see this loot. Liv chomped on a chunk of chocolate.

Chewing, Liv hid the chocolate and the cookies in the tea-towel drawer. 'Who's driving the search?'

'Me, of course. I've already got a few ideas.'

'You?' She swallowed, choked briefly then laughed.

Duncan laughed too, as, spluttering, Liv raised her hand and Duncan slapped it.

'Well done, husband.'

To her own ears, she didn't sound entirely convinced.

After a long hug, Duncan shed his shirt and put some towels into the drier. (Sorry, environment!) While their Indian food cooled in the kitchen, Duncan changed quickly, wandering about bare-chested and in shorts. He was out of shape, but so was she. He'd begun folding washing quickly by the time Liv poured wine and gathered herself. A moment later, she sidled to him and kissed his ear.

'What was that for?' said Duncan.

Liv stopped short of thanking him; no one had thanked her these past dozen years. But, despite the flare-up with Cody, she *was* grateful.

She kissed his other ear. 'For listening.'

Curiously, lately, she was finding her husband fetching. It wasn't the undersized apron he'd taken to wearing that read 'Mummy's Little Helper' but, she suspected, his doing of chores. Unasked. The Lists spoke for her now. They'd become like the Constitution. Or a Bill of Rights. Of course, the Constitution was far from perfect and more than a century of case law had grown around it. Never mind. Seeing her husband doing the house-work was oddly arousing.

That was the other item she'd missed off her List, she realised. Which column should it go to the bottom of? Weekly? Monthly?

Chest out, oblivious, Duncan delivered a stack of T-shirts to their room. Liv followed, closing the door behind her, although a wrung-out Cody was asleep and they were otherwise alone. A habit. The twins needed to be collected in twenty-five minutes. The Indian food was coagulating on the bench. Liv dropped the blinds and whisked off her clothes.

'Have you had a haircut?'

Grinning stupidly, Duncan nodded. 'What about dinner?'

Then he raced her to nakedness. They dove into their bed as if into clear water. Which was apt, as the freshly laundered sheets smelt of a new 'sea breeze' detergent, courtesy of Aldi.

Rolling beneath clean, blue linen, Liv was relishing the sea change.

41

Tuesday: Week one

Liv

First thing, Vic, Jess and Liv met with Lloyd, and Ethan Humphries. Liv had been disappointed to see Ethan but, as head of Year Eight, he couldn't be avoided. Silently, Liv debated whether Gunhild was needed, given Vic had arrived and Tony was on board. Overnight, Vic and her assistant, Roxy, had prepared a list of proposed changes to the physical environment, as well as a list of classroom norms that needed to be enforced, and other lists for specific subjects. Said lists were long and detailed. Vic Cato was probably one of those people who didn't sleep.

After the pleasantries, Vic presented Lloyd with her first list. He listened, his face unreadable, as she explained: the science and food tech labs needed to be redecorated, with posters of Elizabeth Garrett Anderson and Barbara McClintock to be hung alongside Albert Einstein and Stephen Hawking. Posters of female chefs needed to be hung alongside posters of the male TV cooks. Mirrors needed to be installed in the boys' bathrooms, identical to the girls'; and the pink-silver-lined wallpaper had to go. The assorted trophies and sporting paraphernalia around the school needed to include women's sports and women generally. And half of the old principals' portraits needed to be replaced with portraits of women. Photographs would do. Perhaps alumni who were artists could be commissioned? If female leading teachers were thin on the ground, then female school captains, female board members and female former students who were now luminaries were all options. Female world leaders would work, too, past and present, though less Margaret Thatcher, more Jacinda Ardern.

'I like your vision,' Lloyd said, finally, 'but people are used to having the old boys up there.'

'People can adapt,' said Vic.

'We can't afford to redo a bathroom at the drop of a hat,' interrupted Ethan, his gaze dropping below Vic's eyes.

'The school's pockets look deep to me,' Liv said, monotone.

Ethan regarded her coolly. 'Wallpaper's got nothing to do with . . . with gender equality.' He arched a vampiric eyebrow.

'Oh, but it does,' said Vic. 'Broadly speaking, "everything matters".' Vic grinned. 'Small, seemingly insignificant details can have major effects on our behaviour. Let me go back a step.'

Ethan turned to Lloyd as if he felt they were in the presence of madwomen, but Lloyd merely smiled. Meanwhile, Jess looked as if she was at a stand-up show in the front row, 'Don't pick me' stamped on her forehead.

With a glance of pity – or maybe surprise – to Jess, Vic described to the men how research had shown we could change the environments in which we live, work and learn to better achieve specific goals. We could make it easier for our biased minds to 'get things right'. The power of these small details, she explained, came from focusing attention in a particular direction. Giving people a nudge, on a wholesale level. Vic gave the example of how the introduction of 'blind' auditions for top professional orchestras in the United States led to a significant increase in female musicians. And how etching images of small black flies on urinals in the Amsterdam Schiphol airport improved people's aim and therefore significantly decreased mess. Also in the US, how cleaning up empty lots and abandoned houses had reduced gun crime in those neighbourhoods.

Ethan frowned. 'Did you say gun crime?'

Before Vic could answer, Lloyd purred, 'Good to know. But Vic, as you've said, our school is spectacular, extremely tidy, and our students are very well-behaved.'

Liv let that one go through to the keeper. Jess blinked, still mute.

'To that point,' said Vic, 'may I tell you what I saw yesterday?'

Lloyd's smile didn't slip. 'Please.' He sat back, crossed one long leg over the other.

Vic listed what she'd observed the day before: in a corridor, two boys pinching girls' bottoms, and a third lifting a skirt; behind the bike shed, four boys wrestling mightily as a filming trio watched; in Mr Waring's class, another pair of boys passing a note about a chubby, cross-eyed girl. In Humanities, three boys dominating a classroom discussion and ignoring the female teacher at the whiteboard. Two girls teasing a third girl about the length of her skirt. Several telephones and iPads hidden and in use during class, including half-a-dozen boys playing a first-person shooter game. In the science lab, a girl was photographing her cleavage, while the teacher called on boys exclusively for answers. Another teacher – Liv suspected Mr Humphries – was calling girls 'Pet' and 'Sweetheart'. Oh, and three older boys had been watching something fleshy in the library.

Vic seemed to have super-powered women's vision.

'I can go on.' Vic's tone was gentle but unyielding.

Jess's eyes were filling, Ethan's arms were crossed.

Lloyd's renowned grin was gone. 'Oh, I'm very, ah . . . disappointed. Let me get back to you.'

He plucked a blue pen from a sparkling glass containing nine identical others, and scrawled onto a notepad. Liv watched him admire his calligraphy.

'Thank you,' continued Vic. 'I also want to observe the teachers teaching. Cameras need to be set up in, say, two classrooms. I'll watch as many of the Year Eight teachers as I can and give feedback in the evenings.'

'We do that ourselves, from time to time.' Lloyd scribbled again with a flourish.

'Fantastic. Let's do it now. I also want cameras in some black spots. Like that south-east corner of the Middle School library.'

People behaved better when observed (or when they thought they were being observed), mused Liv. Would the likes of Waring and Humphries put on a show? And what about the students – would they notice? Liv was curious to see what Vic learnt. Usually, Liv found meetings a drag, but this one was a hoot. Jess, though, seemed to be suffering. Out of her depth?

'I'll meet the teaching staff, too, as a group,' said Vic. 'We don't want people's noses out of joint. I also need to be across the syllabus. We need to make sure these young people are learning about women in History. Reading fiction by women. Seeing art by women. By all types of women.' Vic's stare bored into Lloyd and he gulped. 'You get the drill. Who teaches Year Eight Science, by the way?'

Jess looked up, her eyes smouldering.

'That's me, and one other,' said Lloyd, his blue pen still.

'Fantastic,' said Vic. 'And English?'

'Giles Waring, Head of Year Nine.'

'Brilliant, looking forward to meeting him. You'll see, on the list headed *Data*, that I'll need to see the breakdown on how both boys and girls are faring, in the various subjects, over time.'

Deep in thought, Lloyd caressed his bald head while Ethan's gaze strayed again. Vic didn't seem to notice. Perhaps she was used to it. Vic took in Jess ironing a piece of paper with her fist. As far as Liv could recall, Jess hadn't uttered a word since the start of the meeting. Ethan's eyes remained locked on Vic.

Vic adjusted her silk blouse, retied its knot.

'Ethan Humphries,' said Liv. 'Stop staring at Dr Cato's boobs.'

Ethan coughed as if a hunk of steak was caught in his throat. The meeting became very quiet.

'What was that, Liv?' said Lloyd.

Four sets of eyes locked onto Liv's, including Vic's.

Liv had read that two voices raised in protest in a meeting were far better than one. She could retract what she'd said, she supposed; say, 'Nothing, forget it.' Or she could take a stand and flip that hovering humiliation back to its rightful owner.

'In conversation, people need to keep their eyes above the neck.'

The silence absorbed this second shock, then Jess squeaked, 'I agree.'

Lloyd burst into laughter, while Ethan huffed as if he had been offended. Liv smiled at Jess.

'I'll speak with Tony,' said Lloyd, wiping his eyes, 'and get back to you.'

Meeting over.

42

Jess

Dr Cato's first class was already underway when Jess slipped in. Her head was still swimming after that meeting. Teaching was teaching, she'd thought, and high school was high school. You had to survive the bitchy girls and horny boys, and not get a bloodstain on the back of your dress. But education in the twenty-first century was way more complicated than that. No wonder the children were stressed. Thank goodness for Dr Cato. She was very . . . impressive and scary. Liv was too, in a funny way. Calling out Mr Humphries! Jess wished she could do that. But writing a post or going on the radio or emailing an opinion piece was one thing. Saying something face to face, woman to man, parent to teacher (or assistant principal) was another.

Armed with a staple gun and a roll of posters, Jess tiptoed to the back of the room, where Miss Lee was doing some marking. Overnight, Jess had been wishing she'd pulled out of this. She'd planned on slipping home after that meeting, but Vic had other ideas. Jess had a feeling Vic was sizing her up and could see her reluctance to be here. Outside, gardeners and delivery people were working; doing things Jess could relate to. Dr Cato was pointing to a cartoon on the whiteboard. It showed a female astronaut plunging a flag into the moon's surface, with a caption that read, 'One small step for a woman . . .' In the next frame, below the caption 'One giant leap for mankind', other rockets were flying around the moon as occupants at their windows were saying, 'Show us your tits', 'Hey baby how about it', and 'Ugly bitch'. Boys were laughing, but Jess didn't get it. The cartoonist was Horacek. Jess had never heard of him.

As quietly as she could, Jess shot a staple through a poster into a cork-board wall. The gun made a quick thud but no one seemed to notice. Or acknowledge her. Moving quickly, she shot another round. From across the classroom, one person tossed her a quick smile. In public. Grace.

Jess made herself slow down. Dr Cato was placing pieces of paper in stations around the room. Different experiences were described on the papers. The students had to choose the descriptions that best matched their experiences, and stand in that area. Discreetly, Jess watched as the boys and girls wandered. Grace moved slowly until she made her selection by the windows. Most of the other girls Jess knew – led by Hannah Appleby – joined her. Much hair tossing was going on. Dr Cato smiled at the group as she waited for the boys to make their choices. With a subtle nod, Dr Cato acknowledged Jess watching. Jess busied herself unrolling another poster.

Finally, with a swagger, Taj Low propped against the wall in the opposite corner to most of the girls, followed by a sulky looking Oscar Winsome. These two seemed to be doing some eye-rolling. The girls were looking askance at each other too now. A couple of frumpy ones were scowling at Grace and Hannah. Taj and Oscar were pointedly not looking at the girls or Jess. Or Vic.

Unobtrusively, Jess read a quote on the next poster. It was from Dr Cato's *Popular is Not the Answer – Be liked for who you are, not for who you think you should be.* Jess was thinking that over, when Dr Cato turned to the boys. 'Who's heard of objectification? Who knows what it means?'

The boys muttered but didn't answer. In the corridor, Liv strode by, humming and purposeful. Grace watched Liv.

'Girls?'

Over the shoulders of some of the girls, Jess read the sheet that hung in their corner. *People freely comment on my body/looks.* Other girls stood near sheets on which was written: *I've been referred to as 'it' or 'that'.* And: *I have been told to: smile more; watch what I eat, how I sit, what I wear; remove most of the hair on my body.*

Objectiwhat? Jess couldn't remember being taught this when she was fourteen. Or seventeen. Or twenty-five. Though she might've heard the word somewhere, once. Dr Cato was waiting as the teenagers eyed each other. Eventually, Grace raised her hand, lifting her forearm though her upper arm stayed pinned by her side. Taj muttered and Oscar scowled, as he was meant to. Some girls looked self-conscious, others indifferent or accusing. Hannah seemed smug. Jess felt herself getting flustered as Dr Cato tossed a mini-basketball to Grace.

'Yes?' said Dr Cato. 'What do you think?'

As Grace answered, Jess listened while she crept nearer to one of the boys' corners. Grace seemed confident of her definition. Taj Low stood next to the words, *In ads, I often see myself portrayed as physically strong and active.* Other boys stood near the words: *If I was the Prime Minister, it's unlikely people would comment on my body, clothing or hair.* And: *I haven't had sexual comments yelled at me from vehicles.* And: *In the media, the bodies of the sex and/or gender I identify with are usually fully clothed.*

'Fabulous. Thank you . . .?'

'Grace.' Grace tossed the ball back.

Jess felt the tension leave her shoulders. It seemed Grace had made a reasonable go of it. Maybe thanks to Liv? Jess looked again to one nearby group of girls: two girls were plain, one very pretty. The moment Jess had seen them, she'd assessed their looks: ranked them in a heartbeat. What did that make her? Sexist? She'd done it to the boys, too.

Everyone seemed to be listening now, even Miss Lee.

'Who'd like to tell us of a time . . .' Dr Cato began, as Jess tuned out.

Confused, she was thinking of Grace's photograph. Grace had been proud of it; she'd felt free and daring. While Jess could understand that, deep down she still thought Grace looked . . . slutty. How did sexy selfies fit with objectification? She'd have to ask Dr Cato later, she supposed, or, better, Liv.

Jess's head was swimming again as she hung another poster, and Dr Cato tossed the ball. Did she really want to be involved in all this? Then, one by one, girls described being leered at, yelled at and touched. One or two boys talked about their muscles being squeezed and about shortness being a thing. Some of the boys laughed, but Dr Cato shut them down. Taking in the pink faces, Jess mostly felt bad for the girls: poor loves. This was just the beginning.

In her first job, as a waitress, Jess had been groped. While working in admin, she'd been told her boobs were too big – more than a handful was a waste, according to her boss. Afterwards, aged nineteen, she'd started running. But then trucks and taxis tooted at her and she hadn't enjoyed her jogs. As a receptionist at an accountancy firm, she'd been told she dressed too conservatively. And then, after she'd adjusted, 'This isn't a fashion parade,' and 'You're a distraction.' She'd felt confused and, yes, ashamed. That feeling had never gone away. There wasn't a woman alive, she realised, who hadn't experienced some of this. By the age of *fourteen*.

Next to her, Taj Low was smirking. Jess raised her gun and stapled: bang, bang, bang.

Hannah Appleby, holding a sheet of paper, was taking a selfie, as Dr Cato wrote on the whiteboard: #MeToo. When the #MeToo thing was in the news, Jess hadn't paid much attention. She was a middle-aged mum from the suburbs. Being pinched on the bum or cuddled by her boss's husband wasn't news. Jess looked to Bella, sitting to one side in her corner, re-reading the scattered sheets.

'Sunlight is the best disinfectant,' said Dr Cato, with a quick glance to Jess. 'What does that mean?'

By the time Jess shot the final staple, the genie within her was dancing on hot coals. She didn't have the courage of 'Gunhild' or the brain of Dr Cato. She didn't want to say the wrong thing, lose her temper or keep being hated. She didn't know what objectification meant until ten minutes ago. But, drat it, she did want to be a part of what came next! She'd helped shed light on that Insta account. She didn't want to go back to living in the dark.

Only problem was, she was out of posters.

43

Duncan

On her phone, Liv was sitting by the shallow end of the busy pool. Cody was thrashing about – over-swimming, if that was a thing. Duncan dropped to the bench beside her.

'Hello, you. You read the wrong List?' Liv smiled.

'No.' He watched Cody sinking mightily. 'Does he do that for half an hour?'

'Every week.' Liv returned to reading her phone.

Duncan took off his jacket and sagged slightly.

'To what do we owe this pleasure?'

'Spoke with another headhunter. It's going to be tougher than I thought.'

She pulled her focus to him. 'Why?'

'Well, senior associates are still being battered but not leaving; or they're leaving and are not prepared to believe we're any better.' He sighed. 'Some are happy staying where they are, hearing the right noises and heartened. But, not counting those who have already left to have a life, or babies, and haven't returned'—he rubbed his face—'doesn't leave a lot of suitable women.'

Liv seemed to run the numbers in her head. 'Yeah, makes sense.'

'I guess I hadn't thought much about it.'

A mum ran by, chasing a wet toddler. 'No, no, no,' shrieked the toddler. 'Not doing!'

'Sounds like you need someone ambitious but unhappy,' said Liv. 'Though not completely disillusioned.'

'Yeah.'

'Lucky woman's out there somewhere.'

Duncan put his head in his hands. Perhaps what the headhunter had said explained why Maggie Koh wasn't calling him back.

Liv rested her phone in her lap. 'While you're waiting for Wonder Woman, why don't you change what you can? Like the office environment, and how you're working in there. You said you're more efficient at home. Use that insight. Make small adjustments; be creative.' She tapped her phone. 'Little changes can have a massive effect – on how people feel. Behave. Perform.'

'Huh?'

And then, she was overflowing with words. A Dr Vic Cato and something called behavioural design featured heavily. As did the words *tweak* and *nudge*. Liv also recommended some book that advocated working in ninety-minute *sprints*. He listened, intrigued. He was far less sceptical than he let on. Everything was on the table, as far as he was concerned. And Liv seemed to have a lot of answers, though not to the problem of how he could reposition his clients from being demigods to reasonable humans.

Listening to her, Duncan did feel better. He rolled up his sleeves. Liv's second-hand stories were remarkable, her optimism infectious.

After a few minutes, he waved at Cody, who, against the odds, had made it to the other end. But, standing at the pool's edge, Cody either didn't see him or didn't want to. Instead, the littlest Winsome put his arms above his head and executed the worst dive Duncan had ever seen.

44

Wednesday

Liv

Forsaking work, Liv tailed Mary MacBeth as the teacher passed The Prove-dore and made for the cafe furthest from the school. Humming softly, Liv strolled into the coffee shop, which was furnished in exposed brick, unpolished timber and jutting metalwork. In a booth, Mary was apprais-ing the light fittings, which may have been deconstructed birdcages. Liv hoped Mary wasn't meeting anyone. Mary had taught the twins English in Year Five; she was a beloved teacher, and one of the few Liv knew as a human being.

Liv ordered a takeaway coffee then approached the booth. 'Mary? Hello there.'

Looking up, Mary's round face was pink in patches. Poor Mary. Liv smothered her surprise. She'd had similar eczema herself once, as a baby solicitor.

'Oh, Liv, if this is about Oscar, I'm sorry,' said Mary. 'But you need to talk with Miss Lee, his home room teacher.'

Mary fiddled with a knife as Liv tried not to stare. 'Oscar? Okay. Will do, thanks. I didn't know – Is it serious?'

Mary waved a scaly hand. 'Friendship issues, dropping basketball and whatnot. Don't worry, he'll find his way.'

Wrong-footed, Liv thought of her sons an hour ago: Oscar had showered for too long and used too much deodorant, fussed with his hair and left, without Jai, without saying goodbye; Jai had been texting from the moment he got up, stopping only to bathe. They'd both swatted Cody away as if he were a rogue drone. Situation normal? Not quite, but not dire. But since when had Oscar dropped basketball? Mary was eyeing the booth as if she was considering wriggling around it and away. Liv sat opposite her.

Up close, the teacher's eyes were veiny, like peeled green grapes.

'What is it, Mary?'

Mary MacBeth put her elbows on the table and forehead in her hands. 'Don't be nice to me!'

Liv leant forward. 'Mary, what is it? You can tell me.' Liv took in Mary's thinning, caramel-coloured crown. 'I'm an excellent listener, if a tad boastful.' Liv gave an encouraging smile.

Mary's concerns weren't really for her ears. But Liv had never seen Mary look so miserable.

'What the hell.' With a wheeze, Mary glanced about the cafe. 'I thought it would get better,' she whispered. 'But it's not.'

Mary scratched her pitted forearms. Liv tried to remember what she'd used to clear up her rash. 'What creams have you tried?'

Mary's watery green eyes were empty.

'Sorry, what's not getting better?'

Mary sighed. 'I love that school. I do.'

Mary had been at Carmichael for more than twenty years. She predated Tony and the first female students. Having arrived the same year as the tennis courts, Mary was as much a part of the school as the bell tower and the elm trees. It was Carmichael lore that Mary knew every child's name, their siblings' names, and their pets'.

'Everyone knows you live and breathe Carmichael, Mary.'

Liv was trying not to sound buoyed, but an unhappy Mary was a perfect conduit.

'At this rate, I'm not going to last till mid-year. But how can I leave those kids?'

'How can I help?'

Mary shook her head, then looked around the cafe again. Three tables of four were filled: all women, of various ages and sizes, mostly in athleisure wear. This type was much maligned beyond Bayside, but Liv could understand the appeal of those stretchy legs. Liv didn't recognise any faces among the chatting women.

'Yesterday, one of the young ones had a run-in with some Year Eight boys,' Mary whispered.

'Oh dear, that's no good.'

Deflated, Liv sipped her macchiato. She wasn't expecting students' issues. Mary was a dab hand with students. But who or what was a young one? A Year One? Year Seven?

'She's very new.'

Having trouble hearing, Liv leant in.

'Her office is adjacent to the woodwork room. Through the one-way glass,' mouthed Mary, 'she'd seen a boy showing his friends something on his phone and being lewd.'

Mary threw in a few lurid hand gestures. Liv nodded, pretending to get the gist of it. It seemed that Mary was talking about a teacher.

'That boy's collecting pics like footy cards . . . needless to say, she told him off. And he didn't take it well. Wouldn't give up his phone, stood over her, gave her a fright, basically. These boys are big now, as you know.'

Mary moved the sugar bowl aside, as if it were bugged. 'Straight after, she came to me, distressed, and the boy in question went to Palmer.'

Liv was confused again. She had a jab of worry.

'No one had warned her, you see,' whispered Mary MacBeth. 'He said to her, "You don't know who I am, do you?"'

Mary's eyes glistened – with frustration, disappointment, perhaps shame.

'What could I say to her? And the little thing's straight out of uni.'

Mary banged the table, and the cutlery holder jumped. So did Liv. Mary covered her mouth.

'What happened then?'

Mary shook her head.

'You can't stop there!' said Liv.

Mary spoke from behind her hands, as if someone might be lip-reading from across the room. 'Liv,' she said, 'don't let Oscar get swept up with him.'

Mary cocked a wiry eyebrow.

'I don't understand,' said Liv. 'Are you talking about Taj Low?'

'Hell's bells. You didn't know?' Mary struggled around the booth.

Liv was trying to keep up. If Taj was a troublemaker, how had she missed that?

'I know his mum but not him.'

'Please, don't tell anyone,' whispered Mary, on her feet now.

'Mary, I can't make that promise.'

Mary's face crumbled like pastry. Liv was about to apologise, but for far too long the wrong people had been apologising. For far too long, the wrong things had been confidential.

'Was Oscar with Taj in the woodwork room?'

Mary shook her head.

'Phew!' said Liv. 'Okay, listen, Vic Cato's working on this. Tell her what you've told me; she'll get Taj Low into shape.'

'I was at the briefing; we all were. But Dr Cato's just another of Tony's little projects—'

'She really isn't.'

Mary inhaled. 'Liv, it's a boys' club. Dr Cato or not, that's not going to change.' Seeing Liv's face, Mary seemed to soften. 'It's stacked against us, don't you see? We work absurd hours. Part-timers are discouraged. The young ones look ahead and don't see a future. Have you noticed the attrition rate among the junior teachers? They don't last two years.'

Liv blinked, processing.

'I know you mean well, but I'm sorry. It's too far gone.' Mary picked at her scaly hand. 'But your boys need you, Liv. They may be bigger, but they need you, now more than ever!'

45

Duncan

Duncan began his work day determined. First thing, he closed the door to his office, pulled its blind and worked, undisturbed, until around 11 am. Got a lot done. Sipping an apple juice, he was ready to try Maggie Koh again. He dialled and, this time, she picked up! Briefly. They agreed to speak further, later in the day. A video conference, of course. Though he disliked being on camera, he was used to it now. When she ended the phone call, he hopped up, opened his door and stared at his painting for five whole minutes. It was going to happen. It was! After lunch, he would read his juniors' work, hold their hands and discuss their careers. But he'd tell them that, from now on, he'd only look at something *once* on any given day. And he wasn't going to let Red ambush him in the hall, or the Men's. Or sneak appointments into his diary. Not anymore.

Around 3 pm, after a few chats and another satisfying *sprint*, he went for a brisk walk through Treasury Gardens. As an experiment, he left his phone on his desk. The day was mild, the sky cloudless and the birds raucous. He watched the wide-winged creatures flutter and swoop. One bird tried to filch a chunk of his hair, and he laughed as he ducked.

When he returned to his office, all was well and he felt reinvigorated, clear-headed, with a spot of poop on his shoulder for good luck. Scrubbing it off in the Men's, he couldn't wait for his video conference. He hoped that, in Perth, Maggie Koh was miserable and far-sighted, but feeling plucky.

46

Liv

Hot off the bus, Jai bounded into the kitchen, shot his lunchbox across the bench then burrowed into the fridge. A minute later, Cody came in and dove onto the couch for his daily quota of TV. When Jai re-emerged from the fridge with a jar of gherkins and a block of cheese, Liv counselled herself: give him a minute. She'd been looking forward to the boys coming home. This was, she suspected, a Winsome first.

'Someone mowed the lawn.'

'Yup.'

Having declined a suite of files, she'd also managed to have the fence paling fixed, order a new washing machine and change three light bulbs. After speaking with Mary, she'd snuck in a mid-morning yoga class too. Spent the whole session in corpse pose. So far, no one had noticed she wasn't rushing off to interview allegedly injured people and their defensive bosses. She'd mustered the courage to call Stella, too, to see how the Havelocks were faring – Blake at his new school, Stella without her – but Stella hadn't picked up, and Liv couldn't bring herself to leave a message.

'Where's Oscar?' Liv was bent over a black sports sock. Beside her was a stack of shirts and buttons, and a spool of pink cotton.

'Taj's, maybe.'

'When did they become so chummy?'

'I dunno. Since they both hate me? Taj's a dumb-arse.'

'Okay.' Liv felt a spike of worry. Since when did the twins hate one another?

Jai hesitated, held her eye. 'You know what he said the other day? "Who knew Grace Charters was hot?"' Jai shook his head. 'And now he's pissed because she doesn't like him.'

Liv was beginning to see a pattern. 'Did you have woodwork yesterday, perchance?'

'Nah, don't do woodwork.'

'Pleased to hear it. How was school otherwise?'

Jai plucked a pickle from the jar. He tossed his head back and ate the fat, green worm, thinking as he chewed.

'We had Dr Cato today in Health. She's good. Funny.'

Liv stitched her sock. Vic had said the classes were going well. Her first text had said, *Killing it!* In another life, Dr Cato could've been a loose cannon. Her second had said, *Big boys still fawning,* with a smiley face and fist bump. Liv hadn't had any update on Vic's interior decorating requests, though, or feedback on her draft charter.

'Dr Cato played college basketball, did you know that? For UConn! She was a Husky!' said Jai.

'Awesome. Anything else?'

'I heard she caught Taj passing a note about Bella. Notes happen all the time, but she's banned them. Taj has to "help out" in the Junior School playground at lunch *every day* this week.' Jai laughed. 'He's super pissed.'

Jai assembled a plate of cheese and crackers, then put a box of savoury Shapes and an apple on top and walked to the table. The tower wobbled. Sometimes Liv wondered at the workings of her boys' brains.

'If you muck around, you lose game time on Saturday, too.' Jai darted to contain his precarious snack.

'I love that woman already.'

'She is kind of like you: a bit weird. No offence.'

Ha. The box of Shapes hit the ground. Jai bent to retrieve them.

'We had to test these headsets for the IT department, too. Had to nod our heads as we listened to stuff.'

'What sort of stuff?

'A few tunes, and some radio editorial about gender equity, respect for women and stuff.'

Liv tried very hard not to smile. Vic had told her about a study analysing how behaviour affected thinking, not the other way around. Specifically, the effect of nodding. How, at some university, three groups of students were told that a market research company wanted to test headsets. The students listened to music and then an editorial about raising tuition fees at their university. While listening to the editorial, one group was told to nod vigorously; one group shook their heads; and one group had to keep their heads still. Lo and behold, the simple act of nodding revealed a big positive difference. The head-nodders agreed that their fees should go up! Similarly, shaking heads revealed a negative attitude, and the head-still folk were unmoved. How Liv loved these studies!

'We have a stack of new headphones to test, apparently.'

'Money well spent.' Liv grinned; she wondered if Vic was planning on letting the students in on the study's findings.

'You should see Mrs MacBeth. She sat in on our class after lunch. Brought another teacher with her. And Miss Lee took notes!'

Liv couldn't wipe that smile from her face.

'The teachers are being filmed, too. This new IT woman's setting up cameras.'

'That's wonderful.'

'I bet that'll stop Mr Waring and his skirt analogy!'

Analogy! Liv was close to tearing up. Out of sight, Cody screamed and thumped: what was he doing in the lounge room?

'What does Grace think?' Liv paused, her needle in the sock.

Jai shrugged, became bashful. 'We're not in the same class. But, yeah, I think she's into it. And she's talking to Bella again, so that's good. Dr Cato's not loading us up with facts and figures. She's telling stories, about her own life. Stuff like that. But, Mum, Grace still can't get her head around Rowan Whittaker-Smith being her boss one day. She's really bummed about it.'

'I should probably speak to her again.'

'No, please don't.'

Liv shrugged, resumed stitching.

'Thanks, Mum.' Jai grinned. 'It was hilarious, actually, Dr Cato taught everyone how to raise their hands, like we're in kindergarten. Because girls mainly do this.' Jai kept his elbows by his sides but raised his hand. He pulled a pouty face.

'And they have to do this!' He shot his hand into the air like a launching missile.

Liv laughed. Her son seemed energised in a way she hadn't seen before.

'And, guess what? I'm doing a survey,' he said, 'of everyone in Year Eight!'

'Wow!' Liv stabbed her left thumb with the needle. 'Did Dr Cato ask you to do that?'

'Yep.'

Liv sucked the pinprick of blood, then high-fived her son. 'What's it on?'

Jai glanced outside, and his leg began to jitter. 'You know, stuff.'

The great wall of blocked communication was rising from the kitchen tiles.

'I still don't get the link between what Blake did and housework, though; and why Dad's hanging around all of a sudden.' Jai hammered a grimace.

Liv snorted. 'The picture will get clearer.'

Vaguely, she remembered something. 'Didn't I ask you to write to Blake?

'Nah.'

Liv was pondering the difference between writing to Blake and writing to Grace and Bella; and why she hadn't pushed for it, when Jai nodded towards the lounge room. 'I hope Dad's not too mean to . . .'

'Don't worry, he won't be.'

Telling an anxious person not to worry was like telling a toddler in the midst of a tantrum to calm down.

She wrapped her arm around her son's wide shoulders. Hugs within the family were given freely. And this one, she thought, really knew how to work her.

47

Jess

A fresh pumpkin quiche was in the oven, a spinach salad was ready to be dressed, and the table set. Soon, her family would descend like hungry hotel guests. Morrie from meeting a new client and Grace from unspecified, possibly boy-related, activity at school. Grace had taken to riding her bike home, with Bella, which terrified Jess, but riding was safer than walking alone. Wasn't it? With one eye on the time, Jess continued her emailing. She hoped the dots were lining up the way Liv wanted. She'd dashed home from work for this, but hadn't made much of a hole in her contacts list. Two and a half messages later, Grace wandered in, eating an apple, and carrying her helmet and sax. Jess smiled.

'No basketball after school, hon?' Jess kept her eyes on the screen. Her desk was in a corner of the sunroom.

'Jai had to go.' Grace slumped into a beanbag.

Jess read a reply from Charvi. *I see what you're saying, kind of. Anyway, I'm happy if you're happy. Speak soon about that conservation thingo.* And another from Penny: *Thanks for the update. Missed you at training. Big game this week.* And from Alison: *WTF? You're friends with that woman now? Going to choir on Thursday?*

No one seemed particularly interested in Dr Cato/V. N. Kovach and her books, or what she'd be saying at Carmichael. Perhaps they knew of her already. Or perhaps they were living as Jess had been – with their head in a bucket. Along with the school's psychologist, Jess was organising

Dr Cato's parent talk. The turnout for these meetings at the school was normally around fifty people, but Jess was determined this one would be different. In Year Eight alone, there were 180 students, which meant 360 parents, give or take. Holding her friends' and acquaintances' attention, though, was proving to be a challenge. She began another email, upped the tempo. If she zipped, she could do another half-dozen before dinner. The trick was to personalise them: How was the snow in Hokkaido? Hope your Achilles is on the mend. Remember that broker we spoke about? Here's her number. By the way . . . She picked up *Bringing Up Gen Z*. There would be a good quote in there.

'Mum?'

'Mm?' Jess smiled at the book as she typed. 'Give me a sec.' Jess lost her train of thought. Backspace, backspace.

'Mum?' Grace's tone was urgent.

'What? What's the matter?' Turning to Grace, Jess noticed two things: Grace was staring at her, and wasn't connected to a phone.

'Everything alright, hon?'

'What are you doing?' Grace was barely moving her lips, as if the effort to speak was too much for her.

'Sending some emails. About Dr Cato.' Although modest, this was, Jess realised, a 'bid'. A moment when Grace was open to her and wanted to chat. She tore her fingers from the keyboard.

'How's it going?' said Jess. 'Do you like her?'

From a pocket, Grace produced a bottle of nail polish – a curious development – and proceeded to apply it. Slowly. 'She's okay, I guess . . .' Two fingertips later, she added: 'Did you tell her?'

That Jess hadn't managed, yet. She hadn't been alone with Dr Cato and, in the scheme of things, Lloyd Palmer's off comment was a blip on the radar. 'I haven't. But I will.'

'Yeah. Don't bother.'

Jess pushed her laptop aside. 'Did I miss something?'

Grace concentrated on her pinkie. Jess had guessed Dr Cato's objectification class would've either fired up the children, as it had her, or depressed them. She'd expected the new Grace to be firing. But Grace was as blue as the nail polish bleeding from the edges of her nails.

'You'll only make it worse,' Grace muttered.

'No, honey. The more we know, the more we can make school better. I promise.'

Grace shrugged and, dissatisfied, splayed her hands on her knees. To Jess, those fingers did look wrong, blue-tipped and without a screen. Grace sniffed at Vic's book.

'I'm going outside.'

'Outside?'

'Mum, half the boys at school are cocks.' Grace's stare became earnest but tinged with something hard. 'Cocks or losers. That's what we're stuck with. That's not going to change.'

'But, sweetie . . . It can. Have an open mind! We're just getting started.'

'Ugh.' Grace wandered outside and flopped onto the grass, as if she'd been shot.

48

Duncan

That evening, Duncan whistled as he readied himself to go home. He couldn't believe his luck. Maggie Koh *was* unhappy! Better still, she was *bored*! Boom! Rearranging his bookshelf, Duncan thought back to their video chat. It turned out that she was actively looking to move to Melbourne or Sydney, for personal reasons. Duncan had been delighted but tried not to look it. He'd made his pitch, outlined the firm's needs. Maggie hadn't baulked. She'd done a spot of homework, too. Asked a bunch of pertinent questions – about culture, targets, client mix. She cut to the chase, which he quite liked. It seemed slow, careful wooing wasn't for her. He was very mindful not to mislead her. He hoped he'd looked sufficiently friendly yet professional, high-achieving yet interesting. And functional. Being a people-person was a drawcard in this profession; the longer you stayed, the fewer well-adjusted peers you had. He'd also propped his bush painting behind him – and she'd noticed it! Surely a good omen. They'd arranged to meet the following Tuesday, in Melbourne. She'd put together some paperwork about her practice. If he liked her, he'd wheel in Michael and Henry. Unfortunately, those were the two she really had to impress.

Jacket on, bag over shoulder, Duncan sprang about the floor – eyeing the décor (beige and black) and the front desk (bare). He noted the mood of his staff – chugging coffees, looking drawn – as he said goodbye. They all should've taken themselves out for a mid-afternoon walk, he decided.

In bed that night, he planned to read more of that book Liv had recommended. Perhaps he ought to bring it into the office, share it around.

He was heading towards the lift when one of the headhunters called. Finding suitable, interested candidates wasn't being helped by Michael's reputation, she explained.

'You don't say?' Duncan said, with his hand on the button. 'Not much I can do about that.'

'To be clear,' the woman said, as if Duncan missing something. 'It's the firm's brand, too. W&U is known as a sweatshop.'

For a moment, Duncan felt defensive and irritated. Theirs was a 'hyper-competitive culture', pure and simple, like lots of others. Then the lift doors sighed open. 'Yeah,' he said. 'Now *that* I'm working on.'

49

Liv

For the first time that month, Duncan and Liv enjoyed the relative ease of a typical weekend. Friday night basketball passed reasonably smoothly, being a short drive away and a win; and Jai shot the lights out. Oscar had pleaded food poisoning, though Liv suspected the PlayStation was calling to him. Everyone deserved a week off every so often, Liv figured, so she let him be. Hoping his new basketball apathy would be short-lived, she opted not to feed it with attention. Otherwise, Saturday sport and Sunday training and footy came and went. Jai was in good form again, firming up new friendships at school, and a 'still recovering' Oscar made scones. In and out of his study, Duncan was mysteriously upbeat, and Cody's excitable antics were amusing. Their littlest spent most of Sunday on the trampoline.

'Bet you can't jump for forty-five minutes straight!' Liv yelled to him.

Wildly, merrily, he jumped. 'Can too!'

She sat, timing him and reading the newspaper. Once he was done, grinning and hot, she'd said, 'Bet you can't do that again.' And off he went again. Having a win here and there was important, Liv decided. Success was a tolerance–goodwill multiplier. And, that particular weekend, she was brimming with bonhomie.

When Liv's phone rang on Sunday evening, she was watching her show, but she found herself hoping it was Stella. She longed to share her news about Vic Cato and Carmichael, and celebrate their boys' near-miss. But, she realised, it was impossible. Losing a friend was like experiencing a death. A small one, like a cat's. She wondered how Jai felt about that. Was Blake more of a dog than a cat?

Fortunately, these questions were moot. It was Jess.

'Sorry to bother you,' Jess said. 'But something's wrong with Grace.'

Liv glanced to the twins' closed bedroom door. She paused her television program.

'She seems, I don't know, depressed. About school. And some loser called Rowan.'

Liv pushed aside her mug of tea.

'I don't think he's being mean or anything. I didn't quite get it . . .'

Liv relived the stepped-on-mouse sound Grace had made in her kitchen. She sighed. Jai wouldn't like it. But Jai didn't understand everything, yet. Least of all the Art of the Difficult Conversation. Besides, over the phone was a gentler option. And Jai was in his room.

'I could have a word, if you like? Is she there?'

'Oh, would you? Thanks so much.'

Liv stared at the fair woman frozen on her television screen. No make-up. No 'do.

Two minutes later, Grace's faint, breathy voice came on the line. She sounded as if she'd been drained and only her dregs remained.

'Grace, I want to apologise. For the other day, I was a bit blunt.'

Liv looked around her large, quiet house. Down the hall, Duncan was at work in his office and unlikely to come out. Ditto the twins. Cody was already down. Liv sat up.

'What I meant to say was . . . You don't need to do a hundred after-school activities, or get ninety per cent in everything. You sure don't need to take raunchy pics or look like a doll. What you do have to do is use your voice, go for what you want and not take no for an answer.'

'Okay.'

Liv rubbed her cheeks. That last bit didn't sound right. Context was everything.

'What I mean is, don't give up on your dreams, Grace; because it's going to be tough. It is. The Andrews out there have a head start. And you're going to fail sometimes. You will. But fail fast and get up again. Have a go at lots of things. See where they take you. Because you're a smart, hardworking girl. You can go far! But make sure you work on yourself as much as your studies. You know what I mean? Develop a strong sense of yourself. There are lots of amazing girls and women out there, Grace, taking a stand. Be like them! And practice being uncomfortable and assertive and, hey, even unlikeable! But not unkind, you know? And don't take any notice of the idiots. Stand tall and keep your eye on the main game.' Liv hesitated. 'That's what your mum and I are trying to do. So you have it better than we have. And then your daughters and sons can have it better than you, you know what I mean? We're a chain, Grace. We're links, you and me. Okay?'

Liv wondered if she'd got carried away.

'Grace?' Liv prayed the girl wasn't crying again.

'Okay. Bye.'

That went well, thought Liv, hanging up.

50

Tuesday

Duncan

The day came, not a moment too soon. Duncan chose his favourite suit, cleaned his shoes and left early. The drive in flowed, the traffic was light and the bay, a wash of mauve, was topped with streaky, pink-fringed clouds. He sang along to *Hamilton* the whole way in. Didn't think ahead to what he'd say to her, nor to their meeting with Michael and Henry. Made himself stay completely and utterly in that car. Years of training.

Ten hours later, at the Flamingo Bar, a buzzing Duncan was ordering champagne. He couldn't wait to tell Liv, to play Uno with the twins, to tickle Cody. He had years to catch up on. But first he wanted to toast their mutual good fortune. Retrieving his wallet, Duncan realised he was always the one buying the drinks. The guy at the table facing the wall, the last to help himself, the first to offer his seat. His mum called him 'Gallant'. But maybe there was another word for it. This evening, he felt like casting it off.

'Come on buddy, come on,' he said softly, as the bartender roved for an ice bucket.

He put the pitter-patter in his stomach down to excitement. Michael and Henry had been blown away by Maggie Koh, as he had. Armed with a bottle and two glasses, Duncan wove through the filling bar.

Maggie raised her hand, as if he'd lost her. Across the cocktail lounge, she looked sophisticated and bright and confident. The closer he got to her, the more he wondered if this was such a good idea. Down the track, when the deal was done, they'd all go for a proper dinner to celebrate.

But he didn't have anywhere to be tonight, he reminded himself. Didn't have a deadline looming. Or a pick-up. He slowed, conscious of an uptick in that pitter-patter. He wondered if he was more excited than he ought to be. But his sabbatical was one step closer and, soon, he could be freed up! If that wasn't exciting, he didn't know what was. Pouring the drinks, he sat with his back to the bar. He raised his glass and the noise seemed to drop.

'To many successful years at Winsome & Ueland, together.'

Maggie clinked her glass on his, firmly. He didn't know why he'd said that. He hadn't told Maggie about his plans for a sabbatical and, after, the lessening of his workload. Maybe that was dodgy of him. But he wouldn't be heading off for months yet. Besides, Winsome & Ueland was perfect for her: boutique and still punching above its weight, despite its staffing hiccups. He sipped from his glass; the champagne seemed to evaporate on his tongue. Maggie smiled at him, as if she was enjoying the same sensation. He remembered what he'd said that morning: how, together, they could rebuild the mergers and acquisitions practice. How in adversity there was opportunity. He'd become quite swept up. The idea wasn't unappealing, though, he thought as he looked into her perfectly round, licorice-coloured eyes.

'A partnership is like a marriage,' Maggie was saying. 'A leap of faith. Except profitable, for all parties.'

'Too right.' Duncan felt as if he'd inhaled a bubble. She clinked his glass again. She certainly seemed to know what she wanted.

Already, this decision felt fateful. Winsome & Ueland would be reinvigorated. He thought of Liv and her efforts. Maybe he wouldn't need a break. Closing his door more often, bringing in Maggie, having a rested George back. Things *were* looking up, and he could introduce more small changes. While he wasn't necessarily convinced of their power, they couldn't hurt. Liv's stories were persuasive.

Maggie was talking about champagne. About an old stone winery. About eating truffles by lantern-light. Duncan caught himself staring at her jet-black, cascading hair. There was so much of it. You could lose your fist in there.

Maggie's thick eyelashes fluttered. 'Duncan . . . what is it?' she said. 'You look stricken.'

'No, no. I'm great. Couldn't be better.' He pushed his chair back. Made himself stare at the pearly light above her head.

It wasn't his fault Maggie looked as she did, he told himself; and it wasn't her fault either. Just as it wasn't his fault she let him hold the door open and pull her chair out; and he'd enjoyed her appreciation. Granted, he didn't pull out his male colleagues' or clients' chairs. But he bought their beers. Lately, everything had become complicated, he decided. People were overthinking everything.

'Where are you and the family looking at living over here?'

She listed her options. 'But I'm leaning towards Bayside.'

Duncan dabbed his lip. 'Good-o.'

Were uninvolved men and women meant to live and work in close proximity? Didn't he read in one of Liv's books that simply putting two people together constantly can lead to something blossoming? Particularly if what they did together was dangerous. Did flying count? You bet it did. Especially for him. They'd better fly separately on those occasional trips to Perth. Maybe he ought to avoid meeting her one on one outside of the office, too.

He felt like a teenager again; this time, one who'd taken a wrong turn and ended up in the girls' dorm. At shower time.

Speaking of which, partnership meetings at Michael's men's club would need to be relocated. He hadn't thought of that. Was this buyer's remorse? They hadn't even signed yet. He shoved his chair further back. Treat Maggie Koh like one of the guys, he told himself. But what did that look like? Little eye contact? Small talk about football? He didn't even like football.

A waiter deposited nibbles, with a shy glance to Maggie.

Why hadn't he noticed that hair and those eyes earlier? He'd been in too much of a rush, he supposed – wanting to woo her. Unbidden, the words *shotgun wedding* crossed his mind.

Maggie was checking her phone. He could see a wallpaper image of a child of four or five.

'It's a huge thing you're planning to do,' he said, thinking aloud. 'Uproot yourself. And your kids. No second thoughts?'

Maggie shook her head, smiled. 'Not bringing the kids.'

'No?' He tried to contain his reaction as she explained, once she'd settled in, she planned to spend five days in Perth every month. 'If it all works out,' she said, 'they can come later.' She seemed to hold his eye. He wasn't sure what she meant by 'all works out.'

'Politicians do it,' she added. 'Spend twenty weeks a year in Canberra.'

It struck Duncan that she was planning on spending less time with her kids so he could spend more time with his. Was that a win? Though he'd resisted doing so up to this point, not wanting to pry, Duncan asked about her children's father.

'It suits him. He doesn't have a proper job.' Her eyes pierced his again. 'No ambition.'

For several fuzzy reasons, her answer made him nervous. A sour waitress deposited more hot titbits.

'Have you noticed yet,' said Maggie, leaning forward conspiratorially, 'how women don't tend to like me?'

'Ah, no, can't say that I have.'

He'd put a few feelers out about her. No one had mentioned that. However, all three of those he had asked were male, he realised now. He watched the waitress depart, scowling. Maggie's reception at W&U this afternoon had also confused him. When he, Henry and Michael had emerged jubilantly from their meeting with her, half of the admin staff had seemed noticeably nonplussed.

'They think I'm going to pick their pockets.' Maggie threw back her head and roared.

'No? Is that right?'

Sitting back, Duncan swapped his half-full champagne flute for a battered pepper. 'Next time you're over, you must meet Liv.'

51

Liv

After dinner, Liv was at her desk when she heard the call she'd been expecting for almost a week. Of course, when it came, Duncan wasn't home.

'Mum? Mum! Can you come here?'

This was a cry Liv had heard many times, daily. Liv dreamt these words. She heard them when she was on the toilet, in the shower, asleep at 2 am. She'd been hearing these words since the boys could first speak. Before then of course the sounds were cries. Having heard them so many times, she rarely responded on the first refrain. Before the Lists, she'd sigh, thinking, What now? (Was that Cody, again?) And then, Bad mum. And she'd get up. Post-Lists, the cry had eased, but it wasn't dead.

After the third call, Liv rose from finessing her charter. (At least Vic had given her feedback.) This caller could have been either twin, but Jai called more often. And was the one with the special, now possibly overdue, homework. She found him at his desk, while his brother snored on the top bunk. It didn't occur to her children to whisper around their sleeping siblings. Just as it didn't occur to them to move their bodies to find her. More items for their Lists. *Whisper when people are sleeping. Move to me. Call for Dad.*

'What's up?' she whispered.

'This stupid survey . . .' Jai looked predictably freaked. 'Kinda been avoiding it.'

'And how is this relevant to me?'

'I haven't made a survey before!'

'Shush, I know that . . .' Jai had probably never asked ten consecutive questions of anyone other than her before, either. 'You can do it, Jai. It won't be hard.'

She retreated to the door.

'No, I can't!'

Jai was willing her to pull up a seat and 'help'. Because that was what the old Liv would've done. The old Liv wasn't alone on this. Some of the homework projects Liv had observed at Carmichael over the years had been spectacular. But the one on the gut, made of coils of pink and white marshmallows, had been particularly memorable. She'd outdone herself – and earned an A-plus.

'When's it due?' she whispered from the hall.

'Tomorrow.'

Liv huffed. 'What did Dr Cato say to do?'

He pointed at his screen. 'She told me to use this site.'

'So . . . read it carefully and go for it.'

Jai pulled an ugly face. 'I don't know what questions to ask.'

Liv sighed. How was he meant to know what to do? He did need her. It didn't matter that she hadn't made a survey before either.

She tiptoed to his desk. 'Well, what did Dr Cato want you to ask – what's the topic?' Liv rubbed her scalp.

'Something about sexual harassment.'

Liv pointed at Jai's handouts, including one of her favourite cartoons by Judy Horacek. Then she scanned the website. It sounded as easy as filling in a form. 'Have a go.'

'Can't you stay?' Jai fluttered his lashes and pouted his prettiest pout.

'Jai-Jai,' she said. 'You need to work this out for yourself.'

'I know, I know. Just stay, okay? Please . . .'

On the top bunk, mumbling in his sleep, Oscar put the doona over his head.

'Oh.' She dropped her voice. 'For a few minutes.'

She retrieved her laptop, sat on the floor and half-watched him work. At one point, he read a series of startling questions to her. Following

Dr Cato's advice, Jai had tried to keep his language simple and direct, and avoid double negatives. His initial questions were: 'Have you had your bottom pinched, or boobs squeezed, or pussy grabbed or otherwise handled by a person of the opposite sex or any sex?'; 'Have you never experienced touching that was not welcome?'; and 'How often have you felt unsafe at school because of sex?'

'You might want to have another go,' she said.

Jai shuffled words, read aloud what he'd done, and rewrote it again.

Gradually, the questions improved. Jai opted for multiple choice answers. Questions ranged from, 'Have you been sexually harassed: a) at school; b) on the way to school; c) at camp; or d) everywhere?' To, 'Have you been subject to: a) sexual comments or jokes; b) unwelcome touching; c) unwelcome staring; d) actual sexual assault; or e) all of the above?' He asked who they should report harassment to, either as a witness or participant: a) a teacher; b) a parent; c) a friend; d) the school crossing lady? He wasn't sure that 'participant' was the right word but he didn't want to write 'victim', and 'harassee' sounded weird. Liv agreed. They settled on 'harassed blameless person'. After another hour, Jai was whizzing along. A switch had been flicked in him. The reason why Blake was pseudo-expelled seemed to also be clearer to him.

'I'm going to offer a chance to win gold-class movie tickets for people who do this within a week,' he said. 'What do you reckon?'

'Good idea.' Liv yawned, but she was impressed.

At the last minute, Jai decided to add six more questions. Off-subject but relevant, apparently. 'We're getting new posters for the science labs,' was all he said.

'Well done, good night.'

Liv kissed his cheek. The survey might not be A-plus material, but Vic would straighten it out.

'See you in the morning,' said Jai. 'I love you.'

These words had been uttered every night for three years. The sole remnant of his first fierce bout of OCD, which involved, among many other things, saying those words twenty times every bedtime. It'd taken her a month to tease out what the fear underlying his various bedtime rituals was – that he'd die overnight in his sleep otherwise. It'd taken them another month to get the twenty declarations of love down to one. Liv could live with one.

'See you in the morning. Love you too.'

She checked Oscar was breathing and kissed his fuller cheek. She realised she hadn't had a real chat with him in days. Hopefully, Duncan had.

52

Wednesday

Liv

The next morning, poorly slept, Liv rose early. Vic had asked her to come in and watch the first footage of the teachers – Mr Waring, in fact. This was something she could do from home once she'd mastered it. Her job was to count facial reactions – smiles, nods and scowls; the participation of boys and girls in answering questions, and being asked questions; and the types of questions asked. A curious job, but Liv, an excellent note-taker, was happy to oblige.

To her surprise, a bloodshot Duncan was pulverising apples and carrots in the kitchen.

'Been working?'

'Nope. Paying bills. But guess what?' he yelled. 'We've found her!'

'What? Already?'

Duncan turned off the juicer as Oscar emerged, dripping, in a towel, and nicked a muffin.

'Turns out, we're very efficient.' Duncan kissed her nape. 'Everyone, ah . . . loves Maggie Koh . . . even Henry.'

Liv filled a glass for Cody. Where was he? She clasped the glass, tight. Only days ago, hadn't this process been floundering? Time was disappearing in chunks. 'How many other candidates did you meet?'

'In the end? Yeah . . . none.'

Unease ran across Liv's shoulders. Where was Jai? From the lounge room came the sound of gunfire.

Startled, Liv turned. 'What was that?'

'Ha . . . mm,' said Duncan, mishearing. 'Doctor of Laws. Ten years in mergers and acquisitions. Finalist in Young Lawyer of the Year a few years back.'

'Jai, time to get up!' yelled Liv. 'Oscar, you need to get dressed. Anyone seen Jai's iPad? And Cody?'

'Henry reckons she's the full package.'

Liv froze. Once, she'd been described as the 'full package' herself. Then, it'd seemed high praise even though she wasn't quite sure what it meant. Today, she decided, it was at least one part insult.

She also had a hunch W&U's due diligence wasn't what you'd call exhaustive. One inappropriate question was burning her tongue.

'How old?' said Oscar.

Liv beamed.

'Huh? Oh, I don't know. Hard to tell. Early thirties.'

'Old,' said Oscar, morosely, as Liv said, 'Young.'

'Married?' asked Oscar, who was chewing with his mouth open, though Liv didn't mind.

'Just separated, two little kids. It's timing, you see.'

'Yeah, I see.'

Gloomily, Oscar eyed his reflection in the oven. Poked his dark rings. 'Left her husband for her career, hey? Typical.'

WTF? Where did that come from? Liv took a bite of a muffin.

Oscar continued, 'What does she loo—'

'She's from Perth, did I mention that?' said Duncan. 'She's moving across. On her own.'

'Wow.'

'Yeah.'

'Where does she stand on quotas?' said Liv. 'On work–life balance? On women helping women? On shaking the place up? Is she going to support your efforts?'

Oscar groaned, and Duncan wrestled with him.

'Dad!'

Oscar scrambled to keep his towel. Sheepish, Duncan got to his feet.

'I have to wash my hands!'

'You just had a shower! Duncan . . .?'

'Oh, well, hopefully she's up for it.'

Liv pulled herself back. 'Hopefully?'

'We've never asked the men.'

'Ha!' Oscar flicked a tea towel at Liv.

'Ouch! Well, you should have!' Liv felt increasingly confused. She looked from her son to her husband to her muffin – it looked like chocolate but tasted like coffee.

'Where's my second muffin?' Cody sprang, as if by magic, from the lounge room. (These kids of hers were hell-bent on equity. 'He had two, I want two.')

'No!' said Liv. 'Oscar, are they mocha?'

By way of answer, Oscar tossed another muffin to his brother before pilfering another two and stomping off.

'Noooo!' said Liv.

Duncan raised his hands. 'I thought you'd be happy.' He pulled her close. 'Liv, already people are saying Maggie Koh could be the best thing to happen to W&U in years. I'm bringing her in, to free me up. So I can hang out here with all of you.'

His breath was unusually bad this morning, riddled with alcohol.

'Awesome.' Liv tried for a smile as she wriggled free. 'Where's Jai? He's going to miss the bus.'

53

Duncan

En route to the ensuite, Duncan unearthed Cody. Wedged between the couch and wall, the boy was concentrating, hard, on Jai's iPad. That wasn't a bad thing, was it? Duncan gave him five minutes to finish up, and headed off. In the bathroom, yawning, he undressed slowly, ran the water. The pressure was firm but he waited. It was chilly out and lukewarm in. Someone had used up the hot.

Naked, tired, Duncan was committed. Bracing himself, he stepped in, head first. Made a caveman yelp. He was ignoring the pain when the bathroom door opened. Oscar. The underdog. His favourite son, truth be told. Oscar was holding a toothbrush. Twiddling it. The boys usually bathed in the family bathroom next to the twins' room. This infiltration of the ensuite was curious. Oscar was looking in the mirror at him in the shower. Oscar opened his mouth, but no words came out and the toothbrush didn't go in.

On Oscar, more hair had sprouted; he seemed stretched, too, if also less toned. His face was changing as well, more angular. More spots on those cheeks. Duncan marvelled. Was he like that once, another body ago?

Cody's scream filled the space. 'No! No! No!' Bangs. Thuds.

'You need to stop!' Liv was loud, but not yelling. 'Give me that, please. Now.'

'But Dad said—'

Uh-oh, thought Duncan.

'Dad—' said Oscar.

'Shut the door, will you?'

Oscar looked to the gaping door. Kicked it shut. Stuck the toothbrush in his mouth.

The sounds of Cody's screaming faded. Duncan had hoped, when he gave Cody that old iPad, that the *Fortnite* cat hadn't snuck out of the bag. It'd taken Jai and Oscar a year to give up that all-eclipsing shooter game. Part Hunger Games, part opioid, if that game had Cody in its clutches, they were screwed.

Oscar was still looking at him.

'Thanks, matey.'

Duncan closed his eyes, and the water dwindled as Oscar turned on the tap. He'd work from home today.

It was high time for those gifts.

54

Liv

As soon as Liv stepped into the twins' room, she saw Jai's screen. On his bed, still in his PJs, Jai was furiously thumbing his phone. Liv pointed at his desk. 'What's that about?'

Jai rose and, bent at the waist, studied the early results. 'Not sure, but it's going crazy.'

'What is?'

'It's the survey.'

'What?'

Startled, Jai tried to read her face. But Liv was reading the numbers over his shoulder. Already, people were completing the survey and uploading responses. Presumably, at the tram stop and on the bus, in their parents' cars and on the toilet.

'Didn't you have to show Dr Cato first?'

'I don't know. Was I meant to?' Jai began to flap his arms. 'Oh, shit. Oh, shit.'

Oscar marched in, still half-naked; on Jai's screen, graphs and tables and pie charts were evolving by the minute. The technology was rather spectacular. And the results were coming in so quickly. Who knew so many kids wanted gold pass movie tickets?

'Wow.' The muscles in Liv's gut were grinding like industrial mixers.

'What?' Oscar mumbled, tugging up his shorts.

Liv moved to Jai's side. Watched the results tabulate. If she was reading the data correctly, more girls than boys were answering. Had Jai somehow skewed the test to draw in girls? Maybe. But the numbers of respondents who'd experienced harassment were high. Maybe these girls and boys were motivated to do the survey because they'd been harassed. Someone had even clicked 'sexual assault' as a response. Liv checked that one again. Sexual assault! She moaned. How had Jai defined that?

As the responses poured in, Liv sank to the carpet. 'What's that table about?'

Jai bit his lip. 'Maths. People's grades. What girls think . . . I dunno . . . I shouldn't've added it.'

Hugging herself, Liv re-read the results. To her mind, harassment and STEM weren't natural bedfellows. Then again, maybe they were.

Oscar peeked over Jai's shoulder.

'What've you done now?' Oscar gave his shorts a final tug, and the button flew off. 'Shit.'

Liv had to admit, Oscar was right: Jai had done it again. And this time Blake had nothing to do with it. Liv wrapped a hand over her mouth. Was her son courageous or completely thick?

'How did you send it to so many people?'

'I put it on Instagram, made a private story . . . added everyone at school.' Jai shrugged as Duncan sauntered in, wrapped in a towel. Oscar was shaking his head.

'What's going on?' Duncan's skin was very pink.

Liv searched Jai's face. His distress was no doubt a version of hers.

'What's up with him?' said Duncan.

'Sexual harassment,' she hissed.

Oscar rolled his eyes, as he walked out.

'What?' Duncan's pink turned scarlet. 'When? Where?' He looked about the room, as if for a mouse.

The sound of yelling bounced down the hallway – again. A second later, Cody hollered. Then something slammed. Twice. Another complex emotion skittered across Duncan's face. Guilt?

'Ah ... at school.' Liv looked up, her mind jamming. 'Not by Jai; though, he has royally screwed up this time.'

'Where were you, when all this screwing up was going on?' Duncan's face was a cryptic crossword, and she gave up on it.

'Same place I always am. Where were you?'

He waggled his now ringing phone at her and strode off. So much for his fledgling emotional literacy.

'Did you say Cody could play *Fortnite*?' she yelled after him.

Jai sank into his swivel chair and spun. His anxiety was hoovering up hers, Duncan's and anyone else's within five kilometres. The chair was practically airborne when Jai collided with the bed. He shrieked, 'Ow, ow, ow!'

Liv's hands curled into fists. Why was everything so fraught this morning? She took a deep breath. 'Jai-Jai, you okay?'

Jai's toe was dripping fat, red tears onto the floorboards. Good thing Oscar, squeamish at the sight of blood, had gone. Jai looked six years old and bursting to cry. Until recently, Jai hadn't cried since last winter, when his team lost the footy grand final by a point. Over the past year, Liv had wondered where her boys shoved their tears. But here they were.

'Mum?' Jai's voice held strains of anger. 'Mum! I've got *blood*!'

55

Jess

Jess was meant to be at work, tallying cinnamon and turmeric. But this was an emergency. Boys caught out behaving badly, again! Grace hadn't done the survey yet, but she'd told Jess about it. (Grace had been sunnier, lately, thank goodness.) Secretly, Jess was glad Grace hadn't done it. She simply would not cope if Grace had been *molested* at school, and was only now telling anyone about it, anonymously! (On that, Grace had assured Jess she hadn't been *molested*. Jess hoped Grace understood what that meant.)

Outside the school, Jess saw Bella. Something jarred as Bella walked in the main gate. Gaining on her, Jess observed tween girls sizing Bella up and giggling. When Mr Crisp emerged from the underground car park, he did a double-take, too. In a black suit and spotted blue tie, Mr Crisp was late. Most mornings, you could see him in his office through the stained glass window, surrounded by people and books. He was, judging by his usual speed-walking, a busy man. But, this morning, he was moving slowly. 'Bella?'

'Good morning, Mr Crisp,' said Bella.

On the driveway, Bella stopped a metre from the principal. She seemed taller, somehow; her shoulders were back, her chin up. Two curious teachers passed, along with a dozen students, regarding Bella as if she were a new and exotic plant. Jess smiled at those she knew. Mr Crisp considered his watch. He moved his tongue and lips about, as though he might have a seed stuck in his teeth.

'In my office, now,' he said.

Then it dawned on Jess: Bella's legs were covered by grey, slightly long trousers. She was wearing a thick, navy jumper beneath her jacket too. The trousers must have been her older brother's.

'I'm going to miss home room, sir.'

'Yes, you are.'

Bella's big doe eyes turned to Jess.

'Oh . . . do you mind if I come?'

Mr Crisp pivoted, wincing.

'I have a meeting,' said Jess. 'But I can join late.' She kept her gaze steady and absolutely did not giggle. 'I've been thinking of bringing up this very thing.'

Mr Crisp nodded.

In Mr Crisp's office, again: twice in one term and never before in five years. Jess didn't want to make a habit of this. Especially as she was pretending to be Bella's second mum. She hoped the girl wasn't in too much trouble.

'What's this about, Bella?' Mr Crisp said.

'Pardon?' Bella's glance swept to Jess, who nodded.

'What is your objective in wearing those pants?' he said. 'The boys' uniform, Bella, is for boys.'

'I know that, sir,' she said. 'But I want to wear it.'

'That's not the way the world works.'

Jess wanted to say that, she was beginning to realise, the world could be changed. But the silence wasn't inviting. Besides, she didn't know much about the winter uniform code, except boys wore long pants and their hair mustn't touch their collar, while girls wore skirts, tights and no earrings.

'Bella?'

Bella coughed. 'I'm sick of having my bra strap pinged, my breasts perved at and my skirt lifted.'

'Ah.' Mr Crisp sat back. 'Indeed.'

Jess felt a jolt of energy.

'What's brought this on? That Instagram business?'

'No. I've been thinking about it for a while.'

'Your timing is curious.'

Bella shrugged. 'I got boobs in Year Six.'

Mr Crisp raised his eyes to the ceiling. 'Yes. Well.'

Jess tried hard not to smile.

'You told me the other day to think carefully about how I wanted to dress.'

'Uh-huh,' he said, solemnly, to the ceiling. 'Where did you get those trousers?'

Bella's eyes flashed at Jess. 'From Blake Havelock.'

Surprised, Mr Crisp let his eyes drop to Bella's. The girl held his stare. His briefcase remained unopened on the desk. His computer was off. Jess was trying to catch up, too. Mr Crisp shook his head. On a side table, the local papers were folded. Their headlines: 'Local Grammar in damage control'; and 'Can Carmichael turn the tide?'

Crossing her legs, Jess rearranged her skirt. In skirts, you were more conscious of how you sat, she thought. And the weather. Wind. Eyes.

'I don't see why girls can't wear trousers,' Jess said. 'They are warmer, and more comfortable. And they're not limiting like a skirt. I really was planning on bringing this up.'

That small lie again; Jess forgave herself.

At that moment, Dr Cato rode her bicycle up the driveway. She was pedalling merrily, wearing yellow pants and no helmet.

'I need to think about this,' said Mr Crisp.

Jess smiled at Bella, who swelled.

'If you hurry, you should get to first period on time. I'll see your home room teacher knows you're here.'

'Thank you, sir.' Bella rose, straightened her jacket and left.

'Thank you . . . Tony.' Jess extended her hand, not something she usually did. 'That was fun.'

'Thank you.' His smile flickered.

His grip was firm, firmer than she'd expected.

56

Liv

Bursting into Lloyd Palmer's office, Liv was too wired to sit, so she jiggled. The assistant principal moved around her as if she were flicking a blade. What she held was in fact a piece of paper. Watching, Vic was sitting calmly, Ethan Humphries was teaching, thank god, but Jess was running late. So Liv jiggle-paced. On her way in, speaking with Vic, Liv's reaction to the survey results had shifted. This wasn't about Jai, or her. This was about culture again; the culture beneath this school's five-star veneer. Vic's data analysis was bearing that out, at least in relation to STEM. Exasperated, Liv took in Lloyd's tasteful office. The only things it revealed were his two athletic sons and a passion for cycling. The cycling paraphernalia outnumbered the happy snaps. She glimpsed a framed jersey. Silver trophies – silver men on silver bikes.

Someone knocked, then scurried in: Jess, beaming. A quick flurry of greetings ensued before Lloyd sat forward, his big shoulders slumped, his hands clasped. 'I'm all yours.'

'If I may,' said Vic. 'Last night—'

'Do you know what this is?' Liv cut in, flapping a piece of paper at Lloyd.

Politely, Lloyd turned from Vic to Liv.

'This is a travesty. A two-pronged and dreadful indictment of this school.'

He looked at her hand, as if the blade had become a pistol. His face changed – in a split second Liv saw fear. Vic was watching as if Liv might blast off a finger.

'These are the results of a survey of Year Eights,' Liv said. 'A broad-ranging survey covering everything from squeezed boobs to future Physics dropouts.'

Lloyd's face mottled. Liv gave him the page of – regrettably – pink and blue graphs and tables.

'Who created this?'

Liv took a deep breath. 'My son, Jai.'

Lloyd's face twisted like a dish cloth.

'I asked him to,' said Vic. 'I realise I should've had it authorised—'

'But he sent it out,' said Liv, 'without running it by Vic. He wasn't thinking. He was tired and excited and . . .'

She stopped, recognising her over-invested old form. Still standing, she put both hands on Lloyd's desk and leant forward. Another power pose. 'You need to read it,' she said. 'Now.'

Lloyd frowned as his gaze flicked from Liv to the page. They each stared at the paperwork as if at a Petri dish where something smelly grew. Liv wished again Jai had chosen yellow and green; and hadn't mixed the two combustible issues.

Lloyd's long index finger followed the lines of data.

'I guess you're in charge of pastoral care.' Jess's smile quavered. 'But who's responsible for Year Eight Science?'

Lloyd didn't look up. 'That's me too.'

The women let the words hover between them for thirty seconds. Finally, Lloyd sat back; his colour returned.

'I don't know what's worse,' said Liv. 'The harassment numbers or the STEM.'

'Oh, definitely the STEM!' said Jess. 'Especially those girls good at Maths, being turned off.'

'That's not news, you know, Jess,' said Vic.

'Is to me,' said Jess, embarrassed. Fleetingly, Liv felt for Jess. But at least Jess was speaking up.

Lloyd opened his jacket; four coloured pens stood to attention in his pocket. He plucked the green. Put a star next to a blue table.

'For me, it's about safety first,' said Vic. 'Many girls *and* some boys don't feel safe here.' Vic looked about, as if a groper might spring out of a cupboard. 'How can they learn to their full potential if they feel unsafe? While I'm here to address some of this, the school needs to own the prevalence of the problem and take on those targeted tweaks across the board.'

Lloyd put a green star next to another table and sat back, nodded benignly; a news reader waiting for his cue.

'Lloyd?' said Vic.

He pushed the page to one side. 'Ladies, thank you for coming to me with this. I can understand your disappointment.' He dialled up his smile. 'These are complex issues. Human nature, to an extent. But Carmichael is on it. We are, one hundred per cent, doing our bit.'

He started clicking away on his screen. Liv frowned as a printer began to whirr.

'We mustn't forget the role of biology,' he continued. 'These students are undergoing great change at their age. We need to respect that, and their passion, their *curiosity*. I mean, it is only natural. We must let kids be kids. Teenagers be teenagers.'

Liv's frown deepened as Lloyd smiled and stacked the printed pages into neat lots.

'My niece, who is in Year Six in that building there,' said Jess, pointing, 'texted this morning that Science is boring and boys like it but not girls. Girls aren't *brilliant* enough, apparently.'

Jess shook her head, incredulous.

Lloyd stapled documents with yellow staples. 'Now, Jess, we do have to recognise the differences in our students. Girls can't kick as hard as boys. That's a fact. But I'm a dad. I get it. And I can make them better. I can make anyone better. But not at anyone else's expense.' His mouth turned down. 'You have to be careful how you go about these things. These days it's all about consensus. Working together for a brighter future.'

Liv fired a look to Vic: We have to work with this? She sat.

Vic was about to speak when Jess said, 'Lloyd, my oldest sister, who lives in Canada, is a leading chemical engineer. Like our mother was.'

'Oh, yeah? Nice.' He grinned as he set out the documents in a precise row. 'Ladies, we're on the same team here. And no one in our team is unsafe, or not getting a fair go. Look out there . . . what do you see?'

The women turned to the window. Lloyd faltered, only briefly. 'On the other side of those curtains are happy kids.'

Liv had learnt, over the years, that there are some people with whom you can debate, and others with whom it was pointless. She crossed her arms. Thank god Vic's toolkit included strategies that short-circuited the need. They could skip de-biasing minds, one by one, and cut to what worked: those evidence-based interventions, which nudged people in the right direction – without them even knowing it!

'This school's meant to be world-leading,' Jess was saying, bless her. 'I thought it'd be *encouraging* girls, not scaring them off . . .' Her eyes were glassy. 'No wonder Iran has a higher percentage of female engineers than Australia does.'

Liv frowned. Vic was studying Jess as if to be sure Jess had finally finished.

'Iran, eh?' said Palmer. 'What d'you know?'

With a chuckle, he flipped through the documents. Put a series of coloured tabs on different pages.

Liv wondered how they'd moved from upskirting to gobbledegook to Iran. And that Iran was somehow faring better in the gender relations stakes. She gauged her anger at around six out of ten. Palmer had stunned it out of her. Jess had helped.

'A lot of people don't understand this sort of data,' said Palmer. 'And it's not reliable. Probably best we keep this to ourselves.' He winked at Jess.

'Lloyd, as you know, a lot of this is why I'm here,' said Vic, loudly, as if to drown out any interruption. 'But I'd like to broaden my remit. I understand boys and girls do comparably here in literacy, which is fantastic, so it's only the STEM side we need to address. On that, I'd like to begin a short Science intervention for Year Eight girls. Jess knows someone who can run it: a Nobel Prize–winning physicist.'

'Yeah, no. Not necessary,' said Palmer. 'Thanks, though. Here, have a read.'

He offered the stack of prettily tagged policies. Only a dazed Jess took them.

Vic raised the survey results. The single piece of paper buckled, like limp lettuce. 'I may have already shared this.'

'Oh, yeah?' Lloyd gave his high-vis smile again. Outside, a bell rang. They waited.

Just how dense was the man? From a distance, Lloyd had seemed so engaged, passionate and inexhaustible. The kids seemed to love him, and not only because he turned girls into professional footballers (despite their limitations in kicking, apparently); and played that tiny guitar.

'How about I have a chat with Tony,' he said. 'Let you know by lunch?'

'Yes, you do that,' said Vic, standing.

Liv collected her bag. Perhaps he suffered from selective stupidity as well as selective coaching. She noticed then the half-dozen photos of middle-aged men in lycra. Among them, Lloyd and Tony, arm in arm. Following her gaze, Jess recoiled. Liv put out her arm and Jess took it.

'Oh, and, ladies,' said Lloyd. 'Permission's granted to change the bathrooms.'

57

Duncan

The boys had been home half an hour by the time Duncan's meeting ended. Rising stiffly, he left his office and headed to the garage. Three minutes later, he wheeled out two bikes. Through the windows, he could see Jai bent now over his books while, phone in hand, Liv circled the house, and Cody hid beside the couch, where he was engrossed in Jai's old screen. Oscar, for unknown reasons, was dragging a mattress down the hall. Duncan wheeled out the final bike. Leaning against the fence, the five of them looked terrific, shiny and new. This was it. He waved to Liv, doing another circuit. But she didn't look out. He tried the back door, but it'd shut, self-locking. He strolled to the front and found that door locked too. He rapped on a window. Cody scowled, without looking up.

'The door,' said Duncan, pointing.

Cody didn't move. On the coffee table was a plate of muffin crumbs.

'Cody!'

Cody flinched but his eyes stayed down. Neither of the twins emerged. Cody's fingers worked away. Duncan banged. 'Cody! Let me in!'

'Cody!' Duncan bashed so hard the window frame shook. Fear and something else – anger? – flashed across Cody's face. The boy sprang up, his silly fringe bouncing.

When the door swung open, Duncan took a deep breath. 'Thank you.'

'You made me die!' yelled Cody. 'You made me *die*!'

'Come outside, now.'

Cody dove back to the screen. Duncan could see a character hang-gliding to earth. Yep, as feared. Duncan vaguely remembered then banning Cody's technology. Why hadn't Liv hidden it? He could feel a roar building.

'Cody. I have. A present. For you . . . Outside. Now.'

Gunfire flared from the iPad. Cody's avatar was under attack, on two fronts. Duncan snatched the screen.

'No! No! No!' Cody jumped, on the spot, frantically. His face was straining, his neck a mass of veins. 'You made me die again!'

Duncan hugged the device to his chest. No one else appeared.

'NO! NO! NO!' screamed Cody. 'I HATE YOU! I HATE YOU!'

Cody continued to jump and holler, then began slapping his own head. Which was rather disturbing. Counter to every atom of his being, Duncan kept his mouth shut and waited for Cody's fury to peak. Incredibly, after a few minutes, it did.

'Finished? Good. Let's go, soldier.' Duncan made his voice deepen. 'You, out, now.'

Cody gave a weary sniff before marching outside. Duncan smiled. In the scheme of things, that wasn't so bad. He'd hadn't lost his cool; nothing was broken. Cody wasn't bleeding.

'Wait here.'

Cody stood upright on the driveway.

'Good-o.' Duncan saluted. 'Don't move.'

Cody half-raised his arm, torn between saluting and not moving, as Duncan bolted inside and locked the door.

Duncan was similarly successful with the twins. They both ignored his first two requests and only answered his third, once he growled. Jai was allegedly studying for a Maths test, while Oscar was in the middle of redecorating Duncan's study. How Oscar could think Duncan didn't need a study anymore was mind-blowing. When the twins finally grumbled out, Duncan felt his chest constrict; every second with these children felt crazy-difficult; and now, he going to have to time-share his home-office too. Seriously?

•

The boys stared at the five bikes as if regarding cousins they didn't recognise. The mountain bikes were red and black and, other than varying in size, identical. A black helmet dangled from each bike's handlebars.

'What do you say, boys?'

Oscar rolled his eyes. 'We're not ten, you know.'

'Hey, that's no way to—'

'Are they from Aldi?' said Cody.

Duncan could feel his temper rousing. Some of the guys at work talked endlessly about their bikes. He'd be a laughing stock if they saw him now. He'd bought five bikes for a fraction of the price of one of theirs. But he didn't really care, and his family had to start somewhere. Only . . . he hadn't expected a nine-year-old bike snob.

'Thanks, Dad,' Jai cut in. 'Can I go? I've got to finish the practice test before domestic training.'

Already in uniform, he trotted off. Oscar shadowed him.

For a split second, Duncan was wrong-footed. 'That's it?'

'I hate bike riding,' Oscar said, over his shoulder. 'How can you not remember?'

Duncan tugged his hair. Why was family time that much better in his imagination? An image came to him, then, of a gravelly hill. A dam. Somewhere here was the provenance of the scar under Jai's chin. And Oscar's fear of blood.

He turned. That left Cody: his least favourite son, if he was honest, which in this context he wasn't. 'What do you reckon?'

Cody sized up his bike while wiping his nose with a vertical palm swipe. Duncan shuddered.

Inside, Liv, his busy bee, appeared at the window. He'd forgotten to include her. He gestured: come out.

'What are you doing?' she mouthed.

Cody's lips parted, revealing small, long teeth. Duncan raised his palm to Liv.

'Wanna go for a ride, Dad?'

●

The two of them rode for forty-five minutes, hardly spoke, pedalled and puffed. Duncan could feel the wind around his ears and his nose begin to run. The bike wasn't too bad, he told himself, only a bit heavy. Leading the way, Cody bolted along the unmade path beside the golf course. Cody was faster and fitter than Duncan expected. Whizzing along, they could see the manicured greens through the wire fence, and long-legged white birds clustered by a lake: few of Bayside's many golfers were playing. The water rippled.

Cresting a hill, Cody looked back at him: grinning, surrounded by green.

His bike wobbled.

'Turn around!' said Duncan, with a laugh. 'Brakes, Cody, brakes.'

'Brakes, Dad,' sang Cody, looking ahead again. 'Brakes.'

As Cody disappeared over the hill, Duncan let go of the handlebars: nine again. He took a moment to congratulate himself. He'd found it. It was in his bloodstream, moving through his body. His joy.

A minute later, Cody crashed into a tree.

Back home, dirty and bloodied but heartened, Duncan wandered the house. He'd tended to Cody's grazed knee, asked how he'd felt, and listened to the protracted answer about how scary-fun those five seconds of air had been (impossible, more like one); then, in amicable silence, they'd limped the bikes home. On balance, the venture was a success. It may've been his imagination, but his home now felt calmer. Liv was grilling steaks; basket-ball in hand, Jai was double-checking his practice test. Only Oscar was MIA. Duncan paused outside his office. Knocked. Within, a young man was talking. Was Oscar FaceTiming maybe, or Skyping . . . Google-hanging? The voice sounded aggressive yet friendly – as if he was hamming up his macho-side. Who was that? Lately, Oscar didn't seem to have many friends in the flesh. Duncan turned the handle but the door was wedged shut.

'Hey Oscar? You ready for training?'

The unfamiliar voice stopped. 'Not going and you can't make me.'

Duncan inhaled slowly. 'Don't be like that.' He threw his weight against the door. 'Oscar?'

'I emailed the coaches last night,' said Oscar. 'I've quit. Rep too. And footy.'

'You didn't.'

Oscar wasn't the best at basketball, but the Friday night and Saturday evening games kept him out of trouble. Training and games gave the boys' weeks shape. Basketball and footy kept them in shape. Plus, watching those games was one of the few family activities Duncan enjoyed. Most of the time. He counted lamingtons in his head to stop himself from yelling. Already, the inoculating effects of his ride were wearing off.

'But why?' said Duncan. 'Osc, why would you do that?'

Duncan waited. Heard that voice again. Then rap music instead. Something sharp lodged in the pit of his stomach. Phone in hand, Jai emerged from the toilet. Duncan shuddered again.

Jai took him in. 'Not like he was gonna play for the NBA. Or AFL.' He gave his half-smile, kept walking.

Duncan could feel a lecture coming on. The words *quitter* and *disappointment* niggled in his throat. 'Come out, right now!' he wanted to shout. He counted lamingtons again, until he heard the shower and the reedy voice of his youngest, singing.

58

Liv

On Monday of week three, Professor Griffin, Jess's boss's husband's sister-in-law, was teaching Intervention Science. It seemed Tony Crisp was much more of a flexible thinker than anyone expected. The Year Eight girls were having an extra double-class each week of Physics. Rather than designing bridges, or other standard textbook fodder, the Nobel laureate was asking them to design ramps for old people's homes, so the cute old men and women could be pushed in and out in their wheelchairs. To Vic's and Liv's delight, even some of the previously uninterested girls were taking on the challenge.

The survey results, while not made public, seemed to turbocharge Vic Cato's program. The students were abuzz and the school's counsellors were flooded with interest in the upcoming parent meeting. On the designated night, a record number turned up. Jess seemed to be particularly thrilled. Even Jilly Saffin was there. Within minutes, Vic won nearly everyone over. De-biasing the environment and demolishing gendered norms was for all, she explained, not only girls. 'If you don't like the word feminist,' she said, with a smile to Jess, 'think of me as "fair-ist". Who doesn't want fair – for everyone?' Who could argue with fairness, insight and designing for equality? No one did.

Though Bettina Low wasn't at the meeting, the following week Taj and two of his buddies were taken out of the program. Liv half-expected Oscar to make a case, but he didn't.

Across Year Eight, Vic's classes were gathering pace. Despite the odd grumble from a parent online, the students weren't complaining. As the days passed, Vic instigated a process of gathering students' feedback on the teaching they received. Already, some fascinating kernels were turning up. 'Don't talk when we're writing notes. We can't multitask!' was one comment; along with, 'Don't teach us when you're having a cup of coffee.' Vic loved these titbits and so did Liv, especially the more meaty stuff – 'Mrs P. talks nonstop for the entire class' and 'Mr R. favours the girls.' Some of the staff, not so much.

At home, Liv watched the vision of teachers in action. The findings were compelling, and largely unexpected. Some of it was predictable: yes, Mr Waring did let the boys dominate discussions, while discounting the girls' input and discouraging their participation. This was shown to him second by second and he was asked to adjust. Mr Humphries was touching girls on their shoulders/backs/arms at a rate of 9 to 1 compared to physical contact with boys. This was put to an abrupt death by Vic, who fed back her thoughts to individuals in the evenings, after school. One or two male teachers and a few more female teachers were asked to speak less in class and ask more of their students; most teachers were asked to demand more from the boys in terms of behaviour and more from the girls in terms of participation, especially giving answers on the spot. It transpired that teachers consistently disliked putting girls under pressure with tough questions. This was a surprise to Liv.

There were other unexpected findings. Most teachers were cranky by about midday. Three teachers (two females, including the Health teacher Miss Lee, and, yes, Mr R.) were far harsher on the boys than on the girls for the same behaviours – talking out of turn, being late and fidgeting. Some boys were getting a raw deal consistently. Some girls (and the odd boy: hello, Taj) got away with murder. All of this was charted and graphed and explained to the working group. Lloyd had become an avid note-taker, working those coloured pens and tags, and said little; while busy Ethan was often absent. Neither of which bothered anyone.

Tony Crisp had given Vic's program his blessing. And, like it or not, his staff were expected to oblige.

For the first time in a fortnight, time accelerated again. Over dinner each night, Liv shared her Carmichael stories and Vic's fascinating insights, while Duncan sat, unblinking, like a kid listening to fairytales. Do we humans have *that many* unconscious biases? He asked, as around them, the boys variously cleared the table, cleaned up and broke things.

'Uh-huh,' she said. 'And they're not all bad. Eighty to ninety per cent of the human mind works unconsciously, apparently.'

'Wow.'

One day turned into another and nothing calamitous happened. No more police visits or scandals or impromptu surveys. During the day, most of the week, Liv had the house to herself; after school, Oscar retreated to his room to watch unspecified talking heads online, while Cody rode around the streets and Jai was engaged by school, mates and Grace. Of course, Duncan worked. The household was relatively calm.

After a week or so, Duncan's listening at dinner bordered on avid.

'There's *that much* wrong with the place?' he said one night over seconds of tuna pie, once the boys had bolted.

'Yep.'

'And you really think you can fix it, with a bunch of tweaks and feedback, breaks and Dr Cato's classes?'

'With Tony's backing, absolutely. And Mary MacBeth's. Vic knows so.'

He chewed thoughtfully. She passed him one of Vic's books: *Power to the Small Change.*

By week four, more girls were wearing trousers, including Grace Charters; and Liv could see change afoot. Girls were being asked harder questions on the spot. Boys were behaving and not being allowed to dominate discussions or waste valuable class time. Miss Lee was more tolerant with the 'naughty' boys, and lightening up. The passing of notes was easing; the pinging of bra straps non-existent. The bathrooms had been revamped by then. They were still waiting on the new posters of scientists and chefs, and for portraits of luminary alumnae to be put in the principal's wing. Meanwhile, Jess reported that Grace had become positively perky, and her friendship with Bella was going from strength to strength. True, Oscar was largely underground, and had become more negative and distant, but he was going through puberty. How were you meant to recognise problematic behaviour change versus bog-standard teenage unpleasantness? (Liv didn't have time to read up on it right now.)

Overall, the cumulative effect of these minor changes was exhilarating. Occasionally, the arched eyebrow of a lead teacher could be seen behind a parapet.

Around week five, Jai bounced home with stories of 'funny warm-up exercises' they'd had to do. Scrambled-sentence tests. Jai shoved a sheet in front of Liv's nose. They'd had to put the words into four-word sentences. Liv read the first few:

1. him was happy she always
2. ball the throw toss confidently
3. we love do to dance

'No idea why,' said Jai, inhaling an orange.

Liv smiled. She knew why. The positive messaging in the resultant sentences would prime the students to feel happy. According to Jai, it'd been a super chill day. Other teachers were introducing wacky games and writing random words around their classrooms, too. Mrs MacBeth was asking the students to tell their neighbours they 'respected' them, once a week. Jai didn't mind, particularly. Dr Cato had instigated a Random Act of Kindness competition, and people could nominate each other for recognition. Everyone seemed to be in a better mood – except maybe Oscar, who'd begun telling offensive jokes on the bus. Embarrassed, Jai missed his twin. Not that he seemed to know what to do about him, nor want to talk to Liv about it at length. She needed Oscar back on her List, she supposed. But, mainly out of sight, Oscar and his problems were easy to forget, and didn't seem too serious. Otherwise, Hannah Appleby and Taj Low were the only other grouchy ones, Jai explained. Everyone else was getting on.

'It must be the weather,' Jai said. 'Kicking around in those red and yellow leaves.'

By week six, Vic reported that the Year Eight cohort was noticeably more upbeat, and the passing of notes and giving of detentions had ground to a halt. Some of the previously sceptical teachers were also coming on board. The classrooms felt refreshed: girls were louder in class; phones were left in lockers each morning and the covert playing of video games fell off a cliff. A snack break before noon was curing crankiness. Guest speakers were cropping up, too: Jess was doing an incredible job of finding people in the wider school community who were chemical engineers, orthopaedic surgeons, IT entrepreneurs, and a CEO of a bank: lovely women, with eye-opening stories.

One barrister gave a cracking presentation. 'Don't muck about getting overqualified at uni if you don't know what you want to do: get out, get a job, plan if and when you would like to have a family, and be financially independent,' she told the girls. 'And step up!' she snapped at the boys. She explained where Australia sat on a world gender equality ranking that ran from Iceland (1st) to Yemen (153rd): sandwiched between Laos and Zambia at 44th. She told a legal horror story about a woman in the United States being charged with manslaughter when her unborn baby died after someone shot her. She talked about female members of the Emirati royal family who had tried to flee Dubai and its patriarchy, not making it and then not being seen again. Her stories were so graphic and passionate, the girls and boys were ignited. One girl shot up her hand: 'What have you done about all this, then?'

The barrister fell silent. 'I'm here now, aren't I?'

The mood in the other year levels was changing too; big brothers and sisters weren't immune to their siblings and teachers' vibes. Three Year Twelve girls visited a Year Eight Science class to talk about university and their career plans. Absolutely everyone listened. An infectious positivity was moving from the Middle School to Senior. Everything was ticking along, with the exception of a formal response to Jai's survey and the endorsement of Liv's charter.

'We're on it,' was all Vic could get out of Lloyd.

●

From time to time, as the term swept by, Tony Crisp looked dazed. A grandfather watching a seven-year-old set up his new TV. But, to his credit, his support didn't waver, and most of his staff toed the line.

At home, Duncan kept pumping Liv for updates as he dried up, dusted and hung the washing. And she shared her small victories. His interest, Liv realised, wasn't so much in Carmichael's progress or even Vic Cato – for him, the quest for change had become personal. His growing little fiefdom at Winsome & Ueland was undergoing its own metamorphosis – in the office. Thanks to his reading, Duncan was quoting studies to her and building in more breaks at work, swapping the cakes for birthday walks, and encouraging his people to sprint, then rest and re-energise. On the walls, he'd put photographs of rainforests and waterfalls. For his team, he was shooting for improved productivity to translate to shorter hours. Balance. He was more disciplined working from home, too, working less, squeezed into the good room. While Liv didn't catch what his new partner, Michael or Henry thought of these changes, and she could see a disconnect here and there, she couldn't be prouder.

At recess one morning in week seven, outside the admin building, Liv observed four smartly dressed men greeting Lloyd. Board subcommittee members? Dads? Definitely not teachers. Lloyd was doing a lot of hand pumping and shoulder squeezing. Tony was at a wellbeing conference. The mood between the men seemed sombre, out of step with the children skipping about. Not that any of the men acknowledged a student. One of them, dressed in a silver suit, had curly hair like Duncan's and was doused in cologne. His hard eyes lingered as she passed. Stinky sleazebag.

In week seven, over tea in the staff room, Vic, Liv and Tony were having a discussion about bias. Unconscious biases.

'I'm very confident I don't have any unconscious gender bias,' the principal said. 'And nor does the school.'

Liv snorted her Earl Grey. Ever diplomatic, Vic suggested Tony complete a test, which the students had already done. A world-renowned test, which

Tony had never heard of (Harvard's Career Implicit Association Test) and nor had Liv, who volunteered to do it too. It was simple but illuminating.

'Oh dear,' said Tony, wiping his glasses, when it was done. 'Oh dear.'

Vic smiled graciously. 'Don't beat yourself up. No one's immune. Liv got a very similar result to you . . .'

'No!' Liv glanced across at Tony in dismay. 'Can I do it again? Do you get better?'

Vic shook her head. Gathering herself, Liv understood something then afresh. No wonder she'd felt so exhausted and overwhelmed. On top of everything else, she'd been pushing against these biases every day, and in every facet of her life.

That afternoon, Liv was delighted to learn from Jean Anderson that, after eavesdropping on a fiery leadership meeting in Tony's office, Jean had been given the go-ahead for the posters for the science and food tech labs, and photo-portraits for the principal's wing.

The following week, taking a break, Liv snuck into a corridor to watch one of Vic's classes through a window. The students were divided into one group of girls and two unequal groups of boys, and Vic was walking between the groups, asking questions. Liv was surprised by the affection in Vic's voice. The girls were laughing, and the boys were complaining, but not with real vehemence. Liv couldn't hear what Vic was asking, but bursts of laughter punctuated the pauses, and girls' hands flew into the air. Liv craned to read what was written on the board. *Members' votes: 12 to 4. Motion passed!* Liv couldn't read the smaller blue scrawl. But the boys were grumbling. 'It's rigged,' snarled Oscar. 'How come every one of them can vote but less than a quarter of us?' said another. 'And on jock straps!' Oscar glowered, as Vic threw a mini-basketball at him. 'Ouch.'

Liv sighed. She was disappointed by her son, nursing his thumb. For the first time in their lives, the twins could be told apart in a millisecond. Jai seemed to be getting taller every week, his muscles more defined, his voice deeper, while Oscar's softening torso, burgeoning spots and bad breath were hard to miss. What was Duncan doing with him? It was obvious she really needed to step in: prise her son open, listen, try to understand. But honestly . . . she felt a twitch of annoyance. Duncan had to learn how to do it somehow. If she kept stepping in, he wouldn't. Ever. Just then, Oscar saw her. She gave him a small, guilty nod.

Liv pulled back slightly to watch the other students listening. Near universal eye-contact, smiles and nods – no headsets required. Not a single eye was watching the clock and counting down the minutes.

In the corridor, three women appeared carrying cylinders, including Mary MacBeth. 'Two months ago, the students didn't know these people. Now they're excited they've arrived!' said one, unrolling a poster.

The other glanced into Vic's classroom, lovingly. Together, the women affixed the posters with a series of satisfying thumps.

Mary passed the staple gun. 'It's a shame we have to give her back.'

'Do we, though?' said the second.

Bang, bang, bang went the gun. Mary lingered over the final poster, giving it a wipe. 'Maybe not,' she said, with a wink. 'She's loving it here; told me this morning.'

The women moved on, smiling at Liv as they passed. Alone in the corridor, Liv could feel their residual optimism, their pride and sense of ownership of this new world.

On pause in Vic's office, Mr Waring and his English class awaited Liv. The man was huge, bearded and long limbed, more like a mountaineer than a teacher of literature. His manner, while improving, still held the whiff of a Neanderthal. The truth lay in his microexpressions; the tight smile to the bright girls, the light in his eyes when a boy answered correctly. Could the man ever be cured? If it were possible, thought Liv, surely now was the time.

Re-energised, Liv examined the fresh faces on the wall: from Malala Yousafzai and Emma Watson to Chimamanda Ngozi Adichie and Simone de Beauvoir, Roxane Gay and Greta Thunberg and Jacinda Ardern. She picked a piece of tissue fluff off Jacinda's chin.

Finally, welcome.

By the end of week eight, everyone agreed: the school looked and felt altered, thanks to what could only be called fine-tuning.

Next week, the last week of term, Vic's program would wrap up for the Year Eights, and the cohort would complete a Science test to see if the science intervention had had any effect. Though Liv had nearly flunked Science herself in Year Seven, she could scarcely wait. Strong results would surely bolster the rollout of Vic's program across the school. A meeting was scheduled next week for Vic and Tony to discuss that very thing. All Liv would have to do then was get paid, sit back and enjoy the ride. The penny had dropped for Liv that Carmichael had been exploiting its mums, for years; now was probably the time for her to speak up.

59

Duncan

That Friday afternoon, as he finished a walk, Duncan was mulling over Maggie Koh. She had slotted in at W&U like a corner piece of puzzle. The clients he'd hand-balled seemed delighted to have her on board. Passing the Flamingo Bar, Duncan congratulated himself for keeping Maggie at arm's length, too – no drinks after work, no lunches (other than the partners' weekly catch-up in the boardroom), and no long meetings one on one. And it'd worked. He was no longer noticing her full eyelashes or shapely ankles.

Entering his building, he opted to take the stairs. Thanks to these daily walks, and weekly mountain-biking with Cody, he was getting fitter and more clear-headed after lunch. Boldly, in the office, he'd stuck with his blind-down, locked-door routine most mornings. And he'd encouraged his staff to take more, regular breaks – walk, nap, read a novel. Though initially confused, his group seemed happier and were finishing earlier but getting more done.

Unsurprisingly, Henry didn't seem to understand Duncan's new ethos, or why you'd want it. You were meant to sweat the assets, not under-utilise them! True to form, Xavier and George were looking worn out, pulling all-nighters, as Michael cracked the whip. Duncan felt for them both, but especially for George. Xavier lived four doors down and preferred it here to his share house. But there was little Duncan could do for George. He had enough on his own plate, keeping Michael at bay.

For now, Duncan's tinkering around the office was a curiosity, puzzling, but he'd probably be called to account sooner or later. Especially if Red kept overdoing the mid-afternoon snooze. Shortly, Henry was going away for his annual jaunt north, which helped.

Duncan accelerated up the stairs. Despite Michael's antics and slogging staff, Duncan was enjoying his time at work in ways he had never before. True, he felt busy, juggling home duties and work, but his plans were evolving. South Australia (or was it the East Coast?) was fading.

Puffing pleasantly, he stepped into the foyer – to find Maggie in a meeting with Michael. As far as Duncan knew, the two had had relatively little to do with each other, outside of the partners' meetings. Probably because Duncan had warned Maggie, though she'd seemed unfazed. Maggie tended to keep her head down and work late each night. Duncan had tried to introduce her to the shorter, more efficient workday too. But Maggie hadn't gone for it.

'I didn't move across the country to bill less,' she said, 'or walk around the CBD with you.'

'No, no, of course not.' Duncan had felt like a twit. He suspected being *at work*, and working, was Maggie's happy place. She seemed to relish cranking out huge numbers. He'd opted not to debate the point. And she didn't seem burnt out. Yet.

Like a peeping Tom, Duncan hesitated in the foyer. He'd been dreading this, especially Fridays when Michael had been at his club. In his office, Michael was on his feet while Maggie sat, nursing a notepad. Duncan wondered if he ought to stick his nose in. Make up a meeting. Maggie was speaking when Michael started to yell. Duncan couldn't make out any details, but Michael was jabbing at the administration cubicles. Each sentence seemed to begin with 'You. . . .'

As Michael's rant grew, Maggie rose. Beside Michael, she looked petite, though she wasn't. In her pointy heels, she was almost as tall as Liv. But Michael was six-foot-three last time Duncan checked, while Duncan was five-eleven. Duncan thought of George. He didn't want Maggie keeling over. But he hadn't challenged Michael since he was thirteen, after which Michael locked him under the house. Overnight. Without the dog.

Duncan was equivocating behind a pot plant when Henry tap-danced into the foyer. Clearly, he'd been at Michael's old farts' club as well. Henry took one look at Duncan, then at Michael's office. 'Uh-oh.' He tucked in his shirt.

A second later, Maggie threw back her head and howled. Duncan and Henry darted closer. But Maggie was laughing, wiping her eyes.

'Feel good, does it? My daughter loved losing her shit – when she was two!' Maggie made herself stop, with a sniff. 'Do that again, and I'll put you in the Cranky Corner. You need to get a fucking grip.'

Maggie left. Silently, Michael watched her go. Then he sat down where she'd been sitting.

Duncan had to stop himself from clapping.

Beside Duncan, Henry burped softly. 'How's the language on her? Fuck me.'

60

Duncan

In the dusk, the bay was crisscrossed with currents. Its surface reminded Duncan of a wildly vacuumed carpet. He turned the music up as, beside him, Jai sang softly. For the second time that day, Duncan was aware of his own contentment. He'd made it home in time to take Jai to this week's game, an early one on home turf. He smiled across to his son. Jai seemed happy, too, maintaining his girlfriend and studies and basketball. And so was Cody, thought Duncan, at home on his bike. The biking was channelling the kid's energy for good rather than evil. He seemed . . . soothed. Honestly, Duncan was enjoying his company on their drives to Lysterfield Park and its excellent tracks. Duncan chuckled to himself. Cody was an observant little mite: noticing how Duncan was getting better at going uphill, and wearing the same pink Aldi bike shorts as the woman in front of them. The only child who did not seem to be doing so well was Oscar. His twice-weekly cooking was giving him away. One night it was too spicy, another too creamy or too salty. Plus, he seemed to be wrapping whatever he could in puff pastry: sausages, steak, spag bol. Yeah, the changes in Oscar were a worry. He had two chins now and was on his way to a third. Duncan knew it was up to him to help, but had yet to figure out how. Or find the time. He hoped tonight's dinner was more palatable.

Driving one-handed, Duncan swivelled his wedding band. Oscar was falling between the hairline cracks between Liv and Duncan. Last weekend, showing some initiative, Duncan had organised a date night and intended to bring up Oscar. He and Liv had ridden to their favourite seaside restaurant, watched the sun set behind the rusted shipwreck and been home by 9 pm. They'd chatted. Didn't overeat or drink. Laughed. And kept the conversation away from their boys. Duncan hadn't wanted to jeopardise the mood. He'd felt fifteen years younger. It was like the old days, before the kids.

Duncan pulled up at a red light. Wondered if he and Jai had time for a conversation now.

It turned out Maggie Koh was one of those people who offered advice, whether you wanted it or not. 'Go for benign neglect,' she'd said about Oscar, over apple danish in the coffee room, that afternoon. 'Give the kid space. He'll come to you when he needs you. Works for mine. They're happy as Larry – self-reliant, confident. My eldest was doing the household budget for me, and he's ten.' Duncan tried to remember what she'd said about conversations in cars. Something like speak less, listen more. Don't treat speaking to them like a duty. Don't overdo the advice. Let them in, so they can give *you* advice. But don't be phoney or try to be their friend. Or cool. Duncan, you are not cool. In the coffee room, Duncan had wished he'd brought a notepad. It was almost worth going into work just for those chats.

Duncan snuck a look at Jai, staring dreamily as he sang. He thought back to last weekend's close game. Jai's team had done well despite Oscar's departure. If anything, they might've been doing better. Eyeing the bay, Duncan wondered how Jai managed his on-court nerves. Maybe that was a way in to a chat about Oscar. He almost asked, but hesitated. Another Maggie pearl of wisdom came to him: notice something about them. People like being noticed.

'Are they new socks?'

'Yeah. Grace gave them to me.'

'Thoughtful of her.'

Jai glanced at him, but Duncan kept his eyes ahead. Mouth shut. Counted lamingtons. They sat in pleasant silence.

They were almost at the stadium when Jai said, 'Dad, something's wrong with Oscar. You know that, right?'

'Oh . . . well, I had noticed something.'

Jai nodded, seemingly pleased by this answer. Despite himself, Duncan began assembling a lecture on commitment, hygiene and diet. He stopped. Cleared his throat. 'What do you reckon's going on?'

'Um. I think I know, but I don't want to say.'

'Right.'

Duncan swallowed. He had rarely, if ever, had a heart-to-heart with a twin. But thanks to his drives with Cody, he was getting better at chitchat. Only last weekend he'd learnt from Cody that three Year Twelves had been caught 'dealing drugs' at school. 'What's weed, Dad?' Duncan had needed to remind himself Cody was nine.

Too soon, they were in the car park. 'Why don't you want to say?'

'I don't know. Because Oscar wouldn't like it.'

Jai picked up his bag but didn't reach for the door.

Duncan switched off the engine. 'What's the worst that could happen, if you tell me?'

Jai shrugged. Duncan's mind roved from drugs to self-harm. Maybe they shouldn't be letting Oscar loose in the kitchen.

A group of girls in Bayside basketball uniforms swirled by. Jai snapped down the sun visor. One of the girls was small, muscular and very cute. She reminded Duncan of a child star, pre-adolescence. She smiled at Jai through the windscreen.

'Do you know those girls?'

'Pack of bitches.'

'I beg your pardon?'

'They're Grace's frenemies.' Jai sat up, went a bit red. 'That last one, Dad, she's super mean. She picks on Oscar. Calls him the "fugly" twin.'

Duncan frowned. 'Fat and ugly?'

'Fucking ugly.'

'Oh.' His instinct was to laugh, but Jai was staring at him intently. 'That little girl is picking on your brother?'

'Yes, Dad.' Jai's eyes darted. 'Like, *all the time.* And she's not little. She's in our year.'

Duncan dropped the chuckle. 'Got it.'

Jai shoved open the door. 'I'd do something but, like, she's a girl.'

Duncan tried to salvage the moment. 'Yeah. Know what you mean. Thanks for telling me.'

Jai gave an abrupt nod. Belatedly, he noticed Duncan hadn't moved. 'You coming in?'

'You know what . . .' Duncan cocked his head, considered the time on the dash. 'Not tonight. Mum might come back to watch. Good luck in there. Go hard.'

61

Jess

Jess was heading for the bleachers as Grace and her team warmed up. Until half an hour ago, Grace had still been revising for the Science test. Jess couldn't wait to see how the girls fared next week. Already, Lloyd Palmer had pulled up his socks. (Grace had said, 'Teachers are different when parents and other teachers are around. We love those cameras.') The second piece of good news was that Grace's pre-game jitters were fading. Even tonight, with Bayside playing their arch rivals, the Tigers, Grace was calm. But some things, like Hannah's preferential treatment, hadn't changed. And so, for the first time in Grace's five-year stint as an elite basketballer, Jess had brought a tripod and iPad – for evidence. Two of Grace's friends had also come to watch: Bella, and Blake Havelock.

Jess didn't know what to make of that.

At the other end of the court, the girls' opposition was warming up too. In orange singlets, the Tigers were loud and intense. Other clubs described the Bayside girls as 'princesses'. Grace's teammates did look well cared for, with ornate hairstyles and icy smiles. Jess used to think it was a compliment, but now she wasn't so sure. She watched as Hannah put up long shots. Counted as one in ten dropped.

Jess tested the camera. She could identify each girl by number, if not by face. She zoomed in on Jai, running in, greeting parents on his way to his game. Liv had done a good job with him, she thought. She eyed Blake, further down the court, chatting with Bella. He looked thin but pleasant enough, sharing his hot chips and blanket. All seemed forgiven between them. Bella was strong, Jess realised. And kind. Jess wasn't that kind.

Her thoughts turned to Dr Cato. For weeks, curious parents had been calling Jess for the inside word on Vic's program. How's she doing it? What's the secret? Some of the students weren't sold, and some dads. Hannah wasn't on board. 'Is it a crime to be pretty, these days?' Penny Appleby had said. 'Hannah tells me she's old. Doesn't understand the popular girls.' Jess had wanted to defend Dr Cato, and remind Penny that Grace was popular too, these days. But Penny Appleby, Jess had come to realise, scared her as much as Dr Cato did – in a different way. The woman didn't blink.

If Hannah Appleby was the most popular girl in Year Eight, thought Jess, why wasn't she one of those 'Top Ten Sluts'? One day, Jess supposed, she could ask Grace or Bella. Or Blake.

With a roar, the Tigers took to the court and Jess stirred. As usual, when Bayside's starting five left its huddle, Grace was on the bench. Grace stayed off until the last minute of the quarter. Penny Appleby hadn't noticed Jess sitting up in the bleachers. She also must not have noticed her own daughter's five consecutive missed attempts at a three, and four turn-overs. Or Grace's steal and fast-break lay-up the moment she'd graced the court. In less than thirty seconds, Grace had managed to score. Because if she had, Penny wouldn't have benched Grace again for the entire second quarter. Jess sat, fuming, as Bayside lagged at half-time.

Jess was tempted to yell. But she couldn't stand aggressive, shouting basketball parents. 'They're fourteen-year-olds!' she'd wanted to tell one particularly noisy dad, earlier in the season. But opposing clubs mostly kept to themselves. Jess could see that man and his wife tonight sitting down the court, and yes, yelling. The coach of the Tigers was even worse. You could hear her now, at half-time – bailing up players, giving it to them between the eyes. Those girls would come back out like rockets. And the Tigers had improved since the beginning of the season, too. Jess watched them returning to the court.

A tall man in cycling gear and a beanie climbed the bleachers to sit three rows below Jess. He wasn't one of the Bayside dads, and definitely wasn't from the Tigers, though he did look familiar.

In the second half, Hannah and the other starting five did what they could to lose the game. Jess checked the iPad was filming the wild passes and rushed long shots; and Bella, shaking her head at the sidelines. She'd take this vision to the club if she had to. 'Grace's getting a raw deal again,' another mum had said to Jess recently; 'You can't compete with the coach's daughter,' said another.

In the dying moments of the third quarter, Hannah went off glowering and Grace returned to the court. Grace intercepted a rare loose ball from the Tigers and passed hard and straight to one of the talls. It was a beautiful assist, and the shot was neat and efficient. The shooter had been fouled, so had a plus-one.

'Beautiful pass, Grace, darling!' Jess yelled. Grace looked up and glared, embarrassed. 'Keep *passing*!' said Jess, with added emphasis in case Hannah was listening.

The man sitting below frowned up at her. Jess ignored him as the shooter made her foul shot. Clapping, Jess jumped to her feet, nearly upending her iPad. The man's gaze swung her way again, but Jess blanked him.

The Tigers passed the ball in, and Grace and the shooting guard, Coco, pressed hard on the ball receiver, forcing a wild pass that Grace managed to get a hand to. Grace pivoted, put up another shot and it dropped. Bayside's bench went crazy. A minute later, the press worked again and Bayside had the ball. The girls swung the ball around the key, waiting for an opportunity.

'Do something, Grace,' Jess said.

Then Grace called for the ball – out loud!

Grace wasn't one to shoot threes. Too risky. But Grace received a pass and put up a three. The shot was long, and high, and beautifully arched. It dropped through the hoop, and the bench jumped to their feet. Jess did too. Her iPad bounced on its stand. Bayside was back in the game!

Unsurprisingly, the coach of the Tigers called a time out. Jess sat, wishing she could tiptoe closer. She could hear the yelling. On the other side of the court, Penny Appleby was on one knee, encircled by the girls.

Twenty seconds later, Hannah returned to the court and Grace to the bench. Jess unleashed an anguished, internal scream. It was stupid to wish desperately for something that hadn't happened in the same situation for the past twenty-four months, and believe it still might. But that was what Jess did. She wished desperately that someone would tell Penny her subbing decisions often cost the team the game. She wished the assistant coach wasn't Penny's sister-in-law. But you couldn't change the world by wishing.

Jess stood. Again, Hannah over-dribbled the ball up the court.

This time, Jess yelled, 'Come on Bayside, move it.' Girls walking along the edge of the court looked up. Players from the Tigers looked up. From the bench, Grace looked up.

'Pass the ball, Hannah, now!' Jess screamed. 'Pass it! Pass it!'

Startled, Hannah jolted to a stop and passed the ball – to a Tiger. Hannah stomped her foot, and Jess winced as the Tiger pulled off an excellent fast-break lay-up. The man in front turned around and put his pointer finger to his lips.

Stunned, creeped out, Jess sat.

In the dying minutes, Bayside lost by eight points. Which was a surprise to no one except Penny Appleby. By the final thirty seconds, Jess was swearing softly. Her recording would be ruined by her screaming and s-bombs, but she didn't care.

Trembling, Jess watched the two teams shake hands. She watched Grace shake the other coach's hand, and exchange a word. She watched Hannah alternately glower or smile, depending on who walked by. Moments later, Grace joined her teammates in a post-game huddle. Most of the girls stood apart from Hannah and Penny. Jess saw Grace put her hand in for the final team yell. As the Bayside girls left, Grace climbed the bleachers to Jess.

The man below gave Grace a long stare. When he got up, Jess worked out where she'd seen him before, and her tremble became a shake. For a moment, she thought he was going to speak to Grace. But he left. Grace sat as Jess packed up.

'Oh, hon . . .' She made herself smile. 'You played so well.'

Grace was taking off her extraordinarily expensive basketball shoes and slipping her feet into slides. Soon, in her socks and slides, she'd look like a British tourist at the beach.

'Mum, seriously?' Grace gestured to the iPad. 'What were you doing?'

'Nothing.' Jess kept her eyes down.

'The whole stadium could hear you.'

Jess zipped up her bag. 'I had to do something.'

'No, you really didn't.'

Jess frowned, turned to Grace.

'Mum. I've got this . . . and I'm out.'

Jess watched the tall man in the cycling gear greet Penny and Hannah, courtside, and leave with them. 'Sorry?'

'I'm out.'

'Because I was yelling?'

An angry laugh burst from Grace. 'No, Mum. I'm going to the Tigers.'

Jess looked at her swan-necked daughter. She looked at the team of tall and intimidating girls, still laughing and chatting beside the court. The ones with the mouthy parents. The coach who yelled.

'Their coach said to call her next season, when tryouts start . . . and I'm going to.'

'You're quitting, mid-season?'

'Yep. And I'm quitting guitar, and concert band too.'

Grace's barely pink face was aglow; her frustration and anger were mixed in with something fresh.

Jess was all for courage. She was. But if Grace stopped these activities, she'd be left behind. Her bright future was in danger of sailing off, without either of them.

'These are big changes, hon.'

With a shrug, Grace rearranged the contents of her basketball bag. What was happening? In one hour, the family's week had been redesigned; Grace's week would be empty. No more dashing from school to the stadium to guitar lessons.

Jess shouldered her bag. At least she didn't have to watch Penny Appleby present Hannah with the trophy for Most Valuable Player – again.

'But what are you going to do with yourself?'

Grace propped her hands on her hips. 'Bella and I are starting a collective.'

'A what?'

Down below, Blake and Bella waved to Grace, who waved back. 'I'm coming,' she sang out. 'Mum, we're going to call out the cocks at school.' Grace's look was an unmasked challenge, as she stepped away. 'They're hiding, but we know who they are.'

Jess thought of that man in the cycling gear; his finger on his lips.

'Oh, gosh.' Jess gulped. 'You do?'

62

Duncan

'Anyone told you lately, we love what you're doing here? You're smashing it.'

Duncan smiled, realising he'd opened with something less than completely true. If Oscar had been surprised to see him back early from the game, he didn't show it.

'And?'

The mood in the kitchen was one of concentration, rap music and isolation. Self-imposed. Duncan had been debating for fifteen minutes how to insert himself into it.

'Want a hand?'

Oscar shrugged. 'I don't care.'

'Good-o.'

Duncan donned a child-sized apron. Oscar's apron was new; on it, a headless, fat-bellied man held a beer in one hand and a spatula in the other. This seemed at odds with Oscar's tucked-behind-the-ears bob. But then, Oscar's own body seemed at odds with that look too. Oscar was decapitating a carrot, as, unbidden, Duncan took to a bunch of parsley. At Duncan's suggestion, Liv had gone to catch the last of Jai's game and bring him home. Cody was having a bubbly soak, after riding his bike with Harry. These Friday night comings and goings were normal. If the Winsomes had been asked, when the twins were ten, whether they'd like to dedicate the coming years' Friday nights (and then Saturday nights as well) to their sons' basketball, perhaps the whole family would've taken up tennis.

Which was why, tonight, alone with Oscar, Duncan needed to get cracking.

'Something happened at work this week,' said Duncan, rinsing the parsley. 'Got me thinking how I should've done things differently eons ago.'

Oscar eyed a pan of rice, vegetables and foreign matter. 'And?'

'And, well . . . how I should've dealt with Michael.'

'Uncle Michael?' The knife in Oscar's hand stilled. Half a carrot remained. 'Why?'

'Because he's an arsehole.'

Oscar hooted. *'Don't speak like that about your brother!'*

An unkind but fair imitation of Liv. With effort, Duncan suppressed his smile.

'How's he an arsehole?' Oscar was chopping again.

Duncan was regretting his choice of descriptor. 'Standard way: he's moody, and yells. Calls people "poofters" and "rangas" and "curry-munchers". He's your garden-variety bully, I guess.'

Oscar nodded. 'He like that to you?'

'Sometimes.'

A thoughtful Oscar scraped carrot into the pan. He moved the various creatures about in their rice bed. He prodded what looked like a baby bird, as if to wake it up. (Where did he get this stuff? Who was paying for it?)

'You work with him every day?'

'For fifteen years.'

Oscar banged wooden spoon on pan. 'Why?'

'That's what I've been wondering . . . I dunno.' Duncan left the silence for Oscar to fill.

Oscar looked up. 'You gotta call him on it, Dad.'

Duncan straightened, chuffed that his strategy seemed to be working. 'Yep, I think you're right. But I need to be – I don't know – smart about it. Creative . . .'

Through the steam, Oscar's stare became unfocused. Duncan felt as if he'd found his mark.

Then Liv strode in. 'Hello, hello. Smells good. What's cooking?' Liv tossed her keys onto the bench.

That was quick, thought Duncan. Too quick.

'Paella,' Oscar mumbled, storm clouds reappearing in the kitchen.

Jai burst in too, red-faced and beaming. So they'd won.

Liv peeked in the pan. Duncan watched her identify chicken legs, discs of sausage and quails. She grimaced. Looked from him to Oscar. Duncan couldn't help enjoying this moment: Liv behind the play. He hummed, as Oscar stirred.

'Call me when it's ready.' Liv retreated, a touch irritated, maybe, or hurt.

'What, no puff pastry?' Jai sloped off. 'Tomorrow,' he yelled, 'I'm going vegan!'

Oscar rolled his eyes, but added a half-smile. The parsley in Duncan's fingers dripped.

'Ready in five, Dunc. Plate up.'

63

Monday

Liv

At 9 am on Monday morning, the Year Eights sat the Science test. Neither Winsome twin had missed the bus. As usual, no one had wanted to drive with her, not even Cody. Watching classes file in, Liv regretted telling Grace not to excel in every subject. To quell her nerves, she busied herself collating materials for Vic's meeting with Tony, and willed those girls to shoot for the stars. Later, around four-thirty, back home, Liv served the boys carrot and cucumber, red pepper and hummus, as she had done when they were five, and asked after the test.

Jai said, 'It was fine.'

Oscar said, 'No one cares.'

Cody blurted, 'Miss Laghari is so sexist!'

That got the twins' attention. Apparently, Cody had tried to sit on his seat after lunch just as Milly sat on it too. He'd given Milly a shove and she'd 'told on him'.

'Miss Laghari said I had to give Milly *my* seat,' he said.

'There you go,' said Oscar.

'Does it matter that much?' Liv asked, with a glare at Oscar.

'Yes!' Cody yelled. 'It's my seat! It has my name on it!'

Liv recognised the righteous indignation, as akin to her own. Laughed. 'Okay, what happened then?'

'I had to sit in the corner. On my own.'

'That'd be right,' Oscar muttered, through a mouthful of capsicum. Liv looked from Oscar to his impassive twin, chewing, mouth closed. Yay.

'And what'd you think about that?' Liv was trying to stay focused.

Cody swiped at his floppy fringe. 'I thought, *What a dick move.*'

Despite herself, she laughed and so did the boys, together.

64

Duncan

As soon as the phones fell quiet and the admin staff left, Duncan directed Maggie to a seat. A revolutionary idea had come to him overnight. It would be the crowning glory of his changes at W&U. He was busting to share it. Test it. The more he thought about it, the more wedded to it he became. Though not the ideal candidate, Maggie was the only person he could think of to tell.

Maggie smirked as he closed the blind at the door. 'I thought you'd gone.'

'Not yet.'

He smiled. He'd been thinking about her. How she didn't tolerate fools and didn't seem to exercise. How clients loved her and women in the office were warming to her, too. They knew where they stood and she was generous with her praise. Under her care, Julia was coming along – speaking up, asking questions – though Maggie had left Red to his mediocrity, and to Duncan. Most notable, Michael's attitude had lifted. He hadn't publicly shamed anyone in weeks. He was like a big pussycat around Maggie now: bringing her coffee, dropping her home, apparently. Duncan had been floored. For a moment, he'd wondered if Michael and Maggie were becoming a thing. Or teaming up to build a power bloc at W&U. She was getting a lot of love for her big numbers. But then he decided, probably not. Regardless, Maggie Koh was the best change he'd made in his fifteen years at Winsome & Ueland. She knew who she was and what she wanted. She was a hugely positive influence. True, they didn't see eye to eye on this topic but he hoped she could be talked around – for the common good. Or her children.

'Is this office smaller than mine now?' Maggie said.

He looked about. 'Could be.'

Over the weekend, Michael had people in to reconfigure the fit-out, now they'd down-sized slightly. Duncan suspected Maggie's office had moved a few metres away from his. But that didn't matter. Duncan sat beside her, rather than across the desk. He wanted to take her unadorned, ring-less hands in his. Appeal to her heart. Worry flashed across her face.

'Who's walking?'

'No one.'

He'd tried to guess how she'd respond – defiantly? Or with astonishment? He was getting better at reading emotions, but predicting Maggie's was a stretch. And this idea was a biggie. It would, at first no doubt, face resistance.

Maggie hopped up. She looked as if she might open the door and wander out.

'Where are you going?'

'You're about to make an announcement.'

Duncan frowned.

'If I had a dollar for every man who told me he loved me, I wouldn't need to be here.' She drew her mouth in, like a child trying not to smile. 'Loved or felt intimidated by me.' She twirled her hair into a rope. 'Duncan, the last thing I want is a relationship. I just got free. I get to do what I want, when I want.'

'No, no—'

Embarrassed for her, he eyed his blind. He needed to explain himself, quickly. How out there most of the legal staff were still grinding away, but nearly everyone in their group had gone even though it was only two past five. How the recent tweaks he'd made – from encouraging their people to exercise whenever they needed to, to bringing in professional masseuses, even updating the pot plants – had made him *feel*. How seeing his people chatting more and laughing and getting things done in record time – in the office – had astounded him and been far easier than he'd thought possible. How these adjustments had emboldened him. Given him a sense of control he'd never felt before. But it wasn't enough. Despite a level of contentment, the itch had remained. It'd come clear, over the weekend. What he needed more of was *time*.

'Maggie, I don't want us to lead this life anymore. I want to refocus it.'

'Oh! Sorry.' She began to laugh, stopped herself. 'Misread that one. What life? Focus where?'

Michael's voice sang from the corridor. 'Maggie K? Where are *youuu*?'

Duncan flinched, despite his brother's playful tone. But Maggie opened the door. 'I'll be ten, Mike.' She shoved it closed. 'He the real problem?'

'A part of it.'

He looked from her to the car park below: Michael's Jag, his second-hand Volvo, her Mini Cooper. She perched on the arm of a seat. Crossed her legs.

'I want us all, everyone, the whole place, to work less hours.'

'Less? *Less?* For fuck's sake! Why?'

'Work is important, Maggie. But it's not the whole pie. We need bigger slices for family. Friends. Partners. To do nothing. Be in nature. Exercise. Give back. Have fun.'

Flopping onto a seat, Maggie looked genuinely stumped. 'How much less?'

All he really knew was, he didn't want to work five days a week anymore. Five days bled over seven days. And he did carry it around with him, even though he'd thought he didn't. He didn't want his people to live like that either – like always having homework. He wanted to be *exclusively* available to his family, at least three days a week. At home, he wanted to be completely in the loop. He'd missed some years with his boys, and lots with Liv, but he could make up for it. Teenagers needed parents as much as little kids did. And wives needed husbands. Husbands needed wives. They weren't flatmates or co-parenting shift-workers. He wanted to live in a more nourishing way, generally. And he wanted his staff to, as well. What that looked like – and how to say as much to Michael and Henry, and to Liv – he didn't know, yet. But everyone working less would mean a profound change in how Winsome & Ueland operated, and how the Winsomes functioned as a family. As people. He couldn't wait.

'I'm thinking four days,' he went on. 'Probably shouldn't close for a day, obviously. But we can get the teams together to come up with ideas. Trial options. It won't be for everyone, but I mean, if we can, why wouldn't we?'

Dazed, Maggie shook her head. 'Duncan, Michael will never—'

'I can put a strong case. We've already made real productivity gains, plus costs are down – travel, entertainment, rent – we can share these gains with our people. Everyone could work four days a week – *on full pay!*'

Her face shifted, a tiny expression he couldn't interpret. Maybe she was doing some internal calculations, running some numbers.

'I know Michael and Henry won't leap at it, but if the rest of us are onside, they might give it a go. What have they got to lose? I'll speak to them, when Henry gets back.' He cleared his throat. 'Can you think about it? Please? I know you love what you do but wouldn't you like more time – to yourself? Or with your children? Honestly?'

She lifted her beautiful, dark eyes to his. 'Same money?' she said. 'That's possible?'

'Yep. One hundred per cent productivity, eighty per cent time, one hundred per cent pay. We can do it.'

Her head was shaking but something may have shifted, as his phone rang: Oscar. 'Thanks. I need to take this.'

65

Friday – last day of Term Two

Liv

Mainly mothers, grandparents and the odd dad were milling beneath trees. Strolling across the field, Liv didn't search the faces, lest she recognise someone whose name she didn't know. She ducked to the far end of the tents and sat on the grass. Teachers and students in matching coloured T-shirts filled each tent. Soon the fourteen-year-old girls would run, followed by the boys, and then they could all go home. Jai was the cross-country runner in the family, and Liv expected him to place; Oscar, not so much, especially not lately. Briefly, she'd thought Oscar wasn't going to turn up. But somehow Duncan had managed it. Well done him.

Parents seemed to be smiling at her from across the track, while, seated, the kids wriggled, half-listening for their race. Even Tony was here to watch, weaving like a seasoned politician – touching elbows, smiling graciously, patting dogs. Liv had to admit he'd surprised her over recent months. He'd broadened his mindset, accommodated the data, and supported Vic wholeheartedly. Which hopefully would continue . . . And now, here they were: the last day of a very busy and productive term. Though not particularly productive financially for her. On the first day of next term, fees were due again. Soon, she'd have to tell Duncan about her little sabbatical.

Watching the mums chatting, Liv felt a pang of grief, missing Stella. So much had happened – much of it thanks to Blake's dodgy Instagram account. Liv realised then she could have written Stella a letter. And perhaps Blake, too.

Distracting herself, Liv eyed the time on her phone. Any minute, the kids' academic reports would be uploaded to the school portal. Her stomach skipped as if the grades to come were hers. But this time she hadn't crammed with her sons. She hadn't read their novels or taught herself their maths. In the specifics of her sons' lives, she was now as hands-off as she could be without being neglectful.

Surveying the field, Liv tried to find Jess. This past week, Jess had been busy at work. How much did these assembled parents know of the school? Liv wondered. How many had Jess spoken with? Two hundred and fifty had come to the information evening, when Vic first started. A record. Had those parents noticed their children's happier moods, and sunnier attitudes towards learning and each other? Or were they too busy managing their children and houses, careers and spouses? Not working had helped Liv focus, she supposed. But not working was a luxury many people couldn't afford, herself included.

Sitting on that damp lawn, Liv could feel her nerves spiking.

The thirteen-year-old boys were finishing their run. Liv's eyes welled. Some of them looked so young! And they were trying so hard, their short legs pumping, puny arms swinging. They were naked in their innocence and hope and effort. Liv wiped her cheeks as some of the boys hobbled in face-saving clumps, while the wiry, running-club types streaked ahead. These boys were at an age where they might remember this experience. Liv was struck by that. Her defining childhood memories were mostly injuries: breaking a collarbone by falling off a horse; or dislodging a boy's tooth on the soccer field. She remembered sporting highlights, too – winning best and fairest for hockey – and receiving prizes for History. This mishmash of lowlights and highlights formed the fabric of her adolescence, her reference points. Which of today's moments, she wondered, would these kids take with them?

Her phone vibrated in her pocket: probably Jess or Vic. But the next race was being called. The girls in Jai and Oscar's year rose in orderly groups. About eighty of them, of all shapes and sizes, in their unisex sports uniform. They would start before the younger boys had finished. The school was running to a schedule, and kids had buses to catch. At the starting line, the girls fell silent. Those at the front looked serious, with their eyes on the first turn. Those at the back and in the middle would be swamped by a choppy sea of moving limbs. Liv spotted Grace towards the front. She was taller than most, and was standing on the outer edge. A man barked then the gun fired.

Grace made a strong start and was in the first six by the turn. Liv wondered if Grace would last the distance at that pace. Was Grace a runner, like her mum? Liv couldn't recall. Bella was there too, Liv realised, in the middle of the pack. Not an athletic child, Bella was nevertheless giving it a go. Her arms were pumping, her face determined. Parents began to move to different parts of the course to watch. As Liv walked, she heard a group of mums behind her.

'Have you met her?' said one. 'Daisy doesn't stop talking about her.'

'I hear you,' said another. 'It's like a light's been switched on: ping!'

The women laughed, but Liv had lost the thread. Glancing behind her, she saw one mum nod a greeting. Coco's mum? Liv didn't trust herself to respond, so she accelerated. She gained on another group. 'It's been special having Professor Griffin teach them. Lulu has got so much out of it . . .' said a dad.

Liv checked her phone. *Call me when you can, V xx.* Liv smiled: how quickly you could go from 'Regards' to 'xx'.

The girls were rounding the final bend. The crowd was cheering and names were being yelled. As in: 'Keep going, Carmen, you can do it!'; and 'Come on, Daisy,' and 'Go harder, Hannah!' Liv watched a small, scowling girl straining to keep with the group ahead. She looked for Grace, found her still in the first batch of runners. She was within fifteen metres of the lead runner, but those fifteen metres must've felt like five hundred. The effort was plain on Grace's face too. As she passed, Liv yelled, 'Go Grace!'

Grace's heels kicked up and her arms swung faster. The girl wasn't going down without a fight; Liv beamed. Grace gained on the group of three ahead and then was gaining on the leader, too. Fifty metres were left and the cheers grew louder. Grace was five metres behind the leader now. Some were no doubt cheering for the girl in front, but most, Liv realised, were yelling, 'Go Grace, go Grace, go Grace!'

Liv felt those tears coming again. She tried not to lose it among the rows of well-dressed parents and elegant grandparents. This was not her daughter. This was not her niece. This was her son's girlfriend and a new friend's daughter, who she'd met only once and had made cry; but in that moment, Grace could have been Liv's. She was the girl who had been in the back of Liv's thoughts these last almost three months. She was the girl whose photograph had begun this entire shift in Liv and the world she lived in. This girl's self-experimenting had inspired new and wonderful experiments at Carmichael Grammar, and very soon the results of those experiments would be made public. Liv found herself running at the edge of the crowd, heading towards the finish line. 'Go Grace, go Grace, go Grace.'

And Grace went . . . To come second by half a ponytail.

Liv missed the beginning of her boys' race. She wasn't the only one. The crowd encircled the girls and cheered, clapping every one as if they'd crossed the continent. The mood was festive. Mums and dads were laughing and talking to each other as if for the first time. Meanwhile, the boys were running around the first turn; a handful of parents cheered and followed. Liv stayed with the girls.

Jess emerged from the crowd, with Jilly Saffin following behind her.

'There you are! Congrats,' said Liv. 'Grace was amazing.'

'Not bad for a girl who hasn't trained,' said Jess, with a bashful smile. She looked different, out of her work clothes: in a black beanie and big sunglasses. Liv almost didn't recognise her.

Jilly Saffin extended her hand. 'Hi, Liv, I'm Jilly . . .'

'Yes, hello, I remember.' Jilly looked more robust than Liv recalled. Fuller in the face. Less brittle. 'Bella did great, too. She came – what – eleventh?'

Jilly's eyes were wide. 'That gets her through to the next level.' She didn't seem to understand quite how that had happened.

The women smiled in disbelief, as their phones beeped, simultaneously.

'The reports are up,' said a nearby woman. A hush fell over the crowd as people consulted their phones. Liv watched the woman click through to the portal, and her children's pages.

'Oh my god . . .' said the woman.

'Coco too,' said another mum, comparing her phone with her friend's. 'Wow!'

'I owe my husband fifty bucks!' The first woman laughed.

The girls' mums and dads were huddling and laughing and comparing glowing screens. Adults clapped their girls, as they appeared puffing and sweaty alongside them; some hugged them, some showed them their phones. Some squealed. Some of the boys' parents looked on, bemused, amused, curious, their attention split between the girls' reactions, their own phones and the race unfolding on the sports field. More parents began to cheer the runners. A few were muttering and glaring at the pods of girls and mums. A small group of parents encircled Tony and took turns shaking his hand. Among the group were Carly and James Whittaker-Smith, who clapped Tony on the back.

The principal himself looked proud, if stunned. The change had happened so quickly, Liv could understand his jet lag. No one could've predicted such an enormous turn in events. Except Vic. ('It can happen fast,' Vic had said. 'You watch.') As the crowd parted, Liv glimpsed Tony, and he waved. A moment later, Carly saw Liv and smiled too.

Liv was in danger of choking up again, so she walked to a nearby tree, then checked Jai and Oscar's results. She was flicking through them when, a hundred metres away, the boys rounded the final bend. By the time she looked up, Taj Low was thrusting his chest across the finish line, with Jai on his tail. Nearby, Bettina Low was bouncing up and down, flanked by a pair of scowling, oversized men.

'Nice one, Taj-ie.' Bettina waved her phone at her son. 'Let me take a pic.'

Liv wasn't surprised to see the boy keep running.

66

Liv

By 4.15 pm, The Provedore's tables were full of coffee-quaffing women and milkshake-slurping children. Jess, Liv and Jilly demolished jam and cream scones as they compared notes about the afternoon's races and academic reports, and waited for Vic. Jai and Grace both wore red ribbons bearing medals. Bella was pleasantly surprised by her eleventh placement, while Oscar hadn't finished at all. Rowan had fallen near the second bend and lost a shoe, and Oscar had stopped to help, which was a welcome return to old form, if slightly suspicious. Of late, he seemed to be taking a break from being a grump.

As for the academic results, Grace and Bella had both done well across their subjects. Grace's results weren't a surprise, though she'd shifted an A-minus in Science to an A-plus, and Jess couldn't stop patting her back. Jai too had done well, as he usually did, but his A in Science had remained an A. Where Jai tended to get straight A's, Oscar usually got straight B-minuses. But Oscar's B-minus in Science had turned into a NN (did not complete), which needed to be addressed, immediately. (*I'm on it*, Duncan had texted. *Sorry I missed the race.*) The biggest surprise, though, was Bella. She'd gone from a C-minus in Science to a B-plus, and was high-fiving any available hand.

Liv sipped her chai latte. Nearby, boys' and girls' mums chatted. Teachers mingled among the parents – mostly female teachers, but a few of the blokes too. Even Carly, James and Rowan were here. The mood

was festive, as if they were at a sweet-sixteenth or bat mitzvah. Noticeably absent, besides Vic, were Bettina Low and Taj; Penny Appleby and
Hannah; and Waring and Humphries, et al. Liv felt a faint ripple of appre-
hension as she chalked up that list.

Liv checked her phone as a group approached their table.

'I don't know how you've done it, but we're very grateful,' said Coco's
mum, her arm slung around her daughter. 'Yeah, what she said,'
Coco added. A second girl, Daisy, gave a nod.

'Don't thank me, the girls did it themselves,' said Liv. 'Alison?'

'That's me.'

Liv gave Alison a thumbs up. As the women left, another group
replaced them.

'Well done,' said James Whittaker-Smith. Rowan and Carly were
standing behind James, sheepishly. 'The school's needed something like
this for years.'

Liv filled with pride. She coughed to dislodge it.

'Did you know Dr Cato picked up Rowan's auditory processing problem?' Carly whispered, gesturing to her son's head.

'I didn't, no.' Liv coughed again, shifting from pride to remorse. 'That's
wonderful.'

As she watched the family leave, Liv felt as though she and Vic and Jess
had scaled a mountain, and brought the school with them. The view from
up here was spectacular, the sky infinitely blue. But they were in rarefied
air; and a range of ice-capped mountains remained.

Outside, a pair of puffed-up, suited men walked by, and Jess turned
her back to the window. Liv sipped her cooling, milky tea. Lots still left
to do, she thought. On the domestic front, she had to tell Duncan she
was no longer going to be an investigator. She was going to be a pioneer.
Well, an assistant pioneer. Or a pioneer's assistant. She just needed to
have the chat with Vic, and they were away. There were so many young
minds to climb inside and get between your fingers. She couldn't wait.

At that moment, Bettina Low stepped inside The Provedore, followed
by Taj and Dylan. These days, the older Low was more man than boy.
Dylan's looks were still plain but he was taller and more muscular than

most of his teachers now. In his sports uniform and lace-ups, he looked like a miscast actor. He smiled at no one in particular. Seeing the jam-packed cafe, Bettina turned and left, calling her boys out after her. On the footpath, Taj and Dylan bickered. A second later, Stella and Blake appeared alongside them. Aghast, Liv watched as Bettina pointed Stella and Blake towards another cafe. With a jut of his chin to Oscar, Taj strode off, while Blake hung back, and Dylan looked genuinely discomfited. Blake seemed altered – his hair shorter, his clothes fitting. Bella gave a small wave. Liv may have imagined it, but for a moment Jai looked like he'd bumped an old bruise. Yes, that was a relationship, or two, she'd mismanaged.

Liv finished her tea. Don't fret, she told herself – look how far we have come! Look around. 'Gratitude trumps fear,' Vic had said once. Or was it regret?

A second later, a bicycle flew across the pavement. The cafe hushed. As Vic appeared, girls and boys rose, followed by parents and teachers.

'We're back on next term!' Vic said, with a fist pump, and some rowdy mums cheered. Liv clapped as people surged forward with hugs and Vic threw herself into the closest pair of arms.

That evening, around a board game called *Life*, the kids were singing, Liv was winning and Duncan was close behind her. Liv had a wonderful job, as a vet. Perhaps counterintuitively, she also had five kids. Duncan was on her heels with four kids of his own and a job as a mobile app designer. Duncan had been grinning stupidly all week; tonight, he seemed to be delighting in sitting on the floor around the coffee table. Not once had he complained about her top forty music, either. Meanwhile, Cody was a secret agent, Jai was a racing-car driver and Oscar was a teacher, and the least happy with his selection. But at least he was laughing about it. (Duncan and Oscar were running some sort of in-joke about dodgy co-workers.) And Liv was enjoying getting paid every time she passed a pay day. A virtue of this game was that it didn't distinguish between men and women – a scientist was a scientist and an athlete an athlete. Everyone could choose to have a family and detour off the career course for a few years, or plough directly on.

Liv grinned at the relaxed faces. They'd been at it for half an hour and no one had squabbled. No one had punched anyone. No one had yelled 'NO!' Their fish-and-chips packaging was strewn across the table, and no one cared.

Liv had read that couples who played board games together stayed together, and she could see why. Last turn, her pet goat won best in show, Duncan bought a windmill and Jai went sky diving, risk free. Even Oscar seemed more settled. The turbulence of months ago was gone.

As Oscar spun the dice-spinner, Liv kissed Duncan on the lips and lingered. The boys did not break out of song.

For the two weeks of school holidays, the Winsome family enjoyed a period of relative ease. The boys wandered around in pyjamas and watched movies, played games, communicated through devices and ate. Other than a few minor brawls early in their staycation, the boys were able to coexist. No one was feverish. No one was grounded. Spending less time alone in his room, Oscar seemed better, as if school was perhaps a trigger for his behaviour; and he had promised not to fudge a test again. Overall, time moved by at a comfortable pace. Duncan went to work, of course, but when he was home he hummed around like a man with a sweet secret, and Liv let him keep it – after all, she had her own. Instinct told her not to tell him about working with Vic, until Term Three began. But the good news was that Tony had agreed to pay her too – for three days a week. She would look back on these two mid-winter weeks as a time when nothing memorable happened – and, for a parent (and a wife), that was a blessed time.

67

Duncan

On the day Henry was due back, Duncan soared into work. To his delight, after much discussion, Maggie had come on board. Ever since, Duncan couldn't wait to finally put his case to the powers that be. Yes, it would require a major shift in mindset but it was worth a shot. This simple and perfect idea. Fortuitously, Henry's annual golf jaunt north had gone well, and Michael had just scored a new client from an old rival. The planets had aligned. After Duncan's meeting, he'd broach it.

Of course, together they'd need to rejig their business model, make it smarter and more focused on output, less focused on billable hours. But that was doable, surely, if they put their big brains together. They were already, increasingly, using quasi-fixed-price contracts. Plus, other firms were adopting the four-day-a-week model here and around the world; and it worked. People came to work refreshed and re-energised; these firms had lower absenteeism and turnover, and even increased productivity and profit. They became employers of choice! Win, win, win. Duncan was confident that his clients wouldn't care, as long as their work got done.

All morning, Michael had been with his new clients in the boardroom next door. Duncan's meeting had been scheduled to begin in that room fifteen minutes ago, but was now squeezed into the smaller boardroom. Duncan smiled, serenely. He tried to concentrate on Red and Julia; yin and yang. Julia was running the meeting, while Red wrote it up. For reasons Duncan didn't understand, Red was becoming a stroppy fellow. Maybe because he was on Michael's radar now. Maybe because eventually there was nowhere to hide. Oh well. Julia ran an efficient meeting and soon it was over. Duncan saw his clients out and made for Michael's office. There, Michael and Henry were debriefing.

Duncan felt an inner drumroll as he rapped on the glass. Michael paused, rubbed his monk-style hair. The sky-blue eyes he turned on Duncan were disarmingly pretty. 'Come on in, little fella.'

On a good day, Michael could be surprisingly light-hearted.

Duncan stepped in. 'Thanks.'

'Did you hear about Owen Low?' Michael said. 'Been made a County Court judge.'

Duncan pictured Owen at university – unconscious, under a table at a ball, permanent marker on his cheeks. Courtesy of Michael.

'Yeah, I heard.' Duncan made himself grin. Truth be told, there wasn't a Low he liked.

Michael's laugh boomed. 'What's the world coming to when that dipstick's a fucking judge?'

Duncan had felt similarly. Sometimes the world made no sense whatsoever. He sat down. 'I wanted to tell you both, I've . . .' He cleared his throat. 'I've got an idea, to mix things up around here. I'm thinking we could trial a four-day working week.'

Michael glared from him to Henry.

'You what?' said Henry, as if he was hard of hearing.

'I reckon we could afford a one hundred percent productivity/eighty percent time/one hundred percent pay model.'

Henry's eyes were popping. 'We need more good people, not less of the people we have!'

Michael boomed, 'Pay people for not working? Is that what he said?'

'Are you ill?' Henry said.

'No.'

'Then what the fuck?' said Michael.

'We can get a lot done in a day now, my team at least. If productivity is up and costs are lower, it's the least—'

Michael blustered over the top of him. 'Is he—'

'What's going on, Duncan?' said Henry. 'Why would you say such things?'

'I want to spend more time with my family. I'm sure lots of our people would appreciate the extra day too. They deserve it.'

Henry looked stunned.

'Henry, Liv and the kids need me.'

Michael imitated him, mincingly: '*Liv and the kids need me!*' His brother really was a very juvenile man.

In the silence that ensued, Henry's disappointment was palpable.

Duncan noticed that Henry's hands were shaking. 'We all work too hard. Too much,' said Duncan.

'Pay people for not working,' Michael said again. 'Jesus. Has he flipped?'

'You really want to spend *more* time with your family?' Henry was pale now.

'You don't have to work stupid hours, you know.'

'Duncan, this is still a legal practice!' Henry said, as if in disbelief.

'The answer's no,' snapped Michael. 'No fucking way.'

Duncan pursed his lips. Looked to Henry, who was closing the door.

'You and your pot plants and *productivity*!' said Michael.

Henry tut-tutted as Michael stood and stomped about. 'Some of us don't want to work less! Or spend time with our families! That ever occur to you?'

'Oh.' It hadn't occurred to Duncan that Michael might not like his children. Though, it made sense: no one had liked Michael's second wife. But Duncan didn't want to debate Michael about his lifestyle. It sure didn't look as if it was working for him. At the very least, Michael could do with a hobby. Golf. Meditation.

'I come in here every day because I live alone, as you might recall,' said Henry.

'I happen to fucking like it here.' Michael gestured to the well-appointed offices and the corridor, where, to Duncan's surprise, Xavier was barking at a red-faced Julia.

At that moment, George appeared and, seeing Michael, he averted his eyes. George was thin, these days.

Michael was watching Duncan think.

'The fucking curry-muncher gave you a scare?' Michael whispered. 'Is that it?'

Every so often, Michael's offensiveness slapped Duncan across the face. Hard. He blinked, almost disbelieving. As Michael carried on, Duncan heard the odd word: 'joke', 'irresponsible', 'piss-weak'.

Duncan looked to Henry: Why can't you see. . .

'I can't get my head around it.' Henry seemed dazed himself. 'Let me sleep on it.'

'No way,' said Michael, 'this idea is dead. The people who work here *like to work*! That's who we are, for fuck's sake. This is a high-performance culture.'

Duncan tuned his brother out, as three things dawned on him. First, he forgot to tell them Maggie and two of the other partners were open to a trial. Second, often, you had to give something a real go before you could say you didn't like it. They were fools for not seeing that. Fools who did not seem deeply happy! And third, what he'd really wanted was to talk. To toss around ideas. The way he was now talking with Oscar, and even Cody. For years, he'd laboured under the hope that, one day, he and his brother and Henry could be close, like families in movies. He dreamt of sharing with them his secret fears – keeling over, divorce, dementia – and hopes, without being laughed at. He'd wished today they could've acknowledged his success in re-energising his team and trusted him. He'd hoped they might have said, 'You've done incredible things here, pal. Keep it up, whatever it takes!'

Most of all, he'd hoped, contrary to all appearances, they might've been interested in him. In his inner life, as he was now in theirs. (Why was Michael an arsehole? Why didn't he want to go home? Why was Henry so resistant to change?)

But who was he kidding?

As Michael ran on, Duncan thought ahead to next week. On Monday, Term Three began and they were due to make another payment. He wondered how Oscar would fare back at school. If that little girl would pull her head in, or if Oscar would do anything about it. Lately, Oscar had been sweet: 'How was your day, Dad? Everything okay?' Liv, not so much. He'd clearly been hatching something but she hadn't asked, once. Duncan felt a constriction in his chest: his ribcage was now a boot being laced. Truth was, he didn't know any families like his dream family. Over the years, Liv had tried, but she'd had too much going on. And he'd had his head in the billable clouds. But that was behind them. The past few weeks, all together, had been the best. Easy. Fun. Cheap. On the weekends and in the evenings, they'd done very little. Played cards and *The Game of Life* again. He'd been an app developer twice. Imagine! It sounded so, so . . . hip and free!

When Duncan rose, Michael towered over him. Through the glass, Red and Julia, Maia and George were watching, as Maggie strolled up. Every face wore a slightly different version of dismay, except Maggie's. Hers looked, if anything, expectant.

Duncan took a long, deep breath. 'You know what? I'm done. I'm going, this minute. Because you're *stuck*,' he said to Henry. 'And you're an *arsehole*!'

'You spineless bag of jelly!' said Michael. 'You'll be back.'

'Will not!' yelled Duncan.

'Will too!'

Duncan raised a pot plant, high; had a vague notion of throwing it at Michael. Dirt fell on his head.

On the other side of the glass, Red sniggered to himself while a teary Julia gave him a subtle elbow in the ribs. Ashamed, Duncan forced himself to surrender the fern. He waited for Henry to reprimand Michael for once, or talk him round. He gave himself a split second to pull back – did he really want to blow up his working life, completely?

A tiny muscle in Henry's cheek moved, and Duncan's chest exploded with merry fireworks. Yes, he did. After all these years, it was that easy. He stepped over the puddle of dirt. At the door, he saw shock spread across the faces of his staff. Only Maggie, his successor, smirked – almost as if she'd seen this coming.

68

Liv

Outside, the trees were undressed and the air was nippy. Winter had come as a shock after a mild autumn, and the holidays, almost over now, had been spent largely inside. Liv had relished the break from ferrying people around, and from Carmichael, though she was keen to start again come Monday. In the kitchen, savouring the warmth, Liv was stirring pots and dancing to the radio. In one roiling pot was king prawn flesh; in a second, prawns' heads and tails bubbled happily. This stock took forever, but Liv was prepared to go the distance. In the fridge, her favourite prosecco and Duncan's favourite beer waited. She'd also bought a lemon meringue tart from the local patisserie and made a rocket, pear and parmesan salad. It felt like someone's birthday – perhaps hers. As she stirred, she sang. She hadn't felt this relaxed or optimistic in years. She also hadn't enjoyed preparing a meal like this in months. Cooking by choice, she realised, was remarkably pleasant.

She smooched the arriving Duncan, who smiled at the activity in the kitchen.

'Is it our anniversary?'

'Nope.' She grinned. 'Merely the eve of a new term.'

'Ah . . . Where shall I put these?'

In one of Duncan's hands was a bunch of multicoloured carnations; in the other, a bag from Aldi. While carnations weren't a favourite, at least she wasn't allergic, she thought. But flowers twice in as many months?

She frowned. She'd read once that spouses who were having affairs became more generous with their partners. More engaged lovers.

'What are *you* celebrating?'

With a grunt, Oscar heaved himself onto the benchtop and filched another cooling Anzac biscuit. Oscar had recently hit the age where bench-sitting was de rigueur. Unhygienic, but at least it meant he left his room. Having cooked for himself and his brothers, he would soon be going to a gathering at Taj's (despite Liv's half-hearted protests), but Jai had gone to Grace's, his second home recently. Since dropping half of her extra-curricular activities, the former super-girl had become a permanent fixture in Jai's week, and they were enjoying a rare basketball-free Friday night together. If Oscar wasn't at Taj's, he'd be friendless. Cody was presently in front of the TV, watching young men mountain-bike off cliffs. Soon, he was heading out with Harry to watch a movie (no sleepover). But not gone yet, every few minutes, he barked, 'I need a glass of water!' and 'I want more cookies!' Which Liv was ignoring.

Oscar's lingering suggested he had something to say. But Liv couldn't find the inner space to attend to him. Within the hour, she and Duncan would have the house to themselves.

'Duncan?'

Duncan picked her up and swung her in a loop. 'My exit strategy.'

Liv felt as if he'd flung a prawn tail at her cheek. 'Your what?'

Oscar beamed.

'From Winsome & Ueland!' Duncan laughed.

'Put me down, please.'

'Go Dunc,' said Oscar, his voice breaking.

'Thanks Osc.'

Back on her feet, Liv reviewed their kitchen and son. This was meant to be a calm, enjoyable, R-rated evening of beautiful food and quiet cele-bration. Double dessert.

'*Your* exit?' She poured herself a glass of bubbles.

'Who else's? I told Henry and Michael. I'm—'

'Wait a second,' she said. 'Hold it right there.'

'What's wrong? What's with the face?'

'I have news too. It's gone so well at Carmichael, I want to quit investigating. Work with Vic.'

Duncan swept his tongue around his mouth. 'Right. Full-time? How much is Vic or the school going to pay you?'

Liv scratched her once-bald patch. While she'd gamely had the chat with Vic, they hadn't dug into the nitty-gritty. Oscar was observing her forensically.

'I'm not exactly sure of the pay, yet. But I'm never working full-time again. Kids or no kids, that's no life. It'll be three days. Three days is probably the sweet spot.'

'Oh, okay. Right . . .'

She wondered if Duncan had noticed she hadn't done any investigating lately. No funny stories about Ryan's Mr Fix-it jobs.

On the radio, a singer was bellowing about his lost love. Duncan winced, opened a beer, took a slug. 'Here's what I want . . .' He cleared his throat. 'It starts with a trip . . .'

'Not that again.'

A three-line vertical frown appeared on Oscar's forehead, his biscuit forgotten.

'What are you going to do in the Barossa for two months?'

'Not two months. Not a sabbatical. We can go for as long or as short as we like—'

'What do you mean?'

'If we sell up, we can go anywhere – cheaper. If we're smart about it . . . live frugally . . . it can work. All I know is, I want to be with you and the boys. You're right, they do need me. A lot. I can't do justice to everyone and keep working as I have.' He looked at her earnestly. 'I can't do it all, Liv.'

'Oh, god.' Liv downed her prosecco.

'When we get back, I'll see what'll fit.' Duncan stared into his beer. 'But I'm done with Winsome & Ueland, Michael, maybe even the law. Everything's up for grabs. I want to work less too. Three days sounds good – all from home maybe.'

Bewildered, Liv watched him swallow. 'Three days?'

'Did you bash him, Dad?'

Liv looked at Oscar in dismay. 'Who?'

Duncan shook his head, sheepish. 'Ah, no. But I resigned, on the spot.'

'You what?' she growled.

Liv worked very hard to keep her face still. Tricky, considering she felt as if he'd just proposed their divorce. In Adelaide or Hampton, without his income, their lifestyle would collapse. The boys would have to leave Carmichael. She'd have to work more, not less. She couldn't see a happy place for herself in that future. She hadn't signed up for this, twenty-six years ago.

'Dad, if we have to leave Carmichael, Jai'll flip. Go totally nutso.' Oscar smiled. 'But I'll go to Bayside Sec, right?'

Duncan's face puckered. How much had he thought this through? Liv looked from her son's intensity to her husband's confusion. She turned off the prawns and the radio. Poured herself another prosecco. The only sound was the exhaust fan.

'Oscar,' said Duncan, 'can you give us a minute?'

With surprising obedience, Oscar slid off the bench like melted butter.

'Thanks, mate.'

'Dad, I'm going to Taj's.' With a jut of the chin, Oscar swaggered off.

'Have fun.' Watching him go, Duncan frowned. 'He needs me, can't you see that?'

Liv blinked, more bewildered.

'We need to give notice to Carmichael. Monday,' he said.

'Over my dead body. That school—'

'It's not all sunshine at that school,' he said. 'Liv, there's talk of a coup. Apparently, lots of old boys are apoplectic—'

'Oh, that's . . . that's ridiculous.' Liv folded her arms across her chest. Her brain couldn't accommodate Duncan and Oscar's new bond or disgruntled old boys right now. Dazed, she considered the stove. The prawn carcasses did look rather disgusting. She put a lid on the pot.

'But . . . Why didn't you consult me before you did this?'

'I've tried.'

She sipped. This probably wasn't the time to mention she hadn't done any files this month. Or last.

'I thought you liked your job. All those tweaks . . . You've been enjoying it—'

'I have. But not for the work.' He ducked her gaze, bashful.

Her stomach buckled. 'Is this about Maggie Koh?'

'No, no. It's about me.' He took a deep breath. 'I'd never asked myself how I felt about my actual work. I've worked nonstop since I was twenty-three, you know that. It's what men do. Turns out, I don't really like it.'

'Fuck,' she said.

'I was prepared to keep doing it – I wanted us all to work a four-day week on the same money but Michael vetoed it.'

'And that was a surprise?'

He shrugged, then grinned. 'Nope. But, I guess, it gave me the shove I needed.'

'Fuck,' she said, again.

69

Jess

By 9 pm, Grace, Bella and Jai had been tucked away for hours in Grace's room, but Jess wasn't complaining. The girls were getting along and Jai was a pleasure to have around, though he wasn't sleeping over. In recent weeks, the girls had been activated, like almonds. Grace was filling in the time freed up by giving away Instagram, Snapchat and basketball with reading about global politics and climate science and student activism. Jess wasn't quite across all of these new interests, but reading was definitely better than taking pictures of yourself.

Jess was midway through ordering a potted orchid to belatedly thank Professor Griffin, on behalf of the working group, for her science intervention, when Grace, Bella and Jai tumbled in.

Grace was holding her iPad close.

'Tell her,' whispered Bella, excitedly.

'No, you tell her.'

'She's your mum,' said Jai.

Grace winced at the flowers on Jess's screen, then thrust her iPad towards her mother. 'Look at this.'

'I thought you were off Instagram, hon.'

'We are, but people have been DMing us.'

'For our list, Creeps at Carmichael,' said Bella.

Jess sucked in a gasp. She thought she'd prayed that idea away. What did Vic's book say about parenting moments like this? Something to do with 'Oh'.

'Oh,' she said.

Jai was fidgeting with his cuffs.

'There are heaps of stories,' said Bella.

'Oh.' Jess's face felt tight, as if covered in mud.

'But, like, the same names keep coming up,' said Grace. 'You'll never guess who!'

Jess looked from one expectant face to another. Neither of the girls looked particularly scared, or wary. They'd taken to wearing their hair unkempt and applying heavy black lines to their eyes. They nodded eagerly at her. Stalling, Jess took in their loose jumpsuits. While ugly, these get-ups looked comfortable. And the girls' eyes were striking – electric blue and glowing brown. In tracksuit pants and a hoodie, Jai may have been wearing eye make-up too. His hazel eyes looked enormous, but that also could've been worry. He was flicking his forelock every few seconds. He was the only one who seemed to understand the ball of fire Grace was holding.

'Mum, guess?'

'Oh, um . . . Miss Lee? Mr Crisp? I'm awful at guessing games.'

'Very funny,' said Grace.

'Most of the creepy stuff is coming from *eight boys* and—'

'Oh.'

That 'Oh' was getting harder to maintain. 'Jai, are you hungry?'

'No, thanks,' said Jai. 'I better get going. Just get my bag.' He slunk off to Grace's room.

Grace waved the iPad at Jess. 'Mum? Say something!'

'What you've got there – it's in the past, isn't it?'

Grace's black-lined eyes narrowed. 'We're not done, Mum. You said that yourself.'

Jess smiled. 'But the school's wonderful today, hon, isn't it? Who wants some gelati?'

'Yeah, it's better but . . . people need to see this,' said Bella.

'The main ones aren't in Year Eight. Look!' Grace swiped to a new page.

She thrust the screen under Jess's nose again. Eight names were written in a circle, and arrows shot in and out with more names attached – girls' names. And the odd boy's. One of which, to Jess's dismay, she recognised. She squinted at the smaller writing: 'Pulled down my pants backstage . . .'

She couldn't look at Jai, as he returned.

'Put that away,' she spluttered.

Grace yanked the iPad away. Even Bella, her agreeable pseudo-second-daughter, looked snarky. Jai fiddled with his bag. He also seemed to be grinding his teeth as he flicked his hair.

'But this changes everything. Don't you see?' Bella pointed to specifics on the screen.

Jess shut her eyes.

'What's the matter?' said Grace.

'We've ranked them, in order of worst offenders, see,' said Bella, swiping the screen again.

'See the top?' said Grace. 'Mum!'

Jess read the name.

'Girls, whatever you do, *do not post that list*. Do you hear me?'

In a split second, Jess pictured the backlash. The furious old men, the stalkers and trolls.

'We thought you'd be happy,' said Grace. 'Naming names, shaming boys.'

'Oh, hon, that was before.' Jess gripped the desktop. She felt as if she was being sucked out of the side of an aeroplane. A plane that'd been heading somewhere warm and magical, like the Galapagos Islands.

'Before what?' Grace said. 'Before you got scared?'

'Promise me you haven't posted that. You will be in *loads* of trouble.'

Grace's dramatic blue eyes were avoiding hers.

'If that's online already, you need to take it down. Please. Now.'

Jess imagined Dr Cato learning about this. Maybe even being blamed for it somehow.

'You're wimping out,' said Bella.

'You don't need to do this, girls. We've come a long, long way.'

'Doesn't feel like it right now.' Grace's face was dappled with disappointment. 'You never told anyone about Mr Palmer, did you?'

Confused, Jess opened then shut her mouth, like a gully trap.

'I knew it.' Grace flashed a sharp look to Bella.

'How do you know what you've got there is true?' Jess said. 'Someone could sue you if it's not . . . I think.'

Could kids sue kids? She'd have to ask Liv.

'We cross-referenced,' said Bella. 'At least two people had to be talking about the same person before we outed them. To be honest, I don't know why we—'

'That was Jai's idea,' said Grace.

Jess looked to Jai, who may have been breaking out in hives.

'One person's enough!' said Bella. 'If it's true, it's true.'

Jess swallowed whatever words were coming up. Poor Jai began to scratch his neck.

'I thought you'd changed,' said Grace. 'But you still worry too much! About the wrong things!'

In their gothic-frump, the pair stomped off; a second later, Jai waved and left. Jess looked from her white knuckles to the screen of plants. For the shortest time, everything had been going so well. For the briefest moment, she'd had her daughter in her palm.

70

Liv

The house still smelt of prawns as Liv plucked a long-lost piece of spaghetti from her cleavage. The evening had been a stunning flop, punctuated by awkward silence and phone calls. Over dessert, Liv was trying to grasp their new world order Mark II, when Cody banged on the door like the wolf in *The Three Little Pigs*. Having a son home was actually a relief.

Liv sang out. 'Coming!'

As Cody banged again, Duncan winced but didn't move. Then his phone rang, again. That was something Liv wouldn't miss. Overall, though, she realised, she'd liked being the partner's wife. The wife was the next best thing to being a partner herself. Or was it better? Duncan answered the phone and she rose.

'Let me in,' hollered Cody. 'Let me in!'

Honestly, as much as she needed the distraction, she didn't really want to. This particular child of hers, she realised, got on her nerves. She paused in the foyer to take stock. By staying out of the law, she'd enabled Duncan's partnership; they both knew that. She'd supported him on the way up, managed the home front so he could work on his big deals until midnight, night after night and weekend after weekend. In return, he'd supported them, then, now and *forever*. That'd been the deal; the unspoken deal. Bang, bang, bang went Cody. Liv sighed monumentally. She hadn't foregone her career so he could give up his. Wreck their kids' lives.

'*Dad?!*' Cody shrieked on the dark porch.

Liv yanked open the door.

'Get out of my way!' Cody said, bolting for Jai's bedroom. 'Where's the iPad?'

Cody's mouth was rimmed with red, as if he'd eaten a dozen toffee apples. This was no time for a talk about manners. Liv dashed to the lounge room and kicked all available gaming gear behind a bookshelf. So much for watching a movie! Their youngest had clearly been at Harry's playing that first-person shooter game that turned him into a raging psychopath. Like Gunhild, but louder, smaller and more physical. Damn it, Duncan should never have given Cody that old iPad.

'Let's get you into the shower,' Liv said, wrestling Cody towards the bathroom.

'No! No! NO!' screamed Cody. 'Where's Dad! I want Dad!'

Still on his phone, Duncan pivoted into his old study and shut the door. With a scowl, Liv dragged Cody by his wrist. 'What the hell have you been eating?'

Five minutes later, Cody was strewn across the shower tiles; Duncan was still sequestered away; and Liv was clearing up, when Jai let himself in. Their younger twin was walking fast and grinding faster. He had an intense, unfocused stare, as if he was trying to solve the problems of the universe, without a calculator. He also seemed to be unusually spotty. As he passed through the dining room, he jumped to touch the archway. He did it again from dining room to kitchen. Oh, no. Where had that come from?

Another minute, another son. Their front door had become a turnstile. Before Liv could get to Jai, Oscar arrived. Good thing her R-rated night in had been a washout. Because Oscar was tear-streaked and wearing black pants and a long-sleeved black T-shirt with something in white drawn on it. The male gender symbol with a clenched fist in its circle. WTF! He was also in the middle of a primal scream.

'YOUUUUUUU!'

'Oscar?'

Oscar charged past her.

'Oscar!'

Liv ran behind Oscar as he gained on Jai. For a moment, Liv thought Oscar was going to punch Jai in the back of the head. Everything was about to become monumentally worse. Potentially catastrophic. But it was an arm punch. Hard. Like a fist-sized injection. Jai bellowed, turned and wrestled Oscar to the floor.

'Boys! Don't! Stop it!' Liv yelled.

The twins continued to give their all to each other in the confined space.

At a jog, Duncan appeared. 'Whoa, what's this?'

'No idea. But . . .' Liv gasped. 'Make them *stop*!'

The boys were grunting and slapping and grimacing. Legs and arms were twisting and pounding. The expression on Duncan's face was confusing. It wasn't worry or shock or alarm. It was more akin to guilt. 'What's that T-shirt all about?'

'Not sure. But I could guess.' Liv scowled, as Jai had a handful of Oscar's hair. 'Duncan, do something!'

Duncan tugged his forelock then leant forward, as if the boys were dogs and he didn't want to risk being bitten. After two more grunts, it looked as though Jai had the better of it. Jai was easing up, when Oscar kicked the wall. Plaster crumbled.

'What's wrong with you?' Jai yelled.

'What's wrong with you?' Oscar yelled.

'Stop yelling!' Duncan yelled.

Duncan loomed over his sons, and both boys cowered. Liv moved between the three of them. Gestured to the boys' rooms. The boys crawled and sobbed in opposite directions.

'You rode right past me,' Oscar muttered, over his shoulder. 'Why didn't you stop?'

'Look at you,' said Jai. 'You're a freak.'

Duncan moved to follow Oscar, who, inexplicably, was heading for Jai's room. Meanwhile, Jai staggered for the toilet. Weakly, he tapped picture frames as he passed. Liv felt a twist in her gut. Ritualised tapping had been dormant for two years. Precisely what was upsetting him? If he went into the toilet and started tapping, how long would it be before he came out?

'Which bozo do you want?' said Duncan.

In that moment, the Lists were irrelevant. The pull towards Jai was as strong as gravity. It took an act of significant willpower for Liv to ignore it. But ignore it she did. Eventually, mothers, like everyone else, needed to be fair. As fair as possible.

'That one,' she said, pointing.

Liv whispered through the closed door. 'Osc?'

From within, Oscar yelled, 'Leave me alone!' And then came the sobs. 'What's . . . wrong . . . with . . . me? What's . . . wrong . . . with . . . me?'

This, from Oscar, was particularly dramatic. From metres away, Duncan's groan was audible.

Through the crack, Liv said, 'What *is* wrong with you?'

A thud against the other side of the door. Liv could feel steam coming down the hall. She'd forgotten the exhaust fan. 'Cody,' she snapped at Duncan, who seemed to be frozen. 'Go to Cody.'

'Oh, for god's sake.' Duncan stomped off.

'Oscar, speak to me, please. Use your words!'

'Go away!'

'No one's going away.'

Louder cries.

Liv turned the door handle and it opened. Bare-chested, Oscar sat on the floor. He looked up at her through greasy hair. Liv waited until, finally, more quietly, he said, 'Mum. Just like people don't choose to be gay, or trans, I didn't choose to be a straight, white male.'

'Oh. Okay . . .' It was rather hard not to laugh at that. But she managed it.

Oscar tugged out a box stashed under the bunk bed. Chocolate bread. Liquorice twists. All the Aldi delights. He belly-flopped onto Jai's bed and cried and munched.

'Oh, Osc,' said Liv. 'It's okay, sweetheart.'

Oscar sniffed and blubbered.

'I get you're feeling confused, hey? And sad?'

'Yeah,' he nodded. Then his face distorted. 'Why are girls so fucking annoying? All mean, and judgey, and attention-seeking and bragging!' He made an even more horrible face and stupid squeaks, presumably meant to resemble a girl speaking. Liv was tempted to slap him. 'And everything's always about *them*! International Women's Day! *QUOTAS*! And *we* have to cut *our* hair! I'm so fucking sick of it!'

Liv put her hand across her mouth. You weren't meant to admit it, but sometimes you really didn't like your children.

Liv had so many things to say. Starting with, 'Have you learnt nothing?!' And 'Watch your fucking language!' Followed by, 'I didn't know you needed a haircut.' Though Oscar's hair was touching his collar.

Meanwhile, Oscar fell quiet.

'Mum, Hannah Appleby calls me "the fugly twin",' he whispered. 'Like, *every day*. In front of *everyone*. I fucking hate that skinny bitch. She's nothing but a nasty piece of gristle!'

'Oh, Osc.' Liv made herself stay silent, hold the space for him. It was a challenge.

Oscar fixed his wet eyes on Liv. 'At Taj's, I kind of went psycho at her . . . and he kicked me out.'

Before Liv could respond, with kindness and empathy and wisdom, an enormous crunch emanated from the bathroom. Presumably Cody had knocked himself out, climbing the shower screen. '*DAAAD!*'

Liv frowned.

Whoever said boys were easier than girls wasn't paying any fucking attention.

An hour later, the boys were sedated (two Panadol each for the twins, and one for Cody – Liv had read the tablets were as good for emotional upset as a headache), while Liv scrubbed pots. Given the crisis scenario, they seemed to have reverted to the pre-Lists status quo: when she cooked, she washed up. Duncan stood beside her, faffing about with a tea towel.

'Good job out there,' said Duncan. 'Team effort.'

'Mm.'

They'd managed to get their sons into bed without becoming ensnared in any one impossibly complex conversation. But first, Duncan had screamed at Cody for reasons unknown and Cody had screamed back. Now Cody had lost his screen time until Christmas. That father–son love affair was brief.

Liv felt another hit of irritation. Tomorrow, each of her boys would need a chunk of her.

'They're all going a bit crazy, aren't they?' Duncan said.

'Yep, they are.'

A freshly buried emotion rose up in her: guilt. Recently, she'd let a few things slide. On that list were two of her sons. She'd told herself she hadn't been their designated parent; that one hands-on parent was enough, and had been for fourteen years. But what she'd been these past few months, she realised now, was wilfully negligent, times two.

She attacked the stock pot. Worked up a sweat.

'How do you think they'll fare,' she said, blowing hair from her cheek, 'when their life's turned upside down?'

'Oh, they'll be upset, I guess. Might go a bit crazier to start with . . . But they'll get over it. Long term, they'll be happier, you'll see. There are other good schools.'

Duncan grinned. He'd been working hard to be amiable since his brief but fierce battle with Cody.

When she didn't respond, he cleared all expression from his face, and suddenly he looked old. Vulnerable. Fragile. Her unemployed husband. She paused at the sink, and shivered. This was ridiculously hard. But it had to get easier, didn't it? She made herself breathe deeply through her nose. One. Two. Three. In the not-too-distant future, the boys would be grown. Gone. How much longer did they have together as a family? They needed to make wise choices, now.

'Our boys need security. Stability,' she said. 'We like our life the way it is. And the school . . . you can't pull them out now.' She collected herself, again. 'Duncan, I didn't marry a . . . a part-time worker. We need at least one full-time wage – *yours*. I mean, honestly, you were dreaming! Who's going to pay everyone the same money for less hours?'

Duncan flinched, and she couldn't help feeling that she'd failed a test.

'Well, I didn't marry a . . . do-gooder,' he said. 'Or a suburban activist crossed with a Russian spy.'

Self-conscious, Liv returned to the colander. 'I'm hardly Russian.'

'You were the one who wanted me to mix things up!' he said. 'That was you, wasn't it?'

Liv's face quaked, as the last of her certainty slipped. 'Yep.'

71

Liv

Lying on the trampoline, Liv listened to the night noises: rustling, squeaks, a confused bird. She searched the pockmarked sky. Her toes and nose were cold, her mind restless. Insomnia was something else to attribute to perimenopause, she supposed. On the upside, no one was calling for her. No one was making terrible choices or fighting with his brother. No one was having a middle-aged meltdown. She was alone with her garden's unseen creatures. Using her cold toes, she zipped up the trampoline's net.

Once, a palm-sized spider had fallen on her cheek, back in Duncan's dank flat. She'd screamed as she danced naked around his bed. Duncan had laughed as he tossed the monster out. Only after did he tell her that spiders made him squirmy too. The spider incident had prompted their moving in together. It'd been easy, that transition. Natural. She retraced her thoughts to their knot. She was having more trouble accepting Duncan's decision than she ought. But why?

In the last week of Vic's class, the Year Eight students had discussed what it meant to be a young man today. The perils of manhood and the 'masculine' qualities worth fostering. At home, listening to Jai describe the class, Liv had realised that she'd given little thought to the valuable male qualities. Ha. Had Oscar skipped that class? Most of the time, when gendered behaviour was discussed, Liv wasn't thinking about the male behaviour. She was too busy quietly trying on the female generalisations. Gentle and patient, timid and passive, humble and submissive. Nope, nope, nope. None of these applied to her.

She supposed stoicism was one for the other team. Duncan had taken himself off to work for years, without complaint. He'd shouldered the financial load, without comment. Yes, he'd been grouchy at times. Tough on the kids. But otherwise he hadn't shown much discomfort. She hadn't ever seen him cry. Not when she lost her first pregnancy at nineteen weeks. Not when Pickle's predecessor was hit by a car and had to be put down, aged two. Not when the boys were born. The range of his emotions to which she'd been exposed was limited: to anger, frustration . . . geniality. Was that an emotion? He didn't complain but he didn't fly particularly high either. The most you'd get was a 'Good-o!' And a wide smile. Her boys had a greater range – at least privately. For all their craziness, she was pleased for them. Pleased they felt safe enough to emote at home. Freely. Colourfully. With Duncan, it was like watching TV from the 1970s: black and white versus technicolour.

She thought of one of her favourite moments. Often, when driving the boys around, she'd listen to them singing along to the radio: their voices sweet and cracking but harmonising too. Unselfconscious. Unaffected. Her heart pumped with love for them.

She felt sorry, then, for Duncan. Hater of top forty songs. Perhaps the emotion in the singers' voices was phoney, as he said. But it spoke to people.

Maybe that was what this mid-life reset was about: Duncan stretching. Until today, Duncan had never done anything his mother wouldn't approve of. Liv ought to be proud of him. No longer the underdog little brother. Why then did he suddenly seem so frail and, well, unattractive? She was having trouble imagining him without his suit, permanently.

On her back, she lifted her pyjama-clad legs into the air and let them drop. Her body bounced sideways. Her neck cracked. Ouch. Perhaps she was more attached to the old world order than she cared to admit. Damn it. She rubbed her neck. She could feel the weight of financial responsibility descending. Yes, she was a grown-up, but she didn't want it. It scared her. She felt unprepared. She liked playing second fiddle in that band of two. She sat up, her ears cold now, as, nearby, something fell into the pool. Something small and spluttering.

Liv spent the weekend avoiding Duncan, which was easy thanks to the combined sports and friends and hobbies of two of their sons. Between them, Jai and Cody were delivered to four assorted games and three birthday parties; Jai managed to put his tapping under wraps, just, to get out of the house. Darling boy. Meanwhile, after school footy, Oscar went to the movies, alone, to watch foul-mouthed superheroes. At home, the twins avoided each other and, to Liv's surprise, Oscar would not open up to her again and nor would Jai about his worries. A silent Cody lay in bed watching *Predators in Peril*. Another screen ban not enforced by Duncan. Her wounded husband spent his downtime furtively on his laptop. Liv couldn't be bothered getting to the bottom of him, either; or calling him on his parenting. This was also unheard of in the annals of Liv and Duncan. They didn't discuss his abandoned career or their boys again. They didn't discuss anything.

The Lists were ignored – people ate, people made mess, people went to bed.

At the kitchen bench, numb, Liv watched them come and go.

72

Term Three

Liv

By sunrise Monday, it seemed Duncan couldn't get away quickly enough. He sprang from bed to walk Pickle, then spruced up and left, wheeling his luggage. It wasn't until the Uber drove off that Liv remembered he was jobless. With an elbow, she levered herself up.

In the shower, she was still puzzling over Duncan's departure when Cody, already in his school uniform, shuffled in. Only the other day, he'd trotted in and said, 'I was just watching Pickle chase her tail and she did it for, like, five minutes and I thought isn't it funny how a dog can entertain herself for five minutes just chasing her tail, and then I thought hang on I've just been watching my dog chase her tail for five minutes.' Dripping, Liv had been left wondering if her nine-year-old hadn't just said something profound.

This morning, silently, Cody passed her a towel. His school shirt looked to have shrunk. Liv distracted herself by inspecting the crack in the glass screen.

Bending over to dry her hair, she reflected. Cody hadn't climbed onto a roof in weeks. He hadn't jumped up onto a door frame and done chin-ups. He hadn't kicked a ball over a fence. Notwithstanding the odd *Fortnite* outburst, it was possible his turbocharged ways were waning. This morning, he seemed to have retreated within himself.

'Mum,' he said, when she straightened, 'the other night, why were you dropping the f-bomb on Dad? Over and over?'

'Ah.' She wrapped the towel around herself. Made another mental note: whisper when swearing.

'Dad surprised me with some news; and I was in shock, I suppose. But thanks for asking.'

Cody nodded, as if this explanation was satisfactory.

'Why were you yelling at him the other night?'

'I was mad. I was trying to say why . . . but he kept yelling "Annoying! Annoying!"'

Liv paused, looking at him in the mirror. 'Oh, Cody . . .' She bent to meet his gaze. 'Why were you mad?'

Cody jumped up, energised. 'Because at Harry's these bots ganged up and killed me when I was top five and you're not allowed to gang up playing solo and I wanted to report them. You get banned for life if you cheat, but you wouldn't let me get the iPad and then Dad was yelling, "Enough! Enough!"'

'I heard that bit.'

'It sucks when people don't listen. You end up double-mad.'

Liv felt herself blushing. 'I'm so sorry, Cody. Double-sorry. And you are most definitely *not* annoying.'

You are not, she said, in her head. Though your behaviour might be sometimes. Or often. But she was sorry. Truly. For gritting her teeth. For passing him on to Duncan. Who had, in some ways, made a better fist of it. Of him.

She swallowed a tear as Cody patted her back.

'That's okay, not your fault. And, Mum, look – I broke the shower.'

Half an hour later, juggling sports bags and instruments and self-packed lunches, her boys tumbled off for the bus for another term of school. Despite the weekend's developments, Liv refused to accept that it could be their last at Carmichael. Though the weekend had clearly left its mark. Slow to leave, Jai had tapped and jumped madly for twenty minutes before he could get out the door: school, it seemed, had become a trigger for him, too. He'd done six circuits of his bedroom – checking cupboards, blinds and bed; then two of the bathroom – checking taps, towels and toothpaste. At the gate, he'd said, aloud, like a mantra, 'I don't want to get expelled. I don't want to get expelled. I don't want to get expelled.' From the porch, Liv was watching him through tears, and willing him to move on, when she received the call.

'We need to be at Carmichael, now.' Vic's voice had lost its buoyant, singsong quality.

'We do?' said Liv.

It was 7.40 am. At the gate, Jai was gone.

Thirty minutes later, outside Carmichael Grammar, Liv was sitting in Vic's Jeep. Distracted and uncomfortable, she watched Vic adjust her phone on the car's dashboard. In this world, rules were broken willy-nilly and applied inconsistently, Liv told herself. A certain freedom came from these realisations. A certain recklessness, too, apparently. The phone on the other end of this call was Jean Anderson's. After serving tea in Tony's office, Jean had dialled Vic, slipped the phone under the desk, then left, unnoticed.

Sipping a takeaway coffee, Liv wondered how she'd gone from overwhelmed mum to this: early-morning electronic eavesdropping. Without Jess. It occurred to Liv that Jess wasn't completely in the picture with Vic: being around fewer hours, juggling work. Liv had detected something else, too, in Vic's tone when she asked, 'Where's that Jess Charters today?' It was ever-so-slightly patronising.

Across the road from the school, opposite the oval, Liv listened to the head teachers make back-from-holidays small talk. According to Jean, seven men had been called to this emergency meeting. Liv could hear Tony's voice along with Lloyd Palmer and Ethan Humphries's. She recognised Giles Waring, too, and assumed the others must be the heads of years Ten, Eleven and Twelve. As some new voices entered the room, the talk of specky marks and fluky goals fell away.

'Told you we should've buried them,' said Lloyd. The sound through Vic's speakerphone was remarkably clear.

In the background, Liv could hear people moving about in Tony's office. Sitting in the draughty Jeep, Vic was concentrating, as if listening for a pulse.

'You can't keep hiding what you don't like,' said Tony.

Another voice chimed in: deep, young. Ethan Humphries. Liv could imagine his manicured goatee, his too-red lips. 'But what do we do? The calls haven't stopped. I've been speaking to angry, angry people.'

Sipping too quickly, Liv burnt her tongue.

'Indeed. Everyone has,' said Tony. Others murmured.

'Imagine if they knew the full picture.' This clearly was from Giles Waring, the Pom.

'I was warned, years ago, that this would happen when we let the girls in,' said Tony, wistfully. 'It's taken longer than I expected.'

'Is it too late to ask them to leave?' said Ethan.

A wave of jolly laughter. Vic tut-tutted. Liv was eyeing the doorhandle. Although she'd practised exclusively in tax, she suspected that she and Vic were currently breaking a law.

'Be a shame to lose the lot of them,' muttered Waring. 'Give that Grace Charters a couple of years . . .'

The younger men chuckled; Vic scowled.

'That's enough!' said Tony.

The group fell silent.

'You've had time to reflect. Speak to me about those Science results,' said Tony. 'How the fuck did they do it?'

The principal's *fuck* sounded wrong. Akin to someone's elegant grandmother dropping the c-word. A long silence ensued. Muffled noise.

'Luck?' said Lloyd, his voice high.

'Luck!' Tony huffed. 'Those girls *like* Science now, and they're very good at it. Many of them. It's incredible and, frankly, embarrassing. You need to lift—'

'There's a bigger picture here, Tony,' cut in Lloyd. 'These complaints about brainwashing. About experiments, manipulation and political correctness. It's serious. Our boys feel shafted. Overlooked. I agree those Science results are a problem. Giving the girls special attention was wrong. It makes it look like we haven't been pushing our boys. I had Bettina and Owen on the phone every second day about this. Taj Low had the worst term of his life, last term.'

Vic was sitting very still.

'Then they should have called me.'

'Your phone was running hot, from what I hear.'

'Well, yes, it was.' But Tony didn't sound convinced. 'And it wasn't only complaints.'

Vic nodded to herself.

'But, you have to admit, it's gone too far,' continued Lloyd. 'It's not been fair on the boys. Showing them up. We've got to rein it in.'

'Impossible,' said Tony.

'Between Cato, the Nobel-physicist lady and that serial pest Liv Winsome,' said Lloyd, 'it was too much. Those meetings we had to sit through. What a waste of time.'

'Oh, that Winsome woman. What an unfriendly, rude person . . .' blustered Ethan. 'She's not from around here, is she.'

Liv's blush was instant and prickly. She tried to conjure Gunhild. Today Gunhild needed a thick skin, and a poor grasp of English.

Vic mouthed, 'You okay?'

Liv gave a half-hearted thumbs up. The time to leave had long passed. She waited in vain for Tony to defend her. Then busied herself trying to spot her boys hopping off their bus.

'How do we know that Science test was set up correctly?' snapped Waring. 'Could they have cheated? How do we know the students did it and not some other dolts, like their dads?'

'What, remotely?' said Tony. 'Is that possible?'

'How do we know the results aren't fake?' From Lloyd. Of course.

'I wouldn't put it past her,' said a gravelly voice. 'Some of the things she was doing . . . Talk about out of touch!'

Vic stiffened beside Liv.

'You know what I think?' Humphries's vampire voice boomed back. 'The nuff nuffs are revolting!'

Liv's eyes flared. She was feeling giddy following the different voices and insults.

'Hasn't that woman gone now?' asked Waring.

'No. I'm rolling the program out again this term. Taking it across the school,' said Tony.

'Tony, you can't!' said Lloyd. 'The Lows will go ballistic.'

'It's still my school! Dr Cato's program has been wildly successful. And the Year Nines need it, promptly. Half of them are horrible.'

Vic nodded adamantly.

Someone said, 'But that wasn't meant to happen . . . and not that fast!'

Someone else said, 'Fuck.' Followed by a chorus of the word.

'You all saw it. In *one term*, it was spreading to other year levels,' said Tony. 'It was astonishing. Misbehaviour was at an all-time low. People were being kind!'

Liv wanted to fist pump Tony. But someone groaned.

'*Scott* Low called me, this weekend,' said Lloyd. 'Called Carmichael a "quasi girls' school". He thinks girls are running the show. Someone's cooked up another Instagram account over the holidays, as well. "The Crepes of Carmichael". Posted it on the weekend. It's the final straw.'

'The what?' said Waring.

'The girls are outing . . . it's a creep list,' said Lloyd. 'Mainly Year Eights talking about it, at the moment. We can't see who made it, or who's on it.'

'I'd suggest you have a fair idea,' said Tony.

'The rumours are out, and they're not happy about it.'

A long silence, deep as a well.

'This . . . *experiment* has gone too far,' said Waring. 'You watch. Run it again this term and those nutjob Low boys will do something stupid.'

Liv felt her milky coffee turning in her stomach. Low *boys*?

There was no audible response from Tony.

'Do something! Yank it – or we're fucked!' Lloyd yelled.

'Gentlemen,' said Tony, his voice rumbling. 'Let me be very clear: I need you on side with this. *The evidence is overwhelming.* We have to respect it, move forward. *Adapt.* Otherwise we're sunk. I will deal with these Crepes . . . They are not above the law. Not anymore. There is no turning back on this.'

'Bullcrap,' said Giles Waring.

'In your *opinion*,' yelled Ethan Humphries.

'Opinion?' Tony boomed. 'Opinion!'

A crash – a falling chair? Followed by a scuffle.

Liv gasped like a footy fan watching a dropped mark. Then the voices became muffled and the phone crackled.

73

Jess

The moment Grace rode off to school, Jess headed to her daughter's computer. Morrie was working from home, almost as if he suspected Jess was up to something. In a way, she was. She'd had enough. All weekend, she'd tried to convince herself Grace and Bella wouldn't have posted it. But, on and off, she'd overheard Grace on the phone or FaceTiming. She'd stood outside Grace's bedroom door with a duster, but had made neither head nor tail of what was going on. Morrie had been particularly clingy over the weekend, which hadn't helped. He'd followed her around, talking at her, and each night she'd slept pinned to the bed by his hairy arms. She hadn't given him much attention lately, so that was probably why. But she hadn't had any time to herself, either. She hadn't made it onto the treadmill in days. She hadn't had a chat with Grace. But, by Sunday night, hearing Grace and Bella FaceTiming again, Jess had been convinced those girls, activated and energised, were up to something. Typing quickly, Jess logged in to Instagram and searched. But no new account, or posts, nothing relevant in Grace's feed. Searching across the platform, Jess found a #creeplist and #creepshot. She searched #dodgyboys and #douche-bags. She steeled herself and searched: #Cocks. Nothing. False alarm. She sat back. Closed her eyes and let herself down from the worry-cliff she'd climbed.

A minute or two later, it dawned: the smell was back. She didn't care what the rest of her family said; it was here. Somewhere.

She looked up.

She put a step ladder in the shower, opened the roof access hole and slid a broom and dustpan through. Then she put on a head torch and climbed up and in. Bent at the hip, she stepped along the beams. Up here, the stench was strong: a cross between rotten egg and dead fish. She should've climbed up here days ago; she should've worn a face mask. A few metres along, she found what she was looking for: small, black pellets. The trail of dried droppings was scattered far and wide. Jess held her nose as she swept. She could hear Morrie on the phone, wandering about the house. He must've been on his tenth phone call of the day. Jess followed her unpleasant trail of breadcrumbs to the front corner of the house. The smell was worst here, overpowering; no longer dusty faeces but something much more ripe and foul and meaty. Whatever chemical process was taking place wasn't finished yet. Tossing aside the dustpan and broom, Jess followed her nose. It didn't take her long.

She was above Morrie's office when the saw it: a furry mass of possum. It'd been large once, maybe full-sized. Today it was grey, whitish and lumpy; something appeared to be growing on its coat. Jess gagged, scrambling back to retrieve the dustpan. How on earth had Morrie not smelt this? And then, she heard him: '. . . new client's Carmichael?'

He sounded surprised, but not as surprised as she was. The shock cured Jess's gag reflex, but she kept her fingers to her nose. Morrie's firm did a lot of work for private schools. One big school had six hundred files on the go, he'd told her recently. That was a lot of parents in arrears. When Grace first began at Carmichael, Jess had wandered the grounds, wondering whose fees were ballooning their parents' mortgages. Whose mums and dads were fibbing about their finances. Whose parents' budgets wouldn't last the distance. School fees were one of the last things cash-strapped families wanted to pay, Morrie told her once.

Jess shovelled the carcass onto the dustpan.

'Obviously, I can't touch it . . .' Morrie was saying. 'Some of those names . . . my daughter's boyfriend . . .'

Jess flinched, and the animal rolled off the dustpan and onto her foot. It gave a puff as something cracked open and its innards dangled. But Jess was too dismayed to be grossed out. She thought of Liv and her three boys. It'd never occurred to Jess that Liv's family might be in financial trouble. He was a partner in a law firm, and Liv worked too, didn't she? Jess couldn't recall seeing Liv on her way to or from a job. (If Liv did work, Jess realised, she didn't seem to dress for it.) But they had a nice car, lived in a lovely part of Bayside . . . Then again, if there was one thing Jess had learnt, being married to Morrie: people's finances were often not what they seemed. Partner in a law firm or not. Down below, the house was silent. For a fleeting, awful moment, Jess imagined herself being locked up there, stuck for eternity between the ceiling and roof with that decaying, smelly beast.

Having bagged and binned the possum, Jess was scrubbing her hands when Morrie called out, 'Going for a coffee with Roger. Back in an hour. Do you need the car?'

'No.'

Watching Morrie reverse out of their driveway, Jess knew to move fast. She started with his desktop and squirted his keyboard. She rearranged his notepads and stacked his pencils. She watered his little money tree. She did all this while reading from his screen a dozen family names and amounts owing. A third at least were Grace's acquaintances, several in Year Eight, not that Morrie would know that. But, yes, one stood out. The names on Morrie's screen looked like a set, bound by something. Not basketball. Not the band. She sat in Morrie's chair, swivelled.

Something here was fishy too.

Tapping Morrie's keyboard again, Jess did what she should've done months ago: googled the board of Carmichael. Within seconds, up popped a grid of smiling, 'trust me, I'm a professional' faces: Chairman James Whittaker-Smith; Andrew Whitehead; James Goodfellow; Andrew Le Blanc; Andy Hasluck; Owen Low; Jeremy Sidebottom; Dianne Chamorro;

Belinda Masters. While James looked handsome, the women weren't particularly pretty, and Jess told herself off for noticing. She scrolled down the columns of faces, counted seven men, two women. At the bottom, Tony Crisp – Principal was described as an Attendee. And there, alongside him, was a second Attendee. A familiar head of overly styled hair. No tracksuit or lycra this time. But Jess sprang from the chair as if Mr Vainglorious was a skunk. Looking at the Company Secretary, Jess could smell his cologne and see his finger on his lips. Shush to you, Scott Low. Fear slithered up her spine.

And then the link came.

On a hunch, Jess keyed into Instagram again; this time, she searched using the school's name. And this time it was there: #CrepesofCarmichael. Why hadn't that come up? She looked again and saw the typo. Jess cracked her neck. The account was private and didn't offer any hints as to who'd created it. But she could make an educated guess.

74

Duncan

Duncan fidgeted, standing behind a large man who was carrying two heavy plastic bags. The flight didn't leave for another thirty minutes, but Duncan was bursting to board. Going on his own to another country for a holiday was a drastic act. A marriage-ending act, if he was honest. And the most selfish thing he'd ever done. But he needed to be alone. Totally alone – on his own terms, away from home and work. Though, right now, the departure lounge was surprisingly busy. He stepped forward as the queued passengers were directed to the descending corridor. A family of four from the UK was next – a mum and dad, boy and girl, aged about twelve and ten. Duncan tried not to look. The boy was showing his sister his phone. They were laughing; the dad was telling them to shush. The wife was carrying the travel documents, as Liv would've been if they were all here, together, going to New Caledonia. He'd never done anything like this before. Never made significant life decisions without consulting Liv (or, before her, his mum). At times, over the weekend, he'd wondered if he'd been too hasty. Reckless. But no. Already, he felt indescribably better. Free. He'd be proud of himself for working all this out on his own if he wasn't feeling so angsty.

The large man in front of him barked into his phone. Duncan tried not to listen but the man kept breaking into expletives. Another Michael. The world was full of them. After hours, Duncan usually blotted them out with a glass of beer. But today there were kids about.

Duncan turned his thoughts to the French lessons he'd signed up for. The diving. The cooking class. He'd be able to cook underwater in French by the time this trip was over. He hoped in his heart of hearts he was making the right call. It was a big thing to end a twenty-odd-year relationship. He hoped the boys would understand. It did feel as if he was smashing the container that held them all. They were now going to be loose, spilling everywhere.

But he'd told her he needed a change . . . A trip. He was *resetting*. Maggie had got it straightaway.

He spread his feet, dispersing his weight to keep himself upright.

This was a moment that would cleave his life in two. Before New Caledonia, and after it. Before he ran away, and after. Before the separation and after. Perspiration was pooling in the dip above his collarbones; he patted it with his T-shirt. He'd told Henry. He hadn't told his brother. Henry had been silent. Worried, presumably. 'I'm not going to top myself,' Duncan had added. 'I just need a rest.' The only other people who knew were Maia, his PA, and Maggie. The trip had been her idea.

'You're being very brave,' she'd said.

But he hadn't felt brave, tiptoeing out of the house like a cat-burglar.

The wide, stooped man before him was next. Duncan watched the flight attendant greet him. 'Sir, may I weigh your bags, please?' She was a muscular, trim woman with a name tag that read 'Tiffany'. She looked fast and explosive, like a point guard, and young enough to be the man's daughter.

The man didn't end his call but merely swivelled the phone away from his mouth. 'I'm a Bronze flyer on this airline!'

'Sir, your bags look heavy. As you know, we have weight limits for cabin luggage.'

He put his bags down and stabbed at his telephone. 'I'm taking a picture of this.' He lifted his phone to take a snap of Tiffany's badge but she covered it.

'No, sir – no pictures. If you could step this way, please.'

The man blustered, loudly. The flight attendant was half the body weight of this man. If he sat on her, she'd disappear. But, calmly, she directed him to one side as Duncan was processed by another, plainly unimpressed flight attendant. Watching the man's antics, Duncan felt sorry for that young woman. She was doing an admirable job, with a familiar air of efficiency. But dickheads were an occupational hazard, Duncan supposed. Oh well. And then Duncan was walking across the runway. In a fresh wind, he was climbing the metal steps.

It was a shame you couldn't mountain-bike to New Caledonia. Duncan felt closest to death on aeroplanes. Mortality was all around him, hidden in the overhead lockers, the sucking toilet and the lifejackets under his seat. Without fail, every flight, he watched the robotic staff put on their oxygen masks, point to the exits. The one day he didn't tap the armrest three times before take-off was the day he was going down. He was buckling in when the man from the queue reappeared. He had one bag now, which he was smashing about. Duncan sighed as the man wedged beside him. This would be a long flight. Further up the aisle, the flight attendant slipped into the cockpit. She appeared calmer than Duncan's neighbour. When the cockpit's door reopened, a pilot – a freckly blond in his late thirties – was marching down the aisle.

'Sir, are you sitting in the correct seat – 5D?'

For a moment, Duncan thought Liv had found him. Or Henry or Michael . . .

'Sir? I'm talking to you.'

'Yes,' said his neighbour. 'I'm 5D.'

'Why did you speak to our flight attendant like that?' said the pilot, with beautifully controlled anger. 'She was only doing her job.'

The man seemed to shrink.

'Did you take her photograph?'

The man was looking at the pilot's insignia rather than his face.

'Did you?'

'No.'

'Your phone – give it to me, please,' said the pilot, whose name was Gary.

Gary the pilot was looming over the man; he was tall, and calm but insistent. Liv would've liked him. The man handed over his telephone and

Pilot Gary flicked through it. The man's phone cover was decorated with a blue coat of arms. Duncan tried not to stare. Seconds later, satisfied, Pilot Gary returned the phone.

'You owe the airline an apology, sir, and you owe one to our flight attendant.'

'Yes, okay,' the man muttered, in a whine. 'I'm sorry.'

Up front, Tiffany and the other flight attendants watched – arms crossed, tight smiles. By this time, the plane had filled. The doors were closed. Others were watching.

'You can tell Tiffany yourself.'

When Pilot Gary walked away, Tiffany flashed him a dazzling smile. Someone clapped. The remaining two flight attendants, a man and a woman, beamed at the pilot too, as he took a handtowel. Then Gary disappeared into the cockpit.

In the moments that followed, as Duncan tapped and braced for take-off, he replayed that scene in his head. Each time, he was struck by the pilot's grace and courage, his respect for his colleagues. His fellow human beings. He'd made it look effortless. But for some reason it made Duncan feel queasy.

It wasn't until the plane began to move that Duncan understood why. What he felt was shame.

75

Liv

Words deserted Liv, sitting in Vic's frosty Jeep. This fine school was being run by a divided gang of sociopaths. Was that news? Liv couldn't decide. But her disappointment was profound. She and Duncan had been knocking themselves out for years to keep their sons at Carmichael. They'd overextended themselves everywhere. Duncan had signed the boys up before they were born! She'd lost hair! She rocked herself. (The embarrassing reality that she and Duncan soon wouldn't be able to afford the place was moot.) The advent of the toxic parent made more sense. But it wasn't only parents who were behaving badly. What came first?

Vic was tapping into her phone, presumably ending the call from Jean Anderson.

'Lloyd Palmer calls those head teachers his spies.' Vic was speaking sideways, as if someone might be watching them with a long-range camera.

'Pardon?'

'He gets them to listen to other staff members' conversations.'

Liv could vaguely recall a mention of spies. Except Jai had said they were 'Mr Crisp's'. She'd thought Jai was being melodramatic.

'Jean overheard Miss Lee complaining to Lloyd, last term. She accused Lloyd of sending in *four* spies to check on her during the course of one day.'

'For god's sake. What did he say?'

'He told her it'd been five.'

'Oh, no.'

Vic laughed. Liv looked forlornly at the world-class ovals, alive with happy-looking children.

'Palmer told Jean a few months ago he's planning to bully Mary MacBeth out of the school. He can't stand her.'

'He said that?' said Liv. 'Out loud?' She sounded like Duncan.

'We know he's bullied students, too. Very subtly forced their hand and made them leave. Outlier boys, mainly: butterfly-collecting poets or musical-theatre types. He did it to Jean Anderson's grandson, a chess champion. And, I suspect, Blake Havelock.'

Liv felt woozy. Vic Cato's knowledge of this school was deep and long. And her motivations complex. Liv considered her friend anew.

'How does he get away with it?'

'He's not as stupid as he sounds.' Vic hammed surprise. 'He went to school here with Scott Low, corporate kingpin and younger brother of Owen Low. Not much of a teacher, and late to it, but Lloyd's been an outstanding coach since he was parachuted in. A couple of the boys have gone on to be professional footy players, and a few girls look likely. Scott Low's kids have left now, but one of them was drafted last year. As you probably know, the Lows love their footy. They have high hopes for Dylan, too.'

'Where was Lloyd before here?'

'Working for one of the supermarket majors. Category manager in charge of meat, I believe.'

Liv groaned. This talk of spies and bullying, agendas and revenge – and football – was a bit much. Ethically murky. Vic seemed far from 'out of touch'.

'Mary is fantastic. Brilliant teacher. Popular. But not political. She tried for Palmer's job once, years ago. Then Palmer came along. And now he wants Crisp's.'

Liv wanted to deny this, but her body tingled in a way that suggested to her it was true.

'Know anything about the Crepes of Carmichael?'

'Nope,' said Liv, with relief.

Vic grinned. 'Thanks to those Crepes, the moment is upon us. Time to oust the old farts.'

Liv frowned. 'Has that been our plan?'

'Oh, yeah! You know now this world didn't just happen,' said Vic. 'Someone has made it so.'

'Aha.'

Who got to choose which old fart to oust? Liv was wondering, when Vic's phone beeped.

'Tony's about to call.'

'Awesome.' If this school had spies, thought Liv, they'd better watch out. Vic seemed to have her eye on a bloody endgame, and Jean was a first-class double-agent.

76

Duncan

Duncan stared at the cockpit's closed door as the plane bounced and a man behind him whimpered. To his right, a woman was reading on a device. Beside her, a man was looking out of the window and grinning. 'Like a big dipper, eh?'

Duncan turned away as the man let go of the armrests. 'Look, no hands!'

Duncan had no intention of letting go. Shutting his eyes, he realised his eyelashes were wet. He thought again of Gary in the cockpit and hoped the man's flying was as good as his soft people skills. Maybe it was timing, but the pilot had made quite an impression. High in the sky, Duncan had come to see himself clearly. How slack, embarrassingly slack, he'd been. As a dad, a husband, a boss . . . When the oxygen masks dropped, you were meant to put yours on first. He got that. But *then you were meant to help the people around you.* That piece, obviously, he'd missed. And now he'd left his family (and his staff!) to fend for themselves, right when the plane was falling apart.

Furtively, he wiped his eyes. No one told you working and being married and having children would be like this. You might manage one good week, without a major drama anywhere. Or a month. And then, *wham!* You lost a big client, or your brother humiliated you in front of staff or made a senior associate collapse. Your dopey junior sent out marked-up agreements for signing. People chased you into the Men's when you had the runs. Deadlines squeezed you like a python. You pulled all-nighters. You wife thought you worked too much . . . Because, at the same bloody time, your son was diagnosed with obsessive-compulsive disorder. Your other son, with attention deficit hyperactivity disorder. Then puberty and Instagram and menopause collided. Your wife wanted to change the world, starting with you and your sons. You suddenly had *more* jobs! Your easy son became miserable and fat. Your gifted son became a feminist. Accidentally, you introduced your younger, explosive son to *Fortnite*! You lost your cool, and you and your wife fought more often than you had sex. You tried to improve your world, and you did, until you took one step too far and it blew up.

Welcome to middle age.

He groaned as the lights flickered off and then on. It wasn't often you came face to face with your own limitations. He wiped his eyes. Flight attendants scurried up and down the aisle. The big grouch beside Duncan was snoring loudly, as Liv did sometimes. Somewhere, a latch to a compartment gave way.

Duncan pictured Liv, fourteen years ago, on the day the twins were born: beaming, hair plastered to her head, one eye shot with blood from a burst vessel. How sad that Liv would be if she were to learn where he was. He thought of forty-five year old Liv, overwhelmed, then happier, with that weird way of speaking. Even the new Liv would be sad. And probably angry. His face began to drip.

In dashing off like this, he'd wanted to be selfish. He'd chosen to be selfish. But now he saw he'd been selfish for years. Passive selfish. Wilfully blind selfish. Hiding selfish. Outside, a flash of lightning just missed the plane and the cabin shook. He closed his eyes. This world wasn't his fault, he told himself, and neither was his place in it. But doing nothing about it was no longer an option, he understood. Not a moral one, anyway.

Was it too late? Should he take this revelation home, or were his boys better off without him? What had his barely-there parenting done to them? Guilt washed over him.

What a mess.

He felt a tear feather his cheek. Maybe this was what happened, he thought, when you found your joy: you found its flip side too.

77

Liv

Liv forced herself up the path and into the foyer of the administration building. Alongside her, Vic was shadow-boxing, as if preparing to out-jab the principal in the final round. Waiting in the Jeep hadn't dampened Vic's mood, but Liv was feeling light-headed, thanks, she supposed, to a combination of the leadership team's dysfunction and Vic's bloodlust, her estrangement from Duncan and Jai's flaring OCD. Not to mention, Oscar's gender politics and Cody's relative neglect, as well as the prospect of them all leaving this school. What'd she been doing? Certainly not being an A-plus mother or wife. Even as a revolutionary, she was feeling lily-livered. She had a terrible feeling everything, absolutely everything, was about to fall apart.

Within his office, Tony was speaking, presumably on the phone. Slumped against a wall, in the deserted foyer, Liv tried not to listen, as if to atone for her earlier mischief. But Tony was remonstrating loudly with someone dogged. She felt sorry for the man, as she took in the series of photo-portraits: a renowned opera singer; earnest Professor Griffin; an Olympic water-polo player; a Queen's Counsel; a brain surgeon; and someone who looked like a comedian Liv had once seen perform. Successful women, every one.

Seeing them up there, Liv's nerves eased, but not enough. She planted her feet, hip-width apart, and raised her arms in a V-shape, like a rockstar on stage. Vic, looking over, grinned.

Two minutes later, Liv was still in her power pose when Tony emerged. Quickly, she dropped her arms. But he'd caught a glimpse. Liv gave an embarrassed wave. The principal's hair seemed whiter than it had been last term. A scratch ran across the lid of his lazy eye: a shock of pink.

'Let's walk.'

Liv felt the uptick in her confidence dip again. Who was this man: out of touch but evolving principal, or despot, mid-revolt? And how could you spot the difference? Without his jacket, Tony led them from the building. They walked across the car park and onto the adjacent lawn. It remained a bright and pleasant morning. Recess had just begun. Tony stopped to survey some Year Nine boys playing soccer. 'Kick it!' he said, warmly.

The boy kicked, narrowly missing the goal.

Tony shook his head. 'Next time.' He continued along the path. Tony, Liv remembered, coached the senior mixed soccer teams. Vic skipped to keep up. Liv wondered what plan of attack she had. Worryingly, the principal looked pained, as if someone had slipped arsenic into his morning tea.

Four girls of about eleven years old walked by, wearing trousers. 'Hello, Jenny,' said Tony, with a quick smile. 'Kate, Annabelle, Heidi.' Once, Liv would've been impressed by his memory, but today she was too unsettled to appreciate it. When the students had passed, he said, 'Victoria, a number of parents have come forward over the holidays with serious concerns about your program.'

'They needn't be concerned.'

His boyish face was glum. 'These young people are susceptible. They are sucking in what you have to say. A number of boys, in particular—'

Another three girls passed, two wearing trousers.

'That's brilliant,' said Vic.

He stopped, cleared his throat. 'These parents and their boys feel targeted: being made the enemy.'

Worry-infused irritation grew stronger in Liv's chest. Damn those Bettinas!

'It is not only these boys' parents. Concerns have been raised internally about your interventions, and some of the science underpinning them.'

'How ridiculous,' said Liv.

Vic merely folded her arms.

Tony gulped, as if in quicksand and about to go under. 'In essence, the view is, the school has lost its way.' He didn't sound convinced.

Vic propped a hand on her hip. 'The Year Eights have been transforming this school for the better, and you know it.'

Taken aback, the man fell silent. Liv looked at her shoes, damp from the grass.

'I'll survey the students again. Show everyone how the Year Eights are thriving after just one term. I can guarantee the vast majority now feel safe and supported, connected and heard. In the best possible shape to learn. You can find other spons—'

'We've had enough surveys for one year.'

Liv's unease metastasised from her heart to her toes.

Tony lowered his voice. 'Victoria, we have no choice. We must wind it back.'

The bell hadn't yet rung, but students were moving quietly into the buildings like cows ready for milking. Stunned, Liv watched them, imagining their parents, their grandparents. This community was vast, from Duncan's dentist, to the CEOs, CFOs, COOs of the country's blue-chip companies, and loads of other mums and dads who were powerful despite their lack of initials. Surely most of them were on board? Liv thought back to the last day of term. Everyone had been so happy, parents and students alike. Cows jumping over the moon.

What were the numbers for and against? Liv wondered. Did she and Vic simply need to remind everyone of what they'd done and why: their reasoning, the research and evidence? She felt her certainty shift. The problem was, the world was already awash with reason, research and evidence. With a few clicks, you could learn from the experts how to be fairer and kinder. Happier and healthier.

Only days ago, she'd read findings from a study that'd made her laugh. Apparently, some people were so over-confident and incompetent that when presented with evidence of real competence they were unable to recognise it. She thought of Humphries, Waring and Palmer.

Today, that didn't seem so funny.

She needed to sit.

'What about the girls' Science results?' said Vic.

Tony paused. 'Indeed. But Nobel Prize–winning physicists cannot teach our students year round.'

'It wasn't only Professor Gr—' said Vic.

'You're not listening.'

'If this gets out, your school will be a laughing-stock.'

'In some quarters it already is.'

Vic prodded Liv with a stare. But Liv felt herself sag. What was she going to do? Did she want to challenge the board? Make this fiasco public? Become a whistleblower? That would take stamina. Courage. Commitment. And more time away from her family. Liv took in the scratch across Tony's eye, his slumped shoulders and crumpled shirt. She couldn't recall a whistleblower who'd come out of whistleblowing well.

Tony looked at his watch.

Liv tried to imagine what it was like to be him. The tax on the man's conscience, and perhaps his lifespan thanks to decisions like this one. She felt overcome. More overwhelmed than she ever had. She'd wanted to drag this school into the present, but she hadn't wanted a bloodbath. She'd underestimated the old guards' power and reach. An image of Pickle chasing her tail popped into her head. She rubbed her old bald spot.

She really needed to sit down.

'Why don't we take a break?' she said. 'Revisit this . . . next year, perhaps?' Liv didn't know the words were coming until she heard herself say them.

'No!' Vic's face contorted: her wingwoman was deserting her. Spinning to earth.

'My thoughts precisely,' said Tony.

'We didn't mean to upset anyone, or split the school community again. We're really sorry about that.' Liv gave her most beseeching smile.

'Yes, Olivia, so am I.'

'Liv, what are you doing?'

'You're battle-ready. I'm not.'

'You were.'

Unbidden, an image flashed in Liv's mind of Jai readjusting the toothpaste tube. For the sixth time. Followed by one of Oscar sobbing and gobbling; and Cody yelling, '*Annoying!*' Liv could feel a groundswell of tears. Was she choosing between being a mother and a revolutionary? Maybe she was. Something had to give.

'Things have changed.'

Vic was a deflating hot air balloon.

'Perhaps you and Jess . . .'

Vic waved off the name, exasperated. 'Despite her excellent connections, Jess is still a novice,' she muttered. Liv frowned.

'Victoria, here's what I need from you,' said Tony, with a sad sigh. 'Explain to the Year Eight parents what you've been doing. Nothing *manipulative*, lasting or dramatic. Explain that the curriculum will return to normal this term. Say your goodbyes. I will send a letter to similar to effect.'

The colour of putty, Vic turned and strode towards the nearest fence.

Tony and Liv stood like two lonely pins at the end of a path, beside rubbish bins and the bike shed. They were facing the original buildings of the boys' school. Tony seemed to consider the red bricks. From this corner, his school looked like a small city-state.

'Have you seen the master plan?' He seemed to be speaking to himself. 'The old music rooms and the chapel are going to make way for a four-storey Creativity Centre. Should be magnificent.' He didn't sound confident.

Liv's eyes were on Vic, who, with a neat scissor kick, jumped the fence.

'The process must be closely managed.' Tony's gaze returned to Vic, marching away. 'One doesn't want bricks landing on heads.'

He gave a weak smile before nodding, like a gracious if doddery old man, and leaving Liv to it.

78

Jess

Jess's newer top three fears:
1. Grace is expelled;
2. Grace is expelled;
3. Grace is hurt.

She waited for Morrie to come home, which might've been a mistake. As he changed out of his work clothes, she told him what she'd seen, what she thought. Before he could get mad at her, she said, 'It's a backlash, like the one against me, but bigger. It's rotten at the top of that school.' That was probably a mistake too. By then, Morrie was trimming his eyebrows. She expected him to be angry. To be disappointed by these men. She hoped he might volunteer to speak to them. At the very least, he could tell his office to stop calling those struggling Carmichael families. People were being targeted! Not people: girls.

'If Grace is thrown out of that school,' said Morrie, 'or harmed in any way because of this, it's on your head.'

In his yoga gear, Morrie began to stretch in the lounge room. Jess considered his downward dog. She felt as if she'd signed up to a war only part of the population could see. She was watching his face go red when a voice from within scolded: Get going!

'I'm going,' she said. 'Back in an hour.'

She was through the door before Morrie could respond. She took the car.

It was lunchtime when Jess marched into Carmichael through the back gate. The school looked the same. The buildings were still immaculate. Windows shone. But the noise! In a quadrangle, groups of students were yelling at each other. Boys ran through the crowds and shoved others randomly. Little fights were breaking out, like spot fires. Another boy was scrawling charcoal penises onto the cream wall of the library. Girls were shouting for him to stop. This felt like schoolies week, except the results were already out, and everyone had failed. Jess hesitated as female teachers darted about, avoiding the students. Someone upended a rubbish bin full of takeaway containers and coffee cups over someone else's head. Boys yelled, girls yelled; boys and girls yelled together, over each other. Jess thought to say something to get these children under control, but she didn't know what. And didn't want to risk it.

In the distance, two male teachers were running towards the quadrangle. Jess felt her heart skip a gear. She dashed between two jostling groups, towards the Middle School building. Grace would've just finished Science on level two. Jess sprang upstairs, but the lab was empty; stools were pushed back and equipment abandoned. Seeing the poster of Barbara McClintock ripped from the wall, Jess broke into a sprint. On the way down, she took the deserted stairs two at a time.

Dr Cato's ground-floor office was empty too. Cardboard boxes lined the desk. Three of the boxes had been partially filled with books and a prickly succulent. Dr Cato's chair was tucked in. Her orange coffee mug was gone. Jess tried to get her bearings. She was tapping madly into her phone when Mary MacBeth appeared.

'What's going on, Mary? Where's Dr Cato?'

'They've shut her down.'

Jess looked outside to the knots of children. Beyond the Middle School, bigger kids were playing football and basketball, seemingly oblivious to the spreading chaos.

'Oh, no. How can they?'

Mary was hunting through the desk. 'The official line? The parents. The community wasn't appropriately consulted . . . transparency issues . . . blah, blah.'

Somewhere, glass smashed. 'The unofficial line . . .?'

'You saw it, last term. It was working.' Mary looked to the window, as if she was needed. 'Have you seen a small basketball?'

Jess shook her head. Prayed Grace and that Insta account weren't the cause of this.

'The kids are beside themselves. Walking around crying, holding hands. Not just the girls, either. Across the Middle and Senior schools. But it's the noisy minority we need to worry about. They're in party mode. It's not pretty. Lloyd Palmer's on the warpath, too, by the way. Have you seen Grace or Bella?'

Jess shook her head.

Mary rummaged in a cupboard. 'You'd better find them.' Mary waggled her mouth from side to side. 'Palmer's not the only one after them.'

Jess felt her shoulders clench.

Glancing outside, Mary straightened her two-piece, as if readying for the onslaught. 'You might want to lie low. While the two warring tribes slug it out.'

Jess looked out the window again, to the waves of children crashing into each other. Children were hurling objects now – balls, bags, clothes. Teachers were trying to separate them, without touching them. Female teachers, mostly. Scattered about the margins were smaller groups of students, crying and cuddling.

It was a bit like a prison riot – without the batons.

'There's talk of suspension, Jess. Or worse . . . Bringing the school into disrepute and all that.'

'Oh, no. How'd they know it was Grace and Bella?'

'Palmer claims the girls admitted it.'

'Oh, those girls . . . They only meant to warn people . . .'

'I know.' Mary moved to the door.

Jess wondered what this would mean for her family. 'Any idea where Grace might go?'

Mary's look was grim. 'No. But if she's clever, which she is . . . she'll be hiding.'

79

Liv

Liv dragged herself out of the car. In the kitchen, phone in hand, she thought of Duncan. Oh, Duncan . . . her absent, estranged flatmate. She needed to fill him in and to debrief, unspool her thoughts. But he was probably having a long lunch in Cottesloe, with Maggie Koh. She rang his number. Listened to his recorded voice. They couldn't have been more disconnected unless they were divorced – though, sometimes, divorced people did seem quite connected.

She needed to apologise too, she supposed. Explain they'd work something out. Especially now everything was in flux, her job included. She wondered if he'd checked into a hotel.

Liv tried his phone, even rang his direct line at W&U. The call was diverted to Maia, who put her through to Henry.

Okay, today was *the* worst day of her life.

Hanging up, Liv realised her husband was a single man who was married with children. And she was a single mum with a husband. Recently, she'd thought that'd changed, but no. In an instant, how she felt about Duncan reconfigured. Apologising was no longer a priority. Her marriage was half-happy, half-crappy. Probably had been for years.

Her fresh shock undercut her indignation. But her indignation was real.

This half-good husband was not the kind she wanted. Did that kind exist – a person who listened, and soothed, and said insightful, constructive things? Not, 'Have you fed the dog?' Or, 'See you late tonight.' Or, 'Why are you cutting the tomato like that?' A husband who could've used this crisis to talk with his boys about what he and they needed, what *men* needed, and what men had been given that they didn't need? But no. That wasn't her husband. Her husband was MIA. She was in a far better position to be a good man than he was. Yes, he was grappling with his life . . . but so had millions of other men, forever! Duncan could've learnt from what they'd learnt; and made real and considered changes. But what had he done instead? *Hopped on a plane and flown away.*

If Duncan's Airbus went down over the Pacific, she thought, it wouldn't be the end of the world. He was worth more to her dead than alive now, anyway, provided he'd paid the latest premium. These were probably the least kind thoughts she'd ever had.

She turned off her phone.

Liv climbed under her desk and curled into a foetal position. The underside of her desk had always looked inviting, around 3 pm, when she was a solicitor. She remained under there as the afternoon passed. Soon her sons would come home and yell, 'Mum, where are you?' A second later, one of them would scream, 'What's for dinner?' She couldn't be bothered remembering whose turn it was.

Her phone rang.

It was unlikely to be about one of her boys, now, at home time. It could, she supposed, be another parent. Perhaps someone had heard about the axing of Vic's program. But Liv Winsome the revolutionary was dead. She turned off her phone, scavenged for a pair of earplugs, then hunkered back under her desk with a doona and slept.

80

Duncan

Duncan lay spread-eagled atop a purple hibiscus-patterned bedspread on a king-sized bed. Judging by the strips of light around the blinds, the sun was potent. Only metres away, people padded by on their way to the pool or the sea or to clean a bungalow. The fan above him was whipping the air into a headache-inducing vortex. He was hungry. And thirsty. And cold. But he couldn't move. For a moment he forgot where he was. Despite the whirring fan, the room was too quiet. No one was banging or swearing. The bathroom was his and his alone. His phone was silent. This wasn't home or work. The sound of throaty female laughter from outside the bungalow was a javelin through his gut. Suddenly, any move, anywhere, felt dangerous, lest he make his life any worse.

On his bedside table, *Should You Leave* lay open and face down, as if ashamed of its influence. Minutes ago, he'd started the book again and been startled to read in an early chapter that, nine times out of ten, the answer was a resounding no.

Something else important that he'd missed.

Time for a different type of book.

He wondered how his boys were going. He wondered about Liv. If she would admit she'd been wrong. Hypocritical. Or would she be too proud? Too hurt? He wondered if that concession was a non-negotiable for him. For all her brains and reading, Liv was very attached to her rightness. How it exhausted him.

81

Jess

At double-speed, Jess looked in broom closets and under stairs; in the bell tower and the maintenance sheds; in the drama space and AV rooms; in the library and backstage in the Great Hall. While she was searching, the teachers managed to get the students into classes. The afternoon periods resumed with a thud of silence. The school looked as if a small tornado had spun through it: chairs were upturned, bins were emptied and flowers had lost their heads. Jess had been searching for about an hour when Ethan Humphries trotted out of the admin building with a stack of letters. He strode about like a jolly, loopy postie delivering invitations to a party. The rest of the head teachers drifted out of the staff room. One of them, a tall bearded man, had the makings of a fat lip. Avoiding eye contact, Jess dashed by them, unseen. The school day was almost over when Lloyd Palmer discovered her searching the pool area of the sports pavilion.

'I can help,' he said. 'Where have you looked?'

'It's fine. I'm good,' said Jess. Her voice echoed off the water.

'No, really, I insist.'

Palmer gave his trademark smile. He was carrying a clipboard, for no apparent reason. He tried to make conversation by explaining his dismay at the day's events.

'Not like these kids,' he said. 'Way out of character for this place.'

Jess didn't like the way he was staring at her.

'Excuse me a moment,' she said.

In the Women's, she lingered and rustled plastic loudly; when she came out, he was gone. Under different circumstances, Jess could see how being naughty might be fun. In peace, she searched the lost property cupboard and the indoor basketball courts. But, on the forecourt of the Great Hall, Palmer spied her again and called out, at a jog, 'Hey, Jess, wait up.' She waited, re-checked her phone. Reaching her, he tried his smile again, with less wattage this time.

'Do you think the girls might've gone home?' he said, once they'd done another circuit. He was puffing to keep up with her.

'No.' The thought had crossed Jess's mind, though surely Morrie would've called.

Jess took in the litter-strewn tennis courts and ovals. Gardeners and cleaners, teachers' aides and junior teachers were picking up rubbish and bins, chairs and balls and bats. Nearly all were women, except for the gardeners.

'Good job, mate,' said Lloyd to a nearby man in overalls.

Watching him, Jess wondered when she'd be back at this school. Whether Grace would be back. Whether she wanted Grace back. She clasped her car keys.

'You know, Lloyd,' she said, 'if you'd done your job, Grace and Bella wouldn't have needed a creeps list.'

Lloyd's smile fell.

'Creep.'

She left him standing like a roadblock on the driveway. She didn't feel so cross with Grace and Bella now. She didn't feel scared or worried. But, walking towards the front gate, she did feel tears coming. She longed to sit beneath a huge elm tree and sob. She wanted a hug, and for people to fuss with tissues. She stepped through the gate and read the sign again: Carmichael Grammar. Bayside's most prestigious school. She cracked her neck. Pulled out her phone. Heading for the shopping strip, she called Dr Cato. Maybe Vic wasn't upset with the girls either. Maybe she was having a smoothie with them. She called Jilly. She called Liv. She called Jean. Even Jean didn't answer. She rang Mary MacBeth.

'Maybe the school will come to its senses, Mary?' she said. 'Maybe they'll realise their mistake, get Vic back?'

'No chance,' said Mary. 'They've fired Jean. The minute she finished those letters.'

82

Liv

It must have been around 4 pm, when Liv heard a door bang and someone crying. 'Mum? Where are you?' This voice sounded angry as well as sad. Liv pushed the doona down. Jai or Oscar? Please don't let it be a plane crash. She stretched. More likely Jai had learnt of Dr Cato's fate. She hoped he didn't have a new compulsion. And that Oscar hadn't been hassled about Friday night's brain-snap. Even so, she forced herself to stay put.

'I can't believe they expelled me!' sobbed a twin.

'Because of your shit-stirring . . . you and Mum,' said another twin, his voice thick with tears. 'Why'd you have to get so into it?'

Okay, so the expelled was Jai. A key fear actually realised. Interesting. What on earth had he done now?

'I didn't shit-stir!'

Snotty snuffles. 'Where's Mum? Why isn't she answering her phone?'

Liv could hear their chests working hard. She suspected they'd been holding in these tears on the bus. At least they were openly emoting, in her absence.

'This's all because of Grace!'

'Grace?! Are you serious?'

One of them coughed. Someone was sobbing hard.

'Why didn't you do something? Your friends are psycho!'

'They're not my friends! In real life, everyone hates me!'

'What do you expect, watching those crazies online? You've turned into a mean, fat loser!'

'I hate you! I wish I wasn't your twin!'

Jai possibly laughed, mid-sob, and then spluttered.

Liv would've laughed too, if Oscar didn't sound so miserable. 'Everyone hates me . . .' But truly, what did he think would happen if he let himself go and spouted sexist nonsense? She did feel sad for him, though. Picked on. And she hadn't meant for any of this to make people feel wrong. Or as if their problems didn't matter too.

'Hey, Osc, take a breath . . .'

Oscar was giving this crying caper a red-hot go. Went on, and on.

'Oh, Osc' . . .'

And then Jai moaned, sounding a lot like Pickle, farting.

Oscar laughed through his tears.

'Ha, got you,' said Jai.

Oscar's noises spluttered, became further apart.

'I didn't mean that bit . . . about hating you,' said Oscar.

'I know. Sorry I called you fat.'

Listening, Liv felt proud of her sons. Oscar blew his nose. 'It's Mum's fault,' he said. 'Why couldn't she leave our fucking school alone? She's totally stuffed it!'

Jai laughed. 'Yeah, she has.'

Aghast, Liv waited for Jai to defend her. He sounded quite calm, now. When he didn't, she felt doubly sad. It appeared she'd been a hopeless revolutionary and an awful mum. She hurled her phone across the carpet and it slid neatly under her bed.

'I've missed you, bro,' said someone.

More snuffles and shuffles. Liv imagined her boys were hugging. It wasn't impossible.

A second, louder bang could be heard as the front door hit the wall.

'Cody? You okay?'

A higher-pitched wailing now filled the house. Liv could picture Cody grey and bleeding, looking like a child zombie. How he'd hurt himself today between the bus stop and home was a mystery. But if anyone could, it was Cody.

'Oh, fuck. Where's Mum?' That was Oscar, sounding angrier again.

Liv sat up, bumping her head, and hesitated. While secretly she was pleased they weren't asking for Duncan . . . was it up to her to rescue them? Who was rescuing her?

'Is it bad?'

Liv held her breath as one of the crying twins examined his crying little brother. 'Nah. Just looks it.' Someone sniffed. 'That knee's the worst. I'll get the band-aids.' This had to be Jai. 'What happened, little man?'

'Milly pushed me over,' Cody said, with a fresh wail.

'Of course she did.' That was definitely Oscar.

Half an hour later, Liv had checked her email and found the key paragraph of the shameful letter: *We wish to advise that your child's presence at Carmichael Grammar is no longer viable. Therefore, his/her last day at Carmichael Grammar was today, Monday . . . Grounds for our decision are to be found in clauses 13.2, 13.## and 14.3# of our agreement dated . . .* Liv stopped reading. Was the survey the reason for this decision? Whatever the reason, she was disappointed. They'd turned full circle. As she closed the laptop, she mused: You would've thought they'd proofread the thing and personalise it.

For a nanosecond, she felt relief. Then she wondered, what would Duncan the Deserter make of this?

Another hour later, the boys worked out she was locked in her bedroom. In the intervening minutes, presumably, they'd gutted the pantry and burnt a hole in their devices. One of them had been doing a lot of urgent, one-sided talking.

'What are you doing? Can you come out now?' Cody pleaded through the door. 'Mummy?'

'Did you hear Jai's expelled?' said Oscar. 'For punching Mr Waring?'

Ouch. Well. That was ironclad.

'Everyone at school went nutso,' said Oscar. 'They fired Dr Cato, and Grace and Bella posted a list of dicks, and Taj hunted them d—'

'Mum, they're expelling, like, everyone! You have to do something!' yelled Jai.

Liv stared at the underside of her desk, where Cody had scratched his name with a 'b' instead of a 'd'. She had a little cry. She'd tried, hadn't she? She'd wanted a revolution . . . but the loyalists had more firepower. Tenure. Her boys waited. She felt a tad bad – guilty, remorseful, selfish – but nothing she couldn't learn to live with. She was unspeakably stiff. The floor was much harder than it used to be.

'MUUUM!' A three voice scream. 'We need you!'

'I quit, guys,' she yelled. 'Find another mum.'

She slumped against the desk. It was cold. Hangover cold. She rested her forehead against it. She had the beginnings of a hangover even though she'd had nothing to drink. Middle age was cruel.

'You can't quit!' cried Cody.

'Ha! Try me!' said Liv.

It really was a lousy job – overloaded and poorly paid; *on* twenty-four hours a day, seven days a week; alternately pestered, berated and ignored. With no fucking privacy. Who agreed to these terms? Where was the paperwork?

'Mum, what's for dinner?' said Jai.

She refitted her earplugs. 'Ask Oscar!'

The house was incredibly well stocked. The Lists were on the fridge. She tried very hard to sleep but couldn't. No one mentioned Jai's footy training. She stayed where she was for the rest of the night. After a while, the boys started slipping notes under the door, and she slipped replies back. They delivered her dinner, too – Oscar's mushroom risotto was better than hers – and when the boys were not around, she returned the empty plate to the hall and found, at her door, a stack of her clothes, clean and folded. After dinner, she heard Jai ask Oscar and Cody if they wanted to hang out in the garage, and they headed off, which was a pleasant surprise; and kept the house quiet. The garage still contained a pool table, an empty fridge and that couch Pickle had once vomited on. Otherwise, nothing much happened, besides, no doubt, a chocolate raid in the kitchen, and the occasional whine and crash.

83

Jess

Mum I'm sorry I'm at a friend's. I know you said this would happen but stuff went down and we had to run away . . . I don't want you to worry if that's possible trust me I'm ok sort of but I need to think this out it's NOT OVER pls don't be mad

At The Provedore, Jess had re-read that message twenty times, as she ate. It didn't get any clearer. She'd answered it, straightaway. But Grace hadn't replied and neither had Bella. Jilly had been surprisingly calm. 'They'll be home tomorrow,' she explained. 'That's what Bella told me, and these days she's one tough cookie. But they're at a friend's. Parents must be away or at work, I guess. Call you when I know more.'

Arriving home, dazed and tired, in the late afternoon, Jess had found Morrie at his desk. He'd bombarded her with questions she couldn't answer, then became cross. He didn't seem to understand what was going on. Or that their daughter was her life's work, but *Grace* needed to be in charge too! Jess couldn't be bothered explaining. And she refused to call the police. She'd retreated to the spare room and started running. Two hours later, she was still there. Thud, thud, thud went her feet on the tread-mill. She was running at 7 pm, when Morrie started banging things in the kitchen. She couldn't stop wondering: how much had she and Grace brought this on? Running, Jess thought of the thousands of fears she'd had over the years. This evening's main fear was one of the original top three: kidnapping . . . Which was, she supposed, quite unlikely.

She felt herself getting angrier at those Carmichael men. Thud. Thud. Thud. Grace was right, she realised: she'd spent years worrying about the wrong things. For a kilometre, Jess beat herself up for being overprotective. For over-mothering. Was that a word? Thud. Thud. Thud. It was going to be difficult, but she'd have to trust Grace tonight. In her heart of hearts, she knew she could. By the time she stepped off the treadmill, Jess had sweated away two kilos and ninety per cent of her fears.

Jess's remaining top three fears:
1. The school goes back to how it was, or worse;
2. Grace can't achieve her dreams, because of all the Andrews;
3. Grace becomes as fearful as Jess was.

84

Liv

Persistent tykes – around bedtime, the boys were trying again. Liv could hear feet thundering down the hall.

'Dad's on the phone?!' said a twin through the door: presumably Oscar. Liv tossed aside a novel she'd wanted to read, a year ago, and crawled out. She snaked a hand around the doorframe. It was dark in the hall. Pushing the door open, she saw her boys standing in a line. She reminded herself to be calm. Dignified.

With a sniff, Oscar passed his phone.

'Where are you?' she said into it.

'Oh, hi, um. It's called . . . Château Royal Resort—'

'What are you doing in New Fucking Caledonia?'

Cody scowled.

'Oh, well . . . I was going to have a rest,' said Duncan. 'Be alone. Learn French.'

'How lovely for you.' She tried to ride the wave of fury to the shore without being dumped. But how many times, in the past fifteen years, had she needed 'a rest'? How many times had she wanted to 'be alone' on a tropical island? That number was in the millions.

Duncan sighed. 'Liv, we need to talk. In person.'

He was sounding rather subdued for someone in paradise. She wondered how the flight over had been; or was it the food, or his room? You'd never know this man had once been a seasoned traveller.

She eyed her empty supper plate on the carpet. She thought of that psychologist friend, years ago, and her three vases. The vase Liv and Duncan had been creating was worse than a platter, she realised. This trip, this dash across the ocean, had hit upon their marriage's weak spot. And smashed it to bits.

'You know what?' Liv said. 'Not having you here isn't that different to having you here. In some ways it's actually easier . . .'

Silence.

'You and me – us. We're not holding water anymore, Duncan. It's broken. Kaput.'

Silence. She felt a tad mean.

'Do you have anything to say?'

'That wasn't very kind.' He cleared his throat.

'No.'

'You'd like it here,' he added. 'It's beautiful; tranquil. Why don't you come?'

She shook her head. The man still had no idea. Was oblivious to, or untouched by recent events.

A layer of steel formed around her heart.

'Duncan, did you hear me? I can't see us coming back from this. First your job, and now this escapade . . . You're not thinking about us, at all.' She closed her eyes. 'You've broken it.'

Something slapped, like a magazine on a desktop. 'I wish you'd never read those stupid books and their smarty-pants studies! I mean, half the famous ones are fucking *bogus*.'

Tears pricked her eyes. They're what?

'Oh, forget it. I'm done,' she said. 'I give up. I want a divorce.'

In the silence that followed, she could hear the ocean between them. And then he was gone.

In the hallway, Oscar, Jai and Cody bolted to bed; but not so quickly that Liv couldn't see blotches around Jai's eyes, a tissue balled in Oscar's fist or snot dangling from Cody's nose.

About then, her calm and dignified front collapsed.

•

Around 1 am Tuesday morning, Liv crawled out of her bedroom. She checked her three sons were breathing, turned off the outside lights, and face-planted onto the couch. Between two and three o'clock, she was on the old iPad, googling. When she was done, she stared at her bookshelves as if at friends who had betrayed her. Not all of them, but definitely some. It turned out, some of the world's most renowned psychological studies couldn't be replicated, or were wrong or fraudulent. From that famous Stanford prison experiment to priming. And power poses! Mortified, Liv sank lower into her couch. The intellectual bubble she lived in popped, leaving only a mist of uncertainty. Oh dear. Her faith in humankind, in the social sciences, in Vic Cato, nose-dived. She felt rather stupid.

Miserable, after a few minutes, Liv switched on the television and surfed, as she had many years ago, while breastfeeding. She surfed until she came across the blindingly youthful face of Clint Eastwood as Dirty Harry. Around 4 am, wide awake, she watched the man walk around, chewing gum and shooting people. Ruthless. Expressionless . . . droll. She sat up, sniffed, squinted. There was something unnervingly familiar about the unorthodox cop. She paused her smart TV. Studied the deadpan arrogance. It wasn't merely that Clint was an iconic actor in his prime. It was something more. Something deeply, intimately familiar. She pressed play again. Her arms tingled. Her heart bashed about. She imagined Dirty Harry with pale eyelashes and long blonde hair . . .

Tossing her tissue at the TV, she grabbed the iPad again. Googled 'Nordic noir'. Alone on her soft couch, she felt a blush begin at her toes and creep upwards. Not one but two of the actors playing those wonderful Nordic detectives had drawn on the dirty man himself as inspiration. Which meant, for months, she'd been walking around Bayside, around Carmichael, around her marriage, spouting outdated studies and pretending to be . . . Dirty Harry.

Shit.

'Mum,' said Cody. 'Mummy, wake up.'

Around 5 am, seemingly only moments after Liv managed to fall asleep back in bed, a posse of sons in pyjamas stood over her. Their facial expressions had the tone of an intervention. They were each holding a torch, as the lights were out.

'What's the matter?' she said, feigning stupidity.

'We don't want you and Daddy to get a divorce.'

Liv sat up. 'I know. But sometimes crappy stuff happens.'

Oscar and Jai flinched. But Liv was done with niceties. With choosing her words . . . and with being Dirty Gunhild. She was going to be real Liv: unabridged, expressive and, damn it, yes, assertive.

She looked from one torchlit face to another. They did look rather ghoulish, her sad spooks.

'Okay, here's what that means. We're going to have to sell our house. Which was your dad's idea, anyhow. You'll all have to give up Carmichael, not just Jai. Which isn't the worst thing in the world, obviously, particularly for you, Oscar. And, of course, your dad won't be back.'

Cody began to cry, silently, while Oscar welled up.

'And I'm going to need to get a steady job, with benefits. No more part-time contract work to fit around you guys. I need full-time, ongoing employment. I'll have to dust off my law degree and work my butt off to convince someone to hire me, given I'm forty-five and haven't worked in the law in fifteen years. Can't remember a damn thing, really. Anywho! I'll probably end up working hours like your father was . . . in some god-awful firm steeped in the adversarial system and patriarchy. Which means you won't see me much. And I'll get very tired. And maybe slightly bitter. So you'll have to lean on those Lists. Especially as Dad's pathetic list will need to be dished out.'

Oscar and Jai swapped identical worried looks.

'We won't have much money, of course, because single mums with three kids tend to struggle. And that's a fact!' She eyed Oscar. 'I'll be way down the ladder. I may not be able to afford another house. I have next to zilch in my superannuation. Truth be told, I'll probably never return to the financial position I'm in right now.' She paused. 'In ten years, I may end up living in the Audi. Or couch-surfing at your place . . .'

This last was said with a finger pointed at Cody.

'Why are you doing it, then?' he said, wet cheeked. 'I don't have a couch.'

'Because, Cody, darling, your dad is a douchebag.'

Oscar's eyes popped, as if perhaps a crack had appeared running across her forehead. But she felt better, post purge – if light-headed.

'I think what Mum's trying to say is that relationships aren't easy,' said Jai.

'And women get a shit deal and end up broke.' Oscar's face lit up, as if the penny might finally be dropping. 'So don't break up, then . . . heaps of people stay together and aren't happy. Can't you?'

Liv wobbled her head, uncommitted. She squinted at the clock radio. It was closer to six now. Outside, a door banged. She realised then that Jai still wasn't tapping or jumping or grinding. Getting expelled had done it, of course. Also, Oscar wasn't on a screen. Cody was quiet.

'Why are you lot up?'

Jai handballed that one to Oscar.

'Dad rang again,' said Oscar. 'Said he was sorry he left. That it was a bad call.'

'He did?' Liv swallowed an avalanche of tears. Maybe she hadn't cornered the market on regret.

'And he wanted us to say his side.'

'Oh?'

'Yeah, how he's allowed to be his own man,' Oscar said. 'How you should respect that. You're not the boss of him, Mum.'

'Uh-huh.'

'How it's the person you marry, not his job.' Cody added.

She clamped her mouth. Couldn't tell if a laugh was coming up or a sob. Or bile.

'He thinks you've got more in common with Uncle Michael than—' said Oscar.

'Uncle Michael!'

'He's an arsehole,' Cody whispered.

Liv stopped herself from nodding.

'He doesn't think people really do change, or can change, or want change. I dunno. He was going on a bit,' said Jai. 'But you don't think that, do you, Mum?' Jai's worried eyes returned.

Liv wondered if she might cry. So many parts of their life had been renegotiated, these past few months. Some of those changes had tripped her up too.

'I . . . don't . . . know.' She bit her lip.

Concern skimmed from one pair of eyes to the next. For once in their lives, she didn't have all the answers. Or even one good one. No study to quote. Her mind was silent. Then Jai and Oscar and Cody wrapped their arms around her, making a teepee of warm limbs. She buried her face in her youngest son's neck. It smelt surprisingly clean; and he was surprisingly calm. How had it come to this? Her sons in close, attuned, yet her marriage and their world splitting apart. It'd all started at that school; with her fresh eyes, and then Vic's fine-tuning. They'd made such great strides. But now almost everything was worse than when she'd begun.

With that dawning, the final spark of fire inside her was snuffed out.

Cody said, 'Don't give up on us, Mummy.'

Liv laughed then and cried. Giving up wasn't really her style. Through tears, she read the faces of her sons. They were beautiful boys. All of them. But the fire was out. She couldn't imagine being ignited again.

85

Jess

After a long, childless night, Jess was back on her treadmill first thing the next morning when her phone beeped. Finally! She read the message, then ran through the kitchen and outside. She ran across the short path and onto the footpath. She didn't often wish they had two cars, but today, with Morrie at an early pump class, it would've helped. Cold air rushed by her bare stomach. It'd been twenty years since she'd jogged outside – in another life. But she'd been summonsed! Jogging along South Road, Jess wondered what to say. Prayed she didn't get tongue-tied.

Thirty metres ahead was a construction site, where hard-hatted men were taking a break on the pavement. Jess counted her strides: one, two, three; one, two, three. One of the men was sizing her up. A stocky and sun-damaged fellow, shovelling fruit from a Tupperware container. She saw him mutter and his workmates look her way. Twenty years ago, Jess would've crossed the road. Twenty years ago, she might've turned around. Today, she could feel perspiration trickle into her bellybutton. She was going quite fast.

As she approached, the man blocked her path. 'What's the hurry, beautiful?'

Only months ago, Jess would've stayed silent. A fortnight ago, she would've thought, I should say something . . . but do I have to? Today, Jess didn't break her stride. Without thinking, she looked the man in the eye and said, 'Out of my way, buster. I'm not here for you.'

Mid-chew, the man froze, then leapt aside. Something fell from his mouth. Slurping from thermoses, his workmates laughed as Jess passed, accelerating. Not bad, she thought. For a first go.

Jess was relieved to find Dr Cato on the sand. Her message had sounded . . . a bit potty. Green Point was still and, being midweek, quiet. Only one kayaker was braving the cold. A bike was nearby, one of its pedals turning. Staring out to sea, Dr Cato was wearing a trench coat, long boots and huge sunglasses. Her hair was dirty and scraped back from her face. Jess tried not to judge her for it.

Walking across the sand, Jess hoped this wasn't about the Crepes of Carmichael.

Turning, Dr Cato smiled. 'Hello, Jess,' she said. 'I'm so depressed.' She yanked off a boot.

'Hi . . . Vic. It is depressing.'

Jess was hot in the cold air. Her skin tingled. She felt alive, alert and, beside the ocean, small. A lovely feeling. For some reason, it was easier now to call Dr Cato Vic. Maybe it was the dirty hair. Or the one shoe.

'But . . . you know,' Jess smiled. 'It's only a setback.'

Vic hopped about. 'You tell Grace sorry from me, okay?'

Jess frowned. Vic didn't know about Grace and Bella's disappearing act. Jess wondered if she knew about the Crepes. Vic took off the other boot as two women jogged by, chatting. They looked Vic up and down.

'Vic,' Jess said, 'what are you doing?'

Vic pointed to the sea.

'Oh . . . hon.'

Jess couldn't see a towel. Vic didn't look like a swimmer. Unbuttoning her trench coat, Vic gave Jess a hard stare. She took off her jacket to reveal a beige, knee-length body stocking. Jess tried not to look at her pendulous breasts. Vic tossed her clothes by the bike, then stepped towards the sea. 'Want to join?'

Jess gulped. 'Me? No.'

Doubly confused, Jess darted in front of Vic. 'The other day, Grace and I were talking about scientists.'

Vic gave a sharp, what-now type sigh, as if she really had to get in that water.

'About how, you try and try, and fail and fail for years and then you have these breakthroughs . . . Unexpectedly. Sometimes thanks to luck. Like that man with the mould.'

Vic stopped. 'Fleming.'

'Yes, him. Grace was saying how he went on holiday, or something, left dirty dishes in his lab, and came back to find bacteria-killing mould.' Jess laughed, marvelling.

'Schoolchildren around the world know that story, Jess.'

'But don't you see? That could be us . . . on the cusp . . . of growing mould!'

Vic frowned at the water's edge. 'You realise it took *decades* after Fleming's discovery for the first patients to be treated with penicillin.'

Jess nodded. 'But people *were* treated. And saved. Millions of people!'

Vic seemed to soften. 'Jess, the people who own the lab are spreading the bug . . .'

Jess felt like a child being reminded of the big, tough world. Vic often spoke to her like that. But, sometimes, adults needed to think like children.

'We can still stop *them*. Find a new lab . . .' Jess thought of how happy those Carmichael students had become until this week, their many lovely, hardworking teachers, and those marbled science labs. 'Or we take back this one.'

'Fighting words, Jess Charters.'

Fighting and bugs, science and hope. Jess didn't recognise herself.

'There's something else you need to understand – you and Liv,' said Vic. 'Science itself is a human construct, right? It works imperfectly.'

Jess looked to the distant kayaker paddling away. 'As long as you do no harm, hon.'

Vic took off her forgotten sunglasses and considered Jess, as if Jess was stepping out of darkness and into light. 'I did underestimate you, didn't I?'

Chuffed, if confused, Jess smiled.

Vic tossed her glasses to the pile of clothes. 'But it's too late. They fired me. I thought I'd brought them with me, but I hadn't. I didn't even have Liv!'

Liv? Jess didn't understand, hadn't been able to reach Liv. But now wasn't the time.

'Haven't you been teaching the children about failure? About how women tend to give up; take failure personally . . . and we get judged more harshly for it too.'

Vic took a step into the lapping water and, ankle-deep, winced. Not knowing what else to do, Jess picked up Vic's clothes and offered them. 'Liv will have James Whittaker-Smith's number, hon. You should call him.'

'Oh, Jess.' Vic Cato was scowling but smiling too. 'I thought you'd need a reset, but you're doing better than me! Back in two.'

With a shriek, Vic hurled herself into the icy bay.

86

Liv

Meanwhile, at the Winsome household, Jai knocked before entering with a tray of sliced cantaloupe, muesli and juice. Moaning, Liv dragged herself up the bed. Their future looked so bleak, she was considering never getting up again, especially now she had room service.

'Byyyeee Mummmm,' Cody yelled, a split second before the door slammed. Duncan was right about one thing, she supposed: they really did need to give notice. ASAP.

Jai hesitated with the tray. Stood perfectly still. Teenage code for *talk to me.*

'Jai-Jai . . .' She sighed. 'Why'd you punch Mr Waring, yesterday?'

Jai peeked through his enviable eyelashes. 'Because he told us boys we 'got our school back'. That the wicked witches were dead.'

'The wicked witches . . .' Liv munched. 'Wow.'

Jai appraised her as her blood began to warm.

'He really said that? In front of you boys?'

'Yep.'

Liv wriggled higher. She *was* a role model, here, she supposed . . . albeit a flawed one. And, yes, her boys probably wouldn't last the distance at Carmichael, but lots of people's would . . . She took in this son's bated breath. Look at him, she thought. Flawed or not, Vic's program had done wonders. A tiny spark fired inside her. Jai was watching her closely. Their gazes fused. A flash of insight lit his face.

'You sure you're up for this?' Liv said.

'Yep! Yep.' Jai beamed.

'Okay. That's it.'

She flipped down the covers.

Liv was springing around her room when Jai returned from the kitchen. 'But, wait, Mum, we need to talk.'

She sank to her knees, searched under the bed, as Oscar appeared. Both boys were, she realised, wearing their school uniforms.

'I thought you'd gone already?'

'I walked Cody to the bus. Just made it.' Oscar actually smiled. 'Took a few wrong turns there, Mum.' He took a big breath. 'I was really, really sad and lonely.' He shot a look to his twin. 'Should've talked about it. Sorry about that. But I'm back.'

'Thank god. Well done you!' she said, and both boys grinned. She sobered. 'I'm sorry I haven't been there for you, Osc. I should've been talking to you too. I kinda dropped the Oscar ball.'

Oscar shrugged, but she could see he was pleased. She gave him a cuddle and he didn't fight it. After, her boys smiled at each other. And, for the last time, Liv admired the twins together in their Carmichael best. They had looked the part. Handsome, well-tailored, ready for business – even if Oscar's uniform had grown too small and his hair needed cutting.

She sank to her knees again, stuck her hand under the bed. 'Jai, why are you wearing your brother's school uniform?'

Jai gave a half-smile. 'Mum, Grace and Bella . . .' Jai looked at Oscar, 'are kind of in hiding.'

Mission accomplished, phone in hand, she clambered up. 'Because?'

'They made a creeps list. Grace was scared her Mum would freak.'

'Uh-huh. Makes sense.' Liv gave Grace a telepathic fist-bump. 'And did Jess—'

'Not yet.'

'But now Mr Crisp and Mr Palmer are getting rid of everyone, including Grace and Bella,' Oscar continued. 'We think Mr Palmer might be getting rid of Mr Crisp.'

'Uh-huh.' She switched on her phone.

'There's some meeting on Thursday night. Taj kept saying, "Bye-bye, Crispy. Mr Palmer's going to run the place like a footy club."'

Liv frowned, tried to work out whether, today, that was good or bad.

'But we're not going to let him,' Jai said.

Liv eyed the phone in her hand and turned it on; buzzing with missed calls, it felt like a grenade.

'Mum, lots of kids are super pissed – about everything,' Oscar added, with a pointed look to Jai. 'But especially about them firing Dr Cato.' Oscar blushed, slightly. 'She did make a few good points.'

'Uh-huh.' Liv grinned.

'Taj and his gang are total nutjobs, by the way.' Oscar grimaced, as if he'd witnessed things he'd rather not discuss. 'They're, like, as mean as Hannah! And you think we're bad for chewing with our mouths open!'

Liv marvelled at how Oscar could link such disparate ideas.

Oscar and Jai were staring at each other. The unsaid was loud. 'Boys . . . what?'

Oscar shook his head, prompting Jai to consult the time on her phone. 'Yesterday was a mess,' said Jai. 'But today we're getting organised. We're gonna boycott classes. We've started a petition, too. To get rid of Crisp *and* Palmer. Bring Dr Cato back.'

Wow. Worry danced a jig through her thoughts. Her boys could get in significant trouble. Which would make it a learning opportunity, she supposed. She took in the twins' matching expressions: earnest, expectant, waiting on her. What rules applied here? Well. Rules only worked when everyone played by them.

'What about Taj, his knucklehead buddies?'

Oscar gulped, with a look back to Jai. 'We'll deal with them.'

Liv nodded slowly.

'We won't do anything dumb, promise,' said Jai.

'You can't get expelled twice, I suppose,' she said. 'How are you getting there?'

'Gonna ride,' said Jai. Despite herself, Liv smiled.

'What are *you* going to do?' Oscar asked.

She shook her phone. 'Call whoever I can think of.'

A puff of sadness crossed Oscar's face. 'Like Dad?'

'No, Osc, not like Dad.'

She unlocked her phone. Her background picture was a photo of the five of them – at a beachside restaurant, grinning over watermelon mocktails. They looked so young, but it was only two years ago. Back when their hair was well-cut, their teeth professionally cleaned, and they did things together. It felt like a decade had passed. Her outward breath became jagged.

Would any of this make a lasting difference: to the school? To Duncan? To them?

'We're going to show him, Mum.'

It was spooky when Jai did that.

Liv saw herself in her sons' eyes. Mother, revolutionary, estranged wife. Ex-lawyer, ex-investigator, ex–Dirty Harry. Could she integrate those roles into one cohesive and effective whole; and a role, a life, she wanted?

She shrugged. What else was she going to do? Go back to sleep?

She gave both boys a kiss. 'Remember, my darling Oscars, they do have spies. Everywhere.'

After, Liv took a long shower then dressed in khaki cargo pants, a black T-shirt and belt. As she dressed, she banished thoughts of Duncan the Doubter/Deserter. Instead, she imagined the school as a town in an old Western film. It was her job to gather the townsfolk, warn and prepare them for the gunfight ahead. She began by ringing Vic: 'I lost my nerve,' she said to Vic's voicemail. 'Felt swamped, all over again. And confused. But I'm back. Please forgive me.' Then she rang Jess: 'You okay? If you are, help! Come over!' Phone in hand, Liv thought of the others to call. Hundreds of parents. Teachers. Board members. She hesitated. Reaching out to people was Jess's forte. Vic had the powers of persuasion. What did she have? She'd outgrown Dirty Gunhild. All she had really was a head full of random, occasionally outdated, research, a passion for sharing it and a habit of cutting people off.

She looked at her phone's wallpaper. People were going to think she was that parent. That mum. Perhaps she was.

Sometimes, despite her foibles, that mum was on the money.

Her next call was to Jean Anderson, who, to Liv's surprise, was at the hairdresser's. Jean had just got off the phone from Vic, who had apparently cast off her shock and was ready to fight back too. Thank god! Together, foil by foil, Jean and Liv finessed a plan. Oscar was spot-on: apparently, an emergency board meeting had been called for Thursday. Which was perfect. Liv would write a letter on behalf of Mums for Equality, demanding Tony Crisp, Lloyd Palmer and the Low brothers senior resign, by 6 pm Thursday. Failing that, Liv would lead a delegation to the meeting and demand action, including the reinstatement of Vic's program and the acceptance of Liv's charter. Legal action wasn't out of the question either: wrongful termination of Vic's contract, wrongful expulsion of Jai . . . of Grace and Bella . . . and whatever else Liv could think up. It was an audacious plan, admittedly, and not exactly the school's protocol for addressing grievances . . . but why not? Lots of people had been delighted with the school's near-transformation; surely, given all the information, the community would support a spill?

Liv's first bold move, therefore, was a letter. To James Whittaker-Smith, Chairman of the Board of Carmichael, and his fellow board members, with Tony Crisp copied in too. Her next email was a letter to the parents of Year Eight. Then she wrote to the Old Grammarians Association. In the latter two letters, Liv cited the results of Jai's survey and fleshed out the school's STEM position. Thanks to Jean's snooping, Liv had all the addresses and the STEM data Vic had gathered. It turned out STEM at Carmichael was going *backwards* . . . the number of girls *and* boys choosing not to do Maths in their final years had tripled in recent years. For boys the figure had moved from three per cent to nine per cent, while for girls the figure was forty per cent. Forty per cent of the senior female cohort at this school was not doing Maths! Vic had been designing interventions to tackle this. Liv felt as if she might burst an artery. She emailed these letters to as many people as she could. Fearless Jean was an excellent help, having somehow walked out with her laptop and access intact; happily, the school's incompetence knew no bounds.

Next, Liv worked the telephone. She went through every old class list – twelve lots of twenty-odd sets of parents. She even left a message for Stella and for Carly. She knew people were at the office and in meetings, on the ward and playing tennis. But, in every call, she told the story of the survey. She told people about Vic Cato. About the STEM figures. She spoke about Professor Griffin's Science intervention. She touched on the creeps list. Finally, she called on everyone to join her at the school to protest, Thursday night.

This would be their moment of truth.

The response wasn't overwhelmingly positive.

Some people wanted to talk about the Low family. Some people were very disappointed in Tony Crisp. 'A polarising fellow,' they called him. Some people thought Lloyd Palmer should succeed him. But lots of people *didn't* want to speak about the Low family. Or about the problems at the school. Some people sounded scared. Or bored. And hung up.

Liv tried to keep the conversations focused on cultural change, on the vastly improved relationships between the boys and girls since the unearthing of sexual harassment. On the environment of kindness that had been fostered. Respect. Mostly people said, 'Wow, they did all that? That's great.' Some said, 'Sexual harassment! When will it stop?' And, 'Girls in Science is a tough one.' And, 'Thanks for calling, but I have to go. Good luck with it.' A number of emails bounced and calls rang out. A few said, 'Not interested,' as if she were a telemarketer. A few more said, 'Thursday? That's short notice. I think we're busy.'

But quite a lot of mothers were angry, especially the girls' mothers. Some of them knew about the survey, the science intervention and the creeps list. They could see the progress that had been made and wanted more. They understood the need to get in early with education – to break down gendered norms and nip in the bud future harm. They knew about the link between attitudes indulged now and, say, domestic violence later.

But they were all unsurprised by the harassment at Carmichael. 'It's everywhere!' they said. As if sexual harassment was like wildfire or the flu. Regrettable but inevitable.

'But there are so many things you can do. It can be stopped,' Liv said. 'Join me! Join my Mums for Equality. We can do this!'

'What about the dads?' someone said.

'Oh, they're invited too!' Duh. 'Mums and Dads for Equality.'

Some girls' mums spoke with a level of resignation that Liv found distressing. They didn't seem to appreciate the urgency of the situation. 'We need to act!' she said, a few hundred times. They didn't seem to grasp the effect Vic Cato had had. How it could happen that quickly – in one term! They didn't understand, as Liv did now, that you didn't need to squish around in every single brain. You could do this laterally. *Scientifically.* And there was more to do.

By mid-morning, she had been hung up on by dozens of people.

Liv had never argued so much with people she was not related to. She'd never been this angry before – not when the twins put the garden hose through the window and saturated her mattress; or even when they chased Pickle through the kitchen and upended the Christmas pav.

What more did these people want?

By lunchtime, Liv sensed her protest would be puny. Her rallying cry to the board a fizzer. Just as bad, Vic hadn't called back and Jai had texted, *Link to the petition's broken and the boycott's tanking.* At least Taj and his mates had gone to ground, inadvertently helping the cause. Mr Waring, having spotted too many Oscars, had just sent them both home. They'd grabbed some hot chips and would head off soon.

Defeated, Liv played phone-tag with Jess and boiled the kettle. Thoughts of Duncan sneaked in. There was a chance he was more right than she'd given him credit for.

As the water bubbled, she wondered if she ought to apologise for turning into Dirty Gunhild; for not going to work. She wondered who her husband was becoming. This work-in-progress man. She wondered if she and the boys should give up on Carmichael. Move out of the

Bayside bubble and into the country, somewhere cheap, and start again. She could work in a library or cake shop. Find a school that was practically free.

She was pondering these thoughts, when the garage door opened.

87

Liv

But first the doorbell. It chimed, twice. Confused, Liv walked in a small circle. Was it Duncan? She wouldn't put it past him. Did she want to see him? She wasn't sure. She braced herself as she opened the door. But, no; there, on the welcome mat, was Stella Havelock and a boy who could've been Blake. Except this boy was wearing well-fitting clothes and looking her in the eye. Whatever Blake was on, Liv wanted some.

'You called,' said Stella. 'About time!'

Stunned, Liv leant against the door; no one moved.

'The minute that Crepes List was up,' Stella said, 'Blake started talking. If only Dylan Low had been sprung three months ago, it would've saved us a fucking bomb in family counselling.'

Family counselling? Liv wanted to congratulate her lapsed friend and high-five her son, but neither seemed appropriate. 'Dylan Low?' She'd forgotten about him.

'Turns out we needed to learn how to say no, and mean it.'

'You're not alone in that.'

Stella smiled. 'Guess we ought to thank that little creep . . . er, Crepe.'

Dylan Low was far from little. He was six-foot-two. Probably eighteen. Probably drove a better car than hers.

'I don't get it. What'd Dylan do?'

Stella elbowed Blake's ribs.

'Set up that Insta account on my iPad.'

Liv gasped as Blake kicked the ground, ruefully.

'Said he'd bash me if I told anyone. He was always at me, when no one was looking. Dacked me last year backstage at the recital.'

Liv hadn't heard Blake utter this many words in a year. Stella curled her arm around him. Liv could see some of his residual shame.

'That sucks, Blake. But how . . . No. Was Dylan Low your fill-in manny?'

'Lasted one weekend. Got Blake stoned. That he admitted to.'

'Oh, Stella, I'm so sorry.'

Stella adjusted her glasses. 'Dylan should've been the one to leave Carmichael. Not Blake. But Bettina can't see it. Not her uber-son.'

As Liv processed all this, she studied Blake's ruddy face. His cheeks had filled out. His butt chin had softened.

'How are you, Blake? You do seem . . . better.'

'Yes, I'm good thanks, Liv. How about you?' He smiled like a benign Stepford son.

Stella was watching as if he was performing a complex soliloquy.

'Yeah, not bad.' Liv glanced at her front garden. 'How's the new school?'

'Kids are nicer. Don't have to wear a uniform. The English teachers don't throw things at you.'

Liv laughed, gestured for them to enter.

'Hey, Liv, I thought you might've worked it out,' Blake said. 'You being an investigator and all.'

'Oh.' Liv pulled a face. 'Sorry.'

'I gave you a few clues.'

Liv coloured, frowned. What else had she missed?

'Doesn't matter. Jai home?'

'Should be soon. All things being equal.'

Stella embraced Liv. 'Missed you,' she said. 'You fucking know-it-all.'

'Yeah, missed you too,' said Liv.

None of us were without flaws, she thought. Or beyond reform.

88

Jess

'She's here . . .'

Jess's eyes filled. After her powwow with Vic, Jess had spent the morning waiting for Grace to turn up, and trying Liv. She'd been very brave and calm, and her house was very clean. But when the call back finally came, she couldn't help herself. 'Thank you,' she'd said, over and over.

At Liv's, the front door was wide open. Stella and Blake Havelock were sitting on the couch and folding what looked like flyers. Liv was darting about the kitchen. The house smelt of eggs. Butter. Pancakes? Omelette?

Jess let herself in. 'Hello?'

Blake and Stella stared in silence at her.

'In here,' said Liv.

Jess waved sheepishly at Stella and Blake as she passed. Then she saw her. Hunched at the kitchen bench, in a cap and oversized boys' clothes, patting a dog. And next to Grace, Bella, in a similar outfit. While Bella was grinning, seemingly having the time of her life, Grace didn't look so happy. Something was off. Jess sprang to her.

Grace's eyes flickered up and filled. 'Hi, Mum.'

Liv flipped a pancake.

Driving over, Jess had been telling herself to stay calm. Don't make a fuss. Don't dump twenty-four hours' worth of questions on her. Jess wrapped Grace in her arms. 'Oh, sweetie.' She inhaled, squeezed to the count of three. 'What's been going on?'

The peak of Grace's cap was digging into Jess's shoulderblade.

Jai whispered to Grace. 'Want another pancake?'

Grace shook her head. Liv had done a really wonderful job with that boy. Jess's worry lifted. Grace was holding her tight but wasn't dissolving. Liv flipped the pancake again and tipped it onto a plate, which she passed to Bella. Liv splashed another batter-load into the pan. Jess pulled back from Grace.

'Are you okay, hon?' said Jess to Liv.

Liv did not meet her eye. Jess felt a squeeze of fear again, as she looked back to her daughter. She gasped.

A split second later, Vic marched in, followed by Blake and Stella Havelock. 'Hello, hello.' Vic tossed her bag onto the table. 'People, takeaway for the day: we're not living if we're not failing sometimes.'

Liv gave a small smile. Failing and learning – may she never stop. The teenagers nodded, looking mildly confused. The mums stood together.

'Smells fantastic in here.' Vic pointed her laser-stare on Grace. 'You. Tell us about those Crepes. Now.'

89

Duncan

It was late afternoon on Wednesday, when Duncan lurched in, weary and flower-less, to find half-a-dozen women and their teenage children on their phones in his lounge room. Everyone was speaking or texting, or both. Every available surface was occupied. Smaller children eating chocolate scampered through the house. Though Liv looked exhausted, she also seemed to be in her element, though what you'd call this particular element eluded Duncan. Obviously, it was something to do with the school. But this wasn't a fundraiser. The mood resembled a cross between wedding preparation and a military operation. People were ticking items off lists. Everyone was wearing red T-shirts with white slogans on them – *VIVA LA REVOLUCIÓN!* He knew Liv loved a bespoke T-shirt, but *revolución*? Oh, god. What'd happened? On the phone, Jai had mumbled something about being expelled, which Duncan had found shocking, if convenient. He'd suspected Jai was catastrophising. Now he wasn't so sure. This war room may explain why Liv wasn't calling him back. Duncan was tempted to retreat, return later. Except he had nowhere else to go, except maybe Aldi.

A squealing Pickle hurled herself at his shin as he parked his bag. Where was Jai? And Oscar? Cody? When the kids were little and still awake when he came home, he'd felt like Santa Claus. Often, he'd felt guilty that, figuratively speaking, his sack was empty. In more recent years, the boys would scarcely have noticed if he'd arrived home with teeth missing. Today, he'd been hoping for a hug.

A stately woman stood by the windows. She was looking across his lawn, with her hands behind her back. People queued to ask, should they meet on the street? Did they need a microphone? Who would speak? Something about this woman commanded attention. She seemed firmly anchored to the ground by long, flat shoes. You didn't tend to see glamorous women without heels. Duncan stopped. His bladder was bursting, but he wanted to hear her answer.

Her voice was soothing, and warm. 'Liv will lead the questioning.'

Liv stirred, doubt flickering across her face.

'Keep it short and sharp,' the woman said. 'And don't interrupt their answers.'

Liv gave a thumbs up, and the seated worker bees buzzed.

'But, hear me – we are unapologetic!' The woman beamed, then lifted her arm in some sort of salute. It made her look like a gorgeous, albeit ageing, commandant.

'Spot on, sister!' said another woman, wearing invisible braces. Was she a teacher, a mum or an unfortunately aged child?

'Finally, heads are going to roll!' said an older woman with streaked blue hair. 'No more Low pressure systems!'

Duncan blanched. He hoped she wasn't talking about the Low brothers. Scary bastards.

He found his boys and Grace sandwiched on a couch. Astoundingly, they weren't texting; Oscar was grinning, and may have lost a kilo, while Cody looked serene. Maybe they *were* better off without him. Duncan's mouth went dry. Something was different too about Grace, who was nursing a poster: a cartoon version of Tony Crisp. Alongside the cartoon was written, *One bad egg too many!* And, *Time to ditch the old roosters!*

Duncan's legs wobbled as if he'd been cycling uphill.

Spying him, Liv rose. 'What are you doing here?'

'More to the point, what are you doing?' His voice was shaking. When they'd last spoken about Carmichael's reinvention, she'd said it was going well. The girls had smashed the Science test.

'You and your mates have been asleep at the wheel,' said Liv. 'It's time to move over, Dunc.'

'What? *My* mates?' He sounded confused, like his father in very old age. What mates?

It seemed she couldn't look him in the eye. She returned to her troop of telephoners.

He reconsidered Grace, wearing one of Jai's caps, and the animated women in his lounge room. The children eating his dark chocolate. One or two of the mothers impaled him with a stare. A young girl poked out a brown tongue. His three sons were watching him, as if expecting a rousing speech. Liv was bent on one knee, chatting to Stella Havelock.

'Ah, Liv?'

Had she had a chance to miss him? To reflect?

Fleetingly, her face seemed to soften, or maybe that was wishful thinking. 'Not now, Duncan.'

She turned away, giving him no choice but to creep upstairs. The twins scattered – Jai to his phone, Oscar to the kitchen. Feeling Cody's eyes on him, Duncan took the stairs two at a time. In the ensuite, he relieved himself. Down below, with unfortunate timing, the room burst into laughter and spontaneous applause.

Then, at the door: 'Dad,' Cody sang. 'Dad?'

'In a minute, mate.'

Duncan sat on the toilet lid and took off his shoes and socks. The tiles seemed to sway. Whenever he travelled, even to Sydney, he felt as if he was moving long after he'd disembarked. He felt this way whether he'd been on a plane, or a train, or a boat. He put his elbows on his knees and rested his forehead against his wrists.

'Dad, you okay? You crying?'

Laughter and cheers continued to waft up the stairs. Duncan felt as though he was in the midst of a mutiny. He stared at his wide, pink feet.

'No, mate.'

What to say to his youngest son?

He tried to listen to his new and faint inner voice. What'd he come home for? Clothes and a cup of tea, a chat with his boys, and with Liv.

To say he didn't want to be stingy or passive or selfish anymore. But Liv was still too busy to listen. Or couldn't hear him. Too much static.

What'd Maggie said, when last they spoke? 'Give love to love, Duncan. Ditch the rest.'

He leant forward. 'Door's open, Cody-Codes.'

90

Thursday, 8.25 am

Liv

Mary MacBeth was waiting by the coffee machine at The Provedore when Liv and Vic burst in and hugged her.

'Morning, ladies. We need to be quick,' said Mary, over Vic's shoulder. 'It's the Wild West back there this morning.'

'We want you to put your hand up, Mary,' said Vic.

Mary spluttered into her scarf. A group of teachers waved at her as they left the cafe. Students rushing by waved too. Everyone was wearing green armbands. School was about to start.

Liv leant in close. 'You'd be wonderful. Parents love you. The staff love you. And the ones that don't can . . .'

The coffee machine roared to life.

'I admire what you two achieved. I do,' said Mary. 'It's been breathtaking.' She gestured to more green armbands darting by outside. 'But I can't see you removing the unholy trinity this evening.'

'Have faith, Mary,' said Vic. 'Sometimes it's counterintuitive. But it can happen, just like that.' Vic snapped her fingers.

Liv gulped. At length, Liv and Vic had discussed tipping points: how a social movement, just like a disease or a trend, could reach a critical juncture and spill over, spreading wildly. How it could happen suddenly, prompted by some small adjustment. But how did you know when you were there? Liv kept wondering. It wasn't something you could bank on. Liv thought of Duncan, who she'd been avoiding since his return.

In a similar yet different vein, how did you know when your marriage was over?

Liv felt her breath catch. She made herself tune back in.

'Mary, you'd make a brilliant leader. The best! Sixteen hundred students need you. Their futures need you leading them, now.'

'Almond milk double espresso,' called the barista. 'With honey.'

Mary was blushing as she took her coffee. 'Keep talking,' she said.

Liv took a deep, centring breath as Vic continued. They were so close. Liv could see an enlightened and diverse board appointing Mary to run the school, the school embracing Vic's program, testing to see what worked, and fostering a love of science and maths, art and literature, and music and sport in its students. A school where discriminatory biases did not prevail, men and women were leading teachers in equal numbers, everyone was treated with respect and kindness, and no one perved at boobs. Or grabbed pussies.

Utopia!

Liv would work day and night to keep her boys at that Carmichael, she decided. She'd go there herself, if she could. She'd return to the law *and* work with Vic. She'd put her hand up for the school council. The Parents' Association. Canteen. School crossing. Though, she'd have to speak with Duncan, she supposed, at some stage in that future.

'You two have no idea how much work principals do,' said Mary. 'Not to mention, the stress and the abuse . . . and that's from the regular parents.'

Liv shot a look to Vic. 'That'll change . . .' said Vic.

'Is there nothing you can't fix?' Mary chuckled. 'Ladies, what I can tell you is, no one else at that school wants the job, besides Palmer. Whatever life you have outside of school is wiped.'

'But you still love Carmichael, don't you Mary?' said Liv.

Liv and Vic were nodding.

Mary nodded too, and, noticing their influence on her, laughed. 'More than ever. But my vision isn't Crisp's. I'd wind back that building schedule, up the teachers' pay, make the school more accessible for many more families . . .'

'Oh, music to my ears,' said Liv.

Mary rested her coffee on the window counter. 'I'd still want to teach, too.'

'Of course,' said Vic. 'Be clear about what you want. Ask for it.'

Mary's phone beeped and she read a message. 'I have to get back. Taj's on the rampage with a claw hammer.'

Liv and Vic shared a galvanising look.

Mary sized them up. 'If you got rid of that unholy trinity – if Crisp, Palmer and the Lows were gone *for good* – I'd give it serious thought.'

'Deal.' Liv hoped the tremor in her smile wasn't visible.

Mary shook Vic's hand, then Liv's. 'Good luck! Send my love to your boys. Ta-ta.'

And off she strode, enviably clear-skinned and perky.

91

11.30 am

Duncan

Jai and Oscar darted in, and Duncan waved them to stools by the window. Outside, seagulls were being terrorised by a pair of overdressed toddlers at the beachside playground. A dad sitting beside an empty double pram blew onto his cold fingertips and half-watched. Duncan could remember that stage. The early mornings and lingering in parks. Picking up spills and changing the odd nappy. In retrospect, he'd quite liked it. The kids couldn't talk much and didn't argue. Didn't pay any attention to girls, pretty or mean. Weren't at an expensive school or lobbying to change the world. You were their world. Yeah, he'd missed a button occasionally or put them to bed wet. But he hadn't meant to, and they survived. He forced his face into a smile.

'We don't have a lotta time, Dunc,' said Oscar.

'Yeah,' he said. 'I've ordered.'

The hot chocolates came within seconds. Duncan watched Jai speed-scoop pink-grey froth, while Oscar drowned his marshmallows. Duncan wanted to say, 'Don't rush. Let's enjoy this moment.' But he was loath to upset them any more than he already had. They were so fresh-faced despite their wispy moustaches. While he'd apologised for running away, then dragging them into it, he hadn't discussed his presence in the good room. They didn't understand the pressures of marriage. Just as they didn't understand that their mum's coup tonight was unlikely to come off. Yes, change could occur, drip by drip. But not on this scale, and not that fast! No matter what'd happened.

He reminded himself to call Maggie again; to see how everyone was doing. Though, in hindsight, he thought, Maggie had been awfully happy to see him leave. That wasn't really a surprise, he supposed. Her agenda had always been crystal clear, and he'd had some heavy-hitting clients. But still, he wondered if she hadn't given him the odd bum steer. Not that he regretted anything. He'd called her yesterday. But she hadn't called back. He'd called Henry, too; same thing. Overnight, Crisp hadn't returned his calls either. It seemed he'd become persona non grata everywhere. Is this what happened when you didn't work? he wondered, stuffing marshmallows into his mouth. Was this how middle-aged women felt, out in the world – invisible?

With a sniff, Duncan eyed the remaining flyers. The boys had been at it since 7 am: posting and tweeting. Now hand-delivering. He didn't have the heart to tell them neither he nor Liv would be able to afford that school next term, even if they did succeed. He'd been going through their bank statements. Liv wasn't as squeaky clean as she made out.

Despite the odds, though, he was proud of them. His boys were engaged. Thinking. On.

Two men sitting outside with pricey bikes seemed to be staring.

'We need to keep going, Dunc,' said Jai.

'Yes, understood. Give me two minutes.'

He took a quick sip. Would any of them want to live with him? Hopefully Cody, at least. He'd managed to get Oscar to agree to French cooking classes with him. In part, to help keep Oscar off those screens. He swallowed. Liv would probably laugh about the cooking classes. She thought she was so progressive, but deep down she wasn't. Maybe he wasn't either.

Oscar checked the time. 'Want to help? We can talk and walk?'

Duncan gave a sad smile, shook his head. *Move over, Dunc.* He hadn't understood that but it'd hurt. The boys gave each other a salty stare.

Duncan had planned to lead in with why he'd quit his job. How, as an adult, he hadn't asked himself the hard questions, and how he'd overlooked his joy. How they should each unearth theirs, early; and listen to themselves. Really listen. But Jai's stare was a two-eyed prod, a lot like his mother's.

'Boys, I—'

A group of cyclists poured into the cafe. This lot were rowdy and around sixty years old, looking as if they hoped to fend off an early death with exercise. The rest of the cafe's patrons watched them. Oscar drained his hot chocolate as Jai stood.

'We get you want to talk about how you feel and all,' said Jai. 'But can we do it tomorrow? We've gotta go.'

'Oh. Well.' Duncan wondered whether to yield or insist. He rose as, outside, a car horn sounded. Turning, Duncan saw the driver snarling at a dawdling pedestrian. Jai frowned at the man.

'Idiot,' Duncan muttered. 'I got yelled at like that riding this morning, minding my own business. Some guy in a van.'

'Yeah?' Putting on his coat, Jai was studying him. 'Make you feel bad?' His tone was brittle.

Duncan frowned.

'Girls get that all the time, you know.'

Oscar headed for the door. But Duncan wasn't following.

'Whistled at, catcalled . . . guys hanging out of cars . . .'

'Oh, well, that's different . . .'

Jai snatched the flyers. Oscar turned. 'Yeah, no. Not really.'

Duncan hadn't seen his boys like this – unguarded and, well, passionate. Oscar had swapped sides with impressive speed, too. Flummoxed, Duncan said, 'What I mean is, this guy was aggressive. Hostile. What you're talking about might be embarrassing for your friends, but not . . . you know . . .'

He looked to the water for an answer.

'It's shit, Dunc,' said Jai. 'That's what it is.'

He wished the boys' education had made them more articulate. Jai rolled his eyes. Shocked, Duncan reflected. In his cycling shorts, feeling conspicuous, he had hightailed it off the road. Pretended to be injured.

'Why do you think Mum's doing all this?' said the boys, at the same time.

'Doing what?'

Jai shook his head, as if incredulous, while Oscar sighed. Duncan wanted to explain himself. How he'd slept badly and got up too early to ride. How he'd spent his life focusing on the wrong things and sometimes missed a cue. But he was trying now. They weren't cutting him any slack.

'It doesn't matter. Look, I do want to talk about your mum and me. The five of—'

'We know. We get it!' Jai slapped his sides, exasperated, in the middle of the cafe. 'But it's not always only about you or us, is it?'

Duncan frowned.

'I mean, are you *happy* with the way things are?' Oscar gestured to innocent coffee drinkers.

Rattled, Duncan cast about. He saw the three or four women on their own with prams. None of them looked showered or refreshed. He considered the men and women in suits, having a coffee and reading, alone. The cashed-up cyclists, holding court. And then he thought of bloody Pilot Gary, again. Not everyone got to wear a uniform.

He groaned. Did they want him to be a Gary, too? Increasingly, he wasn't sure he had it in him.

'Look, Dad,' Jai sighed. 'We get you're sad. Mum's missing you too.'

It sure didn't look like it. Duncan pulled out his wallet. Could've been his imagination, but the leather flaps felt lighter already. He wondered what else that Dr Cato had been teaching his boys. Did she mention the statistics around male suicide, violence or lower life expectancy? All he'd ever wanted was to be a good son and a good husband, a father and provider.

'She knows she's stuffed it, too.' Oscar folded his arms.

Duncan stirred. 'She does?'

And then, right there in the cafe, he was crying. He plucked a napkin from a nearby table. Dabbed it across his eyes. The boys moved closer. Jai put an arm around him, lightly. They waited for him to compose himself.

'Here.' Oscar passed the flyers. 'Come on.'

Duncan considered the half-stack of paper. Most people didn't change, he thought, especially if they didn't think there was anything in it for them. But, seeing the hope and care on his sons' faces, he took the flyers. The boys shared a smile. He didn't want to disappoint them again.

'Boys,' he whispered. 'I'm not getting through to her.'

'So try harder,' said Jai.

'And be creative,' said Oscar, with a half-grin.

A man in lycra passed them, headed for the counter. 'Keep up the good work,' he said, clapping Oscar on the back. He wore a green armband. Duncan was lost.

'Dad,' whispered Jai. 'You do realise, men are happier and live longer when they're married, right?'

Duncan nodded as Oscar pointed him towards the cash register.

92

3 pm

Jess

Jess sat staring at the screen. For hours, she'd been tossing it up. Here at Liv's, everyone was on the couch or scattered across the carpet: Vic and Liv, Grace and Bella, Stella and Blake, Jai and Oscar. Even Liv's husband, Duncan, though he may've been meditating. Everyone but Duncan was messaging, uploading information, reading from screens. Jess consulted the ring of faces. Though they'd discussed this already, she still wasn't sure it was worth the risk. Would it really make a difference? Only Grace and Bella looked up, and, for no particular reason, nodded. Jess cracked her neck. Felt a hot zap of anger. Her heart bounced against her ribcage. She was about to do something she'd sworn she'd never do.

'Here goes nothing,' she said to herself.

She typed quickly and tagged all those media contacts who'd hounded her months ago, including Kristy at *Fresh and Local*. She tagged as many of the parent class-representatives as she could remember. She tagged teachers. She tagged board members. She tagged the Mayor of Bayside. She'd already emailed everyone and texted everyone. But she hadn't done this. And she'd never tweeted before. She read back what she'd written.

Then she added the clip and played it one last time. It went for seven seconds. It was a glimpse. Barely a snapshot. The school's IT manager, a very clever young woman, had found it within an hour. Copied it. Shared it with Vic. Jess had never felt so angry, or so grateful to modern technology.

She took in Grace across the room. Her beautiful swan neck, her intense focus. This was for her.

Every little bit helps, Jess told herself as she hit the blue 'Tweet' button.

Jess chose two images from the Crepes of Carmichael account, too, hit the button again and sat back. She allowed herself an angry, vengeful smile. Maybe she wasn't a very nice person. Maybe that was irrelevant. On her screen, for a final time, she admired the girls' handiwork. Many of their pics had been lifted from other websites, but the words were theirs. Jess's personal favourite, one she uploaded, was the one with Nutella and banana. She might even make it tomorrow, if they have a win, tonight. She shut her eyes and listened to the clacking of fingers on keys. Morrie wouldn't be happy. But that wasn't her problem. The energy moving between everyone in that lounge room was hopeful. They were throwing a thousand bottles into the sea. Flares into the sky. Every little bit helped.

93

4.05 pm

Duncan

'It still smells . . .' said Duncan.

'Quick – one, two, three.'

Liv and Duncan lifted the green couch and headed out of the garage. He was walking backwards, though he didn't mind; and the couch didn't smell as bad as it had. In silence, they carried it the length of the driveway and put it on the nature strip. That seemed fitting. Their whole world was on display. Everyone seemed to know that he'd left. That he was back, but not quite. He didn't know why moving the couch was this urgent. But Cody had developed a phobia of couches, apparently. Liv had already called the council, and a truck was due to collect it first thing in the morning. He wondered if she was planning on putting him in it – the garage, not the truck. In the approaching dusk, he stood, staring at the couch on the lawn. It looked lonely.

'Okay, thank you.' She dusted off her hands. 'I have to get back.'

They hadn't been alone until now. He doubted they'd be alone again before the protest. He wasn't recognising her today. The Russian spy had gone, but someone fiery remained. He hesitated on the driveway. Someone had weeded.

'Liv, don't you think we should talk?'

Liv stopped, propped her hands on her hips. A pose from one of those books. Except it looked natural now. He wondered if it did work.

'I'm done talking at you,' she said, to the letter box.

'Come on, don't be like this.'

'What do you want me to say?' She glanced inside, where people were overloading their wi-fi. 'You've disappointed me, really badly.'

'New Caledonia was a terrible idea, I see that . . . and I'm sorry. But I've been disappointed too.'

She waved his words away.

'You stopped working. You turned into a Russian spy. What was that about?'

Liv kicked a pebble. 'This isn't the—'

'Leaving me to foot the bills, without discussion, wasn't fair.'

'You quit your job without telling me.'

'Yeah. We jumped out of separate planes, at the same time. I should've told you, but I didn't expect to quit. I didn't have it straight in my head.'

'Well, I concede, I should've told you. I did have it straight.'

Duncan was beginning to envy that about her. He could feel tears gathering. 'Liv, you're making out like you don't need me anymore.'

Liv took a step towards him. Her back arched. She looked like a snake about to strike.

'I did fucking need you,' she said. 'You're my husband. You ran away . . .'

'New Caledonia—'

'Not to fucking New Caledonia!'

'Yep. Yep. You're right.'

Liv took a step back. She hadn't expected that.

'We needed me to work, though,' he said, softly.

She took a deep breath. 'Yes. But not like that—'

'I didn't know I had a choice . . .' He tugged his forelock. 'Not much of one, anyway, it seems.'

She frowned. Confusion didn't suit her. He saw a foothold.

'Liv, you didn't like being a lawyer, half the time. Forget about the hours, the culture and all that. You were scared – scared you'd screw up and get sued. Well . . .' He sighed. 'Guess what? Same here. I mean, you were Miss High Distinction, not me.'

She blinked. Twenty again, helping him study corporations law.

'Something else I had to learn to live with.'

She cast about their front garden, their fence, the sky. 'I don't know what to say.'

One of the boys – Oscar? – was watching through the window.

'That's a first.'

She raised her eyebrows, in what he hoped was a small concession.

He had thought to tell her about his call with Henry. How he'd told Henry to keep those powerful old boys away from Carmichael. 'Do you want to keep creating men like Michael?' To which Henry had said, 'George and Red have lodged a bullying claim.' Duncan had thought, Good for them. But he hadn't wanted to talk about Michael; or Winsome & Ueland. He'd said, 'It's not your school anymore, Henry. Let it go.' Then he'd hung up. He could tell Liv. But, honestly, he didn't want to talk about the school, either.

The house seemed to beckon to her.

'That it, then?' he said. 'Have you got what you wanted? Are things . . . better?'

When she snorted, he thought she was going to say something flippant, or tart.

'All I wanted was us in the thick of it, together. We should've cut everything in half, at home and beyond the bubble.'

She gestured to their green and blue suburb. He followed her hand. Saw the trees, the high branches, a pair of rosellas fighting, or shagging. When he refocused, she was tapping her forehead.

'Yeah, I see that,' he said. 'I do. That could still work.'

Her eyes searched the softening sky.

At the window, their boys popped up, one by one, then dropped down again, like demented jack-in-the-boxes. He gestured to them. Lighter notes played across her face.

'Whatever happens, I like how I feel now. Doing something important.'

She gave him a small smile.

'That's fantastic.' His smile was tight. 'But what do you want from me?'

She opened her mouth, shrugged. Shut it again.

'You're a grown-up now. That's a start. But I'm done talking. Explaining. Asking. You work it out.'

He watched her stride back in. Envied her again. Sat on the fence. If their marriage were a game, he realised, it would be a nail-biter in its final seconds.

94

5 pm

Liv

In the remaining minutes of the afternoon, Liv became a mistress of busyness. She folded up her hurt and confusion, her disappointment and doubt and tucked them into a corner of her heart. She focused on her anger, as she fielded calls and directed helpers. At the designated hour, a blue double-decker bus pulled up outside her house. It was covered with huge red-and-white banners. The team had done an amazing job on ridiculously short notice. Printed on the banners were results from the survey. Four in five girls and three in eight boys on one side; and one in ten girls and one in five boys on the other. On the back of the bus was a cartoon drawing of Tony Crisp and Lloyd Palmer, arm in arm, wearing matching lycra. Written in red paint across the picture were the words, *Time for the hens to rule the roost!*

Facing the bus, Liv was shaking as if she'd had too many cups of tea. She'd delegated dozens of tasks these past thirty-odd hours. Grace and Bella, Blake and her boys had stepped up. Especially Oscar. But what they needed now was for their message to stick. They hadn't yet distilled it to a handful of words everyone would remember, forever. Liv thought of the long-ago O. J. Simpson murder trial: 'If it doesn't fit, you must acquit.'

Perhaps it was too late.

Liv had spent the past half-hour double-checking the school's constitution; its appointment process for principals; its board election mechanism. She'd finessed her questions for Tony Crisp, too. But this wasn't about one man, one principal or his assistant, she told herself; it was about a privileged caste. She hoped that, under pressure, the Lows' hold on the school would crack. She hoped James Whittaker-Smith had what it took. Meanwhile, in her lounge room, indignation had fired the handful of workers. Every time she passed, she heard their furious chatter – about one thing and one thing only. Now *that* had stuck.

Stepping off the bus, Liv directed the driver to drive once around the block then park at the front of Carmichael. There, more posters and printed slogans leant against the fence. Liv looked to the small group of rugged-up people milling about – most were Year Eight girls and their mums. She recognised Charvi, Zhu and Alison. A wave of nerves rose from her feet to sweep through her body. She jumped up and down on the spot. Was anyone watching this, she wondered, beyond the bubble?

She sent Cody to sit under a tree with her phone. Probably a bad idea. Jai and Oscar were already here somewhere. She scanned the faces. One of her jobs was to keep a lookout for Mr Vainglorious et al. She and Jess had convinced themselves those men weren't dangerous in real life. But how could they know for sure? Men who enjoyed scaring women could easily enjoy hurting them too.

By five-thirty, the crowd had grown; but if this gathering was to be a party, it wouldn't be a good one. Reclaiming her phone, Liv learnt six members of the board had scurried in the back. Two had braved the front, but neither was Scott or Owen Low. Apparently, Tony was already inside. There were no letters of resignation. No attempts to communicate. No acknowledgement of the protest at all. Liv wondered if they'd even let her speak to them. And if not, what then?

Recognising another arriving group of mums, Liv waved hello. These were mums of the gentler boys; the less sporty boys; the hearts-on-their-sleeves boys; the gay boys; the musical theatre boys; the smaller boys; the overt thinkers; the too-tall; the too-short; the earnest; the unco; the sensitive; the scrawny; the too-nice; the not-white; the young for their grade; the redheads; the lispers and stutterers; the chubby and the squat; and any combination thereof. 'Thank you for coming. Make yourselves comfortable,' Liv said, as she passed out T-shirts. Four of these mums tugged on the T-shirts, over the top of their clothes, picked up placards and started to march.

A few more students arrived with their own placards too. The mood was becoming nervously festive. Something was different about the students. Boys and girls joked together without standoffishness or self-consciousness. No one was staring at anyone's breasts, which was no mean feat, considering that many of the red T-shirts – emblazoned with cartoon versions of Martin Luther King, Jr or Mother Teresa, Gandhi or Jacinda Ardern, even Dr Cato and Professor Griffin – were, due to some sort of mishap, too small.

Fifteen minutes before start time, cars began to toot their horns as they passed. People yelled encouragement out of their windows. Only one or two raised the finger. Bigger groups arrived; perhaps these were the full-time workers, who had dashed here straight after work. Groups of Carmichael staff members also began to arrive. Ex-staff members. Parent year-level coordinators. Mothers' groups and dads' groups. The students arrived in clumps: basketball teams, football teams, drama clubs, chess clubs, choirs, orchestras. The Parents' Association mums turned up in a gang, wearing puffer jackets. Even a group of old old boys turned up, with canes and gummy grins. Former school captains, female and male, strolled in, with lots of people Liv didn't recognise. Everyone was wearing green armbands. Fielding questions from all and sundry, Liv observed the groups merging, and felt a little sick. Public speaking wasn't one of her favourite things. At least she only had to speak before the board.

As six o'clock approached, no word came from the people in the boardroom. No invitation was delivered on a silver plate. The leaders inside were holding firm. Which was no surprise. On the stroke of six, Liv rang Vic, who had been hiding in the wings like the star before the curtain rose.

It was time.

Warily, Liv eyed the microphone that had been set up near the front gate. Someone needed to manage the crowd while she and Vic went in, she supposed. But people were still arriving. An hour ago, the crowd had been thin; now, it was massive. Stunned, Liv watched the waves of people keep coming. Where would they all fit?

Flustered, Liv rang Mary. Rang Jean. Rang Libby the IT manager. On instinct, rang Ryan – her old boss. Plans changed, rearranged, firmed up.

Then a news crew arrived.

The huge crowd adapted extremely well. In an orderly fashion, hundreds of people filed in to the Great Hall, courtesy of Miss Patterson, the Head of Early Learning, and her master key. The building was flooded with light and constructed of timber the colour of creamed honey. It was part modern cathedral, part world-class recital space. Despite the knot in her gut, Liv felt as if she was moving among the chosen. The self-selected chosen, poised to rise up. At a guess, the Great Hall could accommodate fifteen hundred people, and it was filling.

A message came on Liv's phone: Jai and Oscar's petition was exploding, and the clip Jess had uploaded had gone viral! Woohoo!

Searching the young faces, Liv wondered how to satisfy and reward their hope. She was so proud of them. Out of uniform and despite the hour, the students looked morning tidy and sparkling clean. Every girl with uncovered hair had left it out, she realised; there wasn't a single braid or ponytail or bun. No plaited crowns. Just heads of free locks, kinky, straight and curly.

A few of the boys, she realised, were wearing long wigs.

Vic was dragging out the seconds before she appeared. It was doing Liv's head in. Amongst the masses, she searched for the twins, and Cody. She wanted to share this with them. Stand with them. Another message came through: from Mary. The board had barricaded itself in the admin building and wasn't letting anyone in. Liv's moment in the sun was looking overcast. As the clock ticked further past six, the mood in the hall became twitchy. Liv couldn't see the twins. She couldn't see Duncan.

Tapping her collarbones, Liv tried to centre herself. (She'd read some-where that tapping certain pressure points was calming and, what the hell, it couldn't hurt.) She really didn't want to get up on that stage, but people deserved to hear the truth, and be heard. Latecomers were congregating at the rear of the hall when a hush fell across the crowd as the lights dimmed. A second later, Vic Cato strode to the lectern. Relief flushed through Liv, as Vic raised her arms and gave her customary twinkling smile. The crowd whooped and cheered until Vic raised her hands.

'Good evening and thank you,' said Vic. 'My work here was ushered in on the back of modern technology and tonight, with the help of that technology, we intend to usher out the unholy trinity at this school.'

A large screen descended at the back of the stage. Liv watched the upturned faces around her. Read their puzzled expressions. Whatever this was, Liv hoped it hung together.

She tapped faster on those collarbones.

Liv's phone beeped again as two security guards arrived. They were both alert, their hands crossed, eyes scanning the crowd. She'd owe Ryan one for this. She couldn't see a single Low in the Great Hall, but their supporters could be here. Methodically, she surveyed the crowd until she picked out her own boys. The twins were nursing microphones at the rear, while Cody was sitting in the next block of seating and five rows behind where she sat. At nine, Cody was probably the youngest in the room. She doubted he'd grasp the importance of the moment or would be able to sit for the duration. She prayed he wouldn't spring up and yell 'Yeet!' in the middle of proceedings. She craned her neck to identify who was sitting beside him; perhaps Harry's mum? But no. Running a hand through his hair, dressed in his favourite jacket, was Duncan.

Liv was still considering him when an image formed on the screen. Along with hundreds of others, Liv was transfixed.

The Middle School library was close to empty. Wearing headphones, Grace was tapping on a laptop, her head bobbing. Bella was next to Grace, and a handful of other students sat nearby. Behind them were sliding doors. A second passed, then the doors parted to reveal a group of boys and a handful of girls: Year Eights, and one older student.

Grace looked to the camera and smiled, as if to a friend. A friend Liv now knew to be Jai. Grace put her head down again.

Dylan Low eyed the librarian's empty workstation and muttered to the seated, younger kids, who hopped up and fled. Outside, a familiar Year Eight student peeked through the window. Holy moly. Liv recognised the chubby cheeks and worried squint.

A second later, Bella got up and left the library. Unperturbed, Grace continued to work, as Dylan tiptoed behind her. With something behind his back.

Liv felt a surge of anger. Though she'd seen this part before, her anger grew every time she watched. It seemed people who had seen the brief clip online had had the same reaction.

On the screen, Bella was running in the causeway. Searching.

Sitting tall, Grace was still tapping. Then her head moved, as if from the tiniest tug. Another tug, and her head jerked back. Something was flying. You could see it, midair, like a dead snake. All twenty-five centimetres of it. It landed on her laptop. Grace stared at it, as if it hadn't come from her. Liv still half-expected the braid to spasm or bleed.

Outside, a red-faced Oscar could be seen pinning Taj against a wall.

In the library, dazed, Grace picked up her hair in her fist. She raised the long, fine braid to the camera, her eyes vividly blue and angry.

People in the crowd murmured. That was the money shot.

In the quadrangle, Lloyd Palmer shook his head but laughed as he clapped Dylan, hard, on the back. As the boys ran off, Palmer's face registered a moment's doubt. He looked like an emoji – downturned mouth and big eyes.

Abruptly, the screen went blank. The silence in the auditorium was total.

Oh, Grace.

Liv turned to find Oscar in the back row. Her darling overlooked twin. She'd left him to the wolves. Thank goodness he'd made it home.

When the lights returned, the crowd moved restlessly.

'I'd now like to welcome Grace Charters to the stage.'

The crowd hushed as the girl climbed the steps. Grace's fawn hair was jagged, and didn't reach below her chin. A few people gasped. But Grace's head was high.

'Is there anything you'd like to say, Grace?'

Liv sucked in a breath. This wasn't in the script.

'Yes,' Grace said, taking the microphone. She paused. 'If you take one thing out of tonight, don't make it about this.' She lifted a hank of hair. 'Make it about Dr Cato. She made us happier, and kinder, and calmer. Us, *teenagers*! We have to keep learning from her and . . . and people like her, about all sorts of things!'

Liv looked around the audience. A number of adults were nodding and smiling. Several boffin-types were sitting higher in their seats.

'I mean, like, power to the experts!'

'Hear, hear!' A man nearby yelled.

More boffins nodded and clapped. There were more of them in the crowd than Liv had realised. Liv hoped they were the real deal. She turned back to Vic and clapped too. Meanwhile, Grace was getting quite worked up. She flung off her cardigan. On her own, too-small red T-shirt was a comic portrait of one of her heroes: a certain Swedish teenager, wearing a raincoat, scowling.

Around three thousand eyes stared at Grace's bosom, and clapped. Grace laughed.

Liv laughed too. Greta wasn't exactly an expert, was she – had she even finished school yet? – but perhaps that wasn't the point. The point was, Grace, like Greta, was inspiring people with a mic in her hand. Though she should probably hand the mic back now.

In the crowd, Liv glimpsed Rowan Whittaker-Smith, grinning but looking lost. She thought of James, Rowan's father, in that board meeting. Please, she prayed, let him not be a C-minus too.

Five rows back, Duncan wasn't clapping and wasn't moving. He seemed stunned. She realised then what she needed from him. In a word: solidarity. If anything could rebuild trust between them, that was it.

Liv wriggled in her seat. She was a big bottle of soda, shaken. She was bursting to remind him of the issues at stake. Issues that would define the rest of their lives, their children's future and their grandchildren's. What could be more important? (Saving the planet, perhaps, or global health.) She could feel her agitation growing. That inner hum. Okay, yes, her anxiety.

Say something, Duncan!

Marriage was full of these little and big tests. Practically booby-trapped.

At that moment, the doors at the back of the auditorium opened, and three men and two boys stepped in. Heads turned and people gasped. Liv gestured to the security guards but they didn't react, as if the men were invited or ran the show, and the boys were their understudies. Liv rose as the five walked down the aisle. One man led, striding up onto the stage: Tony Crisp. A step behind him was Lloyd Palmer and, in a cloud of cologne, Scott Low, along with his nephews, Dylan and Taj.

These men, Liv realised, were like indulged children. Making permissive parents of them all.

A fresh-faced teacher in front of Liv stared about, as if looking for help.

Liv gestured again to the security guards, who stopped halfway down the aisle. 'If this goes pear-shaped, you need to get those men out,' Liv said quietly into her phone. 'Or lock them in a shed.'

The closest smooth-skinned guard nodded. But he looked as if he was wearing his dad's uniform. Or his mum's.

At the lectern, Tony lifted his arms as if to embrace the room himself. 'Good evening, everyone.' He tried to move Vic along, but she didn't budge. He took the mic from Grace.

'Ladies and gentlemen, boys and girls. When you disrespect another person, you disrespect yourself. And these boys here, these young men, are very sorry for what they've done.'

The two boys nodded solemnly, with their eyes downcast and hands clasped in front, as if to protect themselves from a wayward snip. Liv wondered, again, why Dylan Low had become a brat.

'Tired of being perfect,' Oscar had said, as if the answer was obvious. 'Taj gets all the fun. Plus, everyone knows Taj is Bettina's favourite.'

They do? Liv had thought.

Back on stage, Vic was sizing Tony up, as if contemplating shoving him off. In a charcoal suit and red tie, the principal looked presidential. Someone hissed at Lloyd, and he jumped. He chanced his famous grin, but stopped when it found no traction. Meanwhile, Scott Low was assessing the crowd. In the middle of her row, Liv climbed over people to reach the aisle. People were beginning to murmur, at a loss; a few were making for the exits.

Tony started again: 'Carmichael Grammar has a long tradition of—'

There was no avoiding it. Liv waved for the microphone. Oscar jogged down the aisle and passed it to her.

'Thank you, my darling,' she said.

'Go for it, Mum,' he puffed.

In her sternest you're-in-trouble voice, Liv said, 'Tony Crisp!' And the man jumped, turned to pick her out. 'We've needed more from you,' she said, 'but we've heard enough.'

Tony squinted into the harsh lights.

A few people cheered; some heckled for the three men to go.

'You've stuffed it, royally. All of you. And now . . . now it's time to share. For real.'

The hall exploded into cheers. Liv felt a surge of energy so strong she swooned. Tony staggered backwards too, as if he'd been shot in the midsection. Lloyd stood, frozen, under a spotlight. His bald scalp shone.

Liv was enjoying the cheering, when a reedy voice sounded through the other microphone. 'Mum's right. It's not fair if you don't share. Everyone knows! It's gotta be even stevens.' Cody's little voice squeaked, but the crowd laughed and clapped.

Someone was beginning a chant. Jai? Oscar? Bella?

Lloyd shouted something, but was drowned out by hundreds of voices: 'It's not fair if you don't share!'

'Wait, what?' said someone near Liv, presumably Rowan Whittaker-Smith.

Liv turned to see James Whittaker-Smith appear in the aisle and nod at her. Four other members of the school board were standing with him – two men and the two women – nodding. Relief surged through her. They'd actually done it!

Seeing James, Tony began mumbling another apology, but Scott Low yanked the microphone from his hands. 'This school used to be—' he began. But then, in the midst of the chanting crowd, Duncan was on his feet. For a split second, looking up at Scott Low, he wilted. On stage, the man looked very big. Then Duncan pressed on.

'Hello, everyone!' His voice boomed through the floor mic. 'I'm Duncan Winsome, and I was at Carmichael with you, Scott . . . you probably don't remember me.' He faltered. 'Anyway, I second what Liv said. I also second this little guy.'

He ruffled Cody's hair and Cody grinned up at him. Duncan took off his jacket. He was wearing a white T-shirt with big black letters hand-written on it: *App designer seeks Vet with pet goat, and nine kids.*

Liv gulped.

Tony Crisp's eyes found Duncan in the auditorium. Scott Low closed his mouth. The crowd fell quiet, as Duncan coughed, mastering himself.

'We know what we need to do. And we know how to do it! We were already on the way. Look around!' Duncan beamed, finding his footing, and more people cheered. 'This school deserves a fresh start. We all do. The old model hasn't worked – there's no shame in admitting that. Together we can create a smarter one. On that, I'd like to nominate Liv to a position on the new board. Paid, if possible.' Cody smiled proudly at Liv. 'None of this would've happened without her becoming incredibly committed, passionate, and unlikeable.'

Liv felt her eyes welling.

'Ditto Jess Charters,' yelled another man, with bushy eyebrows. 'Company Secretary.'

Duncan laughed, heartened. 'And you guys'—he gestured to the men on stage—'being kicked out of here could be the best thing to ever happen to you!'

Lloyd Palmer became a stunned emoji this time, as Tony Crisp began to sway like an old tree, mid-felling.

Vic turned to the crowd. 'Hear, hear!' she shouted. 'And finally, from the wings, I give you Mrs Mary MacBeth.'

Vic's words were drowned out by cheers as she pointed to Mary, standing alongside Grace. Mary MacBeth waved regally. Love spread in that room again, as infectious as a giggle.

Fleetingly, Liv wondered if it looked a bit suspicious that she, Mary and Jess were putting up their hands to rule the roost. Decided it didn't. The children continued to chant.

Tony Crisp had gone from red to a bloodless white. Lloyd Palmer stirred, as if regaining consciousness, as Tony tried to retrieve the microphone from Scott Low. While the men wrestled, Jess rose from the second row. She bent down, curled her right arm back and threw something. Flat and pink. The shoe missed Tony Crisp but clipped Lloyd Palmer's big shoulder. He yelped.

Seeing Jess, Scott Low did a double-take. He stepped towards her, waved his arms and said 'Boo!' Jess didn't flinch. Wrong-footed, the man stood, snarling and ridiculous. People laughed.

A moment later, a heeled shoe flew, followed by a brogue and then a sandal, until shoes were streaming at the men on the stage. Ducking, Scott Low scurried and Tony followed, shepherded by Lloyd. Shoes pummelled them, and the crowd's booing swelled. At the exit, a stunned Scott Low copped a battery of sneakers to the head. Dylan and Taj dodged, tossing the odd shoe back.

People continued to chant, boo and hurl as the heavy doors closed behind the men. Liv's security guards waved their arms about like useless defenders beneath a basketball hoop.

Amid the bedlam, Vic raised her arm in that fist-high salute, and beamed. The mountain of odd shoes on stage grew, as if everyone wanted to be a part of the action now. With a cheer, Liv hopped off the lap of the petite woman she'd accidentally sat on. She felt as though she might explode with delight. She felt as she had on the happiest days in her memory: the days her boys were born; the day she quit the law; and the Sunday night she binned their iron.

She looked for Duncan. He was still holding the mic, beaming. From his seat, he found her in the crowd. He searched her face then raised his arm. She raised hers in return, and laughed. Oh, husband. Soon, he was laughing and wiping his eyes with his free hand. She was jumping up and down. Across the mass of people, they were heading towards each other, again.

Afterwards, on the forecourt of the Great Hall, Liv embraced Bella and the Saffins and Morrie Charters. In another huddle were Mary and Vic and James Whittaker-Smith. Even sweet Carly and the unfairly maligned Rowan were hugging somewhere. Everyone seemed to be various degrees of stunned, angry and happy. Lots of people were walking about in one shoe. Some people were wearing odd pairs – sneakers and brogues and sandals.

It felt like a New Year's Eve party, circa 1999, a stroke after midnight. There wasn't a Low pressure system in sight.

Vic broke from her huddle to run at Liv. Her hug was fierce and warm. Soon, Jess found them too and was wrapped in Vic's long arms. Jean directed one of the news crews towards them. Seeing the camera, Vic pecked Liv's cheek, then Jess's, and slipped into the crowd. As the reporter was readying her crew, Liv looked across the ocean of animated faces and then back to Jess.

'Go on,' said Liv, tapping Jess's chest.

Jess gulped, then adjusted her Gandhi T-shirt.

'What would you like to say to the men you've effectively ousted tonight?'

When the reporter pointed the microphone towards her, Jess looked as if she'd blown a circuit. Liv squeezed her hand.

'Gentlemen,' Jess began, then grinned. 'We forgive you.'

Ha. Forgiveness wasn't one of Liv's strong suits, but she'd give it a red-hot go.

That evening, Jess would be beamed out on the late night news. People across the state, sipping tea, wine, and Milo, would listen. Liv knew some wouldn't care about their elite school and its domestic dramas. They wouldn't understand the power of something as small as a haircut. But many would see in Jess and her shining face what Liv could see: excitement and relief, forgiveness, and something more – optimism. If we can do it, Jess seemed to be transmitting, so can you.

Back home, Liv and Duncan led their family outside and onto the trampoline. For a split second, high in the air, Liv felt daunted. There was much to discuss and much to do: jobs to be found, and quite possibly a new house. But surely the hardest part was behind them . . .?

She touched down and, beside her, Duncan bounced high. Together, in the dark, the five of them jumped, barefoot and whooping.

Acknowledgements

A number of people generously gave me their time when I was writing *Tipping*, so that I may better understand their worlds. I'd like to thank them all, and specifically Kyra, Leonie, Mel, SS and James. Thanks are due too to Aoife Clifford and my agent, Tara Wynne, for early feedback on the manuscript. I'd also like to acknowledge the fantastic team at Penguin Random House Australia that has worked on this book, led by Meredith Curnow. I am so glad that I have finally been able to work with you, Meredith. Thanks especially to Kathryn Knight for her astute input, and to Louisa Maggio for her cover design. Writing a book takes me years, and in that time I tend to bounce ideas off my nearest and dearest. In particular, Jody and Sean, Barb, Vikki and Claire, and Sean O'D. Thank you all for listening, sharing your stories and indulging mine. Finally, to my mum, Maureen George, thank you for helping to foster a love of books in me and for the laughter; and to Jason and our boys, Jem and Lachie, thank you for the moral support, inspiration and fun.

Discover a
new favourite

Visit **penguin.com.au/readmore**